OA 1/16

S
n
o
H
a
A
R
w
N
c:

E 7 MAY 2016

28 MAY 2016

C000227027

DISCARDED

AF

Since she began writing in 2008, Cara McKenna has published more than thirty romance and erotic novels with a variety of publishers, sometimes under the pen name Meg Maguire. Her stories have been acclaimed for their smart, modern voice and defiance of convention. She was a 2010 Golden Heart Award finalist and a 2011 and 2013 Romance Times Reviewers' Choice Award nominee. She lives with her husband, with their son in New England but their hearts in the Pacific Northwest. Cara loves hearing from readers. Until her at caramckenna@gmail.com.

Visit Cara McKenna online
www.caramckenna.com
www.twitter.com/caramckenna

Hard Time

Cara McKenna

piatkus

PIATKUS

First published in the US in 2014 by Intermix,
A division of Penguin Group (USA) Inc., New York
First published in Great Britain in 2014 by Piatkus
This edition published in 2015 by Piatkus

1 3 5 7 9 10 8 6 4 2

A CIP catalogue record for this book is available from the British Library.

ISBN 978-0-349-40619-0

Typeset in Sabon by Palimpsest Book Production Limited,
Falkirk, Stirlingshire

Printed and bound by CPI Group (UK) Ltd, Croydon CR0 4YY

Papers used by Piatkus are from well-managed forests
and other responsible sources.

MIX
Paper from
responsible sources
FSC
www.fsc.org FSC® C104740

Piatkus
An imprint of
Little, Brown Book Group
Carmelite House
50 Victoria Embankment
London EC4Y 0DZ

An Hachette UK Company
www.hachette.co.uk

www.piatkus.co.uk

With thanks to my editor, Jesse, who allowed herself to be convinced that a book about a felon could be romantic.

And with thanks also to Claire, who did the convincing.

And to my agent, Laura, for loving the work.

And with extra big thanks to this book's first reader, Shelley—a librarian so adorable, I hereby invite her to come and live with me in my blanket nest for all eternity. Go on, get cozy. I'll make cocoa.

Chapter One

The rules were forwarded to me in an email.

No makeup. No perfume. No jewelry.

That brought a frown to my lips. Having been raised in the South, the request felt about as civilized as being asked if I could please shave my head bald. Where I'm from, a woman won't flee a burning building in the dead of night before at least putting on some mascara and a pair of pearl studs.

Furthermore, said the email, *No tight or revealing clothing*.

I cheated on rule one, dabbing concealer on a zit and under each eye. I only had to *look* like I wasn't wearing any makeup. I may have fudged the second rule as well—my deodorant was clover-scented but I wasn't about to go without, not with the kind of anxious sweating I planned on doing.

The third and fourth rules I aced—plain top with a crew neck, in gender-neutral forest green. Black straight-legged pants, silver flats that revealed not a hint of toe cleavage. *My ears look naked,* I thought, scrutinizing them in the bathroom mirror. Obscene, with their little puncture wounds showing. Vulnerable like those unfortunate, shivering hairless cats.

1

Speaking of hair, the email didn't mention a policy regarding that, but I twisted mine up and secured it with a wide barrette.

Wait. *Am I allowed to wear a barrette?* Could an enterprising inmate turn that into a stabbing weapon?

Not caring to find out, I ditched it, opting for a ponytail. Until I imagined it wrapped around a scarred, beefy hand as I was taken hostage in a riot, dragged squeaking across a linoleum floor toward certain trauma. *No thanks.* I settled on a bun and studied the overall look in the full-length mirror on the back of the door.

That'll do. I looked nice, but not perilously nice. Presentable. Professional. I could guess what my grandma might say. *You look like a runner-up in the Little Miss Frumpy Pageant. For God's sake, at least put some lipstick on. You might meet the right boy.*

Not today I wouldn't. Frumpy would do me just fine, given that the male attention up for grabs belonged to several hundred convicted felons.

Back home, the last man who'd touched me had boxed my right ear so bad, the drum perforated. With my left, I heard him say he loved me not an hour later. *I'm sorry. I won't ever hit you again.* He said that a lot in the two months I let myself believe it.

I'd been dumb at twenty-two, but I'd gotten smarter since then. And I probably held some record for having achieved spinsterhood by twenty-seven, but I'd rather sport that badge than another bruise. Not ever again.

Romantic idealism? No, no worries there. Dead and buried. But the professional kind . . .

It was August, and I'd graduated in May. I was five weeks into my first full-time job, and still determined to Make a Difference in the lives of the people I encountered through my work as a librarian. Both the library and I resided in

2

Darren, Michigan—the epitome of post-industrial decline and a far cry from where I grew up, a thousand miles to the south in a suburb of Charleston. I didn't like Darren, but a job was a job, and my apartment was dirt cheap, situated two floors above a depressing bar on the main drag.

I did a lot of outreach work through the library, traveling most days to neighboring towns, none of which were prospering. There was a lot of difference begging to be made.

Mondays kept me in the actual library. Tuesdays and Wednesdays I was at Larkhaven, a psychiatric hospital campus fifteen miles outside the city, tucked in a pretty pocket of woods—a welcome change from Darren's boarded buildings and abandoned factory lots. Tuesdays I ran sessions in the kids' wards, from reading to the youngest ones to test prep with the teenagers. Wednesday was a half day, my morning spent with the seniors in the dementia and Alzheimer's ward. Reading, delivering books, penning letters or typing emails for the residents with arthritis or waning eyesight. The previous week I'd helped a man write a letter to his sweetheart, a vivacious redhead of nineteen, he'd informed me. He was going to marry her when he got out of this godforsaken Korean labor camp.

His white-haired wife had sat across from us, hands clasped, smiling tightly with tears slipping down her cheeks. I wondered if she cried for the loss of this bygone romance . . . or because she'd never in fact been a redhead, nor known of her husband's affection for one.

Thursdays were passed in the bookmobile, piloted by my colleague Karen. A divorced mother of two teens, she was crotchety and terse in spite of the cheerful floral-print tops that dominated her wardrobe, but she made me laugh. I liked Thursdays a lot—out on the open road, lots of coffee breaks. It reminded me of bygone summers with my father. He was

3

a state trooper and I was a daddy's girl, and he'd let me ride along now and then on what he called The Hunt. Sometimes he'd let me hold the radar gun. I watched a lot of cops drink a lot of coffee back when I was eleven, twelve, thirteen. I watched a lot of people get arrested, too. Felt them kick the panel behind my seat. Terrified and thrilled, like I was in a shark tank.

Though at Cousins Correctional Facility, there'd be no shatterproof partition separating me and the criminals. A table, perhaps. Not even that, if I were to sit beside them, showing them how to fill out online applications or use a word processor or the digital card catalog. Nothing between me and them but the proximity of a guard. And that might keep their hands away, but their looks? Whispers?

I shivered, wondering what kind of punishment-glutton dingbat would need to be told not to dress sexy when she visited a medium-security prison.

Play with fire, I thought. *Enjoy your third-degree burns.* Bad men didn't take much baiting.

To underline the warning, I shifted my jaw around until I heard that pop. It didn't used to do that. Not until that night I'd shown up at my ex-boyfriend's place with the wrong kind of rum. I'd paid for it in cash at the liquor store, and I paid for it again with that slap—so hard the room turned white for a half minute, my eardrum bursting like a shotgun blast and ringing rusty with feedback.

I won't ever hit you again.

How many times had he promised me that, before I left him? A dozen, maybe. But that shot to my head, that woke me up for good.

I won't ever hit you again.

And I'd thought, *No you fucking will not.* He'd passed out after the usual drunken laments, and I took a twenty from

4

his wallet for the rum, and wrote a rather succinct Dear John letter in Sharpie on the back of the hand he'd struck me with.

FUCK. YOU.

My hearing had returned by the time I moved to Ann Arbor that fall. I'd needed a change of scenery. A place with snowy winters, where the men spoke in honest, sharp-edged Northern accents, incapable of glazing their empty promises in sweet Southern honey.

I never told my daddy why I transferred, because sometimes parents need protecting. I didn't tell my mama, either, didn't spell it out. But a woman can tell. When she hugged me good-bye beside my dad's car, all loaded with my stuff, she'd whispered, "I never liked that boy. You pick with your head next time."

Fine by me, so long as next time was a long ways off.

The car that had moved me to Ann Arbor was mine now—a stodgy maroon station wagon. I climbed behind the wheel at seven twenty with the lazy Northern sun just peeking from behind the buildings to the east, and sat there hugging the tote bag full of books and worksheets I'd packed, timing my breaths. There were more books in the back, donations for the prison's collection. Karen had done her time as the Cousins outreach person—a four-year sentence, she named it—and she'd explained that their so-called library was literally a closet full of books. No shelves, no order, just tall stacks of random castoffs.

"I always told myself I'd find a spare hour a week to fix that," she'd said as we rode around the county in the book-mobile the day before. "Get a collection of the kinds of things they actually like—thrillers and spy novels, war memoirs. Bully somebody in custodial into giving me a cart, go up and down the cellblocks, handing them out. But I also tell myself I'm going to lose thirty pounds, yet here we are."

5

"What are they like? The inmates?"

She'd shrugged. "They're a bunch of men who made dumb-shit, violent mistakes. Stripped of their dignity, crowded into kennels to cross-infect each other with their anger. And to fester. And to wish they hadn't made such dumb-shit mistakes."

"Did anyone ever touch you?"

"No. But I'm a fat, used-up old grouch. Probably remind them of their mothers, or some teacher who told them they'd never amount to anything. I got my share of taunts, of course. And come-ons. One proposal. They're desperate, after all. But you . . . Well, you just watch yourself, with those legs and freckles. Make yourself some friends with Tasers on their belts."

"Did anyone ever try to extort you?" I'd read too many cautionary tales recently about female guards and prisoners' girlfriends who got sweet-talked by charismatic cons into smuggling drugs, drawn in too gradually, too deep, until their families were being threatened by the criminals' buddies on the outside. I'd also been staying up far too late, watching far too much *Dateline*.

Karen had said no one ever tried to extort her. And I wasn't some lonely woman using the prison pen-pal system as a dating service. The nicest, most upstanding, most handsome man you ever saw probably couldn't seduce me, so no worries there. The only action I might care to get went down between me and my right hand, and even we'd grown estranged. There just hadn't been anyone I cared to fantasize about, not in ages. Or else there was no fuel left inside me to catch, sparked by the right attraction. Sometimes I worried my ex had hit me so hard he broke the desire center of my brain.

Nope, I thought, sliding my key into the ignition. *He just knocked the trust right out of you.*

6

I wanted a family someday, so I knew I needed to fix whatever my ex had broken, but I could kick that can down the road. Today of all days, I was almost grateful for how distrustful I'd become.

Before I started my car, I took out my phone. Dialed my mom.

"Hi, Mama, it's Annie."

"Hey, baby!" It warmed me to hear a voice from home. I wished I was back at her and Daddy's house, curled up on our old padded porch swing. "Is today the day?"

"Yeah. My first session starts at nine."

"How long, all together?"

"Full day, done at five. With an hour lunch."

She exhaled a long breath, and I did the same.

"You're gonna do fine, baby. You just do what the guards say, and don't let anything those men say upset you."

"Easier said than done."

"You can do it. You're way stronger than you give yourself credit for."

"I don't know about that."

"Well I do," she said, and I heard the tinkling of a spoon in a mug. I could just about smell her tea. "And if you catch yourself thinking you're not up to this, you put my voice in your ear saying that's bull. All right?"

"Okay. Thanks, Mama. I'll let you know how it goes."

"Good. And good luck, baby. I love you so much."

"Love you too. And Daddy. Talk to you tonight."

"Bye-bye, now."

I turned my phone off. Turned my key in the ignition. Turned my old Escort onto the road and aimed for the highway.

The drive took about thirty minutes, and my stomach balled tighter with every mile. By the time I reached the Cousins front gate, my throat stung with heartburn.

7

I stopped before the metal arm of the lot attendant's booth.

"Business?" he asked.

I flashed the ID I'd been mailed. *Anne Goodhouse, Secondary Staff.* "I'm from the Darren Public Library. The new outreach—"

"G'on through," he said, gate rising. "Employee lot's marked. So's the personnel entrance."

"Thanks."

I found a space and gathered my things. My nerves had me strung taut between fear of the unknown and fear of running late—I'd been told to allow a full hour for orientation and "security protocol" before this first visit.

I was greeted just inside the entrance by a short tank of a female officer.

"Welcome to Cousins," Shonda said after an introduction, sounding like a mother whose children were testing her patience—an aura of displaced, weary annoyance, directed at nothing in particular. Her uniform was khaki and snug, her bun even tighter.

"I'll show you around, but first I gotta search you."

"Sure." I'd snapped into some calm, obedient mode— sounded nearly chipper, like she'd offered me a cup of coffee and not a frisking.

Shonda took me into a nearby tiled room labeled Reception. It had no door, but a short jog around a wall opposite the entrance, like in an airport restroom. Inside it was home to very little aside from a long metal table, a set of lockers, and two security cameras.

"Gonna ask you to hand me your bag and shoes, empty your pockets, then strip. Please."

Damn. I handed her my bag, keys, and phone, kicked off my flats and surrendered those as well. I undressed, stuck standing awkwardly as she took her time examining everything in my tote. She went through my clothes next, eyeballing them closely, feeling every seam.

"I know this seems real invasive," she said casually, "but it has to be, when we're letting you inside the general population."

"Sure." Whatever. Fine by me. God forbid I find out the hard way that something on my person could be turned into a shank on some desperate man's whim.

"Crouch and cough for me please."

I did, face blazing. Karen had warned me about this, but dreading it and living it just didn't compare. I wondered how often the inmates had to do this. Daily? Every time they left the yard or the visitation area? Could you even call that a life?

I survived this first taste of degradation and dressed quickly.

"We'll hang on to these," Shonda said, pulling a small plastic bin from on top of the lockers and tossing my keys and phone into it. "They'll be kept behind the reception desk for you, but you may access them any time you're in the secure zone." She explained this with a robotic passion, clearly a speech she gave many times a week. She locked her eyes on mine, hooking her thumbs under her thick black belt. She spoke crisply, slowly.

"While you are a member of secondary staff at Cousins Correctional Facility, you will abide by the standards set forth for all CCF employees. You will not access areas denied by your security clearance. You will not film or photograph the facilities without a permit to do so. You will not transport contraband items into the facility. You will not accept contraband items from inmates. If you encounter contraband items, you will immediately deliver them to the nearest officer. Do you understand?"

"Yes."

I thought I was done, but she went on.

"You will not provide acceptable items to an inmate without express written permission from a qualified staff member. You will not accept gifts, either material or as promised via verbal or written contract, from an inmate. You will not speak to or touch any inmate in an inappropriate way. You will not encourage an inmate to speak to or touch you in an inappropriate way . . ."

This continued for a full five minutes, after which I was handed a four-page, small-print waiver detailing the many rules, plus indexes outlining what qualified as *contraband* and *inappropriate* and so forth. I read and signed it with Shonda watching, and the second I handed it over, her demeanor softened.

"Okay, then. Let's get you oriented, Ms. Goodhouse."

She dropped off the form and my verboten items with a young, crew-cut blond man behind a half-circle reception desk.

"Ryan, this is Anne Goodhouse, the new librarian."

Ryan smiled and shook my hand. He looked like a guy from back in Charleston, the varsity football type or an eager young Marine, pre-deployment. "Welcome aboard, Anne."

"Thank you."

He took my things, swiveling his chair and jangling keys as he stowed them in one of the cubby lockers banked behind him. "You're Karen's replacement, huh?"

"I am."

"The boys took a real shine to her."

Did they? Karen was never one to paint herself in flattering colors, but she'd given me the distinct impression the inmates had loved her as they might a rash.

"I'm sure you'll do just fine," Ryan told me. "You let me know if you need anything."

"She needs a panic button," Shonda pointed out. Her raised eyebrow added, *You'd have remembered that if you weren't so busy flirting.*

"Course." He unlocked a metal drawer and rummaged for what looked like a pager. He clicked something on his computer, pushed the device's button, clicked some more and typed, and finally handed it to me. I clipped it to my belt loop, praying I'd never find occasion to use it.

Shonda led me through a heavy metal door and into a short corridor with the turning of a key—one of about a million on her overloaded ring. "You'll be holding most of your programs in classroom B, and you can use office four when you're not leading a session. You can't keep too much there permanently—it's shared by a bunch of externals—but we'll clear out a filing cabinet for you."

"Great."

"It's got a computer and printer and scanner, and a land line." Another key turned and another door swallowed us, another white hall. "No cell phones on the inside, not for external staff. Sorry."

"I'll live."

"Your clearance'll get you into the office wing, the break room and kitchen, the restrooms, and the admin wing—we call that the green zone. No unescorted inmates allowed. It'll also get you into the dayroom and the classrooms—that's the orange zone, shared by staff and inmates. You'll be restricted from the yard, cells, gym, and so forth—red zone—as well as all blue-zone areas, which are security personnel only."

"Okay."

"Don't panic if you can't remember all that—the doorways are painted to tell you what zone you're entering." She tapped the metal doorframe we were about to go through. *Orange.* My stomach flipped. My legs longed to spin me around, march

11

me back out into the sunshine. I could hear noises through the steel, random shouts and muted clanging.

"We're entering the dayroom," Shonda said, inserting one last key and punching numbers into a bank of buttons. "It's the best-staffed area in Cousins. Inmates are allowed to move freely between here and their cells, provided they're currently what we call 'compliant.' They earn movement privileges, through good behavior."

This was meant to reassure me, but all I felt was cold, cold, icy cold.

"They're gonna talk to you," Shonda told me, finger poised over the keypad. "Don't you pay them no mind. You'll have an officer in front of you and behind. Keep your eyes forward. Smile or don't, just try to look confident. Fake it if you need to."

Oh, I'd need to.

"You don't seem the shimmying type, but I'll tell you anyhow, walk like God or your mama never gave you no hips or butt."

"Sure."

She shot me a maternal look and added, "No external staffer's been assaulted in the dayroom in over ten years."

Yay.

She jabbed the final digit, and the red light above the keypad blinked green and beeped.

Shonda stepped inside. I followed.

The air stayed behind, its clearance strictly green zone.

The dayroom was long, lined with cell doors along one side and loomed over by two rows of the same, up on a second level beyond a railing. No bars—each door was painted metal with a latched slot, a narrow window, and a pair of stenciled numbers. Bodies milled and loitered—inmates in navy blue, officers in khaki.

12

It was a jungle of relentless noise. My hard-soled flats slapped loudly with each step. *Everything* echoed, a hundred sharp sounds ricocheting off concrete and steel and glass. I was drowning in the volume of it, lost in the thundering waterfall of all those shouts and slams and clanks and thumps.

A dozen circular table units were bolted in place, each with four fixed seats sticking out at ninety degrees from a thick post. Inmates were hunched in small groups over the tables and standing around, chatting.

It was all more *casual* than I'd imagined, and I reminded myself that only men with good behavior were allowed to wander freely. Or to attend the library's enrichment sessions.

There were several officers posted at our end, and one of them, a sturdy-looking black guy of about fifty, strode over.

"You must be our new librarian," he said. "I'm John."

I shook his hand. "Anne."

"Where she headed?" John asked Shonda. "Offices?"

She nodded, and to me she said, "You follow John, and I'm right behind you."

I wanted to beg for a moment to collect myself—for a deep suck of oxygen from beyond the heavy door at my back—but John was already moving. Casual, slow steps, exhibiting a taste of the swagger I was denied, as a woman. I kept my hips tight, my spine straight as a lamppost. I shouldered my tote's handle, letting it obscure the profile of my breasts.

Eyes followed me. Conversations hushed, changing the chaotic auditory rabble into a buzzing hive. There were perhaps forty men on the floor and a dozen more above, leaning along the rail in front of the second-floor cells. Panicky demands begged to burst from my throat. *Why are they allowed out, like this? What does it matter if you take away my keys, when I could be strangled to death inside a minute?*

I felt the stares I couldn't actually see, real as fondling

13

hands, reaching from all angles. I tried hard to look calm. Like I'd done this before. I could never pass for tough, not like Shonda, nor coolly above it all like John, so I didn't try. I aimed for invisible instead, though of course it didn't work.

"Finally," a skinny black inmate said with a clap. "Conjugal Friday. Where we get in line?"

A couple of guys laughed, and at my back Shonda barked, "Keep talking, Wallace. Talk yourself right out of commissary for all I care."

Wallace muttered something, not seeming especially chastised. My heart and lungs and throat hurt, too dry and tight. My entire body hurt, like their stares were bruising me.

As we passed a glass-paneled, octagonal station in the center of the dayroom, there was a demographic shift—all the darker brown faces were suddenly gone, a narrow contingent of Hispanic men at the next couple of tables, then all whites. The division was so obvious, I felt embarrassed.

I felt more embarrassed when one of the Hispanic guys let out a low whistle. I felt menaced when the white inmates didn't say anything at all. Nothing I could hear, anyhow. They whispered instead, or licked their lips, making me nearly miss Wallace and his gregarious breed of harassment. I was grateful my face had gone so cold and numb, bereft of blood; blushing seemed an incriminating act. A declaration of weakness of a dangerously coy, female persuasion.

One inmate stood out among the group, even sitting down.

Stood out in his stillness and his focus, even as a buddy elbowed him in the arm.

My pounding heart went still, eerie as birds fallen silent in the wake of a gunshot.

He was big. Tall frame, wide shoulders—but not burly.

Unlike many of the inmates, his head wasn't shaved. His

14

near-black hair was due for a cut in fact, curling under his ears. Dark brows, dark stubble, dark lashes and eyes.

And he was handsome. So handsome it broke your heart.

A deck of cards was split between his hands, paused midshuffle. Some of the men wore navy scrub tops and bottoms, some navy tee shirts, a few white undershirts. This man wore a tee, with *COUSINS* stenciled on the front, above the number 802267. Those digits imprinted on my brain, burned black as a brand.

He watched me.

But not the way the others did.

If he was trying to picture me naked, his poker face was strong, though his attention anything but subtle. His entire head moved as I passed through his domain, but his eyes were languorous. Lazy and half-lidded, yet intense. A hundred looks in one. I didn't like it. Couldn't read it. At least with the horny jerk-offs, I knew where I stood.

I wondered what the worst thing you could do and still only get sent to a medium-security prison was.

I hoped not to ever learn the answer.

And I hoped to heaven inmate 802267 hadn't signed up for any of the day's programs.

Chapter Two

Once the day was actually under way, my panic eased some.

I was in classroom B all morning—not unlike a schoolroom, though the painted cinderblock walls were windowless and posterless, and the vibe was grim.

Four metal chairs were bolted into the concrete behind each of eight long tables in four rows, accommodating thirty-two men total, with an aisle down the middle. My chair was free moving, but no more comfortable than what the inmates were stuck with—the theme of the décor was *minimalist*. Minimal detachable pieces, minimal hardware. Minimal materials from which to fashion a weapon capable of stabbing me to death.

Before the inmates arrived, an older officer took up his post by the door, hands clasped before him, back rod straight. John had introduced him as Leland. His mustache was steely gray, trimmed to the textbook profile of the top half of a hamburger bun. *I will not be fucked with,* that mustache told the world.

The door was opened from the outside at two minutes of

nine, and my heart leapt into my throat. I forced a smile. Forced a swallow. Forced my hands to stop shaking atop the primer set before me on my small, scuffed desk, and forced my knees to quit knocking.

Inmates filed in, chatting and arguing. The class was full, every single chair, leading me to imagine Literacy Basics must have a waiting list. They came in all sizes and ages. Same navy blue uniforms. I didn't spot 802267 among them.

"Good morning," I said. My voice was warbly. I could hear it, so they could hear it. There was nothing to be done about it.

"I'm Ms. Goodhouse, the new outreach librarian from Darren Public Library. Welcome to Literacy Basics." I took a deliberate breath to stop my words from racing. I wanted to shut my eyes, squint to blur their facial hair and tattoos and stenciled numbers so I could pretend they were teenagers, and that I was in a high school classroom.

"I'm going to hand out some worksheets," I said, giving stacks of four to the men in the first-row aisle seats. "Please pass them down." I held my breath as I moved to the second row, but no one touched my butt. Eyes *everywhere*, and somebody muttered, "Southern gal," but no hands. Third row. Fourth. I strode back to the front of the room, masking my relief.

"This is an eight-week course. If I cover material you're already familiar with, please consider it a refresher. The lessons will intensify as the weeks go on. All right? Now, does anyone here not know the alphabet?"

No one replied or raised their hand, and I had no choice but to assume they were being truthful.

"Excellent. We're going to begin with basic phonics. Phonics is a way of learning to read and write by listening to the sounds of words . . ."

17

My brain detached from my mouth—I'd given this intro many times before, having worked as a lower-grade substitute teacher and private tutor through much of grad school.

It was deeply weird, though. Saying all this stuff to full-grown, incarcerated men, not antsy kids.

As the lesson progressed, some men kept completely quiet—deep in concentration or totally checked out, it was hard to say. Others were chatty, wanting to ask questions for no reason other than to talk to me. Usually to flirt.

"Hey, library lady," one man cut in. "You a miss or a missus?"

His, buddy added, "Yeah. Who you be readin' bedtime stories to when you at home?"

"Shut your mouth," a man in the front row swiveled to say. "Like you got a chance? Shit. Some of us is here to better ourselves, motherfucker." That was another contingent, the hyper-earnest types with no patience for nonsense, quick to demand I explain something they hadn't understood.

No one was outright disrespectful or threatening, not in the way they spoke. I could sense what Karen had said was true—the chance to spend an hour with one's attention locked on an unfamiliar woman was a coveted one. I hoped some of them truly cared about becoming literate, but failing that, their willingness to abide by the rules in exchange for an hour's permission to mentally undress me would suffice. Though let's be real—I wasn't getting paid nearly enough for this.

After Literacy Basics came Composition. I asked the attendees as they filed in to please sit in order of their writing proficiency, by those who found it "very challenging," "somewhat challenging," and "not too challenging." A few nodded acknowledgment, but once again they sorted themselves at the tables strictly according to color.

It was obvious that trying to lead them as three separate levels was a lost cause. Instead I handed out sheets of lined paper and golf pencils—the latter were provided by the prison—and read them a prompt.

"Everyone please write for three minutes on the topic of 'my favorite season.' I just want to see where we all are with our writing skills."

I wandered around, my butt as yet untouched. Some men managed a couple of sentences, writing in the slow, mindful capitals of children, others a paragraph or two. As they set their pencils down, I gathered a few pages of varying length to read aloud. I'd be careful to praise what they'd done well before extracting usage or grammar mistakes to make lessons of.

"'My favorite season is summer,'" I read out, glossing over misspellings, "''cause as a kid we had no school and got to play all day and didn't nobody tell me where to be 'til dinner-time. I hate winter it is too long here in Michigan not like it is in Virginia where I'm from.' Right. This is very good. It addresses the prompt with strong, declarative statements. Now let's have a quick lesson about using punctuation to show the rhythm of our words . . ."

The remainder of the writing session went . . . not disastrously. It got hauled off track when I tried to impart some simple grammar tips. Perhaps sensing my unease, someone took the opportunity to spin it into a political debate on the topic of "the black man's voice," and how street slang was more authentic than what he called, "Your fancy white-people vernacular, you feel me?" Terrified of sparking a fight, I wussily let the inmates engage in a semi-civilized dissection of the subject, butting in with the odd, limp, "Yes, that's an interesting point," before things grew heated and Leland thumped the wall with his baton and told everyone to shut up.

19

The session wrapped, and as the inmates filed out, my smile muscles hurt, and my shoulders were practically hugging my ears. I eyed Leland in the corner, pleading for a sign—any sign, good or bad—that might indicate how I'd handled that.

He offered a thumbs-up, his showy, dismissive frown telling me, *Don't sweat it, kid. You're doing fine.*

I took the deepest breath I could manage, willing myself to believe him.

The next session was Resources. Cousins had a strong—if not revolutionary—rehabilitation ethos, and they relied on the visiting librarians to teach inmates how to use the Internet for job searches, and to practice filling out online applications. It wasn't quite a class, more a free-for-all. There were only two computers, so men had to sign up for them in advance. The rest of the guys came and went freely, asking me to proofread the resumes they'd drafted, to explain paperwork they'd received, help them write letters and so forth.

The morning Resources session wasn't too crazy, but I'd been told the afternoon one was far more popular. "They get restless between lunch and dinner," Leland told me in the staff break room.

"Lucky me." I dumped two packets of instant oatmeal in a mug and nuked it in the microwave. I ate without tasting, standing at the window that overlooked the exercise yard. The men loitered, worked out on push-up and chin-up bars, played shirts versus skins on the cracked, one-hoop basketball court.

Years in this place, I thought. *Years with nothing to do but ward off the boredom by building your muscles, maybe your mind.* But even I could tell, there wasn't much equipment on hand at Cousins promoting the latter.

After lunch came Book Discussion—the only session I was actually looking forward to.

20

I'd been encouraged to pick a story that would speak to the inmates' struggles, but not enflame them. Something roughly suited to men with grossly adult problems but teenagers' reading comprehension, and which also met the standards of both the ALA and Cousins. I'd read the prison's guidelines, and they were fairly liberal. They discouraged "excessive violent and sexual content," but happily posed no real censorship threat.

Librarians love challenges—we're all matchmakers, deep down—and I'd obsessed over my selection for days. I'd picked a book aimed at teens, thinking a story about a young man might hearken these guys back to the days before their lives had taken such awful turns.

Book Discussion was held in a different room than the morning classes—big enough to seat fifty or sixty in plastic chairs, with me facing them, also sitting.

The men filed in at one, and I was given two guards—mustache-of-steel Leland in the front corner and another man by the exit. There was much talking and joking, the guys still in social mode from their own lunch break.

Pretend it's a school group. As the chairs filled up I said, firmly as I could, "Quiet please. Thank you. Hi, everyone. I'm Ms. Goodhouse, the new librarian. Welcome to a new session of Book Discussion. I hope you'll enjoy the story I've picked—"

From the second row, "Here we go! To Kill a motherfucking Mockingbird!" Wallace again, Mr. Conjugal Fridays.

A couple guys laughed, a couple shushed him.

"It's called *Shop Breaker*, by Paolo Bacigalupi," I said. "That's all I'll tell you for now." And I began to read.

The story was set in a dystopian future, its protagonist a teenage boy named Nailer who scavenged copper from wrecked tankers. I hoped the setting would keep it separated somewhat from their lives, but the themes were ones I thought they'd care about—making one's way in a harsh world. Survival, oppression, struggle, triumph. Love.

As I read, the men went quiet. Eerily quiet, apart from when something interesting happened and the room hummed with a dozen mumbled comments.

I'd picked a winner.

My voice lost its brittle stage-fright edges. The room stirred when the dynamics between the young indentured ship breakers and their callous overseers were center stage.

Despite the plan to keep my head down and read, my old storytime instincts proved too strong. I began glancing up, stealing a taste of eye contact every couple of sentences. I kept it brief—a second's glimpse at a random face, just enough to engage, then back to the page.

I was doing fine until fifteen minutes in, when another stolen glance brought my eyes to those of 802267.

My heart froze. My lips stumbled, and I snapped my attention back to the book, resyncing my brain and the printed words.

I tried to keep my face down, but knowing he was there, knowing exactly where his body was in this room, in relation to mine, knowing those dark eyes were trained right on me . . .

I looked up.

That stare. That unreadable expression, an impossible mix of apathy and fascination, coldness and searing seduction.

Wait—what? I escaped back to the page, mouth moving on autopilot.

Cold seduction. Yeah, right. Surely there was a better word for that quality, like oh, say, *sociopathic.*

I was mindful to make eye contact only with the other side of the room for a few pages, but his gaze . . . it stuck to me.

Clung like the heat left by a lover's palm. It made my cheeks warm, and I hoped my blush didn't show under the sallow fluorescents.

My mind raced as my lips and tongue soldiered onward.

Look again—you'll see it was nothing. A trick of your mind. A zing of recognition for spotting a seemingly familiar face among the strangers. And familiar from the dayroom, only.

Though why a man's face should have imprinted so deeply, from so brief an encounter . . .

He was handsome, to be sure. Not to everyone's taste—not all-American wholesome-handsome. Much darker. A knowing and dangerous breed of charisma.

Of course I knew all too well, looks deceived. The ex who'd ruptured my eardrum and left me with a popping jaw, he was all-American wholesome-handsome. Blond. Hazel eyes, green in the sun, and that smile. Give him a yellow Lab and a football, and the tableau was complete.

Hand him a plastic tumbler—half cola, half rum—and he became something else entirely.

That's the only reason 802267 is so magnetic. He's nothing like Justin. Blond, smiling Justin.

This numbered, nameless stranger . . . he'd fucked up. Past tense. Fucked up bad enough to get locked away, and the absolute honesty of that held an unexpected appeal. Because whatever Justin's crimes might prove to be—vehicular, domestic, drunk and disorderly—they were To Be Determined. If he didn't stop drinking, something ugly awaited him, and the certainty of that fact, coupled with the *un*certainty of when it might arrive and what shape it would take, was crushing.

But this man, with his dark eyes, dark hair, dark stubble . . . A man like this one, sitting four rows back, three seats from the end . . . I knew where he sat, and where he stood.

23

I knew where he slept—behind a thick metal door. And that made him safe, somehow.

I stole another glance.

His gaze was strong male hands cradling a baby bird—seemingly innocuous, but shot through with the potential for unbearable cruelty. 802267's expression itself wasn't cruel, but that mysterious stare . . . that could be promising anything. That wasn't to be trusted.

Quit looking.

I met the eyes of the men around him, but he shone in my periphery. The way he sat, legs spread, hips scooted forward, arms draped lazily on his thighs. Like this were somebody's yard. Like he had the collar of a beer bottle pinched between two fingers, the summer sun warm on the back of his neck. His eyes were steady, and I felt them on me. Felt them drinking up every word my mouth formed, licking them straight off my lips.

It felt as though I were speaking other words to 802267, words no one else could hear.

What's that stare saying?

What are you thinking?

What did you do to forfeit your freedom? To deserve this life?

What would you do to me, if it were just the two of us in here? Shiver.

But what kind of shiver?

Quit looking at me. But everyone was looking at me—whether they were imagining things that would make me sick or not, they had permission to look right at me, and they did. So why should one man's attention burn when the others left me so cold?

I glanced at the clock. Nearly half past, time to begin the discussion.

When I closed the book on a cliffhanger, audible groans and one, "Aw, come on," rewarded me.

"So," I said, looking around the room. At everyone but 802267. "Thoughts? Do we like Nailer? Why or why not? Hands, please."

No one spoke at first, but after a couple awkward breaths, a dark hand rose.

"Yes," I said, pointing to the young man.

"I hope he get his back on that bitch, for leavin' him to die."

"Do you think he'd do the same to her," I asked, "if he were the one in the position to maybe profit from all that oil?"

A different hand rose in the front row and I nodded at its owner.

"Naw, man. He understands about allies. He'd'a split it with her and that other chick."

"Fuck them," somebody else said, and I gestured for the big, slope-shouldered skinhead to expand on this thought.

"Anybody can tell themselves they'll do what's right in their head. But then when an opportunity arises . . ." He shrugged. "Survival instincts kick in. You gotta put yourself first. 'Specially when it's life or death on the line. Or your freedom."

"I wouldn't never do my crew that way," came a petulant voice in the back.

"Hands," I reminded them. "That's an interesting angle, talking about allies in a situation like this, isn't it? Because Nailer has to both rely on his fellow ship breakers, but also compete with them for his place. Do we think Nailer's going to try to get revenge on Sloth if he makes it out alive?"

A few nods and grunts, and I called on a raised hand.

"I bet he won't," said the thirtysomething Hispanic guy.

25

"I bet he'll turn the other cheek, right, 'cause he don't wanna be a shit like his old man."

This roused a rumble of collective contemplation.

The next hand belonged to Wallace, and what he said impressed me, proving him capable of more than undermining one-liners.

"This world is like, dog eat dog. He be starvin', man. If he don't get hisself some mothafuckin' revenge, man, ain't nobody gon' respect him. It's like in here. You get one chance to prove what kinda balls you got. You pass that up, you fuckin' dead."

"But then he ain't no better than that Sloth bitch," his neighbor said.

The discussion stayed lively and mainly civil, and there were still hands raised when I was forced to wrap the session. The inmates rose with a scraping of chairs and much chatter, and a large guy from the front row approached me at a respectful distance. In a surprisingly gentle voice he said, "This is a fine-ass book, Miss . . ."

"Ms. Goodhouse."

"Right, Miss Goodhouse. Fine enough to be a movie."

"I'm glad you think so."

He didn't smile, but there was a sad warmth in his eyes as he shuffled past. "I'll be lookin' forward to hearin' what happen next. To see if he gets hisself out, or drowns, or what."

"Oh good." I smiled until he turned away, then scanned the funneling crowd. No 802267. Not that I should have been looking.

The rest of my day would be a partial repeat of the morning—Literacy Basics and Resources, back to back. The former was tense.

Fuses were short in Cousins, and no one was eager to look stupid in front of a twentysomething woman or a roomful of their worst enemies, struggling to sound out words like *bucket* and *ocean* and *seagull*. There were meltdowns—frustrated, self-hating flashes reminiscent of the kids I'd helped decipher these same letters. These men needed my help, wanted my help. Resented my help.

I could feel the tension flash and simmer now and then, like ripples of heat shimmering above hot asphalt. It kept me on edge. Even kept my mind off inmate 802267 for a time.

Until an hour later, when I suddenly found myself face to face with him.

Leland had been right—the afternoon block of Resources was more popular than the morning, and it was twice as long. There were lots of inmates and only one of me, and I could taste the collective impatience as I chose at random whom to help next.

I was quizzing a younger guy for his upcoming GED test, when a tall figure came through the door. I knew who it was without even raising my eyes. Broad shoulders and slim hips, long legs. Overgrown dark hair. Eyes hot enough to singe.

Fuck.

Why was I even so freaked out? 802267 looked no more or less threatening than any of the other men, so it had to be intuition . . . Except he put me on alert one level deeper than mere fear. Made me feel warm and unnerved and restless in a way I didn't trust at all. A way I wasn't used to. A hunger I hadn't been dogged by in years.

He strolled between the tables to a free chair on the largely black side of the room, earning hostile glares as he took a seat. He had no papers or books with him, just sat there with his fingers linked atop the table, patient as could be.

He reserved me with his stare, his silence telling me, *I'll be right here, waiting.*

Others had been angling for my attention for some time,

and I was happy to avoid him for forty minutes or more. And still he simply sat there, hands clasped, eyes following me. I came around to him toward the end of the two-hour block, crossing the floor with my heart pounding. I was wheeling a chair everywhere I went, and I pushed it up to the end of his long table, smiling as I took a seat kitty-corner to him.

"You've been awful patient. Can I help you with something?"

Nearly a smile. Nearly. His voice was deep. Low. Rich and dark as spring soil. "I hope so."

"So do I. Shoot."

"I don't write too well."

"Okay."

"I've tried the literacy classes before, but they weren't much help."

"No?"

"I already know all that kindergarten bull, about sounding shit out. I read all right, but my writing's shit. I have to think about every damn letter like it's the first time I've ever seen it. Dyslexia or whatever."

"Actually, that sounds like dysgraphia."

"Like what?"

"It's like a cousin of dyslexia. You can read just fine, you said?"

He nodded once, like a cowboy or something. The way he never took his eyes off my face made me antsy. Squirmy all over. I prayed he couldn't tell. "I read okay. Not fast, but a couple books a week."

"But you find the letters difficult to form, when you sit down to write something?"

"I can copy them just fine, but they don't stay in my head. Not all of them, anyhow."

"Yeah, that's dysgraphia." Dear God, why had he not been diagnosed by first or second grade? What chance did a kid stand in a school system like that? "Would you like to make a plan for working with your challenges?"

"If you've got one."

"Well, I know this isn't the ideal place for it, but many people with your challenge find that typing makes writing a lot easier, once they get used to the keyboard. Do you have much of a computer background?"

"No. But that's true—it's way easier to type. I can find letters way quicker than I can remember how to make them myself."

"Great. If you come to Resources again next Friday, I'll bring some worksheets and literature about dysgraphia. And maybe you could let me watch you write a little, and that way I can see exactly where it is we're starting from. Sound okay?"

Another dip of his stubble-black chin. "That sounds all right."

With a vivid flash, I tried to picture him on the outside. How he dressed. Baggy jeans or snug ones, leather jacket or a plaid button-up, some freebie shirt with a beer logo on it . . . ? What kind of work had he done before he got incarcerated? Physical? Or were those hard, tanned arms a byproduct of this place, of this existence with its bottomless wells of boredom and danger?

Another inmate interrupted my stupor.

"Hey! Tick tock, library lady. I been waitin' over an hour here."

I opened my mouth to assure him he'd be next, but 802267 spoke before I could. He whipped his head around and caught the guy in the coldest beam of disgust you ever saw.

"You see a number on her shirt?" he demanded.

29

"What you—"

802267 sat up real straight. "'Cause I don't. And since she hasn't got a number on her shirt, I guess that means she doesn't *have* to be here. So treat the lady with some respect, since she's been nice enough to show up and pretend to give a fuck about your incarcerated ass."

The chastised man pushed his chair out with a squeal and headed for the door, muttering. 802267 turned back to me, posture relaxing. "Where were we?"

"Right," I said, face burning. "You come back next week, and I'll come prepared to help."

"Deal."

I paused before adding, gently, "I do give a fuck, incidentally."

He cracked a smile, making me feel a more southerly persuasion of flustered.

I was poised to rise, but his stare nailed me in place—from cool to broiling in a breath. He spoke quietly. Like we were engaged in a conspiracy.

"I like how you talk."

"Oh." I swallowed, cheeks and neck burning red-hot. "Th-thank you."

"Where you from?"

"South Carolina."

"I never met anybody from South Carolina." His voice was deep and resonant, and it required no volume to command my attention. He spoke with a tone that was threat, coercion, seduction, lament. All at once. *I never met anybody from South Carolina.* The way he said it, anything could have come next.

I never met anybody from South Carolina . . .

. . . but I love bluegrass.

. . . but I stabbed a man to death in Tennessee.

30

. . . but I hear the girls there taste like peaches.

"What's the weather like there?" he asked.

"Nice," I said stupidly, nodding. Terrified. Hypnotized. "Real nice."

His gaze dropped from my eyes to my mouth, the weight of it as real as a kiss. His own lips were parted, the lower one looking full and flushed.

"Real hot summers," he said.

"Pretty hot." I swallowed again, parched. "Sometimes."

"I miss summers. On the outside."

"I'm sure."

"Miss beer. Swimming in the lake. Feeling my hair dry in the sun."

He parceled out his thoughts in tiny bites, keeping me hungry, dying to taste whatever came off that tongue next.

"I'm sure you do," I offered.

"Miss lots of things." He said it low, each letter dripping molasses, thick with black, sticky-sweet intentions.

This man . . . maybe he couldn't write, but he spoke volumes with a few murmured words.

The officer's voice broke in with a bark. "Collier. Back it up." 802267 obediently sat up straight. *Collier.* His body heat went with him.

Our elbows had been almost near enough to touch, faces close enough to whisper secrets. And wasn't that what he'd been doing? Had I been whispering back? I couldn't even say who'd brought us so near. I could only tell you I hadn't pulled away. And that made exactly two men in the world whose nearness I didn't shrink from—Collier and my daddy.

"I better move on before the session's over," I said, attention on his hands. On those fingers still linked so benignly. Then his eyes. "I'll see you next week, if you want the help."

"It's a date."

31

I stood and wheeled my chair away, risking only the quickest glance. But that was all it took to braise my body anew in his weird, scary heat. I scanned for the nearest expectant face, so woozy I could've been drunk.

I felt it when Collier was gone, like quenching cool rolling in on the heels of a summer storm, deepening my lungs and welcoming my sanity back.

Chapter Three

That man haunted me.

I revisited our interaction a hundred times that weekend, shocked and ashamed he'd managed to get so close. That it had taken a guard posted twenty feet away to spot it, when I'd been sitting right there, close enough to smell his skin.

That's his way, I imagined. A charmer by design. If I wasn't careful, he'd find out the names of my parents or friends and have me muling drugs for him inside a month. That was how extortion worked. On TV, anyhow.

But the thing that threw me most about the incident was the way it elevated a long-held suspicion of mine to blinding truth—I was attracted to bad men.

One abusive boyfriend and a consumptive insta-lust for an inmate who'd done Lord knew what to get put away . . . That was only two offenses, but it was also *plenty*. I couldn't trust my libido any more than I could Collier. Both had to be approached like the dangerous creatures they were.

I tried to drape my obsession under a practical veil. On Monday I rooted through the library's dusty basement, finding what I was after. I made a phone call to Cousins, and after being transferred to three different personnel, I was connected to the warden herself. I made a request, and it was granted. And the next Friday I arrived lugging a heavy case, its pebbled plastic turned brittle by age and dust. After my morning strip search with Shonda, I set the case with a *thunk* on the reception desk in front of Ryan.

"I got permission from the warden to bring this in for inmate 802267."

He eyed the case, opened its latches. "All right, then. I'll send it on up the chain, and hopefully it'll get where it's going in the next day or two."

As Shonda and a male officer escorted me through the long dayroom, I wasn't nearly as scared as the week before. I got stares, a few noises and murmurs of sexual interest, and a cheerful, "Hey, Ms. Goodhouse!" from Wallace. I couldn't remember all the protocol, but I was fairly sure greeting him back was a violation of some rule or other, so I kept my eyes forward and my mouth shut.

I was feeling as confident as could be hoped, until we passed the central booth. Beyond it lay the white inmates' territory, and among them sat Collier, just as I'd anticipated. Same table.

Same seat, I thought, and the same game of cards, though someone else was shuffling. He watched me, and I watched him. Though to *watch* someone really requires that they be doing something, and he wasn't, so I suppose technically I *stared* at him.

I *wanted* to stare at him. I wanted to study him without anybody seeing, pore over this man who affected me like none had before. He'd come to me in dreams every night that week, those arms and hands and that low voice, and those brown eyes like devil's food batter.

34

I'd had my share of crushes—I was twenty-seven, after all—and I'd been with a few guys. I'd been infatuated, if not to the extent some of my girlfriends from back home seemed to get. Not until now. I knew exactly why.

He's a terrible man. He must be, if he was locked up here, among inmates whose crimes were robbery, assault, major drug offenses, rape, manslaughter. Given that menu, I'd be rooting for robbery, and that was pathetic. He was a bad man, no doubt. One who deserved reform, but not my desire.

And he's a prisoner—that's the other reason. That was why I wanted him. Because he was untouchable, the very urge impossible. *Because he's dangerous, but this crush*—if that's what it was—*is safe.* Because my ear had healed and my bruises had faded, but my heart was still too skittish to invite anything real.

What my body felt for him, though, that *was* real. This attraction positively hounded me. Those dreams. And I'd fantasized about him, too, just the briefest, most intense snatches of contact. Of his mouth on my neck and his words steaming my skin. *I like the way you talk.* What else would he say, if he got me alone?

I like the way you—

"Better this time?" Shonda asked, unlocking the door that led to the administrative wing. I'd barely registered leaving the orange zone, when last week I'd been practically gasping to escape it.

"Way better, thanks. The uncertainty's not so bad now, you know?"

"I do. Have a good one, Anne."

"You, too."

The morning sessions went well enough. A couple of minor outbursts, but nothing a bark from the attending CO couldn't shut down. I delivered a copy of *My Side of the Mountain* to an inmate who'd requested it the week before. It had been his favorite when he was young, and he wanted to read it now, to try to remember what it felt like to be his son's age. They didn't visit, he'd said—his son and ex-girlfriend. He hadn't seen the kid since he was four. The request touched me, and I handed the paperback over like I was giving him a bar of gold, more determined than ever to avoid hearing what these men were in for.

Drug possession and theft didn't scare me too badly—those seemed impersonal. Forgivable acts of desperation. But if I heard a guy I'd begun to feel invested in was locked up for domestic violence or sexual assault, or for abusing a child . . . There was a vast difference between helping someone uncover their potential, and knowing what they were *capable* of. And if I had to contend with the latter, I couldn't do my job.

I took my lunch break in the office, eating a turkey sandwich as I stared out the window at the exercise yard. It was bordered on three sides by the four-story prison. I was tucked into one of the corners, two floors up and perhaps thirty feet back from the area where the men did their calisthenics, beyond chain link capped with coils of concertina wire.

No Collier. Not at first. But as I bit into my apple, an air horn sounded and all the men funneled out of the yard. A minute later, the next group spilled in. And my eyes found him as easily as a compass finds north.

He moved in a small pack of fellow white inmates, breaking off as they headed for a set of bleachers and continuing on alone in my direction. A handful of black guys were already getting to work on the sparse equipment, and he strode right on up to them. Exchanged a curt nod with the biggest of the group, securing some permission I'd never understand. He stripped his shirt, tossing it in a ball on the dry, brown grass.

And he was beautiful.

His body shocked the very breath out of me. Tan and strong and fucking *cut*.

Of course he is. What else is there to do? His powerful shoulders tapered to a trim waist, every inch of him looking carved and honed and dangerous, a tall, strong frame wrapped elegantly in muscle and skin. I felt things I thought I'd only ever dreamed, it had been so long. Hunger, between my legs. Urgency heating every ounce of my coursing blood. He dropped to bang out a couple dozen push-ups, and Lord help me, I imagined my body beneath his pumping one. My hand rose, palm pressing the cool glass. Seeking him. I snatched it back.

It was different, watching him like this—with him not watching me in return. With the fear removed, all I felt was the fascination. His loose pants hung about his hips, revealing a sliver of gray. It shone against his tan skin like silver.

Boxers or briefs? I wondered, unsure if the prisoners even got to choose.

He had tattoos on his back and one shoulder, but I couldn't make them out. Like his sentence, I probably didn't want the details. Didn't want to squint and find evidence of his crime, or spot a swastika.

Or see a woman's name written in cursive inside a heart.

No, not that, either. I could admit it. And as I did, I backed away from the window.

Part of me wondered if he'd even show this afternoon, for our little study session. I wasn't stupid. I knew what a man wanted when he stared the way Collier did. He just wanted to be close to me—to a woman. Close enough to smell me, or scare me, or seduce me. Couldn't tell you which. Didn't care to know. All at once I hoped he wouldn't show for Resources or Book Discussion. I *feared* he wouldn't show. I feared too much about him, both his nearness and his absence.

I didn't spot him as the men shuffled in for Book Discussion

37

a half hour later, but that didn't mean a thing. It was a big group. And my body was ringing, a tuning fork vibrating on what was fast becoming a familiar frequency.

My mouth went dry, but fuck it. I plunged into the next chapter.

When it wrapped I asked the room if someone else would like to read the next one, someone with a strong, projecting voice. I got a couple of volunteers, and picked Wallace. The guy certainly wasn't lacking in showmanship, plus if he was reading, I'd be spared his smart remarks. He didn't speak with the finest grammar, but he read quite well, sitting in my seat before the audience. I stood by, making the odd note to myself about what prompts to use to spark a conversation.

I didn't want to pull the men from the story by looking around the room too much while the others read, so I kept my eyes glued to neutral places—my notes, the floor at the foot of the front row, a blank stretch of wall. That was my excuse, anyway. Really I just didn't want to know if Collier was there. Or more specifically, I didn't want the sensation in my chest confirmed. Didn't want to spot him and realize it was true—something inside me was tuned to him. Primed to rouse when he was close. And I felt roused, then. Charged.

The discussion began, quickly growing heated. It was what I'd hoped for, choosing this book—that they'd get engaged—but it still kept me on edge. I didn't yet understand the bounds of their feelings, and what impulses lay beyond.

"If he don't go after her," one man said on the topic of Nailer seeking revenge on Sloth, "then this world ain't got no rules. They boss don't give a shit. Ain't no cops to give a shit. No consequences—"

"She got consequences," another cut in. "She got nothin' now. The book said so, basically, how she'd have to sell her body and shit."

"Hands," I reminded them, back in the reader's seat, legs crossed. "That's an interesting point, about how there's no real authority where Nailer is. The author's implied that maybe elsewhere in the world, it's still civilized. Where the wealthy people live. Any thoughts on that? Yes." I called on a man in the back.

He began to reply, but I suddenly couldn't hear him. Because just to his left sat Collier.

Collier in his navy tee, with his hot-tar eyes. I stared at him, he stared at me.

Could he tell I was staring at him? Was I far enough away that maybe, just maybe, it looked like I was rapt by his neighbor's analysis?

Silence, and I'd not heard what the man had said. Not a word.

"Interesting," I bluffed. "Responses?" I called on someone sitting very far away from Collier, and gave him my full attention.

The block ended shortly and I smiled as the men shuffled out. Unable to resist, I watched Collier go. I wanted to know what he'd do as he reached the door, and I found out, to my own peril. He was looking at me. Straight at me. Cross hairs. And then it was his entire body aimed my way, cutting through the draining crowd, coming for me. He shot the guard a look, getting a nod of permission. He stopped a couple paces from me, hands in his pockets.

I smiled to cover my anxiety. I had the strangest feeling he knew that I'd watched him, an hour earlier. Watched his bare body in the sunshine, toiling in the yard.

"Good afternoon," I offered, and any authority my voice had assumed during the session fled, my words going reedy.

"Hey. I got that thing you brought."

"Oh, that was quick." Fuck, I could smell him. Summer

39

and sweat. I wanted to lick his neck and taste the salt on his skin.

"What is it?" he asked. "A typewriter?"

"Kind of. It's a word processor. It's about a million years old, but I thought you might want to use it, to practice your writing."

"Does it need paper?"

"It takes it, but I doubt they still make ribbons for those things. You can just use the little screen—it'll show you what you're typing. You'll see when you plug it in. *If* you plug it in. You don't have to use it if you don't want to." I was babbling.

"No outlets in the cells."

"Oh, crap." Of course there weren't.

"But I'll see about using it in the media room or wherever."

"Collier," said the guard. "Let's go."

"Thanks," he murmured to me. "I'll see you later, for that help we talked about. And I got a question for you."

My stomach gurgled and my mouth couldn't form a reply quick enough. He was gone, big frame slipping through the door, and all at once I could breathe again.

A question for me? There were so many I yearned to ask in return.

What do you want to do with your life, when you get out? Are you ever getting out? What are you like, out in the world? How do you dress? What would you order in a restaurant?

How would you approach me, out there? With hollow promises? With roses? With a blade and a steady hand?

And when I saw him two hours later during the Resources block, I posed not a one of those questions. He found an empty seat, sitting patiently. I lost my nerve and avoided him. Kept allowing my eye to be caught by another attendee, putting him off. But with only twenty minutes left before my day

40

ended, I couldn't ignore him any longer. I crossed the room, chair rolling before me.

"Hello again," I offered, stopping but not sitting. "Sorry for the wait. Ready to chat?"

He tapped the butt of a golf pencil against the table. "If you got the time."

"I've got a little." I took a seat across from him, wondering how close our shoes were to touching.

"So about that machine you gave me—I appreciate it, but I don't type right." He air-pecked with two fingers.

"Oh, don't worry about that. I bet half of college grads don't type with more than two or three fingers. Just get in the habit of practicing. Typing something every day."

"Typing what?"

"Anything you like."

He shot me a smile, one that cut the tether from the tenuous hold I'd gotten on my role and sent my focus crashing to the floor. I watched his lips as he spoke.

"I've been gettin' told exactly what to do, and when and where and how quick, for almost five years. You tell me what to write or I won't even know how to start."

"Oh, all right." *Five years. For what?* "Well, if you need an assignment, you could spend say, twenty minutes each night, typing up what happened to you that day. Don't worry about punctuation, and the word processor will fix most of the capitalization and spelling issues. Just get your fingers and eyes used to finding the letters. Work on that first, and maybe in time we'll get a plan together to start tackling your longhand. It's a tricky thing, dysgraphia. Didn't sound like you got much help in school for it."

He shook his head. "No one ever said I have that—they said I had dyslexia."

"They differ a fair bit. Dyslexia is often an issue with

41

perception—people will have trouble reading because the letters seem to move, or rearrange themselves."

"Not for me they don't."

"Right. But when you try to write, your fingers can't remember how to form each letter?"

"Yeah. Exactly."

"But you have no trouble copying?"

He smiled. "I wouldn't have made it to tenth grade without plagiarism."

I smiled too, grimly. "Gotcha. Well, it's never too late to start. Do what I said—try typing for twenty minutes each night. You might be surprised how much quicker you are with it by next week. Meet with me again and we'll figure out what comes next."

I gave him some dysgraphia fact sheets and handouts I'd photocopied.

"Thanks. Now can you, uh . . . Can you help me write a letter? To somebody?" He said it almost primly, humility in his voice. It struck me as odd, considering this man had asked me for help, and been offered it without judgment. Then he added in a near mumble, "A personal letter."

The request was legit, a common one during Resources. I checked the clock. "We can start, at least. But I've only got ten minutes."

He nodded. "You got paper?"

I pulled a notebook from my bag—perfect bound, not spiral, thanks to the thrilling array of deadly implements that can apparently be fashioned from three feet of steel wire. As he handed me the pencil, our fingertips brushed for the thinnest moment—quick and hot as a static shock.

"All righty. Shoot."

"Darling," Collier began, only loud enough for me to hear. His gaze jumped up to pin mine. "That's how it should start."

42

Darling, I wrote. My stomach soured, and even I wasn't deluded enough to pretend I didn't know why. Fuck me, I was penning a love letter to his frigging . . . who knew what. Wife? Girlfriend? Ex? Stalkee? Fine. If this didn't get me over my stupid infatuation, nothing would. I eyed his arm, but his sleeve covered the tattoo I'd spotted from the office window. Whose name might be hiding under there . . . ? *Get a grip.*

"Go on," I said.

"I missed you since your last visit." He watched my hand as he spoke, as his words took shape, drawn by my fingers with an ease he'd likely never know himself. The act felt strangely, intensely intimate.

"A few minutes a week with you is almost more cruel than it's worth," he continued. "I miss—"

"Hang on." I scribbled, catching up. I sensed his posture tighten with annoyance or impatience, and I couldn't blame him. I was a stranger, after all, being asked to transcribe his feelings in a place where emotions were as dangerous to bare as pulse points.

"Okay, go on."

"I miss you every minute we're apart. And I watch the clock every morning when I think I might be seeing you again." He paused, waiting until my hand did the same. "I miss how you smell. Like spring and grass. There's not much grass here. I miss your face . . . And the way you smile sometimes. I want to make you smile like that."

I ignored my jealousy, that hot snake twisting in my belly as I imagined such things. "Okay."

"I miss your voice. The way you talk."

I like the way you talk. Where you from?

The snake slowed. Changed direction, coiling low.

"I wish I could see you, away from here." He put his forearms on the desk, leaning closer, speaking even more

43

quietly. "I wish we could be together . . . in ways I haven't been with a woman in five years. Sometimes, when I see you . . . Sometimes I can't even listen to what you're saying. All I can do is watch your mouth. I watch your lips and I think about kissing you, when I'm alone at night. Though I'm never really alone here. But I imagine I am—alone with just you. I think about your mouth, and about kissing you. And other things."

. . . *other things,* my hand echoed. My neck was hot—hot like sunburn. My cheeks stung. My loose clothes bound me.

"Sometimes I watch your hands," he went on. Watching my hands. "I watch your hands and imagine them . . . on me."

I was trembling, and surely he could see it. His words had turned jagged, pencil pinched between my bloodless fingers.

"I imagine—"

"I think we better leave it there," I breathed.

"We've got three more minutes still."

"Yes, but this is getting . . . I'm not sure it's appropriate that I write this sort of letter for you." *And I'm not sure it's appropriate how wet it's making me. Not sure at all.*

"Right. Well, I guess that's just about what I wanted to say, anyhow."

"Good. I . . . I could have it mailed for you. If you have her address."

That dark gaze jumped from my hands to my eyes and I flinched, too much heat going too many places. For a moment he just stared—not cold, not mean, just . . . *telling.*

"I don't know her address," he said quietly.

I shivered. My hands felt icy, my throat tight. My belly warm and heavy and damning.

His attention dropped to my hands. "Maybe you could hang on to that for me. Until I can remember."

"I can leave it with you." I tore the page carefully along the perforation, but he was shaking his head.

"You hang on to it," he repeated. "It's real personal stuff. Man doesn't want just anybody reading those kinds of thoughts."

I lowered the page, saw it fluttering in my quaking hand and closed it in the notebook. "Fine."

"I didn't get to sign it."

"Oh."

He nodded to the pad, raised his eyebrows. I submitted, pushing the page and the pencil across the tabletop. It was my turn to watch his hand as it formed two short, slow, careful words. Then he slid everything back.

"Thanks . . ." His eyes dropped to my chest, but it was my ID badge he scanned, not my breasts. "Annie." He said it low, made more of breath than sound, as if he were telling himself a secret.

Ms. Goodhouse, I should've said, but the only correction I managed was, "Anne." My parents called me Annie, and my aunts and grandparents and a couple of close friends, but that was all. Not strangers. Not this man whose first name I didn't even know. Whose crimes I didn't wish to hear about. Whose desires I'd just traced with shaking fingers. "I'll see you next week."

And he was gone, long legs striding for the door. This time he didn't look back.

I tucked the letter away in my bag, not daring to see what he'd written.

I won't look. I'll keep it closed in this notebook and not read it, and if next week we speak and he doesn't have an address, I'll throw it out. I'll burn it. I'll do whatever—anything except read it.

I read it in my car.

My butt met the driver's seat, my hands went to my bag, and I slid the page out, fingers shaking.

Darling,

I missed you since our last visit. A few minutes a week with you is almost more cruel than it's worth.

I miss you every minute we're apart, and watch the clock every morning when I think I might be seeing you again. I miss how you smell, like spring and grass. There's not much grass here.

I miss your face, and the way you smile sometimes. I want to make you smile like that. I miss your voice. The way you talk. I wish I could see you, away from here.

I wish we could be together, in ways I haven't been with a woman in five years. Sometimes, when I see you . . . Sometimes I can't even listen to what you're saying. All I can do is watch your mouth. I watch your lips and I think about kissing you when I'm alone at night. Though I'm never really alone here. But I imagine I am. Alone with just you. I think about your mouth, and about kissing you. And other things. Sometimes I watch your hands. I watch your hands and imagine them on me.

Yours,
Eric

Chapter Four

I thought about terrible things, that night.

About a slim iron bed frame, and a man's long, strong body laying atop threadbare covers in the heat of summer. About the waistband of prison-issue pajamas, pushed down by a big, tanned hand to expose an erection—thick, flushed, ready.

A fist stroking slowly to start, then quicker. Rougher.

And that face. Handsome features pained, dark eyes shut.

For the first time in months, my own hand slid low. Me and my hand in my lonely bed, in my lonely room, on this lonely night . . . wondering if a man was thinking of me and doing the same twenty miles away.

Though I'm never really alone, here.

How did that work, I wondered, hitting Pause on the scene. Were convicts discreet, to keep from pissing off their cellmates, or did a man just do what he had to do, and so did everyone else, so who cared? The former, I hoped, preferring the civility of it. Or perhaps the desperation of it. Of Eric Collier stifling his moans and grunts, tensing his body

47

to keep his motions subtle. Of his lips forming two soundless syllables.

Annie.

He'd be thinking about things he couldn't give himself. *Ways I haven't been with a woman in five years.* The wet heat of a hungry mouth. The wet heat of my . . . which word would he use? *Pussy,* probably. Or *cunt.* Yes, cunt. Blunt and ugly, to match his world. I'd flinch if he said it to me, and wasn't that what I wanted, really? No candy coating to sweeten the things he said. All burrs and sharp edges, coming off the smooth slickness of his tongue. His tongue. Did he miss how a woman tasted, after all this time? Would he want to do that, or would he be selfish, concerned only with what I could offer his cock?

Annie, he'd whisper.

And I'd murmur, *Yes?*

He'd say, he'd say . . . He'd say, *Lemme taste you. It's been so long. Lemme kiss you. Down there.* Would he even ask permission? Maybe it would be all needy grasping and bossy hands. No requests, no coy "down there."

On your back. I gotta taste your cunt.

A fever broke out all over my body. I imagined the same happening to him, two towns over in the human kennel he got locked in every night. He'd escape for just a few moments, in thoughts of me. Of us, together.

The twitching of his hand, the buck of his hips. He'd yank his tee shirt up from his waist, expose the taut, flexed muscles of his abdomen. His fist would race, and—

I jumped as my phone came to life, shimmying on the glass side table next to my bed. My hand flew out of the boxers I slept in and I fumbled for the device. *Mom cell.*

I hit Decline. It wasn't late enough to be an emergency, and I couldn't just go from masturbating over a convicted

48

felon to chatting about what was blooming in her and Daddy's garden. I couldn't go from imagining my name on Collier's breath to hearing it in my mother's chirpy voice.

Tomorrow, I thought, and shut the thing off. And I went back to my fantasizing, back to gruff words and warm breaths, a starving man's hungry mouth, approximated by my own fingers. There was nothing else, not tonight. The real world could wait.

I read his letter a hundred times in the next week. I read it so many times, those words in my handwriting, I began to worry it was all a fiction I'd penned. I read it so many times I didn't need the paper anymore. His voice was in my head, clear as a recording, saying all those things. And his voice was in my head every night, saying whatever I scripted for him. Filthy things, romantic things. He called me tenderly by my name, nuzzling my ear. Called me *bitch* and forced my thighs apart with his. Called me *darling,* like in the letter, the word dark and charged and electric as the clouds before a summer storm.

I could only imagine how he might be, in real life—how he'd treat me if we were alone together. Happily there was no possibility of *us,* alone together in real life, and so I imagined everything, every possible flavor, relieved to know my hypotheses would never be proven right or wrong. That he'd never get a chance to disappoint me.

I spent so much time fantasizing about him, it occurred to me on Friday morning that I had no idea how to act toward him, if he approached me again. Play dumb, pretend I really did think that letter had been meant for some other woman? Be stern, shut him down before he grew bolder?

I knew what I was *supposed* to do. I was supposed to tell Shonda or any other CO about it, but I also knew I wouldn't

49

be doing that. Selfishly, I wanted the letter for myself. And recklessly, I even hoped maybe he'd want to tell me more.

It was insane, of course, but when you've not felt sexual hunger for months, for years . . . The idiotic risks people take in the midst of affairs made sense to me, suddenly. Nothing felt as good as this wanting. Logic was impotent. Flaccid. A pitiful, powerless thing.

I saw Collier as I passed through the dayroom, and it was recognition as I'd never felt it. I'd lived out a thousand imagined intimacies with this man, and when our eyes met it felt as though he must have lived them, too.

It was muggy and brutal that day, leaving inmates and staff alike punchy. The convicts bickered and baited, but it was for the best—the discord kept me on my toes, kept my mind off Collier through Literacy and Composition, kept my eyes off him for the most part during Book Discussion.

As always, though, he caught me during the afternoon Resources block. I had to wonder if that was on purpose. If he wanted to be my final memory of the day when I left this place.

Oh, the meaning I read into every crack and crevice of our encounters.

Attendance was down. The Resources room wasn't air-conditioned, and apparently the allure of ogling my breasts and butt wilted some when the temperature flirted with the triple digits. Men still came and went, and most showed up for their computer slots, but for once I had a bit of free time, myself, and I used it to make a list of things I'd need to implement Karen's unrealized plan of starting a cell-to-cell book cart service. I'd nearly begun to think I could put off choosing my stance toward Collier another week. Or indefinitely. *Maybe he pulls that "help me write a letter" shit with every librarian.* Maybe he'd never come calling again.

Foolish me.

50

He came for me at twenty minutes to five. I felt him step through the door, a heat wave and a cold front all wrapped inside one man. He strode to where I was sitting, lazy as you please, and I knew it was him without even looking up. He stood across the tabletop from me, behind an empty chair, his big fingers curled over its back. I raised my chin. Played it cool aside from the pink I felt stinging my cheeks.

"Hi there."

"You free?" he asked, in that voice that had whispered the most brilliant, disgusting secrets in the privacy of my head this past week.

"Sure." I nodded to the chair and he sat. He pulled a folded piece of paper from his back pocket, and a knot formed in my middle. *Another letter?*

"I was hoping you could read something for me," he said, gaze on my hands. "Something I wrote."

"Sure." I realized in that moment, I knew exactly where the nearest officer stood, and not for my own protection. I knew it the way every one of these cons must. The way a criminal keeps his radar tracked on witnesses and cameras when he knows he's on the brink of wickedness. I took the paper from him, but he stopped me before I could unfold it.

"Not now. But maybe you could take it with you. Take your time. It's real important. I want to make sure I say everything right."

Thump thump thump. "Um . . . Yeah. Sure. I can do that." It was lined paper, and I could see the impression of his handwriting. Lots of it. "Whether it needs rewriting or not, this was good practice, writing it all out," I offered.

He nodded. "I used that machine. I wrote it on that, and it fixed my capitals and spelling. Then I copied it down on paper. I didn't have to rely on my head, to know which way all the letters went."

51

"Smart."

Collier's brown eyes swiveled, seeking the guards. Finding them busy with the now departing inmates, he leaned a bit closer. "I'll make this real easy for you," he said.

I felt my brows rise and my heart tumble into my shoes. "Easy?"

"I've got stuff to say. To you." He tapped the paper, his voice barely a whisper. "If you want to hear more, next week, you wear red."

"Wear red?"

"You show up next week wearing red, I'll know what I've got to say is okay by you. You wear any other color, I won't ever bother you again. Not about typing or anything else. I won't be angry or anything. But if you wanna hear, wear red."

"Collier!" The guard shot him a look. "Check your posture, loverboy."

Collier sat up straight, drawing his crossed arms away. "Red," he said. "But only if you want to hear more."

I nodded, tucked the folded paper in my notebook along with a couple other convicts' letters I'd promised to drop in the mail room.

He watched my hands then stood. "'Preciate that," he said at a normal volume, and pushed his chair back in.

"That's what I'm here for."

And he left without a backward glance. The older guard on duty—Jake, I thought his name was—came over.

"He being a creep?"

I laughed too quickly, shook my head. "No. Bit of a flirt, that's all. Harmless." *Yeah, harmless.*

"He's not whispering anything offensive to you, I hope."

"No. He's just cagey about his writing disorder," I fibbed. "Doesn't want it advertised that he needs help, I think." *For the love of God, don't ask to see the letter.*

52

But Jake only nodded. "Funny how some of these boys still hang on to their pride, after we take every other damn thing away from them."

"Does he . . . Should I be worried about him, in particular? Is he known for being manipulative?" *Say no. Say no say no say no. Please don't take this away from me. It feels too good.*

Jake stood up taller, looking thoughtful as he shifted his belt around his belly. "That one . . . He's no boy scout, but he keeps his nose clean. Good behavior since he got in, stays out of the race bullshit as much as a man can, in a place like this."

"So not too bad."

Jake smiled. "Bad enough to get locked up for ten years. So not too great, either. If he gives you the willies, trust your instincts . . . But he's not a known predator. Probably what you'd even consider one of the good ones, in fact."

I nodded, feeling the weirdest mix of shit. Relieved, intrigued, unnerved. It must have shown on my face.

"Still finding your feet, huh?"

I blew out a long breath. I could let my anxiety show, now that all the criminal eyes had left the room. "Yeah. I mean, people try to get away with stuff at the library all the time. But here . . . I dunno. I want to help these guys. I want to give them the benefit of the doubt, except I know how incredibly stupid a move that is."

"Best tool you got in here is your own gut, kid. Listen to it."

I smiled and picked up my bag. Inside it was a letter from Eric Collier. Eric Collier, who'd been sentenced to ten years, if Jake hadn't just been tossing out some ballpark number. *Ten years.*

On the one hand, I thought as I walked to my car, ten years was good. Murder wasn't likely, given that Cousins was medium security, and ten years was probably too little for an especially heinous sexual assault.

On the other hand, ten years meant Eric Collier was *not* in for shoplifting or selling weed, or for unpaid parking tickets.

But he is *in for another five years.* Minus parole, if Jake hadn't been factoring that in, and if Collier was eligible. And even if he was, I really didn't like Darren, so I'd surely have moved on to another city and job in the next couple of years myself, and I wasn't going to encourage and beguile him so badly he'd come after me . . . Was I? Was he the coming-after type? How long a sentence did stalkers get?

But the whole wear-red thing . . .

He'd designed this so I was in control.

Or he designed it so I'd think I am.

I tried to do as Jake had suggested and listen to my gut, but the lust and anxiety had me so edgy, it was hard to know what I was hearing aside from my pulse beating hard, everywhere.

He robbed a bank, I decided as I turned my key in the ignition. Done. Decreed. A desperate, ballsy crime, but the only thing that got shot was the ceiling, to prove his gun was loaded. He never intended to hurt anyone, and didn't. In fact, I imagined, he'd only loaded that one round, as a fail-safe against an accident. And he surrendered peacefully when the jig was up. He'd needed the money to get his brother out of trouble with the mob.

No, no mafia stuff.

He'd needed the money to pay for his grandma's hip surgery.

Perfect.

I spent the drive mentally filming Collier's thwarted heist, and by the time the cops stormed the bank's lobby, I was rooting for him. The fantasy was what I'd need to let myself open his letter, but I caught myself as I pulled up along the curb.

54

This really is some fucked-up, bad-idea imagination game to you. But to him . . .

To him, whatever this was might be the realest thing that had come along in five years. This infatuation that kept me awake nights might be this man's only reason for getting up in the morning, for all I knew.

No. I was giving myself way too much credit.

Just read what he wrote. Could prove the creepiest thing I'd ever laid my eyes on, and all this energy I was spending, writing him into some redeemable script, would prove a complete waste.

I slammed my door and eyed the bar. Though I lived two floors above it, I'd only been in for a drink once. After I'd finished unpacking from my move I'd gone down, hoping maybe the place would prove more charming than it looked, that I'd forge some friendship with the bartender or magically run into a fellow displaced Southerner. Nope. Lola's was a dive, frequented by dead-enders and career alcoholics, folks with too much free time, few-to-nil prospects, and just enough cash to drink themselves insensate for a night.

I used to drink a little in college, at parties. Then Justin had ruined all that for me. Alcohol wasn't fun anymore, wasn't the socially acceptable vice it had been. Slurred words weren't funny. Shots didn't punctuate a good time—they counted down to detonation.

But tonight . . .

I walked past the side entrance that led to the apartments, heading for the front door.

A Friday at Lola's looked like any other night. Almost all the seats at the bar were taken, but I wanted privacy, anyway. I stood behind a vacant stool until I caught the bartender's eye. He was young, maybe thirty, with tattoos on his arms and a pristine white Tigers cap over his buzz cut.

"Do you have iced tea?" Or what passed for it, up here.

He checked an unseen fridge below the bar. "Yup."

"Iced tea with lemon and ice with a shot of bourbon, please."

He looked skeptical, but filled a pint glass with a can of Nestea and mixed it all the same. I paid and took my drink to a two-seater booth in the quietest corner. I didn't want any people or windows at my back, no possibility of anybody reading over my shoulder. I was acting an awful lot like a criminal, I thought, settling into my spot. I took a sip and winced. Goddamn. And I'd thought my grandpa mixed these strong.

I hadn't eaten since twelve, and I felt the drink almost immediately. Felt good. Tasted like family barbecues, not all those nights I wasted with Justin.

I waited until my blood was hot, then drew my notebook from my bag. I smoothed my fingers over the folded paper, felt the lines where Collier's pencil or pen had pressed. I peeked inside, just enough to see blue. I pictured him pinching the ink stem of a stripped Bic—the staff removed the outer plastic tubes because the cons could use them for God knew what. Collier's big fingers around that skinny implement, carefully transcribing his thoughts from the word processor's screen.

What on earth had he wanted to say to me?

I got a plan to bust myself out of here, but I'm gonna need your help. There's twenty grand in it for you—I got profits coming to me from my buddy's meth racket.

Please no. Though that certainly would scare me straight.

Just read it.

What was I so terrified of? Everything. That he'd seduce me further. That he'd prove me an idiot for getting drawn in so deep, so fast, with so little bait.

56

No. That he'd somehow wreck this infatuation I'd come to treasure far too much. That he'd take away what he'd given me, these past couple of weeks—that thing I'd thought I'd lost. My ability to crave a man.

I took a deep drink and unfolded the paper.

His writing was as stiff and mindful as a grade schooler's, peppered with dark patches where he'd scribbled words out to fix or replace them.

Darling,

I took another deep drink, sweat breaking out under my arms and between my breasts.

You probably read lots of books. With way better words in them than I could ever write. I don't know how to make the stuff in my head sound good. But I'll try.

You don't know me. I don't know you either. You're probably one of those girls who needs to respect a guy before you feel something for him. Where I come from people don't think that way. We all just drink and fuck and call it love for however long it lasts. But I want you to think I'm better than that. To be someone you could maybe respect. Crazy as that sounds. So I need you to know I didn't hurt a woman to get locked up. I wouldn't ever hurt a woman.

Anyhow. I don't know you. You seem real nice and it was good how you cared enough to get me this machine. You'd probably do that for anybody who needed it but I think it's real nice all the same. You're pretty too. I meant what I said when I got you to write that letter. All those things. I haven't been with a woman since I got locked up. That's a long time. Saying those things

57

is the closest I've felt to sex in five years. But I don't want to say things you don't want to hear. Maybe I got a chance to say about you wearing red next Friday. I've got lots of things I want to say to you and way more personal stuff than this. Saying it feels good. Like I'm a man again in a way you don't get to feel on the inside. So wear red next week and I'll tell you some of what I think about. If you don't I'll leave you alone.

Yours,
Eric

PS If you've got a man already I apologize. I don't mean any disrespect to him. If you tell him about this tell him I said he's real lucky.

I refolded the page and set it before me, pulse pounding everywhere. In my feet and temples and throat, heart thumping against my ribs and echoing between my legs. All the places that tell your body *run*, and all the places that tell your body *fuck*.

As I took another drink, a fat drop of condensation fell from the glass and hit the paper, and I jumped like I'd toppled an entire pitcher onto a watercolor masterpiece. I dabbed at the spot with the hem of my shirt, unfolded the page, and blew on it until it dried.

Jesus, what was he doing to me?

All at once I didn't want to be alone with those words.

I wanted to call my mom . . . only I so couldn't. After what happened with Justin, no way she'd ever sign off on some clandestine convict romance. She was married to a state trooper, for Christ's sake. My closest friendships from back home had mellowed in the years since I'd moved north, and the ones I'd forged in Ann Arbor had never matched the intensity of those bonds you make in your teens. There was no one I could confide in about this. Not without it being treated like a mental health crisis, anyhow. Hell, maybe I ought to talk to somebody at Larkhaven. Maybe they had a whole ward just for crazy women who fell hard for good-looking prisoners.

I tucked the letter in my bag and moved to the bar, suddenly needing to connect with someone, even a stranger. A couple of people had cleared out, and I took a seat at the very end, open to the bartender but with a wall close to my back. Damn Cousins, training me to think this way.

The bartender came over, eyeing my half-empty glass. "That okay?"

I nodded. "Perfect, thanks."

"Nobody's ever asked for that before. What's it even called?"

"I don't think it's called anything. Just what my grandpa always drank."

"You're not from around here."

I shook my head, sucking a long pull through the straw. "South Carolina. I started a job at Darren Public Library this summer."

"College girl," he teased, all grandiose.

"Grad-school woman," I corrected, warming to him.

"Right on. And here I thought you must be somebody's parole officer, dressed like that."

He tidied the bins of lemon wedges and cherries and I watched, feeling the whiskey buzz. He had a round face, making him look younger than he probably was. Softly muscular, like a high school football star whose glory days were solidly in the rearview. He reminded me of some guys I knew back home. I leaned my elbows on the bar and caught his eye.

"Need a refill?"

"Nah. But do you . . . Do people really do what they do

59

in the movies—get drunk and tell you all about their romantic problems?"

"People get drunk and tell me all kinds of shit."

"When it's romantic stuff, is it always totally doomed, do you think?"

He looked thoughtful. "Yeah, probably. But everybody around here is kinda doomed. Why? You got romantic troubles?"

Knowing half the bar was probably eavesdropping, I told him, "I dunno what I have."

"Is that the trouble?"

"Maybe. Probably."

He stole my glass and cracked open another can of Nestea, but I stopped him before he could add the bourbon. He poured a generous shot in a tumbler instead and slid it to my elbow.

"People tip me better after they unload," he said, one side of his lips hitched in a smile.

I smiled back. "Well, there's a guy."

"There always is. What's good about him?"

"Well," I said, eyes rolling up to the neon signs above the bar as I thought about it. "He's awful handsome. And he makes me feel special. And he's kind of . . . I dunno. Mysterious, maybe."

"Mysterious ain't good," said my bartender. "Mysterious might as well mean he's got a secret family in the next county."

Oh. Jeez, he could, for all I knew. And maybe he hadn't been with a woman for five years, but how many girlfriends might come see him during visiting hours? How many might think he was theirs, once he got released? I grabbed the shot and emptied it into my glass.

"What else is good about him?" my bartender asked.

60

"I dunno. That's it, really. He's handsome and he makes me feel special."

"What's bad about him?"

He's kind of incarcerated. "I don't know much about him, but I know he's been in some trouble before. Plus I can't really be with him."

The bartender nodded. "Married."

"No, he's not." *Is he?*

"Totally married. Secret wife. Twelve kids."

The man on the nearest stool nodded now, a slender black guy with salt-and-pepper hair, dressed in a tradesman's jumpsuit.

I shot them each a frown. "It's not like that. He's just . . . It's kind of long-distance. We talk mostly in letters."

"He deployed?" asked my nosy neighbor.

"No. He's just . . . He's in one place, and I'm in another. But I think I like it, for what it is."

"Say you found out he *was* married," the bartender said. "Would it break your heart?"

"I dunno . . . It'd make me real mad, I guess. And I'd feel awful guilty." I was feeling sort of mad and guilty now, wishing I hadn't asked for an outside opinion. I'd been enjoying my delusional, epistolary fling. They were ruining it with all their perfectly reasonable questions.

"Don't lend him any money, whatever you do," said Jumpsuit.

"I'm not stupid."

"Nah, just horny. Same thing."

I glared at him, but only because he'd pretty much nailed it there.

"Say you had a baby sister who was in your position," said my bartender. "What would you tell her to do?"

I took a drink, and gave it some serious thought. "I'd probably tell her to be careful."

61

The bartender put his hands up like, *There's your answer,* and my neighbor thumped a concurring fist on the counter.

I shook my head and drained a huge gulp. "Y'all are no fun." Shit, I must be drunk. My *y'alls* were coming out. I left a ten on the bar and sure enough, I felt the shots as I slid from the stool.

The bartender grabbed the bill, snapping it between his fingers. "If I'd known you were such a good tipper I'd have lied to you. Said this guy was the best idea ever. Earned myself a twenty."

"That's for the double I didn't order," I said snottily. "Not your opinions."

"Well, I'll lie to you, anyhow. This guy sounds like an awesome idea. I'm sure whatever it is he's not telling you, it's all good stuff."

"Yeah," offered Jumpsuit. "He's just real modest. Doesn't want you to know he's a volunteer firefighter."

"And that he reads to orphans on the weekends," said the bartender.

"Doesn't want you to know he's actually a millionaire." Jumpsuit again. "He's keeping it a secret 'til he knows you love him for who he is."

The bartender lost it on that one, laughing as he said, "Man, that'd be the goddamn best-kept secret. If I wanted to hide a millionaire, I'd sure as shit stick him in Darren fucking Michigan."

Try Cousins Correctional Facility.

"That'd be like hiding a diamond down a porta-potty." Jumpsuit just about doubled the bartender over with that. "Last place you look, man."

I rolled my eyes. "Good night, boys. Thanks so much for your sympathy."

As I headed for the door the bartender called, "Hey!"

I turned and raised my brows, faking annoyance.

"What's your name?"

"Anne. Annie," I corrected, for no good reason.

"Annie, I'm Kyle."

"And I'm Rodney," said Jumpsuit.

"Come back and let us know what happens," Kyle said as he ran a towel over the bar, sounding sincere.

"Yeah. We wanna see the engagement ring," added Rodney, and Kyle whapped him with the towel.

"Seriously," Kyle said. "Let us know."

"It'll cost you a shot," I told him, wanting to leave with the last zing.

"Deal."

"Y'all have a good night."

I headed out and up the side entrance to my apartment, flipping three bolts and switching on the weak overhead light to illuminate my little living room. I dropped my bag on the couch, grabbed the remote, and switched on the TV.

I was wiped. Thoroughly buzzed. I ought to be excited for the weekend, but in truth I wished I were working. The last thing I needed was time to think too hard about everything. Everything Collier had written, and every decent question the two perfect strangers downstairs had thought to ask about him. Questions I'd somehow managed to avoid confronting on my own.

I pulled out his letter and read it again.

If you got a man already . . . tell him I said he's real lucky.

It was things like that, and his promise to leave me alone if I chose not to wear red next week, that made this dangerous. I had no way of knowing if these scraps of deference were sincere or not. All they told me was that he was smart enough to know I deserved them, which could either make him a gentleman or a con artist.

"Who are you?" I murmured, staring at those careful, measured letters. Then I snatched my compact out of my purse and stared at my own face, flushed from the heat or bourbon or from Collier, maybe. "And who the fuck are *you*, anymore?" I squinted at myself. "You're drunk, that's who. Eat some dinner, stupid girl."

I tossed the compact on the coffee table and flopped along the cushions with a sigh.

"I don't own anything red," I told the room. "I look awful in red."

Did I? I wouldn't even know. I'd never owned anything red aside from maybe socks or a hair band.

"Whores wear red," my grandma had told me once—she'd walked in while I was watching *Pretty Woman*. I must have been fifteen. I'd told her, "She *is* a whore, Gram." And she'd nodded sagely and said, "Stands to reason."

I'd thought about it and realized my mom and my aunt never wore red, either, not that I could remember. Funny how mandates you don't even agree with can still chisel themselves across your subconscious.

If I wanted to hear more of whatever Eric had to say to me, the decision couldn't be made without a concerted effort, a mindful purchase. A premeditated crime.

Shopping with the intent to seduce a dangerous felon.

Staring up at the ceiling, I told the fan, "He wants me to be his whore."

It didn't reply.

"I think maybe I want that, too."

64

Chapter Five

By Thursday, I still didn't own anything red.

It was rainy and muggy, and Karen and I were cooking alive in the bookmobile. School was out but we went to youth centers and day camps through the summer break, and we'd hit three stops so far, with five more to make after lunch.

"Lookie there," Karen said as we hit the outskirts of a small city. "Your new best friends."

A line of men dressed in orange were scattered along the median and right-hand shoulder, tending to the skinny saplings tethered at intervals and bagging grass clippings and trash. On the backs of their jumpsuits, *COUSINS* was stenciled in black. And to my mingled horror and excitement, when the traffic came to a halt for a red light, who should be closest on my side but inmate 802267. Outdoors, no razor wire between us, just a dozen paces' worth of pavement and the window glass. It was positively thrilling. Nothing like how I might've expected.

He kept his head down, eyes on his work. His temples and forearms shone with sweat. At once, my ambivalence was gone. All I wanted was a taste of him, outside like this. And

I was wearing makeup and jewelry, and my hair was down. God help me, I wanted him to see me this way, all polished up.

I pushed the switch to unroll my window. "Hey," I called.

"What the hell are you doing?" Karen barked.

When he didn't look, I tried again. "Eric!"

That brought his face up. Brown eyes went wide, then fled back to his busy hands.

"Anne," Karen scolded, and my window rose at the push of her button. "Jesus, have you lost your fucking mind?"

"I know some of those guys. I help that one with his dysgraphia." *And his sexual frustration.* "I thought it'd be nice. I mean, how often do those guys get told hello on the outside?"

She shook her head lamentingly, like I was talking about lifting my shirt for them. I'd never have pegged her for the paranoid kind.

"Jeez. It's not like they're going to stab us for being friendly—even if they wanted to there's supervisor guys everywhere."

"They're not allowed to talk to you, dummy. They're not even allowed to look at you. Man can lose major privileges for that. He could get kicked off work release."

"Oh." My face burned. "No one told me that." I craned my neck as we started moving again, making sure Collier wasn't getting chewed out. Looked like I'd gotten away with it. My polite self wanted to roll down the window and shout an apology, but I'd learned my lesson there.

The whole thing seemed monumentally . . . barbaric. I *knew* these men. Some of them, anyhow. They were people to me, students even, yet the rules demanded I treat them with all the respect of animate traffic cones. It made me feel gross inside, this forced inhumanity.

66

I turned to Karen. "So if some jerk shouted stuff at them, or threw something even, they just have to ignore it?"

"Course they do. Hurt feelings are the least of what those boys forfeited." She shot me a look, stern expression softening. "You're too sweet for your own good. You better watch yourself in there."

Chastised, I shut up for the next couple of miles. But when the embarrassment lifted all that was left underneath was an urge, the same instinct that had made me call out to him. The urge to catch his eye. The urge to connect with him.

"I'm feeling like a BLT," Karen said as we rolled into the next small town. We had an hour before our next stop.

"Fine by me."

She pulled us up along the curbless roadside before a family restaurant. The shop next to it caught my eye. *Divinely Debbi*. Women's wear, one of those stores that's clearly somebody's doomed dream. People around here could barely afford groceries—no way were they shopping at boutiques. I bet it wouldn't make it three months, but for now, it was surely Debbi's pride and joy.

And right there in the window was a red dress.

"I'll just be a minute," I told Karen. "I want to look at something in here."

"Want me to order for you?"

"Sure."

"What?"

"Surprise me," I said, not really listening. My feet were dragging me toward the window display and the red dress.

I couldn't wear that to the prison—it was a knee-length halter. If Shonda lost her mind and actually let me into the dayroom, I'd cause a riot.

I pulled the door open, greeted by country music and a blessed blast of AC.

"Good afternoon!" said an older woman, Debbi perhaps, coming out from behind the counter. I was the only customer. I bet I'd been the only customer all morning.

"Afternoon."

"I saw you looking at that dress in the window." *Whore,* she added in my imagination.

I nodded. "It's pretty, but I need something more conservative I could wear to work. Do you have anything else in that color, maybe a top? Short sleeves are okay, but nothing low cut."

She showed me some options, but everything was pretty summery, embellished with beads or cutouts or just too revealing.

As she went out back to check for something, I poked through the racks.

And I found it.

It was cream colored, a soft knit top with three-quarter sleeves and a boat neck, not wide enough to flash any bra strap. And splashed off-center across the front was a huge red poppy, bright as a maraschino cherry against vanilla ice cream.

"Sorry, nothing," she said, reappearing.

"I'll try this one," I said, holding up my find.

She led me to a booth and pulled the curtain closed. The top fit like a glove, and I scrutinized the shape, assuring myself poppies weren't vaginal-looking, as flowers went.

It wasn't a red top, per se.

But the flower was bold. *Bold as a flag whipped in a bull's face.*

Still. *It's not all red. I'm not a total whore. Just a partial one. Just a splash of whore.*

I liked it. I'd wear it—if not tomorrow at Cousins, then elsewhere. I changed back into my tee and headed to the counter.

68

"Do you have this in a size bigger?" It fit perfectly for what it was, but what it was would let a convict guess my measurements far more accurately than any of the other outfits I'd worn.

"That's the last of its kind, I'm afraid."

I drummed my fingertips on the hanger and bit my lip. I could throw a cardigan over it. Just let a little of the red peek through. A little wink of whorefulness.

"I'll take five dollars off," the woman said, and that was all it took to tip me.

"Deal."

"Cute top," Shonda said, holding it out before her.

It was my fourth Friday at Cousins, and for the first time, she'd let me keep my bra and panties on during the strip search.

As I pulled my jeans and the top back on I asked, "This isn't too snug, is it? I could keep my sweater on, but it's hot today . . ."

She laughed. "A parka's snug enough for these men. They've all been guessing what's under your clothes, Anne. If you want to give them an extra hint, that's up to you. You're not violating any codes in that, but decide for yourself how much attention you're willing to draw."

I'd worn the thing. I wanted some attention. Some very, very specific attention, from one set of male eyes among the couple hundred I'd encounter today. But since I'd bought the top, something strange had hatched inside me. Something invasive, with creeping vines. The tendrils had taken over, wrapping me in a sensation I hadn't felt in five years—feminine mischief.

Five years.

Five years since I'd wanted to feel sexual, and invite that attention.

Five years since Eric Collier had been with a woman.

A long time since a woman had felt like a woman, and a man like a man. A long time for two people to shut their needs in the dark, I thought, buttoning my cardigan over most of the red blossom. Most but not all. It was so hot inside it. And I wanted to bloom.

Shonda led me across the dayroom floor. Collier's energy led my eyes to his. That dark gaze dropped, just for a second, finding so much more than the simple shape of my breasts that the other men sought. His stare shot back up to my face, and I saw red there, too. Lava in that stare.

I felt my hips sway of their own accord and locked my legs back up. Locked my eyes on Shonda's collar until we passed through the next set of locked doors.

I got through the morning sessions, though I couldn't tell you how. My eyes were on the clock, my mind elsewhere. I practically jogged from classroom B to the office. I wondered if anyone had noticed how I'd taken to eating alone. If they thought I was antisocial.

It's not you, I might tell them. *It's just this damned pornography that's always playing outside my window. I can't seem to quit watching it.*

This was the only time I got to feel any control over my infatuation, I realized as I stood before the glass, finding Collier in the crowd now filling the yard. A nod to the black guys in their corner. Shirt comes off. Thirty chin-ups, fifty push-ups, fifty sit-ups, repeat. Then these two-in-one things he did at the end—a pull-up, then drop for a one-handed push-up, double quick. Twenty of those, for dessert. Sometimes afterward he'd jog around the yard a few times, but today he got drawn into a conversation with some of the other men who were working out. He kept his body language neutral, arms crossed over his bare chest, shirt

70

slung around his shoulders—no open hostility but no real friendliness either.

"'Round here if you black," Wallace said during Book Discussion an hour later, on the topic of social division, "you best only talk to the blacks, or else nobody got your back when shit goes down. It ain't even racism—it's just basic fuckin' math. One, two, three, four," he said, pointing to himself and a few neighbors. "And if you white, you best keep to the whites. One, two, three-fucking-four," he said again, waving toward the other side of the room. "Math. Forget that biracial buddies *Shawshank* shit. Chocolate and vanilla don't mix in here."

"And if you some kinda in-between caramel motherfucker," one of perhaps three Hispanic guys in the room added with a grin, "then ain't no calculator gonna save your ass."

The group shared a good laugh at that, united for a moment in their perfect division.

I wasn't comfortable with this discussion, but strangely, every last man in the room seemed absolutely fine with it, like Wallace had simply explained how the sun came out during the day and the moon at night.

I steered us back to the story, but stole a glance at Collier. He was wearing the shadow of a smile. He'd probably laughed at the joke, too, and I wished I'd seen it. Heard it. I bet he laughed real quiet—grudging little huff of air, sidelong smirk. Not sinister, just mischievous.

Maybe I'd make him laugh, one of these days. Maybe this afternoon, during Resources.

Yeah, right. I was lucky when I managed to even take a full breath around the man.

He took so long coming after me during Resources, I'd begun glancing down at my chest, checking that the red flower was indeed visible, wondering if it didn't count. Worrying it hadn't been enough.

71

Then at five minutes to five, that tall shadow came through the door once again, paper in hand. I was helping someone fill out a legal form, and immediately I felt drunk and fuzzy brained, struggling to answer his simple questions. I apologized, blaming the heat. And without even thinking, I unbuttoned my sweater and stuffed it in my bag.

The second I realized it, I froze. I glanced frantically around the room, expecting two dozen pairs of eyes staring at me, all of them as wide as if I'd stripped naked. That was how it felt, with that huge orange-red flower leering from my chest. A few guys were indeed admiring the change, but I was the only one flirting with a heart attack over it.

A bell rang at five and the man I was helping said thanks and gathered his things. I did the same, and Collier wandered close.

"Sorry I missed you," he said, eyes on my shirt, my face, my shirt, my face.

"Me too. Maybe next week."

"Sorry you had to see me yesterday," he said more quietly. "Like that. Bad enough I'm stuck in these pajamas, inside."

"I don't care. *I'm* sorry I tried to get your attention. Nobody told me you guys can't look at anybody when you're working."

Nearly whispering now, he said, "Would've been worth anything they took from me, just to hear you say my name."

I went all warm and stupid at that, too hazy to say anything. He changed the subject.

"I don't suppose I could give you somethin' to read over again?" He held out the folded paper—two sheets.

I accepted them, slid them into my bag. "Sure."

"That's a poppy," he said, eyeing my top.

"Yes, I believe it is. You know your flowers." *Or your opium.*

A little half smile upset my middle in the nicest way. "Been

72

learning all about plants, the past few months," he said. "Landscaping stuff, for work release."

"It must be nice," I managed, suffocating. "To get outside."

Again his gaze dipped to my shirt. "It sure is."

The guard told everybody to get a move on, and Collier took a step backward, another, another, hands in his pockets. "You have a good weekend now, Annie."

I nodded, and the words came out with an effort like childbirth. "You too, Eric."

I stopped at the supermarket on the drive home and made myself dinner at the salad bar, grabbing a bottle of white wine for no good reason.

No good reason or absolute necessity? I wasn't a hundred percent pleased with my newfound interest in alcohol, but on the other hand, at least that meant Justin hadn't ruined it for me.

I turned the fans on high when I got in and opened the windows. The temperature had dropped and the sky had gone gunmetal, a much-needed thunderstorm on the way. I poured myself a few ounces of wine in the fanciest glass I owned, an etched crystal goblet that was the lone survivor from my grandma's antique punch set. I added an ice cube, stashed my salad in the fridge, and settled down on the couch.

Something was missing.

I hopped up and grabbed the votive from the bathroom, checking my reflection before I exited. I looked different, wearing red. But I didn't look like a whore—not a bit. I looked like a frigging virgin, all dewy from the humidity, wide-eyed and scared and eager. Dumb and nervous and innocent as a bunny.

I lit the candle and set it beside the wine. Went back to the bathroom and put on makeup, spritzed perfume in the air, and whipped my hair through it, like my mom had taught me. I put on jewelry, headed back to the couch. To the closest thing I'd had to a date in over five years.

I took a deep drink. Found Collier's pages in my bag, stroked the backs of his words, unfolded the paper and smoothed its creases.

Drank some more.

Breathed in, breathed out.

Read.

Darling,

I guess you wore red. So I'll tell you the things I think about.

First I feel like I should tell you what I'm in for in case you didn't look it up. I know lots of the guards and other staff don't like to know. Makes it easier to treat us half decent if they don't know what we did. So if you didn't find out for yourself I'll tell you straight that I'm in for assault.

I blinked at that word, feeling strangely numb. *Assault*. That explained the ten years Jake had mentioned. I wasn't surprised, not horrified either. Not even disappointed. Maybe a little unnerved, but purely by my own complete *lack* of reaction. I was relieved though, that I'd heard it from him. All the times I'd considered snooping around online, I'd wound up shaky and dry-mouthed, and chickened out.

I read on, bracing myself for details.

It was against a guy who had it coming. You'll have to trust me on that since I'm sure he'd tell you different. Anyhow it was bad and it was ugly and impulsive. If that scares you then maybe it'll help when I say it's real unlikely I'll be getting out anytime soon.

74

Though it made me feel guilty . . . yeah, that did help. And although assault was terrible . . . Impulsive, he'd said. Not planned or plotted or premeditated. That loosened my chest. Maybe it'd been some bar fight gone terribly, terribly wrong. Ten years, though, Jake had said. Hell of a bar fight. I set the worry aside—shut it back its drawer, the one labeled *Massive Denial* that made this reckless affair possible.

Anyhow if you're okay with knowing that I'll get back to the nicer stuff. Just seemed like time you knew if you didn't already. I know I don't know you or what you like so I hope nothing I say offends you. All I got is the truth. I hope maybe you'll like it.

I like to watch your mouth when you read from that book. I can't tell you what the story's even about but I've got your lips memorized. I shut my eyes sometimes and just listen to how you talk. I've never been with a Southern girl but it's like every word you say comes out rolled in sugar. I think about kissing you like I said. Real deep and slow with our eyes closed. Maybe feel your hands on my chest or my back. As I hold your face or your hair. As I got to see if you taste like sugar to match how you sound.

I grabbed my glass off the table, took a deep taste and let the wine coat my mouth.

There's other ways I think about your mouth and about holding your face and hair, too. I think you can guess what I mean.

"Oh mercy."

I'd be real gentle, though. Tender. I promise. It's just that I've felt nothing but my own hand for so long. I'd kill to know how your mouth felt. Warm and wet. Nothing nasty. Whatever you maybe want to do to me.

My hands shook, the letters blurring. I shut my eyes tight, and I let myself imagine it. Us, in his cell, but no one around anywhere. Perfect silence except for his breathing, hitching above me in anticipation. A thumb hooked under that waistband and his strong hand easing it down, that staple of my recent fantasies. Collier exposing himself. Those dark eyes full of hunger or need, aggression or total helplessness. I couldn't begin to guess, so I opened my own eyes, needing more clues to who this man was. And what he wanted from me.

I'd do the same to you.

"Praise Jesus."

I want that even more because then I could hear your voice. I want your hands on my head and my hair and you saying things to me. Anything. Just my name. Or you could tell me faster. Slower. Deeper. Lower. Use your hand, Eric. I'd do whatever you asked for as long as you wanted it. With my lips or my tongue or my fingers. I used to be real good at that. Maybe you could teach me all over again.

My body clenched hard. *Teach me.* This dangerous, hardened criminal wanted to be taught something by little old me? My arousal went from mouse to cat, fearful to wicked. I reached for the glass but found it empty. I licked the inside of the rim.

I bet you taste amazing. I'd treat you so good just to taste even more of it. I'd make you come that way if you'd let me. I'd spoil you so good before I ever asked for anything for myself just so you'd know I care about you. Maybe if I did a good job you'd reward me. Let me inside you. It's been so long since I felt that. And you'd be so wet from what I made you feel. I hope I can say that word to you. Wet. That's probably a rude word to say but I think about it. About making you that way and how incredible it'd feel. Being inside you.

I'm hard now. Typing this. I've been hard since the part about kissing you. I never imagined I'd get hard from writing or typing. How about that. You really are a good teacher.

When I think about being with you it's always away from here. Outside. In the sunshine maybe by the lake.

I changed my own fantasy, rereading everything he'd written, laying my back against the sand and grass instead of some narrow, metal bed. Warm sun on my face, warm dark hair clutched in my fingers. Same hungry man between my thighs, wanting to be taught.

Sometimes I want you on my lap. Riding me. It's been so long I bet I couldn't last a minute. But at least that way it might be like you were doing that to me. Making me lose control. Or maybe if it was real I'd need to be on top. Like I'd die if I couldn't move how I wanted. I'd try not to be too rough. Unless you like that. You seem like maybe you'd like for a guy to be gentle and romantic. I'd do my best to be that man. But sometimes I like it fast too. I'm not the nicest guy but I'm not an asshole either. I'd try real hard to be whatever you wanted.

77

I've been typing for two hours and using an outlet in the TV room. All the guys are pissed off about the noise so I better quit it. Next week wear green and I'll tell you more about what I think. If you don't I'll leave you alone.

Yours,

Eric

PS I like feeling like I'm dressing you. I hope you like it too.

I did. Especially when he said it like that.

I wore green next week, that same spruce-colored top as my first day at Cousins. At ten of five he gave me two more pages without a word—just set them atop a slim stack of other inmates' correspondence with a little nod.

Darling, I read an hour later, lounging on my couch in a silk camisole, hair down and sticking to the back of my sweaty neck. The Devil was whispering secrets, my grandma would say of the day's humidity. And a man who was far from a saint had a few of his own to tell me.

I don't know what women think about when they think about sex, he wrote.

I bet it's nicer than what guys think about. So I won't bother describing my dick or anything. Women probably don't care about those kinds of details. We can talk about how stuff feels instead. I can tell you how my dick feels instead of how it looks. Hard. Harder than I think I ever felt before I had you to think about. Hot too. So hot I bet your hand would feel cool on my skin. I'd give anything to feel that. To kiss you while you touched me. I'd show you what I liked with my hand on yours. Slow and tight to start. Then faster.

Fucking hell.

I reread that first line.

I don't know what women think about when they think about sex . . .

I smiled. This one thought about whatever Eric Collier told her to.

That's how I like fucking too, he wrote, and the room spun. *Slow to start. But by the end you'd have me so wound up I can't promise I'd be gentle anymore. But I kind of want to show you that. How bad I want you and how hard I'd have to work to stay in control.*

I wish you knew what it does to me when you wear the colors I tell you to. I didn't know color could do that. Get me hot as a photo of a woman or someone's actual hand on me. I was out for work release a few mornings this week by the airfield. I was only trimming the weeds but they had flowers planted around the front of this one building. Marigolds. Most were yellow and orange but some were almost the same color as the poppy on that shirt of yours. I saw that red and smelled all that grass and I thought about you. It got me all messed up in the nicest way and made me forget where I was and all the ways I fucked up to get there.

I don't think you've got any clue what it means that you let me write these letters. It gets me so riled up it hurts. But I like it. I imagine it's some spell you've got me under. Makes me want to be all kinds of ways with you. Helpless sometimes. But darker stuff too. Like I want to punish you for making me this crazy. But nothing bad I promise. Nothing you wouldn't be okay with. The

79

kind of stuff lovers get up to. That's how I think of you now. Like my lover. That sounds crazy but you have to understand I can't even remember what it was like the last time I had sex. Not because of how long it's been but because the stuff I imagine about you is just that real. So real it's like I've got the crispest memories of it.

I hope you don't think I'm blowing smoke up your ass with these letters. Or that I want anything more than just to say this stuff to you. If I could think of a way to prove it I would. Since I know me being a convict won't give you any reason to trust what I say.

I've gotten way better at typing by the way. I still only use two fingers but I'm way faster. And copying it down on paper had gotten easier too. I thought it might make you happy to know that.

Wear pink next week and I'll tell you more. If you don't I'll stop bothering you.

Yours,
Eric

PS Wear your hottest underwear too. I don't care if it's a thong or granny panties. Whatever makes you hot is what I want to imagine you in. Say the word and I'd slide them off real sweet and slow or rip them right down the middle. Whatever you wanted. Whatever man you want me to be.

Whatever man I wanted him to be.
One I could actually touch, and kiss, and be with? Or exactly who he already was, and trapped safely behind those bars? A couple of weeks ago I'd have said the latter— no hesitation. But things were changing. My bad idea felt real, now.

I couldn't say exactly what did it.

Maybe, *I'd show you what I liked with my hand on yours.*

Maybe, *I can't promise I'd be gentle.* Whatever the reason, I slid my notebook from my bag.

And I finally wrote him back.

Eric,

I just read your latest letter. I'm glad you write them, and I'm glad to hear it's getting easier. And that doing it means so much to you. I'm sorry it's taken me this long to write to you in return, but I'm sure you can appreciate why I need to be careful. Though that's not the only reason.

When I was younger, I was with a guy who didn't treat me well. I paused, wondering how foolish it might be to tell him this. Could a manipulative convict turn this into a weapon, surely as he might fashion a toothbrush into a shank? Fuck it. I had six days to come to my senses.

He made me not want to be with men, for a long time. Not since you first got locked up, actually. I shut myself off from feeling sexual right around the time you got shut inside a cell. So we've both been missing these feelings. How about that?

You said you'd try hard to be whatever kind of man I wanted. I don't know what I want, to be honest. But I do know I haven't desired anyone in five years. Not until you. I'm not making any promises to wait for you or for this to ever be anything real, but I like talking to you this way, in letters. I'm afraid to say too much. To promise too much. I'm afraid I'm being selfish, enjoying your attention, and using you to feel this way again. But

81

I haven't felt this in forever, and it's hard to just shut it off.

Like you said, we don't know each other. Only how we seem to make each other feel. But sometimes that feels like enough. So simple and right, when real life can feel far too messy.

He'd assumed I wouldn't want to talk about crass things, about our bodies, but he was wrong. I wanted to tell him how I watched him from the office window, when he was exercising. But if someone searched his cell and read this letter, looking for contraband, too many roads would lead to staff, and to me. I'd have to fib, and assume he could read between the lines.

I bet I know what your body looks like, when you're out in the yard. I bet it's beautiful, and I say that as a woman who's not been all that preoccupied by shallow things, like the way a man looks. You make me care about that, somehow. Maybe because I know so little about you. And because our lives are so different. Maybe I want to understand your body because I worry I could never understand what it's like, being you.

I paused, wondering if that even made sense. Whatever. It was true.

I bet when you're outside, your skin is tan and shines with sweat. I bet you have tattoos, on your back and shoulder . . . I hoped he'd realize what I was saying. Hoped he'd feel my eyes on him from now on when he worked out on Fridays, a woman's admiring gaze cutting through that sea of male hostility. *I want to lie you down on a bed and trace my fingertips over those designs, whatever they might be, and*

82

ask you what they mean, and about the man you were when you got them. And if you're the same man now, or someone else. I feel like someone else now, since you started writing to me. I feel alive and vibrant and excited in ways I didn't even a month ago. I'm afraid of what I feel sometimes, but I like that better than feeling nothing.

You said you didn't know what women think about, when they think about sex. I can only tell you what I think about.

My throat felt tight, my head dizzy. I felt as cloudy and wound up as if he were actually here, touching me.

You think about us by a lake, on the grass. I think about us in your cell, sometimes. I can hear thunder outside. Are you in your cell now? Can you hear it, too? It must be such a lonely place, yet so devoid of any privacy. When I imagine it, it's only us, and I bring all those things you miss into a place where you don't get to feel them. I want to lie with you on your bed, and see your eyes from close up. I see fire in them from across a table or a room, and I bet if we were together on that tiny bed, I'd feel it on my face like actual flames. I want to kiss you and feel how hungry you must be for a woman, after all this time. I want to slide my hand between our bodies and find you excited. I want to make you feel a hundred things at once—powerless and aggressive, needy and pushy, grateful and greedy. Everything a man can feel with a woman.

I want nastier things, too. Like you braced above me and your hips pumping hard.

I took a deep gulp from my sweating glass of ice water, fever burning me alive.

I want to see everything as it happens between our bodies, the way yours would fit with mine. How fast you'd go when you were working to please me. And how fast you'd go when your turn came. I want to feel how much you want me, I wrote, hand shaking, *with your cock. Feel how hard and thick and hot you'd get for me.*

Should I tell him . . . ? No, I shouldn't. But I did.

That's what I think about, when I touch myself. Your body. The way it must look when you're in the exercise yard, and how it'd look, laboring for me. And the things you'd say, in that deep voice of yours. You think my accent's all sweet and feminine. Yours is just the opposite to me. Dark and hard and male. I want to feel everything that's different about us in the way we'd fuck.

Christ, I was a mess. My fingers were slippery around the pen. I was wet between my legs, from nothing more than wording these thoughts. I couldn't actually give him this letter—it would push our bizarre affair so far over the line . . . But I couldn't not finish it, either.

Six days to find my senses, I reminded myself. Six whole days.

When I read your letters, I hear them in my mind, in your voice. And I play them back in my head, when I touch myself. I imagine the thoughts you've shared as much as any physical thing I might picture us doing. When I come I'm always thinking about the words you say, and your eyes staring down at me—the parts of you I know for sure. That's what I think about, when I come. Your eyes and your words and your voice.

I hope this letter's found you well, or as well as can be expected. I'll see you as the fates allow. Until then, I'm yours on these pages.

Your darling. In whatever color you please.

Chapter Six

Six days, but I never came to my senses.

I wandered even further from my senses, in fact, and on Wednesday afternoon I made a trip to the mall a few towns over. I didn't own any hot underwear, and for the first time in ages I thought maybe I'd like to change that. Sure, I'd be wearing it for myself. Unseen at Cousins and on my weird, dateless dates on my couch. But Collier had asked me to, and I liked doing what he said, in this safe way. I liked letting him dress me.

Victoria's Secret looked like a magical fairyland—a riot of patterns and flower scents and frilly lace and shiny satin. I wished he'd told me what color, what sort of style, anything. I didn't have the first clue what made me feel sexy aside from his words.

I wandered between the displays, waiting for something to catch my eyes.

What would be the most exotic, to him?

I thought of the poppy shirt, of that inciting, bright red. Nothing like the navy uniforms and the endless drab cinder-block of Cousins. So red, maybe . . .

But no. I stopped before a very different option. Crisp spring green.

There's not much grass here . . .

Green, the color of freedom, of summers by whatever lake he'd mentioned. Grass, the blanket he wanted to lay me down on.

I've been learning all about plants.

It must be nice, to get outside.

It sure is.

I grabbed a bra in my size, nearly plain compared to some of the other styles. A bit of lace at the tops of the cups, and lace panels at the hips of the matching panties. Not a thong—I didn't think I'd like to work a long, sweaty shift in one of those—but not especially innocent in the back, either.

Your personal garden to tend, Eric, I mused as I set them beside the register, feeling high and cheesy and happily dim.

If only you could visit it.

Though thank goodness you can't.

Before I left for Cousins the next Friday, I sealed my letter and wrote *Darren Heating and Plumbing* on the envelope, with my own address beneath it. Added a stamp. Just in case Shonda saw it in my notebook. *Oh,* I'd say. *I'd been meaning to pop that in the mail. Just had a leaky pipe fixed.*

Paranoid, scheming liar. That's what I'd become. And an idiot to boot.

The whole thing was foolish. Terrifically foolish. I'd remove the pages from the envelope before I handed over the letter, secreting it among some other papers, but I had no guarantee Eric wouldn't show it to his buddies—or even to an officer, if for some reason he wanted to try to get me fired. Or threaten to get me fired, unless I did who knew what. I hadn't signed it, hadn't mentioned my job or Fridays or any other incriminating hints . . . But handwriting was hand-writing. And rules were rules. *You will not speak to or touch any inmate in an inappropriate way. You will not encourage an inmate to speak to or touch you in an inappropriate way.*

Double check.

But he's never even once asked me to write back. He'd never angled to get his hands on anything he might use to take advantage of me. He'd kept the evidence flowing in one direction, with me safely upstream.

Shonda didn't so much as take the notebook out of my tote. She didn't check my clothes, either, not the short-sleeved raspberry pink button-up I set on the table, or the flats that were slapping over the cement floor of the dayroom a couple of minutes later.

Slap, slap, slap. Whore, whore, whore, they seemed to chant.

Whores wear red, I told them.

Pink's just red with some cream mixed in, you silly slut.

But underneath, grass green. Clean as spring. Yet so damn dirty.

I found Eric's face, just for a second. *Guess,* I told him with my eyes. *Bet you can't.*

He caught me earlier than usual during Resources that afternoon, and I wondered if he had any clue how nervous I felt. How *terrified.* Terrified of what I was about to hand him, and terrified that I might get caught. When he came over to where I'd just finished helping another inmate with a letter, I started shaking all over, like an honest-to-God train was rumbling through the building.

"Hey there," I said, and smiled. My anxiety had to be plain. *I'm not afraid of you,* I wanted to tell him. *I'm afraid of me. What I'm capable of.*

"Afternoon." He took the vacated seat across from me. He'd brought a book with him, an oversized blue paperback called *The Essential Garden Maintenance Workbook*.

"Is that for your work release?" I asked, pointing to it.

"Kind of. The guy who manages the program lent it to me. Can I ask you to help me read a couple things? There's lots of words in here I don't understand."

I nodded. "Of course." I moved my chair to the end of the table and angled the book between us. His knee brushed mine, and even through two pairs of pants it was the most explicit contact I'd ever felt. I shut my eyes for a breath, heat burning my cheeks. *Act normal. Act normal.* I opened the book.

"Show me."

"I marked a couple spots," he said. He flipped to a dog-eared page, and casual as you please, he slid out what had become an absolute fetish object to me—a folded, lined piece of paper. He set it aside, near my hand.

"This here," he said, tapping a section header. "I don't understand what this is saying."

"'Herbaceous perennials,'" I read aloud. "I don't understand what that means, either. But we can figure it out between us, I bet."

As I skimmed the chapter with him, I felt my mouth moving, heard myself speaking. But with his warm knee touching mine and his voice so close, everything else seemed to fade, like the contents of a cabinet veiled by frosted glass. His knee. Both his knees, I imagined, spread between mine. This voice asking me such different questions. *Like that? Harder? Faster?*

The fog lifted as I sensed another inmate in my periphery. He was standing at a polite distance with a book of his own tucked at his side, watching.

"Is that enough for now?" I asked Eric, sitting up straight.

"Yeah. That's real helpful, thanks."

"Before I forget," I said, nice and loud and casual as I stood, instantly mourning the loss of his heat. "I brought you

89

some worksheets. Up to you if you use them, but they might be helpful." From my bag I drew out a fat stack of photo-copies I'd made, my letter hidden among them. I handed them over, then took his folded pages and slipped them into my notebook, smooth as a grifter.

"Thanks," he said, closing the sheets in the landscaping book. "'Preciate that."

And with a smile that I hoped belied my hammering heart, I turned my attention to the waiting inmate.

The whole drive home, all I could think was, *I really did that, didn't I? I really gave him that letter.* And the adrenaline high went sour in a heartbeat.

Shit, shit, shit.

I didn't know this man at all. Did I?

It felt like I'd walked right up to him, handed him a glinting knife, and asked if he'd please cut the tag out of my shirt collar. Maybe he would. Or maybe he'd grab my chin and slit my throat. He could hurt me so badly with those words that had made me feel so good to write. I'd handed them right over. A weapon custom-made to destroy me.

Sure, there was no ALA law about librarians getting involved with the convicts they worked with—we didn't have a code of ethics the way a counselor or medical professional might—but the entire situation demonstrated a *remarkable* abundance of poor judgment on my part.

It was like a switch got flipped. I went from giddy to panicked, instantly. I couldn't even bring myself to read his latest letter—not until I knew what he'd do with mine. The only thing I did was peek at the very bottom of it.

Wear yellow and I'll tell you more.

Yellow. I didn't even know if I wanted to wear what he told me to, this time. Not when I had no clue what his next letter might say.

90

Wear white, it might say. Then, *Meet this guy, get this key, transport the cocaine from storage locker 707 to this address and only accept small bills. If you don't, I'll send your dirty letter to the warden and get you fired. By the way, I write just fine. Boo-hoo about your mean old ex-boyfriend, you stupid slut.*

Oh God oh God oh God, what had I done?

I checked my phone obsessively through the next week, positive my boss's number would appear at any moment and inform me that we needed to have a meeting. Immediately.

It never did, but I never relaxed, either. I shoved my new green bra and panties way underneath my boring underwear in its drawer, barely able to identify myself as the woman who'd felt so slinky and mischievous buying them. I hid his letters down there as well. I grieved for the loss of what I'd had these past few weeks. This thing that had felt so good, suddenly gone. All my fault.

On Friday morning I stared at the yellow shirt hanging in my closet. I couldn't wear that. But if I didn't, he might think I was through with him, and then he might really get mean.

I compromised. I wore a black short-sleeved button-up, gray pants. No color anywhere, save for the yellow silk flower on the elastic I wound around my ponytail. Just a little wink of complicity. A little insurance policy, keeping him nice.

It was my longest day at Cousins so far. The longest day of my life. A month crammed into eight hours.

I was nauseated, and skipping lunch hadn't helped. My stomach was a clenching fist, my nerves a swarm of hornets. For the first time ever, when Collier came through the door at the end of Resources, I felt cold, not hot.

Oh God oh God.

He had that book with him again, and a big manila envelope. He waited until I was done looking something up for another man, then wandered over to stand by where I was sitting.

I smiled as much as I could, lips hard and bloodless.

"You all right?" he asked, his brows drawing together.

"Yes. Fine. You?"

He shrugged. "I suppose. I did those worksheets you gave me."

He handed me the envelope. Someone had removed its metal clasp—hopefully a staff member. Not wanting to appear suspicious to the officers, I slid the papers out halfway. And he had actually done the worksheets, or at least the top one. It had never occurred to me that he might.

"Great," I said. "I'll take a look before next week."

He stood there a second, not saying anything. A beat later, I realized something that broke my heart. He was hoping I had another letter for him.

I got to my feet right as the bell rang. "I better get myself organized."

A single nod. "Enjoy your weekend."

"Thanks."

"I like that thing in your hair," he added quietly. "Reminds me of marigolds."

I replied with another smile, a sadder one, tight with confusion and uncertainty, and I headed for the door. I ran from the man whose body only last week I'd wanted to feel wrapped around my own.

It had been gray all day, and the rain finally arrived as I was grabbing my things from the office. I watched a sheet of water descend on the empty exercise yard, sudden and solid as a dropped curtain. My car was barely twenty paces from the staff exit, but I was soaked to the bone by the time I climbed into the driver's seat.

I pulled the manila envelope out of my tote and made sure it wasn't too wet. I wanted to rip those pages out and find his next letter among them. Read what he had to say about my own letter. But did it matter what he'd say? Even the sweetest words could so easily be a lie. He still held the knife I'd given him.

The downpour had tapered some by the time I reached Darren, and I hugged my bag to my chest, jogging doubled over to the door.

My clothes felt itchy as I entered my sticky apartment, and I wondered for the hundredth time if I could afford to buy an AC unit. I changed into dry yoga pants and a tank, and I stood staring at the envelope on my coffee table for a long time before I finally sat on the couch and picked it up.

I flipped through the pages slowly, knowing there was a letter from the gap in the stack, from the size difference between the forms and the notebook paper. *A thick letter,* I thought.

Thick with what? Assurances, or criminal instructions? Fuck.

He'd actually filled out all the worksheets, and I'd included nearly twenty of them. This was either a testament to his boredom, or to his dedication to making the ruse look credible, or to his desire to impress me.

I got to the notebook pages. Five of them at least. This must have taken him *hours.* Unless they really were some kind of extortion notice, one he'd composed weeks ago. And maybe not for the first time.

I whooshed out a long breath, and I read.

Darling,
    Thank you for the letter. That meant a lot.
    I was real angry to read about that guy who didn't treat you right.

And just like that, my heart slowed. My head cleared.

I try not to get angry in here but that got my blood up. You deserve a man who treats you however you like. In some other life I'd try to be that man. If you wanted me to. In my old life I'd probably go after that guy who treated you bad, but I'm trying to not be that person anymore. I'd rather talk about you and me anyhow.

I think it's real sad how you didn't want to feel anything for so long. It's real sad that a man like me doesn't get to be that way with a woman, but to hear about a woman just not wanting to feel that is so much sadder. It's fucked up the way men can hurt women and how much longer it takes to heal than just a bruise or a cut.

I started crying. Hot tears of pure relief, like I'd thought someone I'd loved had died, only to hear they were safe and sound. I let them flow, filling the room with my mewling, primal gasps and moans. I cried like a toddler, with no dignity whatsoever, and when my vision cleared enough, I read on.

You're a smart woman but I've got to say, it was pretty stupid of you writing me that letter. It's the best thing I've been given probably ever but now I have to give it back to you. It's safer for you that way.

I read that again. And again. I flipped past the next page of his handwriting, and there was my own. That's why his letter had seemed so thick. I started crying again, then laughing. Hysteria at its most hysterical, like I'd stuck a syringe full of narcotic-grade relief into my vein and rammed the plunger down.

He gave the knife back! He's good, he's good, he's good!

I giggled, giddy, and ran to the kitchen and poured myself a glass of wine. I didn't go to the trouble of changing or doing my makeup, but I spritzed some perfume then jogged back to the couch, bouncing onto the cushion. My date night was back! Twisted as it might be. My lover was back, abstract though our romance undoubtedly was. I snatched up the pages and took a deep, sweet taste of wine.

I read your letter a million times this week. I tried to memorize it before I gave it back and I think I did a pretty damn good job. I copied down a few parts I didn't want to forget, but nothing that might get you in trouble. Don't ever give me a letter that way again. In person and with no envelope. Nobody checked me on the way out and they don't sweep the cells more than every couple months, but when they do they read everything and any letter without a mail room or visitation stamp and staff initials means it must have come through the inside and that's contraband and too many clues. It's dangerous enough me writing all this but I figure if they find this they'll find your letter so I may as well be clear while we're being reckless. Anyhow if you want to write me do it through the mail with a made up name and address.

"Oh, duh." I smacked my forehead.

No rule says I can't get dirty love letters from a woman on the outside. Hell that's what keeps most of these guys going in here. I hope you keep writing. Just do it smarter. Type it. Mail it.

I hope I don't seem angry. Just spooked. I'd hate for you to get in trouble over me. Enough about that.

Indeed.

You said you worry about using me to feel sexual again. Don't ever worry about that. I can't tell you how good it feels to do that for you. I know I'll probably never see you outside this place, or actually be with you, but just knowing I do that for you is the most incredible thing I've felt in years.

If we were together, I'd show you all the good things a man can do for a woman. I'd try to make up for what that other guy did to you. Everything you want and more. I'd make you feel so good and I'd never ask for anything until I got you off. I'd earn whatever you thought I deserved and it'd feel so amazing knowing you were wet because of me. I love that you think about me when you touch yourself. I don't think anybody's ever told me anything that made me feel so good. I bet I don't need to even tell you I do the same. Sometimes when I touch myself all I have to do is imagine you saying my name. Just think about you saying my name while I was kissing you between your legs or touching you or fucking you however you wanted me to. I don't even have to think about what we're doing. Only about your voice.

I hope it's okay I said fucking. I only did because you said that in your letter too. I could say making love instead but I know you probably don't love me. We barely know each other. Plus that's who I am. I probably don't make love. I probably fuck. I'd try for you if you asked me to, though. You'd have to tell me how it's different. It just seems like something a different kind of man would do.

I don't know how to tie a tie, either. I've probably got a lot to learn if I ever want to be with a woman like you.

You said you want to know how I'd be, during the sex. Usually in my mind after I make you come, it gets more rough. I'd never hurt you, not even if you asked me to. But I want you so bad I'd need to go fast. I'd show you with my body how bad I need to come. Inside you. I think that's what you want to see. All the things you make me feel.

I hope maybe I'll hear more about what you want in another letter, but through the mail like I said. If you tried to hand me a letter and I wouldn't take it I hope you understand why now. And if I hurt your feelings I'm sorry.

I'll see you next week, darling. In green again I was thinking. You look so good in green. Even though you have blue eyes they almost look ocean-colored when you wear green. And I've never been to the ocean.

Yours,
Eric

I sighed, long and loud, letting my head drop back against the cushion. I took a sip of wine then nearly choked on it, realizing I still had an entire extra letter of his, the one I'd been too scared to open last week. I rooted through my undies and brought it back to the couch. Though my heart beat hard, it was nothing like before. I was in bloom again, petals spread wide and eager to soak up whatever he had to say. I propped my feet on the table and unfolded his pages.

Darling, he wrote. And he told me about the things he wanted to do to me, the places he wanted to take me, if he could. The things about me that took his mind off his daily life, and roused his body in idle moments. And I wondered if he wasn't a bank robber after all, the way he kept making off with my heart.

Chapter Seven

From there, our paper courtship began in earnest. And our in-person contact—the brushing knees and reckless glances and murmured code words—those became the highlights of my weeks. That and my steady progress in building Cousins a proper library. I'd convinced the warden to let me take over a classroom that I'd never once seen in use. For now it was just a dozen mismatched bookshelves and the most rudimentary of catalog systems, but it grew, week by week. Same as my heart seemed to grow with every letter Eric gifted me.

Darling, he'd write.

It was my birthday on Sunday. I'm 32 now if you were curious. How old are you? There's so much I want to know about you. Tell me about where you're from. Everything about it that's nothing like where I'm stuck now.

That night in bed I imagined you came to me, like magic. You were there and it was us and nobody else, real quiet. You told me you wanted to treat me, for my birthday. We kissed and then you were moving down, your mouth and hands on my neck, my chest, my belly. Then you were pulling down my pants, until you could see how big and hard I was from wanting you. Then it was your mouth on me, so slow and sweet, and you'd stop now and then and look in my eyes or say my name or smile. I asked if you wanted it, what I had to give. If you'd taste it. And you said yeah, let me have it, Eric. And I did. God I have no idea if you'd ever let me do that for real, but for my birthday I let myself imagine it . . .

And I'd write back.

Of course I'd let you do that, on your birthday or any other day. I'd want your fingers in my hair, and your voice telling me what you liked, and your hips under my palms, shifting and giving away how excited you were getting. If you told me faster, I'd go faster. If you told me deeper, I'd take you deeper. If you told me suck harder, I'd do that, too. And when you couldn't take anymore I'd beg to taste whatever you had to give me . . .

I got his pages on Fridays, and wrote mine immediately so they got into the Saturday mail. It was nearly like I got to see him twice a week, since my letters almost always made it to him on Tuesdays, and just imagining his anticipation and reward was as exciting as opening one of his letters to me. I wore green, gray, purple, black, blue, white. Whatever he told me to.

Darling, he'd say. *Your words about made my week. There's so much bullshit happening around here lately, but at night*

99

I can escape into what you wrote me for a little while. I like what you said, about how it smells like fall now. I smell it in the mornings, out on work release. I never liked school and I hate the winter, so I guess I just don't like that fall smell the way you do. But maybe if things were different I could learn to like it. When it got cold outside I could hide out in bed with you all day, where it's warm. When it snowed we could stay inside and I'd find a hundred new ways to make you feel good . . .

And I'd curl up in my covers against the October chill, wondering how it was I'd ever pined for an air conditioner. I'd write, *Sometimes I wish our circumstances were different, so I could come see you during visitation and say these things to you out loud. Of course then we'd have witnesses. We couldn't say all the things we do here. But do they let you touch visitors, at Cousins? Hold their hands? I bet just feeling your foot against mine through our shoes would take my breath away.* And it did, weekly, though I didn't want to drop too many breadcrumbs for the folks in the mailroom. *Lord knows what actually holding your hand would do to me . . .*

He'd tell me, *Sometimes my favorite thing to imagine is just us on a big soft couch. Me on the end and you between my legs, on my lap kind of. I could feel your hair on my cheek while we watched a movie maybe, and I could smell your skin. It would drive me crazy, being against you like that. I'd get hard, I know it, but it would be so perfect, just being with you that way, I wouldn't even care. Maybe you'd like that though, getting me excited. Maybe you'd take my hand and lead it wherever you wanted it. I could touch you between your legs just sitting together that way, feel you get wet and hot and feel me getting even harder. After I made you come, I'd lay you down on that couch naked and take what I needed . . .*

He craved the most intoxicating mix of things—the most romantic, affectionate contact—domestic, even—chased by harsher deeds. Always my pleasure given first, and his earned. His needs sounded more physical and aggressive than mine. Nothing unnerving. Quite the opposite. But that old male-female, rough-gentle dichotomy. After a big, inhibitions-loosening glass of wine, I wrote to dispel this myth.

Eric, I wrote. *I loved your last letter. I love all your letters. Hearing everything you have to say, and everything you want to do. I hope you know I'm excited by the way you talk about sex—about the sex you want, after you've made me come. Sometimes I want that so much more than the sweet things you tell me about. If we were ever together, after you got out . . .*

At this, my heart hitched. A child inside me had picked up the book of matches, and her eyes were nailed to the door, nervous at getting caught. Hands itchy, eager to make trouble.

. . . I'd want to see how badly you wanted me. Needed me. I'd want to see exactly what you were like, after all that waiting. I bet it would be so fierce, and urgent. I'd want your hands all over me. I'd want to feel your lack of control and your need, even if it was clumsy and frantic and nothing like what you'd see in a movie.

I know you're worried about what happened to me with that ex, but the way he hurt me, it was never about sex. He would drink too much and turn resentful, push me or give me a smack—he always said he was teasing, and told me I was being too sensitive, but I knew deep down what was coming. I left him the night he struck me in the side of the head. He burst my eardrum and knocked me to the floor. I never saw him again after that. What he did snuck up on me, because he'd led me

101

there, step by step, letting me adjust to whatever he'd done last. A mean poke, then a pinch, a push. They built up gradually, like the way you develop a tolerance for spicy food or alcohol. What I thought I could handle got modified. I'm almost glad he hit me that hard that night. It was so much worse than what had come before, it woke me up.

It's not even male aggression that scares me. It's the hidden stuff. The potential. It's what a man's capable of, and being tricked into letting myself get led there.

Sweet Jesus, I was writing all this to a convicted felon, wasn't I?

I love what you say, about the things you want to do for me. But part of me wants to hear what you like. Right up front. I don't want to be eased into anything. It sounds strange, but trust isn't a gradual process with me—a slowly, steadily earned privilege. I don't trust things that build gradually. Like the way he hurt me. I like black and white now. Honesty, even when it's not that pretty.

I paused, blinking. Was that why I'd ended up here? In Darren, in such a crippled library system, and at Cousins? This town and those places . . . They didn't come gift-wrapped. They led with their thorns, same as the criminal I was falling for. The first thing I knew about him was that he'd done something awful—why else would he be in Cousins? The wolf had come at me teeth first, and with the danger understood, the fear of a nasty surprise gone, all that was left was soft fur, shining eyes, power, speed.

So tell me what you want, I wrote. *Tell me all the dark things you think about.*

102

It was cold that next Friday, and I was nervous as I climbed into bed and wrapped the blankets up to my armpits. Not scared like after I'd handed him my first letter, but edgy. I'd told the wolf, don't hold back. Took the muzzle off him. I couldn't guess if he'd come at me with his tongue or his fangs.

Darling, I read.

I want to fuck your ex up, I really do. But I can't and I won't, not even if I was let out tomorrow and he walked past me on the street. It sounds like you took care of it yourself, so I'll just keep telling myself that's enough. I'd like to think there's no worse punishment a man could suffer than losing a woman like you. And if that's not enough to make him regret what he did and maybe change, then he's probably too stupid to learn from getting beat down by some angry stranger.

You want to know all the dark things I think about, huh? Does that mean you like dark stuff? I don't want to disappoint you, but I'm not into real dark stuff. When you're a young man and bored and free and figuring everything out about sex, that's when you get fixated on things. About what the best kind of sex is, the perfect sort of woman, complicated shit like you see in porn maybe. Taboo stuff. It's like being able to choose any kind of food you want, any time you want. You start to only want one sort of thing. The best, most perfect thing. Does that make sense?

I've been locked up now for five years and a month. I bet you can guess, the food here sucks. If I got out I'd want to taste everything there was. Every flavor and every kind of meat and every sort of sweet or salty or sour. And after five years without touching a woman, when I get out, I want to try all those most

103

simple flavors of what a man and a woman can do together.

Everything's so hard in here. And mean and ugly and loud. I know you want to hear dark things, but what I say about the romantic stuff I want to do with you, I want that so bad I can't tell you. I want to be in a room with you, so quiet I can hear your breathing and your heart. A place so clean I could smell your skin. And with candles, all yellow and soft after the bright white lights they use in here. I want to be with you someplace that's nothing like my cell. Someplace big and open, with a giant mattress a foot thick and the softest sheets. Someplace cool in the summer and warm in the winter. In a huge bathtub. On the grass somewhere. I want feminine things, because that's what I miss. Because in here, everything feels hard and sharp and bright. I want to escape and go someplace dark and soft and quiet.

I want to escape inside you. I want to feel your hands on me, and your eyes, and feel like there's nobody else for a hundred miles. I want to feel all that, like I'd want to pay close attention to the first few bites of a nice meal in a restaurant. I'd want to savor, at least to start.

But after that first taste, I could do darker stuff for you. You want to feel how pent up I am, don't you? You want to feel powerful, offering to end my suffering. It makes me smile to think about that. You seem so sweet and that's so naughty. You want to watch me lose my mind, so of course I'd let you see that.

I'd go real slow, to start. For me, not for you. Let me savor, like I said. But it wouldn't last long, I promise. I'd explore your mouth and your skin first. I need your hands on me, it's been so long since I've been touched in any kind of nice way. I'd want you to touch my cock

104

real slow so I could memorize every second of it. And when I first slide inside you, looking down at you in the candlelight, your hair down and spread across those big pillows . . . I'd make that moment last a hundred years.

I let the hand holding the letter drop to the side, sighing for every corner of the room to hear. "Fuck me, you're good."

But after I got to feel all that again after missing it, then I'd give you the dark stuff you want. I'd be so fucking hard for you. Inside you. I'd want to make you feel it, every inch of my cock. I'd want to say with my body, feel what you do to me. Feel how deep I want to be. Feel how bad I want to come with your wet hot cunt on me after all these years with just my hand. I'd stare down at you and you'd look like an angel smiling up at me. Or maybe not. Maybe you'd look mean. Wild and on fire. Maybe your hands would be on my ass or my hips, and I'd feel them begging me for more. Deeper. Harder. Faster. I'd give you that, and knowing you liked it would get me so hot. I'd do whatever your eyes told me to. Or your mouth, if it said, come for me, Eric. I would. Then I'd show you with my mouth or hands how grateful I was.

"Oh my."
All the things I hadn't thought I wanted to hear from this man—soft sheets and candlelight and tenderness. The things I'd thought *he thought* I would want to hear. The things girls are told they like, the things men are trained to promise.
That night I wrote, *I was so wrong*.

Wrong about what I'd assumed you wanted when you

said all the gentle ways you planned to be with me. How I'd imagined you were just trying to please me, tell me what you thought I'd like to be told. I've never known those words to come from a man's heart—only his mouth, when he's trying to get a woman into bed. But you really want all that. I can taste how badly you do, from the way you wrote about it.

So yes, I'd love for you to be all those ways with me. Everything you've been missing, for as long as you wanted. And yes, you're right—I do want to feel powerful, making you crazy. I hadn't even realized it myself, but you're right. You're so strong and together, and I want to turn you into a pleading mess. I want to feel your muscles moving under my palms, feel your body chasing your pleasure, faster and faster. I want to watch the strongest man I've ever laid my eyes on shake and tremble and moan, helpless from needing me . . .

Chapter Eight

It was the second Friday in November when everything changed. When the ground opened up, swallowed me whole, shot me out the other side to stare at the universe upside down.

Darling, I read that night.

I've got some news and I don't know how it'll make you feel.

I've been granted parole.

My heart stopped.

Just stopped, suspended like my breath before a plunge into icy water. My fingers shook, my hands, my arms.

I should have told you about it as soon as I knew. My hearing was in early September and I got the official news three weeks ago. I never expected this to happen. My lawyer told me straight up, I fucked my chances ages ago, the way I told everybody I had no remorse about what I did. How I'd do it again exactly the same way. I didn't tell you about the hearing because I didn't like either way you might react. I figured either you'd get your hopes up and I'd probably be denied my first chance at parole, or you'd be scared about me maybe getting released. Then once I knew I was just plain afraid to tell you. I was afraid you'd stop writing to me. I'm still scared of that. I hate writing this. I hate imagining you being afraid, knowing I'm getting out. Maybe I'm wasting my time. Maybe you're as happy about it as me. But I really have no idea, and I know what this place does to a man's head, and that it's foolish to get your hopes up about how things will go.

At any rate I'm being released the Tuesday after next at eight in the morning, if everything goes the way it's supposed to.

"Oh God. Oh God." My body was confused, feeling too many things, too intensely. The Tuesday after next. Eleven days. Eleven days.

It's funny how we never talk about why I'm in here, even after I told you. I guessed you must be okay with it. Or okay enough for us to keep talking the way we do. I've only lied to you once ever, that time I got you to write that first letter for me. I want to make sure I stay honest about everything. I know that's important to you.

I hope you don't feel like I lied to you these last three weeks, about my getting out. I wasn't trying to be dishonest but it was cowardly, not telling you until now. I've enjoyed what we have so much. I was selfish and didn't want it to end.

But more than that, I want you to know I won't come

108

after you once I'm out. I'm not stupid and I know this is going to change everything. Most women who write to cons find them through a program for that. On purpose. I know you didn't get into this on purpose. And I don't want you to worry about what expectations I might have about you and me. It wasn't like we were lying to each other, with the things we said. More like we were telling each other bedtime stories. I'm not dumb and I didn't think you were making me any promises in those letters.

I think I've got a job lined up for when I get out, doing landscaping eventually but at first mostly snow removal and that sort of thing for the city, through the winter. I'm happy about that, since it means I'll be outside a lot. I'll be living in Darren.

"Shi-i-i-t."

I know you live there too and if you see me around, it's not on purpose. My work release supervisor hooked me up with the job, and it's better than anything I might find on my own, especially back home. If we leave things up in the air by the time I get out, I promise I won't talk to you unless you talk to me first, if I see you around. I promise I won't come to the library and look for you. If we run into each other and you want to say hello, or you want to have a drink, or to do anything at all, all you've got to do is ask. But if all this has just been for your imagination, I understand. The last thing I want to do is make you scared of me.

I've got no idea what you're thinking about all this, so I won't write you a letter for next week. But I'll make this as easy for you as I can.

If you already know you don't want to see me once I'm out, wear black. I won't be mad, I swear. I know we never expected this to get as deep as it has.

Or if you do want that and you want me to look for you around town, wear green.

If you don't know what you want yet, don't wear either of those colors. I'll keep away until I get some sign from you that you made a decision. If I don't hear anything by January first, I'll do my best to forget about you. Or at least forget about ever getting to be with you. I'll probably never forget how you made me feel these last few months. It really was like having a window suddenly open after years without any sunshine or fresh air.

Anyhow. See you Friday. For the last time inside here, and maybe the last time forever. If you know for sure you don't ever want to see me, PLEASE wear black. I'd rather get disappointed up front than live in false hope, if your mind is already made up. You seem like the sort of girl who'd hate to hurt a man's feelings. You can hurt mine though. It's okay. I've been through a lot and I survived all of it so far.

Respectfully,
Eric

I read the pages a second time, then set them down. A car honked outside and I jumped.

I rubbed my face, hard. "Oh fuck."

Was it oh fuck? Was that how I was supposed to feel?

Who cared what I was *supposed* to feel—how did I actually feel? I tried to listen to my body, but the adrenaline was deafening, hurricane-force winds.

I felt scared, for sure. Scared of Eric? Maybe. Or scared because in the span of one letter, my shapeless, pleasurable illu-

110

sion had solidified and shattered, and all I held now were shards. Scared because my two choices were both perfectly terrifying.

Wear green, throw myself into his arms. Then find out we really didn't share anything outside these letters. Or find out he was dangerous to more than just that one man he'd assaulted. Maybe not immediately. Maybe slowly, the way Justin had revealed himself.

I finally did what I should've done back when he'd sent me that first letter. I looked up his crime.

Aggravated assault with a deadly weapon, with intent to maim. Sentenced 5–8 years in Cousins Correctional Facility and fined $5,000.

Fucking. Fuck.

Five to eight years? Clearly, Jake had been talking in generalities when he'd told me ten. But the details couldn't help me now. I'd needed them months ago—needed them, but feared them. Put the pleasure of this crazy fantasy above my own goddamn safety.

Wear black, and stay away. Then find out he wouldn't do as he promised and leave me alone. Or find out he would, and then what we'd had would just be . . . over.

Just gone, like we'd shot it between the eyes? The most vibrant thing I'd known in the past five years, dead, cold, the fire doused even quicker than it had crackled to life.

Three choices, I reminded myself. Don't wear green or black, but instead resign myself to the uncertainty. That didn't feel much different than the black option, aside from offering the both of us the cruel gift of hope.

I needed answers. And that meant asking questions, ones I'd been determined never to pose to this man.

*　　*　　*

The next Friday I wore not a stitch of black or green, and I doubt I'd ever been this nervous, walking through the dayroom behind Shonda. Not even on my first shift. I didn't seek his eyes, but I sensed him all the same. I'd never felt so awful in my entire life, striding past that man, ignoring him, too scared to see his face, knowing he must have been dying all week, praying to see me in his beloved green. Somewhere in my periphery, a man was aching. A man I'd loved. A man I'd never really known. A man who owed me answers.

I didn't look for him in the yard during my lunch break, didn't spot him during Book Discussion. That should've been a relief, shouldn't it? But I didn't breathe easier, realizing he wasn't in the room. His attention had become some strange, dark, private treat to brighten the toughest day of my week, and I'd come to crave it. His absence left a pit in my chest, deep enough to feel even behind my nerves.

I watched the clock all through the afternoon Resources block, foot tapping, heart lodged in my throat. If he didn't show, I really was fucked. I'd have no clue what to expect after he got out. I'd have no idea how he felt about my no-black–no-green ambivalence—whether he was sad or angry or perfectly accepting.

Bad and violent. That's what his crime had been, in his own words. Were bad, violent crimes only done by bad, violent men? Could a man who was fundamentally bad make a woman feel the way Eric Collier had made me feel, all these weeks?

Of course they can. Justin had. Millions of bad men made millions of lonely women feel good. Like a drug, pleasurable and reckless, so hard to quit after you start living for the fix. I rubbed my temples, smoothed my ponytail again and again, bit my lip and blew out long, nervous jets of sour breath. I probably looked like a frigging junkie.

To my mingled horror and relief, he came to me during

Resources. Earlier than usual, like he'd known I'd need to talk.

I extracted myself from the inmate I was helping, and though it was rude, I went over to where Eric had sat, passing men who'd been waiting for my attention.

I plopped right down across from him, and I didn't waste a second.

"Congratulations," I said tightly, hands clasped before me.

Though he smiled, he held back some. He could tell from my tone that I wasn't on the verge of planning our first extramural rendezvous. "Thanks."

"That's wonderful news, about your release and your job," I said, then dropped my volume to demand, "What *exactly* did you get incarcerated for?" I knew now, but I wanted to hear how he'd frame it.

"Aggravated assault with a deadly weapon. With the intent to maim."

Exactly as the Internet had told me, word for word. Was it better or worse that he wasn't trying to soften it?

"Oh God," I breathed, squeezing my eyes shut. Then I caught myself, knowing I had to act calm before the inmates or officers got too curious about our conversation. I pulled a random stack of papers out of my tote and set them between us, a prop.

"That's what the judge decided it was, anyhow." He huffed a tight sigh, attention dropping my hands for a moment, then back to my face. "You want to hear about it?"

"No, but I think I have to. Tell me."

"I beat a man half to death with a tire iron."

Oh God. Oh God oh God oh God. This was so much worse than a bar fight taken too far. So visceral. So *brutal*.

After ten seconds' mute stupor, I managed to ask, "Who?"

"This guy I knew from back home."

"And was that your intent?" *Intent!* And he'd told me it was impulsive. "To . . . to maim him?"

"I didn't intend anything. I just knew he had to be hurt . . . But I probably would have killed him if I hadn't gotten stopped."

I mouthed, "Oh fuck." I looked down at my hands, finding them worrying the stack of papers, folding them over and over along a softening seam. I let them go and met his eyes. "Do you regret it?"

"I don't, no."

"Even though you've forfeited five years of your life?"

"It wasn't a choice, how it went down."

"Were you . . ."

"On drugs or something? Nope. Clear as a bell."

"And would you handle it differently, if you had it to do over?"

Again, he shook his head, then spoke the words I dreaded. Words I'd read in his handwriting, but they hurt so much worse out loud. "I wouldn't change a thing."

Fucking hell. I couldn't care for this man. Not a man who'd taken a *tire iron* to another human being, no matter what that person had done to him. I hated Justin, for what he'd done with his bare hand. I ought to *loathe* Eric Collier. I ought to. But I couldn't, not until I had the answer to the most important question of all.

"Why?"

"I can't tell you."

"Why on earth not?"

"Because the why of it is wrapped up in somebody else's business. Business it's not my place to share."

"If you don't tell me . . . I can't process this, if you can't tell me why."

114

"Sorry. He hurt somebody, so I hurt him back. That's all I can say."

"Then . . . Then I don't think I can see you," I murmured. "When you're out."

He nodded once, but unmistakable disappointment passed over his face, dark as a shadow. "I thought that might be the case. That's your choice."

What the fuck was I supposed to say to him now? This wasn't how breakups worked, in a sane world. "What we had . . ."

He sighed, leaning back. "Yeah. Yeah. It was real nice for me, too."

I was about to go on, but he pushed out his chair, stood. Quick motions, but not aggressive. Efficient. And I realized from the way his face and neck had gone pink . . . He might cry. He was leaving so he wouldn't cry in front of me. My heart twisted, as real as if two hands were wringing it, strangling it. So badly I was staggered to imagine how the thing he'd done to that man must've hurt so much worse. It barely seemed possible.

He pushed in the chair, not looking at me. "Thanks for all your help, Ms. Goodhouse."

The name landed hard, all knuckles. "It was . . . It was my pleasure." *Don't go. Don't go.* But he'd already pulled away, out of that conspiratorial bubble we'd inhabited so many times, here in this room. "Good luck," I offered. "With everything."

A half-assed wave as he turned and headed for the door, a limp and dismissive thing.

My chest ached so bad, I pressed a palm to the spot.

I just broke a man's heart.

I broke his heart, but he beat another human being near to death. And he'd do it again. He'd told me so. Without an ounce of regret.

115

An impatient inmate plopped himself down in Eric's seat, and I went through the motions of my job. But in my head all I heard were his words, ones I'd read enough times to engrave across my memory.

I'm not the nicest guy but I'd try real hard to be whatever you wanted.

That's how I think of you now. Like my lover.

And finally, *I'll do my best to forget about you.*

As I drove home that night, I hoped I could do the same. Forget him, forget everything about this affair, except for the way it had returned things I'd thought I'd lost. All the emotions I was still capable of feeling. Lust and longing . . . and maybe even love.

I just hoped someday I'd prove myself wrong about another worry, and find I was capable of feeling those things for a man who actually deserved them. Of course that brought me back to Eric, and forgetting about him. He'd taken up so much of me, there wouldn't be room for anybody else until I banished him from my system.

But there was a far scarier and more pressing concern that needed my attention. What if he decided he didn't want to be forgotten?

He's sad now. But what if he gets angry?

And I now knew what happened when Eric Collier got angry.

And it was so much worse than some drunk boy's fist boxing my ear.

Yet as I drove home that night, it wasn't fear that weighed my body down. The fear stabbed me now and then, but it didn't stick. Didn't linger. Not the way the grief did.

And that made me think about girls who said of their questionable infatuations, *I've got it so bad.*

I wanted to tell them, *Honey, you don't have the first clue what bad feels like.*

116

Chapter Nine

The Tuesday of Eric's release came and went. I thought of him at eight that morning, as I drove to Larkhaven for my day on the children's ward. I thought of him constantly, alternately stung by fear and gnawed by regret. My Friday at Cousins was bleak, cold without the heat of our affair taking the edge off the despair of that place. But there was a bright side to it, in a way.

If Eric Collier wanted to come after me, he knew when and where to do it. I scanned the road on the way in to Cousins. Nothing. I scanned it again in the evening darkness, squinting along the shoulder. Checked for tailing vehicles the entire drive home. Nothing. I looked over my shoulder all weekend, jerked my head at the smallest sounds through my library shift on Monday. Still nothing. Nothing that week, nothing the next. And as my panic eased, fading to a more shapeless shadow of foolishness and regret . . .

I began to miss him.

And in time, my eyes stopped scanning. And started seeking. Four thirty on a Monday, a couple of weeks before Christmas, the sun was already sunk low. I said good night to colleagues and the few patrons who'd braved the weather, pulling on my gloves and hat as I headed for the door. I was eager to get home and finish my online Christmas shopping.

Winter wouldn't technically arrive for a week, but this fact was wasted on Michigan. The parking lot was down a block, the sidewalk half cleared of the mess left by a small storm that afternoon. *Wintry mix*. God, how I loathed that term. Too perky. Ought to be called *hell cake*, all those treacherous layers of snow and slush and black ice.

The glazed white blanket draped over the library's front lawn was stained pink by the dusk. A worker was chipping away the slippery, lumpy crust uncovered by a snowblower, stabbing it apart with a sort of hoe. Behind him another man was shoveling the pieces aside and spreading salt in his wake.

The passage was narrow, and the man with the pick thing crunched onto the snow-covered lawn to let me pass. As he looked up, his dark eyes widened.

I stopped short, nearly falling on the ice. Eric's hand came out to steady me, but he yanked it back just as quick, looking alarmed by the impulse.

I gaped, heart pounding hard, too hard. "Oh my God."

"Annie." His voice. His body. All of him, right here before me.

"You're here. Why are you here? Why are you where I work?"

"I'm sorry. It's my job—I go where the city sends me."

For a long moment we just stared, then he took a breath, seeming to calm. That made one of us. This man I'd thought of nonstop, but not actually seen outside my memories for nearly a month . . . Not since our breakup—if it could be called that.

"I was afraid this might happen," he said. "I'd have warned

you if I'd known how. The last thing I wanted to do was scare you."

My panic eased some, but I was still high as a kite, pulsing with adrenaline. "Jesus . . ."

"Sorry. Feel free to . . ." He nodded down the sidewalk, inviting me to go on my merry way.

It was either take the invitation or stand there, paralyzed, so I took it. "Thank you," I added stupidly. "For clearing the sidewalk. Take care."

And I ran away. Almost literally. I skirted the guy with the shovel and salt and hurried around the corner to the library's lot.

Safe in my wagon, I turned the key and let the heater warm up. I held the wheel and counted my breaths, commanded the panic to ebb.

"That was true," I muttered aloud, startled by my own voice. *He really had been afraid that would happen.* I'd seen it in his eyes. And our last meeting at Cousins, it had been just the same. His eyes had matched his words—full of regret.

"Maybe he'd even started forgetting about me," I told the car, breath steaming. The thought was a sock in the guts. Did it hurt as badly as my reaction just now might have made him feel? My running away and telling that man, *Yes, I am scared of you.* He'd omitted so much, but no, he hadn't lied. Had I lied, with all those sweet words I'd handed him, only to snatch them away in the end? Had my body lied to him just now? Running, telling him I was still afraid, when I knew in my heart I wasn't? Shit.

I could go back.

And say what? There was no question I could think of—and no corresponding answer he might offer—that would make us a good idea. But to go home now, with the edges of everything still so frayed . . .

"What are you *doing*?" I sighed, shaking my head as I turned off the engine. I shouldered my purse and headed back down the block. It was growing dark, Eric and his colleague now little more than silhouettes before the library's glowing front windows. His coworker was a quarter block behind him, meaning I might steal a few words without holding up their progress. But what words?

Guess I'll find out.

I skirted the shoveling man again, high-stepping through the snow to pass Eric, then turned, hugging my bag.

He looked up, went still. Christ, he was handsome. That face I'd memorized, and touched in my imagination on a million lonely nights. So exactly as I remembered, only lit by streetlight and sunset now. His hair covered by a knit cap. His navy uniform gone, replaced by jeans and a black coat. This man I'd maybe known, maybe not, disguised in different clothes and suddenly standing in my everyday world. In the open air.

"Hi," he said, clearly uncertain what to make of my return.

"You're really not coming after me, are you? Ever?"

His eyes widened but he shook his head. "No. I'm not."

"You think I'm scared of you, don't you?"

He nodded, sadness lowering his lids.

"I'm not, though. Not anymore."

"No?"

We stared at each other a moment, the sound of his colleague's shoveling growing closer an inch at a time, nibbling away at our privacy. My gaze dropped to Eric's mouth, his chin. I could see a sliver of his neck, red from the cold.

"You should be wearing a scarf."

The barest crack of a smile. "I'll be all right." A pause, a swallow. He looked nervous, as though a guard might be watching us. A hard habit to break, I imagined, after five-plus years under relentless scrutiny.

120

"I swear I'm not here on purpose," he told me again. "I don't have much say where I get sent, for work. I want you to believe that, so bad."

"I do."

"Do you?" he asked, hope in his voice.

I nodded.

His posture drooped with relief. "When I first saw you, I was like, oh shit. She's gonna think I'm stalking her."

And perhaps I had, if only for a breath. But no need to underline this. Instead I asked, "How have you been?"

He shrugged, big shoulders hidden by his coat yet burned so indelibly across my memory, tan and gleaming in the summer sun. "I'm good, I guess. Got a job. Got a place."

I eyed his mouth, entirely without meaning to. *Have you kissed a woman, since you got out?* It wouldn't be hard. Not in three weeks. He was handsome, dark, dangerous. Magnetic. And was I really so special, now? I'd been accessible, inside. That had been my appeal, hadn't it? An accessible, attractive young woman. A rarity in prison, but now that he was out, maybe girls like me were a dime a dozen. Prettier ones. And ones who hadn't broken this man's heart. The jealousy burned, and its heat was so unexpected, I winced.

"How've you been?" he asked. "Still at Cousins every week?"

"Yup. Same old, same old. Is it . . . Is it okay that we're talking? I'm not going to get you in trouble, right? I don't really know how parole works."

"It's fine, long as I get my job done. Nothing like work release."

"You're a free man."

He made a face. "More or less."

I rubbed my hands, cold asserting itself now with the panic drained away. "When are you done for the day?"

121

He kept his expression neutral save for a tensing of his brows just under the fold of his cap. Hopeful or skeptical or confused, I couldn't guess which. "When this sidewalk's cleared."

"Any chance you'd like to get a coffee?"

"With you?"

"Yeah. Nothing serious, but yeah."

"I'd like that," he said, nodding faintly, then more vigorously. "I have a couple things I want to say to you. Stuff I messed up, the last time we talked."

What else has happened since we last talked? Have you taken a woman to bed? Felt all those things we wrote to each other about, with someone else? Christ, the mere idea made me feral.

"Want to meet me at the corner there when you're done?" I pointed to a chain donut shop across the nearest intersection.

"I'll be there." He didn't smile, but I saw something brighten in his features. "Maybe twenty minutes?"

I nodded and left him, heading to the corner.

While I waited I ordered a tea, and my anxiety was just . . . gone. Lifted like a smothering blanket.

That old giddiness from the letter-writing times was long gone, too, but I could breathe again. He wouldn't hurt me, not the way he'd hurt that man. Not the way Justin had hurt me.

I could see him from where I sat near the front window, a black shape steadily working its way down the block. Once done, he and his colleague disappeared, then he was back, walking to the corner, tools abandoned in some unseen vehicle. I watched him cross the street, jogging between cars, hands in his pockets. Watched his face materialize in the light of the front window, his eyes catching mine. A jingle of the door, and there he was, tall and familiar.

122

I managed a smile when he pulled out the chair opposite me. His coat was dark gray, not black as I'd thought, and as he shed it he asked, "So, how you been?"

I shrugged. "Fine. Just working. Counting down the days to Christmas, so I can see my family."

He nodded for a long beat, staring at my hands or my cup. I studied his clothes in return, ones he'd picked for himself after years in that navy blue uniform. Nothing fancy. The collar of a white tee behind a red wool sweater. He looked good in red. He looked *way* too good in jeans. He'd lost his summer glow, his skin nearly pale against his black stubble and brows and sideburns, and there was that same dark hair I'd imagined between my fingers, overgrown as ever as he took off his snow-dusted cap. Those brown eyes, rippling with every emotion a man could feel.

"Can I get you something?" I asked.

He shook his head, looking flustered. Looking like he'd not come here for coffee and small talk. I sat back in my chair, letting my posture tell him I was ready to listen to whatever he needed heard.

Spreading his fingers on the tabletop and giving them his attention, he said, "I messed up so bad, the last time we talked. Telling you I didn't regret what I'd done."

I toyed with my tea bag's string. "If it was the truth, then it wasn't a mistake. I wanted the truth from you. I *deserved* the truth. Especially . . . especially given the circumstances. Given how intense we'd gotten."

"I know you did."

"And that what I thought was reality—that you weren't getting out for *years* . . . That was unfair enough, you not telling me. I'm glad you didn't pull any punches when you told me about your . . . crime."

"That was so stupid, though. Telling you I'd do it again."

123

"Would you?"

He pursed his lips.

"You would," I said, surprised to hear the exasperation in my voice. I was annoyed. I really *wasn't* scared anymore. "You'd do it again."

"I don't have any choice."

"Can you imagine how I'd feel," I said quietly, "if my ex tried that bull on me? Told me he only hit me because he didn't have any other choice except to give in to his impulses or whatever?"

Eric looked like he'd been struck himself, irises framed all around with white for a breath. He looked so hurt, I regretted my own impulse, blushing.

"Sorry. Maybe that was harsh . . . But for all I know, the two are perfectly comparable."

His features softened. "Did you deserve what your ex did to you?"

"No, I didn't."

"Then it's not the same at all. At *all*. That guy I beat deserved everything I gave him. If I hadn't done that, he'd never have felt what he had coming to him."

"You went to prison so you'd have a chance to realize how bad you messed up," I said. "That you'd done something wrong. And you came out without learning that lesson at all."

He frowned. "I'm different than I was when I went in."

"It doesn't sound like it."

Pink rose in his cheeks, nothing to do with the cold. But his anger or frustration didn't frighten me. It didn't reach his eyes.

"If I went in and came out thinking that guy got more than he deserved, when I beat him down . . . If that's reformed, I don't want to be reformed, then. Call my parole officer and get me sent back to Cousins, because I don't regret what I did. If I had a time machine, I wouldn't change a thing aside from have the common sense to not tell the judge I would've killed the guy if I hadn't been stopped."

My mouth dropped open. "You told the judge that?"

He looked embarrassed, then steeled. "Yeah. I was pissed. And it was probably true."

"But that's so . . . foolish."

"I was young and dumb. And righteous. The prosecution wanted me in for life, for intent to kill. My lawyer wanted me in for plain old assault with a deadly weapon. The judge split the difference with intent to maim, even with my fool ass telling her I wanted the guy dead. She believed my lawyer, that it was a crime of passion. That I wasn't in my right mind, I was so upset."

"You wouldn't tell me why you did it. What he did to you."

"And I still won't. Look it up if you want—it made the local news. Play detective if that's what you need."

"I did—enough to corroborate what you told me about it. But the why of it's clearly personal. I'm not going to get the answers I need in some old news blurb. I want to hear it from you."

He shook his head. "There's business at the heart of it that nobody ought to know. If people find out, it won't be from me."

Jesus, he was stubborn. "Are you an angry man, Eric?"

He gave that a long moment's serious consideration, then met my eyes squarely. "No. No I'm not. I'm actually a real sensitive guy. Calmer than most folks."

"Most folks wouldn't try to bludgeon a man to death." I took my own breath away. My words felt blunt as that tire iron, and I was shocked to hear them. Shocked and oddly thrilled to have found my voice, my spine.

"Everybody gets mad, if you push them the right way," he said. "That guy I beat down pushed me harder than anybody can be expected to take. But I got cranked through three years of anger management classes at Cousins, and I *know* what angry motherfuckers look like. And act like. And I'm not one of them, not outside those circumstances that got me put away."

I wanted to believe him. I really did. But I'd wanted to believe Justin, all those times he promised not to hurt me again. And I'd wanted to believe I wasn't the sort of woman who'd let a man mistreat her. Eric believed what he was saying—I trusted that much. But people were the worst judges of their own characters.

He sighed and stared at the tabletop between us. "It's like we were never anything at all, were we? All that stuff we said to each other . . ."

Even knowing it might be dangerous, I said quietly, "I meant every word I wrote to you. I felt every last bit of it."

He met my eyes. "Doesn't feel that way. The way you look at me now."

"I knew you in a vacuum then."

"What's that mean?"

"I knew . . . In that context, I only knew part of you. One side. And the stuff on the other side is huge—why you did what you did, and how you feel about it."

"You're saying that like, before, I looked okay from where you sat, like some shiny red apple. But now you sliced me open and I'm too rotten for you?"

I opened my mouth. Closed it. My brain thought the simile was apt, but my heart begged to differ. "It's not as cold as all that. But you . . . I dunno. Petals and thorns or something. Some poetic bullshit like that." Like the kind of bull I'd fed myself only weeks ago.

126

"You think I'm like him, don't you? You think if you give me long enough, I'd hurt you like he did."

I shifted in my chair, all at once deeply uncomfortable. "I don't know what I think."

"I'm not a guy who gets mean if you just wait long enough. But if somebody fucks with the people I love, I'm not going to just sit back and let it pass."

My brows rose at that.

Eric seemed to catch himself. I saw color rise in his cheeks and he went stiff, sliding a cell phone from his pocket and checking its screen. "I gotta meet with my parole officer at five forty-five." He stood to shrug his coat back on.

My stomach turned. I felt unsatisfied way down inside, teased by the very edge of a satisfying explanation. As he pulled on his hat, I eyed his neck, still red from the cold. I unlooped my scarf from the back of my chair. It was rich bottle green, a cashmere blend, and it stood out like a jewel against my camel-colored winter coat, against the gray and white of Michigan winter. I loved it, a lot.

"Here," I said, holding it out.

His brows rose.

I gave it a shake. "Take it. I have another at home."

Reluctantly, he let me put it in his hands. "Green."

I thought of you when I bought it.

"It's real soft."

"Use it. Your neck's all chapped."

His fingers squeezed it but his expression was pure misgiving.

"I want to you have it."

He met my eyes. "I don't need your charity."

"It's not charity. It's a woman telling a man he's being a stubborn jackass. Take it before you get wind burn."

A little smirk, a little breath. "I'll borrow it. But only 'til I see you next. I'll find my own by then."

127

"Fine."

He caught my gaze. "Will I?" he asked. "See you again?"

"I'm not sure."

"We don't have to . . . We don't have to be those people we were, in the letters. We can be just who we were today."

If I took you to bed, which man would I get? Shit. I hadn't meant to think that.

"Unless you don't like who I am," he added quietly.

"I don't know who you are, Eric. You've kept things from me—the fact that you were getting out. And why you did what you did, to get locked up."

"That first one—I'll own that. But I can't tell you why. I'm sorry."

I sighed, watching his fingers as they flexed, subtly feeling the scarf. "Just tell me this, then. What this man did . . . Was it worse than trying to beat a human being to death?"

His gaze darted, moving back and forth as he looked between my own eyes. "That's not an easy question, Annie. But he hurt someone real bad. Someone I love, who didn't do anything even half as bad to him. He did something that he had to answer for. And he answered to me."

"Why couldn't he answer to the police?"

"Not my call to make."

I squeezed my eyes shut, weary. When I opened them, he looked as tired as I felt. I stood. I watched him wind my scarf around his neck, its tails so bright against his dark coat.

"That's a good color on you."

He smiled limply. "I remember a time when I used to dress you."

My body responded, humming. He spoke the way lovers do, when their affairs have come to an end. Sad and fond and accepting. Were we lovers? Without ever having touched one another? My scarf had now caressed more of this man's bare skin than I ever might.

"I remember liking that," I said softly.

"I'm still him. I'm still that man."

I looked away. Tears were brewing, and that was just another intimacy I wasn't ready to offer him.

"Look at me," he whispered. And the way he said it, every noise and every person around us went away. I turned. He held out one end of the scarf, brought it to my cheek.

"I love how your eyes do that," he said, voice full of wonder. "How they look green, next to something green. Like that old trick you do with buttercups. Like they suck the color right up." He let the end drop. "Anyway. I have to get going."

I nodded.

We bundled up. He extended an arm and I preceded him to the door, which he held.

"Thanks."

"I'm gonna be around the library now and then," he said. "I can't help that. All depends on the weather, and where the city sends me. With my record and this economy, I need to just go wherever my boss tells me I'm going."

"That's fine. I'm not scared of you."

"Aren't you?"

I shook my head. "No. I don't think so."

"Good."

My lips twitched and I pursed them. I couldn't say if I was on the verge of smiling or crying.

"Do you . . . Do you want my number?" he asked. "You don't ever have to use it. But would you like it? Or my email address?"

"You have email?" Why did that seem so surreal?

He nodded. "My sister gave me her old laptop."

"Um . . . Okay, then. Can't hurt."

He fished for his wallet and took out a business card of all things. *Eric Collier. Contract Landscaping. Odd Jobs.* An email address. A phone number. A free man.

I slid it deep into my coat pocket. "Thanks."

"Maybe I'll see you around, Annie."

I watched his lips as he said it, my cheeks warming to remember how I'd fantasized about kissing them. "See you."

A little hitch of those lips, a little wave, then he turned away, heading for the road. My scarf around his neck, probably smelling of my lotion. His card in my pocket, slippery between my gloved fingers.

The man who'd brought me back to life, crossing the street, leaving me closed in the dark and cold. Leaving me wanting.

Chapter Ten

I made the decision two days later. After a lot of thought, and no alcohol. After weighing the pros and cons and finding no answers there, only more questions. And it was a question I typed into the body of an email.

> Would you like to hang out on Saturday evening? Just as those two people from the donut shop. There's a bar on Benson Street called Lola's. Seven o'clock?
> Anne

I paused. Hit the back arrow key. Added the *i*.

> Annie

I could've called. But writing . . . Wasn't that the only way, really?

His reply didn't come for another two days, sent around noon while I was busy at Cousins. Busy worrying he'd either not received my message or had chosen to ignore it. My heart stopped when I saw his name in my inbox.

I'll be there. And I'll bring your scarf.
Eric

When the night arrived, I was early. But he was earlier.

I spotted his back through the front window, his messy hair. As I hauled the door open, it felt as though I were spreading my ribs wide, heart pounding and slick for the world to see. He didn't spot me until I reached the booth he'd procured. He looked surprised as our eyes met.

"Evening," I said, slipping off my coat. I'd donned it as a formality, not ready for him to know I lived here. And I'd dressed exactly as I felt, a bundle of caution hiding a core of hopeful mischief. Jeans and a fitted sweater saying nothing special . . . but underneath, spring-green lace and satin.

"Evening." He studied me as I sat, his expression tough to read. My scarf was rolled neatly on the table by his elbow, and he slid it over the shiny wood. "Thanks for that."

"You're welcome. You all right?"

"Yeah, fine. I'd just expected to be kept waiting. At least until seven."

I shrugged. "I've been needing a drink." *And to see you. Whoever you are.* The bar was warm, and he was wearing a tee shirt, his winter layers heaped beside him. I tried to not notice his arms.

He looked around. "This is *not* a place my parole officer would approve of."

"Are we violating your conditions?"

He shook his head. "Nah. But I sure didn't have you pegged as a girl who'd pick a dive like this."

I shrugged. "It's close to where I live, and it's not like Darren has a ritzy section. Can I get you something?"

"You sit. I'll grab whatever you want."

My eyes jumped to the bar, glad not to find Kyle on duty. The last thing I needed was him shooting me looks, demanding, *Is that the guy? The one we warned you about?*

"Iced tea with lemon and ice and a shot of bourbon."

Eric looked puzzled at that but nodded. "Sure."

He came back shortly with my drink and a bottle of beer. We sipped in heavy silence for half a minute, then he asked, "Why'd you decide to see me again, anyhow?"

I read your letters on Monday night. Every last one. Wrapped my tongue around each word, then watched us act them out in my mind, all week. "I'm not sure."

His brows drew tight.

"I'm not trying to toy with you," I said. "If I knew what I was after, I'd tell you . . . I think maybe I'm just trying to make sense of you. And us, how we were. What we are now."

"We're whatever you decide we are."

"Would you want to just be friends with me?" I asked, curious.

"Maybe. Until you started seeing somebody."

"What would happen if I started seeing somebody?"

"It'd rip my heart out," he said with a sad smile. "How would you feel if we tried being friends and *I* started seeing somebody?"

Oh God. I felt exactly that in a breath—the meanest twisting in my chest and stomach. We were here already, weren't we? Talking about things I hadn't been sure we'd *ever* be able to utter to one another.

"I'd feel crummy," I admitted. And I realized in the next breath exactly what we were. We were exes. We had a history. We'd been intensely, romantically intimate. We'd felt for each

133

other, and we'd hurt each other. We'd never truly touched, but all the same, we weren't over what had been between us.

"I'll be honest," he said. "If you want to hear it."

I nodded, sipping my drink to try to clear a lump in my throat.

"I'd be friends with you, for as long you weren't seeing anybody. Because I like you, as a person. And because I'm in love with you."

I froze.

"I'd be friends, just for the chance to see you. But the second you got into something with some other guy, I'm out of there. And *not* because I'd flip out and beat him up. Just because it would hurt too much. I'd be out of your life—no drama, no nothing. Just gone. But for now, I'll take you whatever way you'll let me."

"Jesus."

He smirked at that. "Like you didn't know."

"No, I didn't. Not in . . . those words."

"Well, you know now." He stared at his bottle, spinning it around and around by the neck. "But if you feel like being friends . . . I don't even care why. Pity, curiosity. Because you want to fix me, or get back at your daddy. Whatever."

I frowned. "None of those reasons."

"I know I ought to be getting busy forgetting about you, because I fucked all this up so bad, I'm probably never fixing it. But you're the first good thing I've felt in so long. The only colorful thing in this shitty gray world I've come back to. The spring seems such a long ways off. Maybe seeing you will get me through the winter."

I didn't even know if he was speaking in metaphors or not, but again I pictured the green oasis I'd hidden behind wool and denim.

"Well . . . I don't know why I'd want to be friends," I said.

"I don't think I *need* to know why. But we connected on the inside. I want to know if maybe there's some way we could do the same, in the real world."

He held my stare. "That *was* my real world."

Fuck. I blushed, ashamed. "I'm sorry. Of course it was. It was real to me, too . . . in the moment. But I didn't know what I was doing, either. I was too drunk on it. Too close to step back and see what was happening."

"And what was happening?"

I blinked at his hands, still toying with the beer bottle. "I was falling for a man I didn't really know. A violent man. Who'd done something terrible to another human being. Worse than the boy who'd made me not trust myself to begin with."

"Your ex hit a woman. He hit *you*. Why?"

I frowned. "He was drunk. And frustrated, about I don't even know what."

"I beat a grown man, sober. One who goddamn well saw it coming. One who deserved it."

"So you keep saying."

"I'm no saint, but I'm not your ex, either. I'd *never* hurt you." His burning eyes told me this on a level no words ever could.

"Not me, no. I believe that."

"Who do you see, right now?" he demanded. "The me you met at Cousins? From those letters? Or some violent man from whatever dramatic reenactment you've got running in your head, of what I did when I was twenty-six?"

I was tired of this question—the one I'd been asking myself for weeks now. I shut my eyes and rubbed my face, let him see how exhausted the whole thing left me.

"You're the same woman to me," he said quietly. "From our letters."

"I wasn't the one who was keeping secrets."

135

His nostrils flared, exhalation audible. We were quiet for a time, me sipping my drink, Eric staring out the front window at the passing cars. He broke the lull, meeting my gaze.

"I haven't . . . I haven't been with anybody. Since I got out."

Goddamn my heart for rejoicing the way it did. Something inside me gave way, river ice breaking up in a spring thaw. "No? That's . . . surprising."

He shrugged, glancing around the bar. "I don't know anybody in this town."

"No, I guess not." Though why should that matter to a man who'd gone without for half a decade? "You're awful good-looking. I'm sure if you wanted to . . ."

He frowned.

"What?"

His annoyance softened, and when he spoke he sounded defeated. "The way we'd been talking, before I got out . . . That was like we'd been describing a feast. Some amazing gourmet meal I was dying to sit down to, once I got released. Then I do get out, and I can't have that feast—and that's fine. But after all that thinking about it, I don't want to settle for just whatever I might get. I don't know if I'll meet a woman anytime soon who'll make me feel the way you did, but I don't want just anybody, for the sake of it. I don't want the first sex I have after five years to be as forgettable as some drive-through hamburger."

I felt too many things at those words. Touched, to hear I was special. Hurt, to hear he did intend to move on, to look for someone who could replace me. But why shouldn't he? Why wouldn't I *want* him to, if his waiting for me to come around smacked of obsession?

All I managed was, "I could understand that."

"Plus the places a man might go, to hook up with somebody—bars like this one. Those aren't places I need to be hanging out at, now. Those sorts of people. It's too depressing. I've spent too long locked up. I don't want reminding of how people get themselves locked inside their own dead-end lives and bad habits. It's too much like prison. And it's too much like home."

"Sure."

"Did you . . ." He sighed, an aggravated huff. "Have you been with anybody? Any guys, since we quit writing to each other?"

I blinked. "No. Of course not. Not that it's your business." But the bald relief on his face doused any angst I felt.

"I know it's not," he said, voice softer. "But I still wanted to know. It's only natural."

"It took *me* five years to meet you and feel ready to even share those thoughts. To *have* them. I'm not going to jump into bed with somebody and actually do those things."

"I just wanted to hear that maybe that stuff, everything we said . . . That it was special, I guess."

My face warmed. "Of course it was. I wouldn't have risked my job if it weren't." Or my heart. Christ, I was aching for him, all over. Want all twisted up with pain. "It *was* special. But I also don't know you. I don't even know how to parse those two things. Part of me feels like I know you inside out, better than any guy I've ever been to bed with. But also that you're a total stranger."

"A stranger because you don't trust me?"

"Because I've not met so many sides of you. Important ones. The side of you that did that awful thing. The side of you that chose not to tell me you were getting out . . . even though you knew you should. That it would change everything."

"I was selfish."

I nodded. "Yeah. You were." I stirred my drink with my

137

straw. "I was, too. I used you to feel all that stuff again. Alive. And sexual. With somebody I didn't think I'd ever have to worry about becoming anything real with."

"I don't mind being used like that."

I took a deep breath, let it out slowly.

Eric turned his bottle around and around, thinking before he spoke. "Do you know why I beat him like I did? With a tire iron?"

"You won't tell me why."

"No, I mean why a tire iron."

"No."

His gaze sought the traffic. "It's because for that bright, hot moment when I got the news that set me off, I wanted that man dead. Because my bare hands weren't enough, after what he did. And because I didn't own a gun, and I didn't take the time to plan shit out. I just moved my body to where his body was, and on the way I grabbed something I thought maybe I could kill him with—"

"God, *stop*." I cringed, fearing a play-by-play.

"What I'm saying is, I'm not the kind of man who designed his world to be violent. I'm white trash—I know that. Where I'm from, that's just how it is. But I wasn't the worst man you ever met. I never got into any scary drug shit, or knocked some poor girl up, or stole from anybody. Before I beat that man down, the worst thing I probably did was drive too fast and smoke weed a couple times a month. Get in a scrap now and then. Like I said, I'm not a saint, but I'm not . . . I don't know what it is you're worried I might be. But I bet I'm not that bad."

Except what I knew him to be—an attempted murderer? Not that great, either.

"If you won't tell me why," I said, "I don't think I can ever . . ."

"Ever what?"

138

"Get back to where we were. In the letters."

His expression flickered at that. Like he'd not imagined us finding our way back was even the wildest possibility. Like I'd just told him, *There's still a chance. I'm not over you.* Like I'd just admitted it to us both. It made me feel dizzy. Or maybe that was the bourbon.

"Even if I did know why," I added quickly, "that doesn't mean I'd agree with you doing what you did. But I wish you'd just tell me."

He shook his head.

I slumped in my seat, weary all over. We were right back where we'd gotten stuck in that donut shop.

Eric thought a minute, drummed the tabletop with his fingertips. "I could make a phone call."

"To whom?"

He cracked a smile at that. "'To whom.' Fuck me, you're adorable."

I rolled my eyes.

He changed again, seeming suddenly determined, and calm. A man with a plan. He stood, skirted the bench and headed for the door, fishing his phone from his jeans, coat and gloves and hat left behind. I watched him through the front window, his back to the glass. I could see his shoulder blades through his tee, from the way he held his phone to his ear. The neon sign behind him blinked red to yellow, turning his blue shirt from black to green, black to green.

Wear green. Wear black.

Right now he wore both. I'd worn neither. And if I had that final choice to make again . . . Here I was, still not committed to either option, as fickle as that light. Did this phone call really have the power to change my mind about him? Exonerate him? Invite him upstairs, into my bed? Inside my sheets, inside my body?

139

I flushed all over, shocked to have even thought those things.

He was talking. I could tell from how he'd move, then pause. He shoved his free hand in his pocket. I thought about grabbing his coat and bringing it out to him, chose not to. He nodded, shook his head. Looked down the street. I tried to imagine the conclusions I'd jump to about him, if we were strangers. That man beyond the glass, making a desperate phone call in his tee shirt, in the frigid winter air. A guy chasing drugs, maybe? Or a girl?

Suddenly he was gone, out of frame then coming back through the door, phone in hand, still lit up. He sat back down across from me and held it out. On the screen it said, Kristina.

"Go on," he said, giving it a little shake.

I took it, my warm fingers brushing his icy ones. I held it to my ear and said, "Hello?"

"Yeah?"

"Sorry," I said, shooting my companion a look. "Eric just gave me his phone. He didn't tell me who you—"

"I'm Kristina."

"Oh. Hello. I'm Anne."

"I know who you are." She sounded bored and aggressive at once, that rusty voice suggesting she was probably taking long drags off a cigarette between sentences. "Eric told me all about you."

"Oh," I said again, stupidly.

"I'm his big sister. He tells me everything. You want to know why he beat that asshole down."

I swallowed. Did I? I wasn't so sure anymore. "I'm guessing he did it for you."

"That shitbag didn't get any less than he deserved." She still sounded bored, but I sensed tension behind the tone. A

140

tough girl trying to act hard, to cover up the fact that she felt something.

"I don't know what Eric and I are," I admitted, eyeing him. "But we can't be anything if I don't know what made him do such a terrible thing."

A sharp, mean little laugh, one that had me picturing Kristina with a forty at one elbow, a shirtless man passed out on a threadbare couch in the background. Single-wide. Camped in some weedy lot where American dreams went to die.

"You want to hear about the terrible things men do," she said through a cruel sigh. "Oh, I could tell you all about that. But it's none of your goddamn business what happened to me. I told my brother and I told that bitch judge of his, but I sure as shit won't be telling you. Just know there's ways a man can hurt you, ways that don't leave marks on the outside. Ways that make a tire iron look honest. That clear enough for you?"

My throat hurt, but she couldn't see me nodding so I croaked, "Yeah. That's pretty clear."

When she spoke next, her tone lost some of its ragged edge. "You think whatever you want about me. But my brother's a good man. Maybe the only good man to ever come out this place. I don't know who you think you are, but I can guaran-fucking-tee you, you'd be lucky to deserve him. Not the other way around." And she hung up on me.

I stared at the phone as her name disappeared and the call duration flashed. Eric reached out and pocketed the thing.

"She's not a woman whose business you just go around sharing," he said mildly.

"No. I gathered that."

He cracked a smile. "She's wild, my sister. Same as our father."

"I'm surprised she didn't do the beat-down herself."

His smile wilted. "She would've. 'Cept he broke her arm."

141

My body went cold. "Oh."

"I'm done dwelling on all this," he said, sitting back. "But there you go. Whatever she said, that's all you're ever gonna hear about why I did what I did. It wasn't a choice to me. It's not a question of whether it was justified."

"Looking back, do you wish you'd killed him?"

"No," he said. "I'm glad I didn't kill him."

I blinked, surprised.

"It was worth five years, showing him what happens when you fuck with my family. But no, he's probably not worth my sister feeling like I'd forfeited the rest of my life in order to see that guy dead."

"Did he get put away? For what he did to her?"

"No, for other shit."

"Not in Cousins, I hope."

He shook his head. "They wouldn't allow that."

"Good . . . Did you know him? Before?"

Eric nodded. "Oh yeah. I knew him. He and my sister had been something, once upon a time. We cooked out together, went down to the lake, worked on cars. My mom let him crash on our couch one summer, when I was maybe sixteen."

I shivered. That was so much worse to me. For violence to be lurking in someone you thought you knew. It made you question everything. Your own judgment and intuition, why you didn't see it coming, and if it was your own fault, in a way.

"You trusted him, then?"

He shook his head. "Not by the time he did what he did."

"No?"

Eric held my gaze. "You're from a real nice place, aren't you?"

"We weren't rich or anything." Not by Charleston standards. By Darren standards? By that curve, I may as well have grown up in some gated paradise.

142

"I'm not from a nice place," he said. "Little nothing-town called Kernsville, an hour east of here. And there's a plague out there, the way plagues spread through dirty places hundreds of years ago. Only this one gets brewed up out of cough syrup and it's a pipe or a needle that bites you, not a rat. You follow?"

I nodded.

"I'm not saying what I did was any kind of mercy or anything. But if some infectious animal was going around biting people, nobody would hesitate to put it down."

"And he's still in prison now?"

He nodded.

"Is there anybody you have to answer to, back home? Friends of his?"

"No. He'd fucked just about everybody over in one way or another, by the time he got locked up. If he gets out someday and wants to get back on me or my family for what I did to him, he'll be marching up alone. If he's got any uncooked brain cells left in his head, he'll find himself a new town to infest."

We were quiet for a time, the space between us filled with strangers' arguments, with hard rock and laughter and the tinkling of bottles and glasses.

I had my chin dipped, attention on the table, and Eric angled his head low to catch my eyes.

"Yeah?" I asked.

"You look sad."

"I guess I just wish you regretted it," I said quietly, the words surprising even me.

"I can't. It was the right thing to do, no matter how wrong the law says it was. I couldn't live with myself if I hadn't done that. There's natural laws that trump the ones you might get arrested over."

I turned that around in my head. I tried to imagine what my father would have done, if he'd heard about Justin bursting my eardrum, knocking his daughter to the floor, breaking her heart so badly she walled it off for the next half a decade. He served the state. The law. But if he'd known . . . If he'd gone after Justin, hit him as hard as that hand that had struck me . . . I loved my daddy as much as a girl can, but if he'd done that, I'd have hugged him harder than I ever had in my life. Loved him even more, to know what he felt for me went that deep, that it weighed impulse against reason and said *fuck you* to the latter. I'd not given him a chance to make that decision. I'd protected him, because deep down . . . maybe I knew which he'd have chosen. And Justin wasn't worthy of endangering my father's job. He wasn't worthy of breaking my father's heart, either. Not on top of mine.

I eyed Eric's bottle, still full to the neck. "Are you allowed to leave Darren without your parole officer's permission?"

He nodded. "Yeah, just can't leave the state."

"Let's go somewhere."

"What, now?"

"Yeah. Let's drive someplace. Somewhere quiet. With water." Like that lake he'd mentioned in our letters, the one I'd imagined us beside so, so many times.

He gave me a look I'd expect from a protective friend. "You want some freshly sprung con to drive you out to someplace quiet?"

"I do."

He mulled it over a moment, then stood. "All right, then."

We abandoned his barely tasted beer, my half-drunk cocktail. We abandoned the neon lights and sour smell of the bar and the warmth, pulling on our layers outside the exit. He led me half a block to an old silver truck, went around and unlocked my door.

144

"Keep your gloves on," he warned, shutting me inside. He climbed into the driver's seat. "This piece of shit's heater's been broken since before I got put away." He reached behind his seat for his cap. I donned my scarf and the engine stuttered to life.

"Where'm I taking you?" he asked, easing us away from the curb.

"How far is that lake you told me about? The one you missed when you were locked up?"

"Forty minutes maybe."

"Let's go there."

"If you say so." He made a U-turn and aimed us toward the highway.

We drove without talking for a long while, until we exited onto a lonely route, leaving industrial Michigan behind, slipping into hibernating farmland, then woods.

His voice shattered the silence. "Why d'you want to see this lake so bad?"

"I'm trying to understand you. I want to see the place you told me about. It seems like . . . It seems like the place that embodied everything prison took away." And the place where he'd brought our bodies together, in those fantasies he'd written out for me.

"It won't be anything like what I miss. Frozen, dark. Snow all over."

"It'll just have to do."

I sensed his nod in my periphery.

We passed a sign that advertised parking for a public beach, but a metal gate kept us out, so we drove on. A mile later he slowed to an ice-crunching halt along the roadside, and through a gap in the pines I could see a satin ribbon—the near-full moon on the lake, on a frosted plane the wind had blown bald. Eric shut off the engine and killed the headlights.

145

It was the darkest place I'd been in months. No streetlights, no houses winking in the distance. Just the moon. By its glow our breath steamed in the cold truck cab.

"This is nothing like what I miss," he reiterated softly, in a tone as black as grief.

"I'm sure."

"This is like visiting your grandmother's grave and pretending it's the same as seeing her again." I saw him swallow, saw him blink. His face was white and jet and silver, a daguerreotype.

"Why are we here?" he asked, so quietly it could've been my imagination, if not for the puff of his misty breath.

"I need to see you. Here. Away from Darren or Cousins or any other place full of bricks and barbed wire and all that depressing stuff."

"Snow depresses me."

"Not me." I reached for his gloved hand with mine. We rested them on the seat between us. The most we'd ever touched, and even through all the layers, I felt him.

"I love the snow," I said. "The fluffy kind, anyhow, not the brown slush. We never had any real snowstorms where I'm from, not except for Hurricane Hugo, and I was real tiny for that. But I remember it. It was the most magical thing I'd ever seen." I squeezed his hand. "It was like the world had been covered in sugar." Sugar, like he'd imagined tasting, if we ever kissed.

"I hate blizzards," he said. "Meant I couldn't escape the fucking trailer I grew up in. Not the way I could in the summer." He sounded bitter. Bitter now, about this. Never about his sentence, or about the years he'd lost, about any promises he'd read into my letters, ones I'd broken when I turned him away.

I stared at the moon's reflection, smudged across the ice.

"Try to see it through me. The way your letters made me see sex through you. In ways I hadn't felt in ages."

I turned and caught his features soften at that, watched black lashes lower against white skin. When his eyes opened, those brown irises were obsidian-dark and shiny.

"It's not all bad," he conceded, staring at the lake. "It's clean, anyhow. And quiet. And . . . open. And it's good to see so many stars again."

"It's so still."

He nodded, then whispered, "And you're here."

I shivered, the sensation strangely warm in the icy coldness. "I'm here." In an isolated place, with a dangerous man, without informing anyone where I'd gone. Yet I felt nothing resembling fear.

"I took you somewhere," he added, even more softly. "Someplace you wanted to be."

I shifted, collapsing the cup holder tray into the dash so I could turn and rest my bent legs on the bench seat. "You took me all kinds of places, in our letters. Places I worried I might never want to go, ever again."

He turned, too. "I really did that?"

"You really did. Whatever my letters meant to you, stuck inside those walls, I swear yours meant just as much to me. Stuck in my own little lonely box."

"Not possible."

I smiled at him. "You'd be surprised."

For a long moment we watched each other's faces, two pairs of eyes studying, recording. Then his gaze dropped to our hands, resting on the seat. He slid off one glove, and I did the same. Grazing my fingertips along his palm, I felt his warmth for a slim second before the air stole it. Like a child, I fanned my fingers to measure my hand against his, then he zippered us together, squeezing softly. We held tight until body

147

heat came out of hiding to curl up between our palms. His next breath flared, giving away the fire burning behind that cautious expression.

"Tell me what you're after," he whispered.

"I'm not after anything. Only this."

"Tell me where we stand. Are we those two people from the donut shop, or those two people who wrote those letters to each other?"

Good question. "We're someplace in between, I think."

His brows drew together—only the subtlest little movement, but it told me everything. It wrote all his hope and regret and need across his face, clear as black ink on a white page.

"I haven't been with anybody since I got out," he murmured.

"You said." Yet the hot little spark those words gave me was strong as when he'd first told me.

"And you don't think I've changed, from who I was when I got put away, but I have. I don't want to go back to being who I was before I went in. Who I was at twenty-six. Who I was back in my shitty hometown. I want to be somebody who deserves to be with somebody like you." He flexed his fingers between mine. "And not because you're sweet and pretty and seem like, I dunno. Like some good girl or something, all clean and shiny. Like you'll fix what's wrong with me, with your purity or some shit like that."

"Good." Very good. "But why, then?"

He watched our hands, thinking. "Because you're somebody who makes me feel what you do." He frowned. "Because of how you make me feel, not because of how you *seem* like you'd make a man feel. Fuck, I'm not saying this right at all."

Yet it was poetry to me, dizzying in its beauty. I squeezed his fingers and whispered, "Go on."

"I don't want you to think that I see you as this perfect white handkerchief that I think I can use to like, clean away

148

the badness from myself. Because that's how so many guys like me would see you. As some angel that'll fix their sins. That's not how I see you at all. That's not why I want you, or want to feel like I'm worthy of you. I just want to be the kind of man who deserves to feel what you make me feel, instead of just settling for whatever's available, the way people do back home. Did that make *any* sense?"

It made so much sense, I felt tears searing my cheeks. Eric raised his eyes.

"Oh, shit."

I squeezed his hand and wiped my face with my gloved one. "They're good tears."

"How come?"

I shrugged. "Because that's exactly how I've felt before, with guys. Back home. Like I'm not allowed to have any dimensions past whatever fits the mold of sweet, wholesome Southern good girl. Like I shouldn't swear or talk back or say mean things or lose my temper, ever. It's like being on probation, almost."

The corner of his lips hitched. "I read your letters. I know you're not that girl."

I smiled. "And it was nice to be seen that way by somebody. And valued for it."

His gaze fled again, dropping just to my scarf or chin. "Do you think . . ." He trailed off, but I knew what he was asking.

"I think maybe." He'd done everything he could to fix the mistake he'd made, omitting the news of his release, and to explain why he'd beat another human being half to death. Even more importantly, I believed him when he'd said he was planning to move on. And that was what I'd really needed, to trust that what he felt for me was affection, not fixation.

His next words were barely a whisper. "Tell me what to do, to stand a chance of us ever getting there."

I didn't think. Only spoke. "Kiss me."

"Now?"

"We need to know if what we feel goes beyond those letters. If it doesn't, there's no use in us both pining for it."

"You been pining for me?" he asked, and his eyes narrowed in the most charmingly cocky way.

"Course I have. For that man I met on those pages. Show me he's here with me now." I wasn't entirely sure who this woman was, saying these words. But maybe I ought to let her speak up more often.

He held my stare, and that look had me back in a hard chair, in a bleak room, in a mean world. Those hot, dark eyes, the ones that pinned me like a butterfly in a place where I never should've mislaid of flight instinct. He edged closer. I did the same, bringing my bent leg up, resting my knee between us. My seat belt bound me, and I let his hand go so we could wrestle out of them.

My knee on his thigh, heat soldering us together. His other glove stripped, then two bare, cold hands on my jaw, and those lips suddenly so close. His fingertips stroked my cheeks, brows, nose, skirted my lips. No man had ever made me feel so fascinating. He touched me like I was something precious and beguiling. I touched him in return. The contours of his face, the stubble I'd imagined rubbing my skin—so much softer than I'd guessed. I'd memorized the shapes of him, across the dayroom, across a classroom, across a tabletop, but it was nothing like stroking them for real. Feeling his heat, smelling his skin.

A man, touching a woman for the first time since his freedom had been taken away.

A woman, touching a man for the first time since she'd been robbed of her desire.

In a truck no less, like two eager, clueless virgins, parked at the edge of something big.

150

He seemed like he could do this for hours—just hold my face and nothing more. This man who had to be dying for his feast, yet he was enthralled by the candles or the soft cotton napkin, content to delay that first coveted taste a little while longer. He was steeped in awe, and I in impatience. His lips were so near, and I needed to experience them. I needed his mouth to make promises . . . to give me clues to how the rest of his body would feel.

I rubbed our noses together, but his hands firmed, keeping me from coming any closer.

"Kiss me," I murmured, the words thin with desperation.

"I only get to do it once, for the first time."

"I'm going to die if you don't."

His lips twitched and his eyes narrowed, crinkling. "Remind me which of us has been locked up for five years."

"Both of us," I whispered, and it changed him. I watched as he realized it was the truth. I watched as he came to understand I needed this as badly as he did. That he'd been going hungry for a woman's body all this time . . . but I'd gone without the very hunger itself.

His palms cradled my jaw, thumbs on my cheeks. He tipped my face gently to his, like a chalice to obliterate a long, cruel abstinence.

And we met, skin to skin.

I'd thought I'd had the best first kiss a girl could ask for at fifteen—barefoot on a dock in the sunshine, peppermint ice cream on the boy's lips. But as Eric's mouth sought mine in the cold dark of this old truck, it felt more right than anything I'd ever known.

He wasn't cautious, not the way a man gets when he's trying to give a good girl what he assumes she wants. He kissed like he was tasting chocolate, a slow, rich, curious exploration suspended between innocent and dirty. A tease

151

of tongue, another, then deep sweeps, ones that cocked his jaw and curled his fingers in my hair. Everything I'd imagined. Hot. Needy. His low moan made the cab go hazy, and that mouth shifted—curious to ravenous in a beat.

I surrendered to his eager, bossy tongue, dying to feel this again without fear—a man's aggression. And his was so sweet, marinated in so much longing and waiting and mourning. When I'd tasted my fill of his hunger, I stroked him back. I told him with my mouth that if—that *when*—we found ourselves in a bed, I'd be so much more than receptive. That he'd leave those sheets with nail scratches up and down his back, maybe bite marks on his neck. When I nipped his lip, his entire body tightened, pushing a groan from his throat. He wore a hoodie under his coat and I found its drawstrings, clasping them.

He spoke my name into my mouth. "Annie."

"Eric." I stroked his neck, then bit him again, a little harder. Another tightening, another plaintive groan. The roughest man I'd ever gotten close to, yet here he was, so utterly at my mercy.

The me from those letters was back, that girl who'd played with fire and liked the burn. I felt a boldness in my blood I'd never experienced before, ever. I sucked his lip, kissed his chin, his ear, breathed in the frosty, faint scent of his stubbly skin.

"Touch me," I whispered.

"How?"

"Anywhere. My face or hands or neck. Anywhere."

He slid his fingertips from my hair and held my jaw, tasting me deeply with rhythmic sweeps, the motions echoed all through his body. He came closer, seeming above me, somehow. So big. So familiar again, this man I'd thought I'd lost. His hips shifted in time with his kiss. I waited for the pressure, for his hands pushing me back, for his weight on me, his

152

heat. I waited, and waited. I fisted his collar and hood, all but hauling him onto me.

"You hard for me?" I asked against his cheek.

"Course I am."

"Are you big?"

The softest, most frustrated laugh vibrated against my lips, then he pulled away enough for our noses to touch. His lips brushed mine as he spoke. "You'll have to find that out for yourself sometime." He nipped.

I let my palm roam down the front of his jacket, but he caught it at his ribs, his own hand trembling. "Not here. Not like this."

"We're at your lake."

"Not like this," he said again, pressing my hand firmly to his shoulder. "Not all rushed like this. Not after how long I've waited."

"How, then?"

"In your room. In your sheets that smell like you, where it's warm. In a big, soft bed. With candles and music maybe, all that girly stuff that's nothing like how my world's looked for the past five years. Not in the truck I've driven since I was in high school. Not getting watched by all this fucking *snow*."

"Tonight?"

"If that's what you want, then *fuck* yes."

I laughed, rubbing the tips of our noses together. "As soon as we possibly can."

His smile was as dry as it was warm. Dry and warm as those sheets he craved. "I'd speed if I weren't on parole."

"We need condoms."

"And gas." Turning, he redid his seat belt and started the engine, headlights bleaching the pines, scaring away the stars. "Get ready for the longest twenty-five miles of your life."

Chapter Eleven

The ride back to Darren was a blur. Black asphalt, bright white service station lights. The same old decay rolling past, but a shiny little cardboard box now hiding in my purse. Eric was as impatient as I was, catching himself speeding every half mile or so, slowing down with a tight sigh.

"Where's your place?" he asked as we exited at the city's edge.

"That bar."

"Same street?"

"Same building. Third floor."

He laughed. "You weren't kidding when you said you lived close."

We were there inside five minutes, and he found a space right in front of the side entrance.

My hands were shaking as I fished out my keys and unlocked the foyer's two doors. I heard his steps behind me, up two flights. Felt them. Felt *him*, the weight and nearness of his body.

I flipped on the living room lights. "You can just toss your stuff wherever." I waved to the rocking chair by the window.

My coat, then his draped on top. Gloves, his hoodie and hat, my scarf—a big rumpled heap of the two of us. Two pairs of boots leaning into one another like weary travelers.

"It's nice," he said, looking around.

"Can I get you anything? Tea or coffee? Or I might have some wine."

He shook his head, the movement tight. His eyes told me there were things he wanted to taste, but none of them came in a glass.

"I'll give you the tour. Living room," I said with a cheesy sweep of my arm, then a peek at the kitchenette. "Bathroom through there, and my bedroom."

I led him inside and switched on the weak bulb of my reading lamp. I saw it all through his eyes. A full-sized bed, made up in fluffy down and soft sateen, the quilt my grandma had given me when I'd started college folded at the foot of the mattress. Curtains on the big window, blocking streetlight and brick. Perfume bottles and a jewelry box on the old dresser, a silk scarf draped from its mirror. I detected scents I took for granted. My clover deodorant, the facsimile summer of my laundry detergent. Me, in my bedclothes. Me everywhere. I watched his face as he studied my room.

"Is it what you pictured?" I asked. What he'd pictured when he'd fantasized about me. About us, in a place this soft and feminine.

"It's perfect."

"Have a seat." I gestured to the bed, then excused myself to use the bathroom. Smoothed my hair, ran a fingertip over my deodorant stick and dabbed it behind my ears. *I miss how you smell, like spring and grass.*

I fetched the condom box from my purse in the living room and gathered the votive and matches from the coffee table, shutting off the lights until it was just that single bulb,

155

illuminating the man sitting at the edge of my mattress. His eyes went to the box, and I set it and the candle on the side table, feeling awkward. Feeling blatant.

"Be right back," he said, and we swapped places, me sitting nervously on the bed as he used the bathroom. I lit the candle and turned off the lamp. I considered whipping off my clothes and waiting for him, posed seductively in my underwear, but maybe—

He returned, tossing his sweater on the floor.

"Do you want to undress me?" I asked. "Or watch me undress for you . . . ?"

"I want to kiss you, and we'll see what happens from there."

I smiled, loving that. Loving that even though we'd each scripted this encounter down to every last inch of exposed skin and stitch of shed clothing, we hadn't come here to act out those scenes. We were here to explore. To discover.

I patted the covers. His weight again. Then his heat. His lips.

That mouth was hungry. His hands held back, resting unassumingly at my shoulders, but I felt excitement in the way he kissed me—starved, greedy tastes, as though I were a drink he couldn't wait to get wasted on. I held his arms, that bare skin under his short sleeves, all that hard muscle. One warm hand rose to hold my face, thumb stroking my jaw. The other went to my collarbone, fingertips light as a butterfly, making me shiver. The need was spreading through his body, from his mouth, now his fingers, read in his torso from the way he tensed, anticipating. The hand above my breasts grew heavy. I felt a fever breaking out, felt hot in my skin and seared by his excitement. The way he kissed was as raw and dirty as any sex I'd ever had, and I ached to feel his mouth all over my body. Between my legs, like his letters had promised.

I led us down, onto our sides, heads on a pillow. My scent was there in its case, and I hoped he could smell it, too. My sweater was stifling, and I broke our mouths apart to strip it away. Then my jeans. He took my lead, and soon we were down to our tees and underwear. His shorts were slate blue, his excitement apparent. My own arousal pulsed hot at the thought that I'd feel him if we pressed close. The first hard cock I'd touched since undergrad. The first wet, excited woman he'd touched since he was twenty-six.

Our legs locked, mouths seeking. He let me hear his heavy breaths and deep moans, let me feel him squirm, antsy. His fingertips rubbed my collarbone, then with a surrendering groan, he cupped my breast.

The contact shocked my breath away. I'd felt something for every boy I'd gone to bed with, but I'd never felt *this*. Never had a man felt so right, my need for him so urgent. Animalistic and instinctual. The rush of it made me dizzy.

He swallowed, looking a touch drunk. "Jesus, you're beautiful."

"Do you remember," I whispered against his mouth, "when you asked me to wear my hottest underwear for you?"

"Yeah."

"I bought some after you said that, special. Because I didn't own any that made me feel sexy. I bought some and I wore it that next week, just like you asked."

He exhaled roughly, a man in pain.

"And I'm wearing it now."

His eyes caught mine, burning hot. "You wore it tonight, knowing we'd end up . . ."

"I didn't know. But I hoped we'd get back here. Maybe I planned for us to get back here, in a way."

Between panting kisses he murmured, "I want to see."

I let him ease up the hem of my shirt, to take in my panties.

157

He looked overwrought at the sight, the same way I felt watching his lips part and his eyes grow hungry. He tugged at my top, and I arched off the mattress so he could push it up, then I peeled it away for him. With a soft push, he turned me onto my back and knelt between my legs. I was ready for his aggression, but all he did was look at me. Drank me in with that thirsty stare.

"Green," he said with a little smirk.

I smirked right back, nerves gone. "The way you talk about plants, and summertime . . . It seemed more exotic somehow than black or red."

He nodded, stroking my legs from calf to hip, up and down, again and again. "It's perfect. You're perfect."

Worth waiting all these years for?

"I'm almost glad," I murmured, "about having shut all this stuff out for so long. If it means I get to discover it all over again, this way. Feeling it so . . . *intensely*, I guess. Wanting it this badly. With you."

He had no words for that, only actions. On our sides once more, and his leg thrust between mine, two mouths devouring. I pawed at his shirt until he wrestled it away. His hand was warm on my breast, thumb swiping back and forth, quicker and quicker as my nipple tightened. I'd forgotten I could feel so much there, and the way it deepened the tension between my thighs. I stroked his chest and arm, his hard belly, the crest of muscle at his hip. All these gorgeous shapes I'd stolen guilty glimpses of from my office window, suddenly hot against my palm. I imagined him flexing, imagined him pumping into me, and all at once the hunger went from an ache to a painful twist.

"I want to feel you," I whispered, then sucked his lip. "Show me."

His hand was on mine, leading it, pressing my palm to

him. Soft cotton, hard flesh. A thousand tiny things I'd forgotten, like the weight of a man's arousal, its heat, the way it reacted, straining for more. He stroked my hand up and down, slow and light. He was bigger than I'd let myself imagine, harder than I'd remembered possible. He urged my touch lower and curled my palm around that most vulnerable part of him, squeezing softly. Led me back up, cupping my fingers around his blunt, thick crown.

I did this to you, I thought, tracing the cleft with my thumb. *And you've imagined this very moment, same as me. The moment I found the evidence of what we feel for each other, right in my own grip.*

He let me explore, and I did so slowly. Thoroughly. I felt it when he got wet, from the way the cotton dragged against my palm. I freed my mouth to look between us at the dark patch on his shorts, and to let him see how fascinated I was.

"Feel how ready I am for this?" he whispered.

I nodded, swallowed.

"You want to see me?"

I met his eyes, so dark in the low light—black as the sky way out in the country. "Yeah. Show me."

And there it was—the sight I'd been imagining forever. His big hand, big thumb tucked under his waistband, pushing it down. Big cock. He wrapped himself in a fist, eased it up and back.

"You like it?" he murmured.

"I love it."

"I want your hand on me." He moved his own low, circling the root with his thumb and first finger, presenting himself. "Touch me."

His skin was hot. So was mine, and there was friction, even just between my fingertips and his bare shaft. I wrapped my hand around him, wanting us both to see how thick he

159

was in my small fist, how dark and flushed against my pale fingers. How right that must look, after all those years stuck servicing himself.

Soft, searing skin glided along that rock-hard core with my strokes. He dropped his face, nuzzling my neck, kissing and nipping. "Say you like it."

I tightened my grip, made the pulls long and luxurious. "I do. Even more than I'd imagined I would."

I heard him swallow. "Am I as big as you'd hoped?"

"Bigger. And harder." Tighter still, I let my hand tell him the things I had no words for.

He moaned, breath scalding my throat. "I tried to imagine this so many times. You touching me. But I got it so wrong, back then. I never guessed what it'd be like, smelling only you. And your candle. And . . ." He grunted softly, lost to a caress that crested his head. "And how quiet it would be. Quiet enough to actually hear you, touching me."

Indeed. The whisper of spring-green satin, my breast moving against his arm as I pumped him. Of skin on skin. So much breathing, and the rustle of the down comforter as he shifted his eager body.

"What do you want, tonight?" I asked.

"Everything," he said, watching my hand. "What do you want?"

"Whatever you've missed most."

"Everything," he said again. "A little of everything."

"That thing you imagined, on your birthday . . ."

"Your mouth."

I nodded.

"If you like that," he said, filthy hope written all over his face.

"Lie back." *And let me spoil you.*

He arranged a couple of pillows against the headboard,

160

half sitting. *He wants a good view,* I thought with a happy shiver. My own view was a heart-stopper—this powerful, gorgeous body reclined on my bed, taut with anticipation. He helped me get his shorts off, then spread his strong thighs for me.

I moved to my knees and elbows, capturing him in my hand. I'd forgotten the smell of an excited man. I'd forgotten that I could *love* this. I'd stigmatized all but the most gentle, romantic guises of sex since Justin, but as I brought Eric to my lips, I remembered so much. Dark things that had made me curious when I'd been younger. Rough things. Rough men. I'd closed those appetites in a box, not trusting them for so long . . . *But he didn't break me,* I realized, taking Eric between my lips, feeling him tighten like a spring. I'd shut those things away—packed them, labeled them, *Not for me, not anymore.* But they returned in flashes now, a rush of dark desires. *My* desires again.

"Yes." He arched when I closed my mouth tight around his head, and I felt the weight of his palms on my shoulders, then my neck.

It all came back to me, this act. Everything it had made me feel—vulnerable and excited with one boy, a little demeaned by another, powerful once, dirty another time . . . but never like this. Never hungry this way, wanting simply to taste a man's most intimate skin, taste his arousal. Feel his desire against my tongue and between my lips. Hear it in that deep voice, chasing through the shadows like a breeze.

"God, Annie."

His hands were neither pushy nor gentle. Warm fingertips in my hair, following the motions, urging but not forcing. His breath had grown harsh, and every little grunt and gasp lit me from the inside. I eased him out, meeting his eyes.

"Let me hear you."

His face was flushed, lips parted, eyes at once burning and glassy. "Yeah?"

"Yeah. Moan for me. Or talk to me." Just that voice, transformed by what I made him feel.

"I don't want to say the wrong thing."

"You couldn't. I want to hear whatever you're thinking. Whether it's romantic or nasty or mean or any other thing. Whatever comes out."

He nodded.

I took him back inside, rewarded immediately with a long, deep groan. It vibrated through the length of his big body, and the room felt darker, the taste and scent of his excitement sharper.

"Yeah," he murmured, fingertips guiding once more. "I haven't felt this in so long. Nothing this soft, or sweet. Nothing that made me feel this close to anybody."

I took him deep—deeper than was comfortable, and more aggressive, but in the moment, my need to consume him drowned everything else. My need to meet *his* needs. To taste his relief and surrender—

"Stop," he said suddenly, nearly pleading.

I backed off and met his gaze.

"I'm too close. Way too close."

"I don't mind if you . . . Not at all."

He shook his head. "Not like this. Not tonight."

So often he made these decrees . . . But how long since he'd been able to control his experiences? I smiled. "Whatever you want, Eric."

"Face to face."

Warmth bloomed in me, happy hunger. "Sure."

"Let me taste you first," he said, already moving, urging me to swap places. "I'll get you so ready. And get a hold on myself before I lose it."

162

He straddled my legs, and when his hands slipped beneath my back I arched to let him free my bra clasp. His cock pressed along my navel, hot and heavy, still slippery from my mouth. The breath left him in a rush as he lifted the cups away, his lids dropping like blinds, his gaze slivers of heat searing my bare skin. He moved his knees between my thighs, gruff, shoved a forearm beneath my back, taking my breast in the other hand. The rough stroke of his thumb, then the smooth, slick heat of his tongue. I held him, fingers in his dark hair, my own head driving into the pillow as his mouth teased and sucked and spoiled. Then those lips were at my ribs, my belly, his arm peeling free from under me. Strong hands on my hip bones, kisses trailing low to flirt with the lace border of my panties. More lace at the sides, and his fingers curled under it, tugging. I lifted my butt and let him strip me bare.

As he settled between my legs he said, "Tell me what you need."

"Just to feel how much you want this." And I could see it already, the need in his eyes and the hunger in his parted lips. Awe in the crease of his brow.

I'd never done this and felt what I did then. Pure impatience, not a trace of worry. I didn't care how I looked, how I smelled or tasted, and whether those things were good enough. A younger woman's worries. I only cared that Eric discover it all—the flavor and scent of my desire, the shape and feel of this place he'd not visited in so long.

He taunted, breathing deeply, letting me feel the warmth of his exhalation. I gripped his hair tighter. The faintest contact—his nose, then his lower lip, another long breath. My legs shifted and he stilled them, holding my thighs in place. Those hands told me, *You're dreaming if you think I'm going to rush this.*

163

His voice told me, "It felt so good—your mouth on me." I felt each word against my most sensitive skin.

"You felt so good there," I whispered back. "I want to feel you every way I can, before we say good night. All the ways we told each other about—"

I gasped as his tongue moved, a firm, gliding stroke tracing my outer lip. I let his hair go to grasp his shoulder, needing skin and muscle. He mirrored the caress on the other side, and my nails bit him. A greedy sound warmed me. Slow, long licks along the inner seams of my lips, then a deep sweep of his hot tongue, straight up the center. Another, and finally those soft lips closed around my clitoris.

"*Oh.*"

He sucked, tongue flickering. And though my sighs were near silent, he moaned as if he were fucking—as if he could feel precisely what I did.

The air was cool when his mouth abandoned me. "What did you fantasize about most," he asked, "while we were still writing each other?"

I shut my eyes as his mouth went back to work. "Dark things."

His stroking tongue demanded, *What dark things?*

"Always you . . . exposing yourself. Us kissing, maybe, then your hand, lowering your shorts. Showing me how excited you were. Things I never thought about before . . . not the way you make me do." A man's bare excitement, bold as pornography.

He changed his position, leaving me aching as he shifted onto his hip so he could clasp his cock. His flesh looked heavy, and as he stroked I watched it go from swollen to steel. Watched his muscles tense, the ones along his side knitting, his belly furrowed, his arm locked. Excitement glistened at his crown, and I felt the same evidence greeting his tongue as he lapped at my arousal.

"I wondered how you looked," I muttered, head fuzzy.

164

"When you touched yourself. Thinking about me . . . I bet it was never this quiet, or dark." What else must he be wallowing in? "Never this warm, in the winter. On a bed this soft. Tasting me, like you are now."

His pumping fist fumbled at that, his laving tongue disrupted by a deep moan.

"Can you taste me?" I asked. "How much I want you?"

"Yes." His nose rubbed my clit as his tongue drove deep.

I cupped his neck, our skin damp, his hair curling under my palm. "You can't taste me deep enough," I said, the words flowing from who knew where. From some dark place hell-bent on baiting this man. "Your fingers can't explore me how I need you to."

His hand abandoned his cock at that. Two digits slid between my lips, his mouth claiming my clit. He showed me exactly how right I was.

"That's good, Eric. But it's not enough."

"Tell me," he murmured, teeth nearly nipping, making me twitch. He moved his fingers like a cock, steady and stiff. "Tell me what you need, Annie."

"You. All of you." Imagining just that, the pleasure simmering between my legs spiked, tight and grasping.

"I won't last a minute."

"Good. I want to see that. How bad you need this."

His moan was everything—excitement, frustration, awe, aggression. I could taste his need in that sound, as surely as he could taste mine on his tongue.

"Eric."

Another moan, a surrender that curled his body around my leg, muscles tightening.

"Show me," I said softly, and stroked his hair. "Show me what it feels like, to be wanted by a man, the way you want me."

His eyes caught mine, burning bright across the landscape

165

of my naked skin. Strong shoulders rolled as he moved, stalking up my body, arms at my ribs, thighs knocking mine wide. Anticipation roared through me like fire, and getting a condom detached and unwrapped for him took ten lifetimes. He leaned back, chest and abdomen gorgeous in the candlelight, forearm flexing as he rolled the latex down, all the way down. He was big, and the way it hugged him was the best kind of obscene, making me want to feel the same—stroked and stretched and filled with him, every filthy thing.

"You ready?" he asked me, voice thick.

"Yeah. You?"

He held himself steady, held my eyes. "I've been ready for this for months. Though I never really thought I'd get to be here."

"Me neither."

"You deserve a man who'll spoil you rotten," he said. "Make love or fuck or whatever it is you want, for as long as you need it. What you're gonna get is somebody else, this first time. I can't help that. But if you let me, next time I'll be everything you need, I swear."

"You already are," I whispered. "Whatever you are, that's what I want."

He lowered onto braced arms, sealing us with body heat. I opened wider. As his smooth, sheathed head met my lips, I grasped his shoulders, anchoring myself. Holding my breath, memorizing everything. Every ounce of pressure as he pushed, every thick inch of his arousal as I welcomed it. Every pound of muscle as his body sank against me.

His eyes shut as his cock slid home, all the way home. "Oh God."

I could feel him throbbing inside me, the urgent tick of his pulse. It was more perfect and right than I ever could have guessed, the two of us joined this way. Like the electricity I'd

166

felt between our eyes so many times at Cousins, a thousand-fold. It put my fantasies to the blackest shame, the reality of this moment.

"Whatever you want to feel," I told him. "Take it. It can be about you, this time."

"You're so *fucking* warm." His eyes opened. "And beautiful. And soft. Everything."

"Take me. Take me like this is your birthday—like you can have anything you want." And wasn't it his birthday, in a way? A rebirth, a man's sexuality rising up into the light once more.

With a steadying breath, he began to move. He was recording every centimeter of the friction, surely as I was, every sensation, every subtle, mutual stroke of our joined bodies. I rubbed my palms over his chest and belly, feeling greedy.

"You're gorgeous." I drank him in, golden in the candlelight, honed and powerful. His cock glinted each time he pulled out, slick from me. Thick from *wanting* me.

"This what you need?" he breathed, his motions beginning to speed. His excitement had darkened, awe eclipsed by animal appetites.

"Yes."

"Am I big enough for you?" He made it rough—a half-dozen long, smug thrusts showcasing his arousal from base to crown.

"Yes. You're perfect." This needy creature, mine to spoil.

"You make me feel that way. So fucking big. You're so tight."

"From wanting you."

"Yeah." He lowered, weight shifting from his palms to his forearms. "I can feel it." And he made me feel it—the way he could fuck hard, effortless from how wet I was.

167

The only resistance came from how lush and swollen he'd made me, how big I'd made him, but not the tiniest hint of friction.

I touched his back, his arms, his hips, kneaded his ass and urged his strokes. He felt so *male* on top of me, strong body flush to mine, muscles clenching. With another man, one I didn't want this badly, I might've felt overwhelmed—plowed or crushed. Violated by the thick, pounding length of him. But all I felt with Eric was his desperation. He moaned against my neck, something in the sound telling me he'd crossed a boundary. That he was too far gone to pull back.

"Show me, Eric."

A deep grunt answered me, then, "I'm too close. I'm sorry."

"I'm not—let me see you come apart."

"Yeah," he breathed, taking the permission. "I'll show you." His body seemed to rise up, casting me even deeper in its shadow. His angle was sharper, his handsome, fierce face right above mine, eyes on fire behind those heavy lids.

"You're so fucking wet."

I touched his hair, smoothing it back, holding it. Holding *him*. "You made me this way. The things you did. And from wanting you."

"You made me this hard," he echoed, and took me roughly. I palmed his hips, feeling the way his muscles worked.

His forearms butted my ribs, hands sliding under my back. He sealed us together, close as two people can get, holding me tight as his cock took what it needed.

"Oh. Oh, here I come." He was falling to pieces above me. "Here I come, baby."

"Good."

"Fuck, you're so warm." He buried his face against my neck, hips hammering hard and frantic.

I held his head. "Come on, Eric." I could feel his pleasure.

I could sense how hard he was going to orgasm from the way it kept building. *Come on home,* I thought. *Home to me.*

"Yeah. Yeah. Oh God, here I come. Here I come."

Every inch of him seized, muscles rigid and his cock buried deep. A grunt, a spasm, and another, and finally—

"Annie." So quiet. Like a whispered secret, like that very first time he'd uttered my name.

And then it was just his breathing, harsh and labored and wondrous in the dim room. He pushed up, taking his weight off me. His face was incredulous. Drunk. He brushed my nose with his, touched his forehead to mine, panted against my temple. He felt so startlingly right. So meant for me.

He luxuriated a moment longer, then reached between us to secure the condom and ease out. I admired his body as he moved aside and off the bed, ducking out to disappear into the bathroom, returning a moment later. The most gorgeous man I'd ever seen, the candles bringing back that summer tan I'd admired in an alternate reality, in the Cousins Correctional Facility exercise yard. In August. In some previous life.

He joined me, the both of us propping ourselves on our hips and elbows, knees locking, skin radiating heat. He touched my hair, chest still rising and falling hard, though his expression was pure peace.

"Tell me that was worth waiting five years for," I teased, smiling.

"Tell me the same."

I nodded. "It was."

"That was worth way more than anything I can think of." His eyes roamed my throat, my breasts, our tangled legs. "That was so much more than I even let myself imagine, back when we were writing each other those letters. You felt so much more . . . So much more of everything I'd guessed. Soft and warm and so fucking . . . *right.*"

I shivered. "Exactly."

"Tell me what you need."

"Anything." Two minutes of just about anything, I was so wound up. "Your hand, maybe. While you kiss me."

"Here," he said, moving. He sat up, legs in a V, back against the pillow and wall. "Straddle me."

I did, settling so our faces were level. His mouth took mine as two fingertips found my clit, his hard arm flexing against my breast with his teasing motions. I swayed against him, overcome. His fingers curled and dipped, the pad of his hand rubbing me as he penetrated.

"God." I spoke into his mouth, dizzy.

"Pretend it's me," he said, lips moving to my ear. He slid inside me, again and again, and I did as he said, imagined his cock. Remembered his cock, the way it had owned me, flat on my back. My hips were moving then, eager to be the one doing.

"Yeah. Ride me." His other hand rose up between us, not cupping my breast, merely grazing it, the contact sparking each time my motions rasped my nipple against his palm.

"I've imagined this," he whispered, voice so close by my ear, it became the room itself. "You using me, to feel all this. All those things you missed."

"Me, too."

"Next time it'll be my cock," he promised. "Hard as I was before. But for you, not me."

"That's what I'm imagining."

"Hard," he said again. "All for you."

I flushed all over, from his tone as much as his words. From how cocky he sounded, and from knowing he'd not sounded this way for anyone else in so long.

"What else?" I asked, needing this man, exactly this way.

"Whatever you want, like I said. Ride me. Hold my face between your legs until I taste it when you come. Watch in

170

a mirror as I take you from behind—whatever you want to feel. Or see. Or make me do for you."

God, all of that. I nearly asked for that final thing, for the mirror. For him behind me, stroking me home, moving his hips so I could imagine we were fucking, that he was owning me. But *not tonight,* my mind whispered, sounding so like Eric, back in his truck. Tonight, face to face.

"Faster," I whispered. "Use your fingers."

He slid them out, stroking me with my own slickness. "Like that?"

"Even faster."

He strummed my clit, setting my body humming.

"Eric."

"I can smell you."

I folded around him, pressing my face into the crook of his neck, gripping his hair.

"Next time," he breathed. "Next time you come on my dick."

As the orgasm began blooming, I imagined it. All that slick, hard heat hugged inside me. His own excitement, that cock gripped in a tight fist as he pulled out, lost himself all over my belly or breasts. Explicit, possessive things.

"Moan for me," I whispered, teetering on the edge.

He did as I asked, his deep voice right behind my ear, his throat humming. His fingers circling, circling.

"Like you're coming."

He gasped for me, grunted deep in his chest. His hips flexed beneath my thighs, and when he spoke, I unraveled.

"Here I come," he murmured, and I pictured just that. Just as he'd done, not five minutes earlier, and I felt it all. The snap of the tension, the free fall, the plunge. The surge and crest, surge and crest, until I went still, trembling against his chest, hips ground raw.

171

His fingers were gone, both palms whispering over my sweat-damp back as I caught my breath.

"Good," he told me. "Good."

I pulled back and let him see everything I felt, no matter how flushed and crazy and rabid-looking it'd left me. He smoothed my hair away from my face, twisting it into a coil, letting it tumble loose.

"All right?" he asked, and the tenderness in his voice broke my heart, officially.

"So much better than all right."

He smiled at that. "Me, too."

My calf was threatening to cramp, so I shifted to sit beside him, arranging a pillow at my back. He took my hand, linking our fingers atop his thigh.

I sighed for the entire city to hear, dropping my head back against the wall.

"Well said."

I turned to grin at him, giddy when he grinned back.

After a long, dozy silence, he urged me to lie down with him, curling his body around me from behind. All that possession I'd fantasized about just as I came, only so tender, this way.

He froze with a deep breath, then asked, "Can I stay the night?"

I blinked at the dancing shadows of my room, surprised. "Of course you can."

He buried his face against my neck, body going utterly slack, and he growled, "Good."

"I wouldn't dare send you back out into the cold. Not after that."

"Can I take you someplace for breakfast tomorrow morning?"

"Sure. Or I could make pancakes or something."

172

He *hmmm*ed happily at that. "Homemade pancakes. Jesus, it's been ages."

"Then we could stay inside and drink too much coffee. And get to know each other, nice and lazy. Oh—unless you have to work."

"Only if it snows again. And it's not supposed to."

"Oh good."

He pulled away, sitting up a little so he could catch my eyes. "So you really do want to get to know me better."

I nodded. "Sure I do."

"Does that mean . . . I dunno. What does that mean? Are you over the things that freaked you out about me?"

"I'm getting there. I forgive you for not telling me about your release, when you knew. As for the assault . . . I don't know how I feel about that. I don't know that I'll ever understand it. But I don't think it scares me anymore."

"That's something."

I frowned, lips pursed hard enough to tingle.

"What?"

I twisted around to face him. "If we were ever . . . You know. An item." My face went warm. Funny how naming that possibility could feel so vulnerable, after everything else we'd bared to one another tonight. Did people even say that anymore? An *item*?

"Yeah?" he prompted.

"If a man did to me what that guy did to your sister—"

Eric instantly looked horrified.

"Sorry. I don't want to imagine it, either. But just *if* . . ."

"Would I fuck him up?"

I dipped my chin in a nervous little nod.

"Yeah," he said. "Yeah I would. If that ever happened and you weren't even my woman, just my friend, or my ex? Yes. I'd do that."

173

"What if I asked you not to? Could you promise me you wouldn't?"

That one really, truly stymied him. His gaze dropped to my chin, brow creasing.

"Eric?"

He met my eyes. "I couldn't promise that, no."

A little something went dark inside me, even as something else sparked hot. This man would avenge me, to the death. A thought as fierce and reassuring as it was disturbing.

"I'm sorry," he said. "But I know that's what I'd do."

"If we were together, your freedom would mean more to me than another man's punishment."

His expression matched my own feelings—stubborn confusion, frustration, and everything so much bulkier and tougher to process with the sex haze still making us stupid.

"What would you gain from assaulting him?" I asked.

"It's not what I get, or what I need. When I did what I had to, for my sister . . . The kind of man who'd do that to a woman, no sentence can fix what's fucked up inside him. He'd have to be an animal to do that. And an animal won't understand regret the way the prison system thinks he should . . . But he'll understand two pounds of metal in another man's fist, hell-bent on beating the life out of him."

I winced.

"I know you can't stand to hear that," he said, stroking my hair. "But I hid enough from you already. From now on I'm laying it all out, ugly as it is."

"I appreciate that. I think. But my daddy's a state trooper. And a good man. So I refuse to believe the system's completely broken."

He laughed softly. "Jesus Christ. A trooper? Well, I'm fucked. Never getting *that* blessing."

"Don't change the subject."

He sighed. "I'm not going to lie to you, not about what I feel. And as far as I'm concerned, any man who does what that asshole did to a woman has that coming to him, from her husband or her brother or her father."

Her father. My father. Thank God I'd never had to find out whether that good, upstanding lawman was capable of Eric's brand of justice.

"Let's not talk about all that," he said, tone softening. "Let's keep talking about pancakes and shit."

I nodded. It wasn't as though these worries might ever materialize, down the road. And it wasn't as though we even knew if there would be a him-and-me, down the road. The fact that he was holding me now, that our impossible affair had somehow tunneled out from under those ten-foot walls and become this—our two bodies warm and spent in my bed—wasn't anything I ever could have predicted.

And I didn't want to waste this miraculous present, worrying about a future that might never arrive.

I turned back over, enclosed in strong arms and male heat. Wrapped in a body that offered me everything a man could, be it pleasure or desire or the darkest depths of loyalty and honor. Wrapped in uncertainty and inevitability. Wrapped in everything good and bad, beautiful and ugly, black and white and gray. And green.

Everything that made a man worth loving.

Everything that made a woman run. Into his arms, or out of his reach.

Chapter Twelve

"Hey."

The world inside my eyelids was dark pink, and I peeked through those curtains to find the man from my fantasies sitting up beside me in bed. He was cross-legged, sheets and blankets pooled around his waist. And goodness, he looked nice there.

"Morning," I mumbled, wary of my breath and not wanting to waft its offense at my bedmate.

"Morning yourself. I was going to shower, unless you need to get in there first."

"Oh, let me brush my teeth. Two minutes." Leaving the covers, I felt a weird mix of self-conscious and seductive as I skirted the bed, naked. The drapes were closed, but light still leaked in from their crack and from the hallway. I shot Eric a look over my shoulder, admonishing the way he watched me.

"Take your time," he said, a smug half smile on his lips.

He was still sitting up when I returned from my freshen-up, and he watched as I pulled on panties, a bra, yoga pants, camisole. I stared right back as I slipped into a cardigan and flipped my hair from under the collar. I put my hands to my hips.

"Two can play that pervert game," I told him, awaiting my free show.

He smiled at that and drew the covers aside. All the mischief left me then, just to see this beautiful man, naked in my room. Tall and strong and handsome and, for however long it was meant to last, *mine*.

As he passed me, he let our arms touch, his hand catching mine, and he gently turned me around as he moved toward the door, our fingers finally slipping free. My attention caught on his back, on black ink.

"Wait, come back here."

I made him sit at the edge of the bed and I went to the curtains, drawing the heavier ones back, the sheer layer underneath letting in the dawn light but preserving our privacy.

I knelt on the mattress behind him. "I've been wondering what your tattoos were . . ." The one between his shoulder blades was as big as both my palms, a pair of feathered wings flaring out behind some kind of crest, a ribbon woven through it all, with writing. It was more illumination than motorcycle gang, and I traced the Antiqua-style letters. "'Thicker than water.' That's quite appropriate, for you."

The design flexed with his shrug.

"Did you get this in prison, or before?"

"Before."

"And what's the other one?" I shuffled on my knees and turned his shoulder toward me. A staggered stack of words, a trickling river of script. *Life for life, eye for eye, tooth for tooth, hand for hand, foot for foot, burn for burn, wound for wound, stripe for stripe.*

Blood ties and vengeance. Of course. "They're very . . .

177

you, I'll give you that. And I'm selfishly glad neither of them is some other girl's name."

He shot a smile over his shoulder. "Jealous?"

"Maybe a little." I traced the ribbon drawn across his back one more time. "They're pretty. You picked a good artist."

"I'd get rid of them if I could."

My hand dropped. "Really? How come?"

"I got them when I was twenty, twenty-one."

I wondered if perhaps his time served had contradicted these words, if perhaps blood hadn't proven especially thick in his family, not thick enough to stand by a man through a five-year sentence . . . ? Maybe not. Who knew?

"They're still nice," I told him.

"Glad you think so . . . Just feels like they belong to a guy who doesn't exist anymore. Some dumbshit kid who had no clue what those things meant."

"Like a bad omen or something?"

He shrugged again, the muscles between his shoulders bunching. "Nah, nothing that superstitious. I just feel like, I'm never going back to being that kid, the one who thought that stuff—loyalty and blood and all that—was just some crap to get inked across his skin."

"I think I understand."

"They're not bad, I guess. They just belong to someone else now."

I studied his skin, a trace of that golden tan lingering even as the New Year approached. I pressed my winter-pale hand to his back. "What's your lineage, anyway?"

"Bunch of stuff. Mostly French Canadian and German on my dad's side, and my mom's half Puerto Rican, half Irish."

"That's quite a mix." Complex, just like him.

"Bit of everything . . . Ignorant as they might be otherwise, I'll give my family that much—they're color-blind."

I wished I could say the same of mine. My parents would *never* say anything intolerant aloud, and they were both way more evolved than the generation who'd raised them . . . But old biases persisted.

As Eric stood, I let my fingertips trail down his spine, then watched his ass as he strode to the door. I flopped back across the rumpled covers, and listened as the water came on.

There's a felon in my shower. There'd been a felon in my bed. In my *body*. But it was so easy to forget how we'd met, taking it minute by minute. And thank goodness. If this was going to be something, I needed to focus on the future—not the place we'd met or the mistakes he'd made to get there.

He doesn't see it as a mistake, though.

I got up and headed for the kitchen to start a pot of coffee. If I'd welcomed him into my bed, I had to have gotten at least halfway past the cavernous divide between Eric's actions and our two disparate lenses for viewing them. I had to be, or else whatever this was didn't stand a chance. And it deserved a chance. Eric deserved a chance.

It was as I clicked the basket into place and hit the On switch that I found a way around the problem. A philosophy to trump his righteousness and my misgiving.

If he hadn't done that, I'd never have met him.

I wouldn't have gotten my sexuality back for who knew how long. Wouldn't have felt alive as I did now. Wouldn't have felt all those wonderful things with him, last night in bed.

Maybe I didn't approve of what he'd done . . . but I'd be a liar to deny that I was grateful for it, in my own selfish way.

I pulled out pancake ingredients, pleased to find I had everything. I heard the bathroom door open, heard Eric's footsteps creaking through my bedroom. He appeared shortly in the kitchen threshold, dressed in yesterday's clothes.

179

"Have a seat," I said, waving to my little table by the window. "How do you take your coffee?"

"Cream and sugar, if you have it."

I made him a cup, hoping it was a million times better than prison coffee. I wanted to spoil him today, in every way possible.

He sat just as he had back in Cousins during Book Discussion, legs spread wide and lazy, and it felt like August all over again. My heart soared as he took a sip and shut his eyes, pure rapture in his smile.

"Strong enough?"

"I haven't had coffee this good in forever."

"When's the last time you had pancakes?"

"When I got out."

My shoulders slumped. "Oh, darn. I was hoping I'd be your first time for everything."

"Sorry, my mom and sister beat you to it."

I found a whisk and beat the batter in a plastic bowl. "Did they meet you, the morning you were released?"

He nodded. "They brought my truck, with some furniture to fill out the apartment I'd gotten hooked up with. A bunch of old clothes, not that they fit anymore—I was still a wiry kid when I went in. We went to IHOP."

"What'd you order?"

"Sausage. Two sides of sausage." He smiled at the thought. "The meat in prison is disgusting."

"I'll bet. What else?"

"Pancakes, eggs, butter on everything. But the coffee wasn't half as good as this," he said, raising his cup. "Or maybe everything just tastes extra good this morning."

"And why might that be?" I asked coyly.

He smirked, eyes narrowing, and patted his thigh. "C'mere."

I set the bowl aside and dusted my hands on a dishrag. I

180

sat on his leg, feet between his spread ones. Warm palms ran boldly down my waist, over my hips.

"Thanks for last night," he said quietly.

"Thank *you* for last night."

"There's no way I can tell you how much that . . . how important that was, to me." He looped his arms around my middle and rested his chin on my shoulder.

I felt vulnerable in the nicest way, naked and protected at once. "I'm so . . . I'm so grateful, I guess, that you waited for me. Or flattered. Or something. That whatever you feel for me, it was strong enough to be worth waiting for."

"You know how I feel about you. I told you last night, at the bar."

I'm in love with you. I'd barely let myself absorb his words, but I'd felt the truth of them, spoken between our bodies. I wasn't ready to say them back. I didn't yet know if they accurately named what I felt for him. But I could bask in having been told them, at least.

He spoke, breath warming me through my sweater. "You will let me see you again, right?"

I stroked his hair. "Yes, of course I will."

He pulled at my collar, exposing my bare shoulder and kissing me there, then bade me to stand with a soft pat on my butt. I was cooking a man breakfast, obeying his orders to sit on his lap and getting patted on the butt. It would've been kind of ridiculous, if I weren't so damn crazy about him.

"I wish I could afford to take you someplace nice," he said as I went back to cooking.

I ran a melting pat of butter around the pan. "I don't care. There's not any nice places in Darren, anyway."

"Someday, though. I'll save up and take you somewhere good. For Valentine's Day, maybe."

181

I smiled at him, ladling batter into pools with a soft sizzle. "I like the places you took me last night. Without us even leaving my bed."

His cheeks went ever so slightly pink, his grin bashful. "I liked those places, too."

"Don't you look shy?" I teased. "You, the man who tricked me into writing dirty letters for him in a room filled with convicts."

He laughed. "I only tricked you that first time. You can't act innocent about all the stuff that came after."

"You still going to write me love letters, now that you're out?"

He made a game face. "If you want me to."

"You could email me over Christmas while I'm in South Carolina. Tell me everything I'm missing out on, being away."

"I will."

I grinned, turning the bubbling pancakes over. "What are you doing for Christmas, anyhow? Driving home to see your family? And where is home, again?"

"Kernsville."

"Right."

"It's about twenty miles past that lake we parked by. But it depends on the weather. If it snows and there's extra work I could pick up, I'll stick around here. Holidays pay double. I don't really want to head home, anyhow. My dad always seems to turn up, and I don't really feel like dealing with him. Not yet, at least."

"You haven't said much about him."

He shrugged. "He's still married to my mom, but it doesn't mean anything to either of them."

"You said your sister takes after him. What word did you use? Wild?"

"Yeah. He's always up to something. Always waiting for

182

some check to show up, or some scheme to come through. He's not the worst man in the world—never hit my mom or us kids, and he's more of a dipshit than an actual leech. But he's no sort of role model, either. He's a loser, basically. Lazy. Ignorant."

"Bummer."

"He's just how they make them, back home."

"You're not, though."

"I used to think I wasn't . . . but come on. I was incarcerated. Kind of wrecks any upstanding cred I'd built up, always staying employed and relatively sober."

"What did you do, before Cousins?" I asked him. "For work?"

"Whatever I could get. Construction, demolition. Security. Drove a truck for a lumber company for a couple years. Whatever paid half-decent money and kept me outside some, and didn't require a diploma."

I handed him a plate with two pancakes, delivered the syrup bottle and butter dish, found us silverware. I put the third pancake on my own plate and sat down, our knees brushing under the small table.

"Made me nuts," he went on, "the times when I couldn't find work for a week or two, back home. I hated some of my jobs, but I never understood how anybody could stand it, just sitting around doing nothing."

"Me, too." I thought of Justin, twenty-eight now but probably still sixteen at heart, wasting entire weekends drinking and playing video games with his buddies. And how many hours had I sat there, spectating, bored half to death?

Eric said, "That had me more nervous than anything, about getting released—what the fuck I'd do if I didn't have something lined up. If I'd get stuck back home, having to crash with my mom or sister. And how awful that'd feel. Like I'd forfeited all that time *and* wound up worse than where I'd left off. Or like everybody would look at me like I was going to turn into my dad—a waste of space."

"Thank goodness for your work release supervisor, I guess."

"No lie." He sponged at his syrup with a forkful of pancake. "It's been hard. For my family, after five years, my getting parole is like the finish line to them. The goal. For me it's just the beginning."

"And what are *your* goals?"

His eyes went to the window as he chewed, the morning light making them look like the syrup, sweet and maple brown.

"To work my ass off, to start. Get through the winter and see how this job goes, once I'm actually getting to do landscaping. Get good at it. Get *real* good at it, and I dunno. Just see where it takes me. Maybe I'll see about getting some certification. Though I probably need my GED first, and I never managed to pass that while I was locked up. Not even close. I don't think I ever even made it halfway through before the time was up."

"They offer GED programs tailored to people with all sorts of special needs."

He smiled, looking embarrassed. "Special needs? Christ."

"You know what I mean. For dyslexic students and people with ADHD, and even for dysgraphia. I think you need proof from a doctor though, to qualify. But that's not such a hurdle."

"Nah, probably not. Not if I want better work certification. It costs a couple hundred bucks for a professional landscaping course and it's probably all stuff I'll learn on the job anyhow, but if it means I might make more money down the road . . . could be worth it."

"You seem to have found something you really enjoy."

He nodded. "I do. I hope that's not just because it got me

184

out of Cousins a few hours a day, though . . . But no, I like working with plants. It's interesting, the way each one needs something different to thrive."

"Better you than me. My mom's had a garden my whole life, and I still can't seem to keep anything more complicated than a jade plant alive. Do you think you'd do that—build yourself a garden?"

His cheeks flushed again, if I wasn't mistaken.

"What?"

"I sort of have, already. *Sort* of. Much as I can, in my apartment anyhow."

"I'll have to come see sometime."

A funny little smile. "I'm not sure I want you to. My place is such a shithole."

"Oh yeah, and mine's a penthouse."

He shrugged. "I like yours. It feels like a home. It's going to be a while before I can afford to move anywhere nice or decorate. I owe a lot in fines for the assault, and for time served. Plus my truck needs work, and my mom always needs something done—something bought or at least fixed, and driving eighty miles round trip to do the fixing is expensive, with my shitty gas mileage."

"Ah."

"Plus I can't really stand going back home now."

"No?"

He shook his head. "I've been back twice, since I got out. Prison wasn't a step up or anything, lifestyle-wise, but I've been away long enough that it's like . . . I dunno. Like I can see that place for what it is now. Like I brought the world into focus, being away. When I was eighteen, twenty years old, I was almost proud of where I'd come from. Fucking trailer park pride or something."

"Time for a fresh start, maybe."

185

He nodded. "Overdue . . . Is that why you're here? A fresh start?"

"Not exactly. A start in general, to my library career. I got my master's in Ann Arbor, and a job search brought me here, but that was the only reason."

"Think you'll stick around?"

I considered it. Considered my struggling, scrappy library in its struggling, scrappy little city. Considered the people I helped at Larkhaven and Cousins, and out around the county. "For a while, at least. But I don't know if this is where I want to be the rest of my life. I want to make a difference in a place where it counts, but . . ."

"It's a depressing area."

I nodded, feeling guilty. "It is. And the people are just way different than back home. People say that all the niceness down South is fake, but . . . Some days I'd happily take fake niceness over honest jerkiness. Plus winter's so damn long."

He leaned back in his chair. "Let's pool our money, then. We'll buy a little place down South, way away from all the snow and my shitty hometown. I'll be able to do landscaping year-round. You can find some little town with a library that needs fixing."

My body went funny, warm with the pleasure of such a thought. Had he been serious, it'd be a different matter, but we'd just spent the night blowing each other's minds, so when else would wistful future-fantasizing be this appropriate?

"Sounds good. Though between your fines and my student loans and both our salaries, that pool may take a long time to fill."

He shrugged, smiling. "I know a thing or two about patience."

I smiled back, but that light in my middle flickered once more. He'd told me last night, he couldn't promise not to do

186

what he had for his sister, for me. It meant something to him, something about honor or justice. But should anything terrible ever happen, and this was my man . . . He might make a decision that took him away from me, right when I needed him most. His freedom was worth less to him than another man's due suffering, and I wasn't sure I could commit to someone who valued vengeance over staying close to his loved ones.

He must see that as the extent of what he has to offer, I realized. *His violence.* Foolish as it was, I wondered if I could teach him differently. Show him how much more worth he had as a partner than a pit bull.

But if half a decade in hell hadn't taught him, what chance did I stand?

Dumb thoughts. Now wasn't the time to be having them, anyhow. *Now* was a time to revel in what we did have—a growing fondness, an undeniable physical bond. Plenty to explore, for now.

I made another round of pancakes, then we drained the coffeepot into our mugs and retired to the couch to flip channels while we digested. Eric made a piqued noise, and I stopped on football highlights. I didn't care what we watched. I only cared about the warm heft of his arm around my shoulders and the sight of our socked feet propped side by side on my coffee table. I only cared that for the first time in five years, I was close to a man. And he felt so good. Big and strong, reassuring. Warm and right as the mug in my hands.

"You got anyplace to be today?" he asked. "Stuff to get done?"

I shook my head. "Nowhere 'til tomorrow morning. You?"

"Nope. Even if I did, I'd blow it off if you'd let me hang out here with you."

I waved at the TV. "With all the buildup they're giving the

Lions game, I'm pretty sure you *have* to stay now. And I got groceries on Friday, so we have absolutely no reason to leave the apartment, as far as I'm concerned. I'll be happy if I don't even put shoes on today."

He gave me a squeeze, drawing me closer. "I can barely believe we're here, like this. Much as I imagined it. After last week, at the coffee place . . . I thought for sure the fire had gone out of us. Out of you, anyhow."

"Not really. Not completely, even when I got freaked out, about your release. It was always simmering deep down. Embers of it, just waiting to reignite."

"That's awful poetic."

"Back when we were writing to each other," I said, laying my head on his shoulder, "I used to get dressed up, and put on makeup and perfume, and light a candle. Pour a glass of wine. And I'd sit right here, and read what you had to say to me. Like these really weird dates."

"Right here?"

I nodded. "Where you're sitting. But sometimes in bed, too."

"And you dressed up for me?"

"I guess so. Or for myself. I'm not sure. Just to make it special. Or exciting."

"Did you ever go to bed after," he asked softly, "and imagine you were getting undressed for me, when you took your clothes off?"

I bit my lip. "Yeah."

"Did you keep thinking about whatever we'd been saying to each other in those letters, in bed?"

"Yes."

He turned, his far arm coming around, palm warm on my ribs. "You put yourself to sleep, thinking about me? About us, doing all that stuff?"

"Just about every night."

His voice turned low and heavy. "You ever say my name, when you came?"

I nodded, throat tight, head foggy.

"Out loud?"

"Yeah, I'm sure I did."

He caught my eyes, then leaned close to brush our mouths together. "I want to watch that sometime."

I'd never let a man see me doing that before. But I'd never wanted one the way I did Eric. "I'd do that, for you. If you'd do the same for me."

"Anything."

His body felt tight now—set like a trap and ready to spring. I wondered if his cock was as hard and restless as his muscles.

"Why are we watching football highlights?" I whispered, mouth at his jaw.

He smiled against my lips. "What would you rather be doing?"

"Terrible, filthy things."

"Like what?"

"I won't know 'til we're doing them."

A warm, gloating little laugh. "Your bed's still all messed up from what we did last night."

"It is."

"I've thought about that. About you, naked on a big pile of sheets and covers."

"Is that all?" I asked innocently.

"Your hair all messy. And the smell of you just . . . everywhere."

I studied him fondly. "You were always the strangest mix of things, in my fantasies. Like, desperate and rough at the same time. Like you could beg me for something in one breath and boss me around in the next."

189

"Because you didn't really know me then?"

"No, not that . . . More like, you were just everything I wanted from a man. Helpless and powerful, and sweet and nasty, all wrapped up in one lover. Like I could make you feel all that."

"You did. You still do."

"Yeah?"

He nodded and kissed my forehead. "Take me to your room and I'll show you."

I stood, his hand slipping from my waist to my hip before I captured it in mine. We left the TV droning, padded down the hall and into my room. Christ, it still smelled of sex. Intoxicating.

He turned, big arms snaking around me, chest brushing back and forth against my breasts, lighting me up. "Tell me how you want me." His words caressed my temple.

I spoke thoughtlessly. "Hungry. And like you can take anything you want. Anything you've been missing."

"All those times I told you, I wouldn't ask for anything 'til I got you off first. But last night . . ."

"I loved how you were last night. All crazy."

"Not today, though," he murmured. *Growled*, more like. "Today you make me work for it."

190

Chapter Thirteen

Eric's hands were between us, freeing the one, two, three little pearl buttons on my cardigan. He felt so tall, so damn tall. His chin at my forehead, his body seeming to cast a shadow even with the sun coming through the gauzy curtains.

I let him unwrap me like a gift—sweater, camisole, bra. His hands slid from my face to my shoulders, over my breasts to rob me of air. Down my belly as he dropped to his knees. Down to my hips, where he slipped his fingers under the wide band of my yoga pants. He kissed my navel as the stretchy fabric slid over my thighs, cool air tensing my skin. My boy shorts were red with white polka dots, and I'd picked them on purpose. Utterly silly compared to Eric's utilitarian world at Cousins, and different surely than the lingerie sported by the models in whatever magazines made the rounds inside. Exotic, I hoped. Some goofy flavor of feminine he'd forgotten about. Unique to me, maybe, as oddly possessive as the notion was.

I ran my fingers through his hair, nails raking his scalp. He made a hungry noise that heated my belly, and slid my

191

pants and underwear to my ankles. I stepped out of them and pushed off my socks. In a breath he was on his feet again—hand on my butt, a mighty motion, a gasp from me, then my legs were wrapped around his waist and my arms circled his neck, and he was carrying me the half-dozen paces to the bed. We lay down as one, the rumpled sheets cool at my back, Eric hot and eager above me. He sat back on his heels and peeled his shirt away. My hands on his face, in his hair; his mouth claiming mine, our bare chests brushing. His hips grinding, forcing me wide, and Christ, his cock—hard behind his jeans, insistent at the crease of my thigh. I felt him shudder, a soft moan thrumming between our mouths. I shuddered, too, just to feel this with someone again.

He leaned back to grasp the outsides of my thighs, working his excitement against mine. His muscles flexed—abs, chest, arms, shoulders, and those just below his ribs. It was like the sexiest scene from a racy movie, only real. Happening to *me*. I could watch his body for hours. But what he'd said, about being smaller before he'd been put away . . . If it was prison that had rebuilt him this way, was I bad for rejoicing as I was? Reveling in this glorious physique he'd cultivated out of boredom—or worse, in self-defense?

Fuck it.

"I love your body," I told him, and let my eyes and hands wander wildly.

"Good. I love the way you look at me." As though wallowing in the thought, he slowed his motions, rolled his hips in a brash show of power. I clamped my palms to his sides, feeling him work.

Gorgeous body and damn, that face. I drank him in, those features that so perfectly matched the rest of him—strained now and dangerous, dripping with sex.

I let my hands slip low and unbutton his fly, and he did

the rest—jeans and underwear lost over the edge of the mattress. Just us now. He tangled our legs and turned us onto our sides. As we kissed, a smile overtook me, so broad he must have felt it. He pulled away.

"What?" he asked, his own curious smile blooming.

And then I did the worst possible thing I could.

I burst into tears.

Through the blur, I watched his eyes widen, his surprise perfectly mirroring my own. His body went slack and he stroked my hair. "Hey, hey. You okay?"

I nodded, burning face all screwed up. I sucked an ugly breath, trying to get my voice working.

He didn't panic, just kissed my temple and cradled my head as I gulped and gurgled. The tears ebbed and my clenching jaw loosened.

"God, sorry." I wiped at my cheeks, surely beet red. "I'm not upset, I swear."

"Just feeling too much?"

"Not too much, even. Just . . . a lot. More than I've felt in ages. I think maybe I just boiled over."

I heard a little noise in his throat, a speck of a laugh, and he held me tighter. "Go ahead and cry, then."

"I'm done, thanks."

He pulled back then kissed my mouth, probably tasting my tears. His neck was warm and smelled of my soap as I rested my cheek against it and caught my breath.

"We've got all day to do what we came in here to do," he murmured. "If you need to keep relaxing."

"I just want to lie right here for a minute."

He ran his hand over my hair, smoothing it away from my face. "You got it."

After a minute, my voice broke the calm silence, the words coming without intention. "The last time I cried, it was after

I got your letter. The one after I messed up and snuck a letter in to you."

His stroking hand froze. "Because I chewed you out?"

"Oh, no. No no no." I pulled away to meet his eyes with my surely pink ones. "No, I cried because I was so relieved . . ." Oh shit, did I really want to say all this?

"Relieved because . . . ?"

I took a deep breath. "Because after I gave you that letter, I freaked out. The second I left it with you, I realized I'd basically handed you a weapon you could use against me. And I was so scared all of a sudden, that everything you'd written to me, maybe it wasn't true."

"Oh."

"Sorry. I shouldn't have brought it up. Jesus, this is so unromantic."

"It's okay. That's smart stuff to be freaked out about."

My tense muscles softened some. "Then when you gave me that letter back, it was . . . It was the most relief I've ever felt. It was like I'd treasured this thing so much, then thought maybe I was about to lose it, tortured myself over it . . . And then it was given back to me, like, threefold."

"That's kind of how it's been for me, since I got out. Like we had all that, when I was still inside, then I fucked up, thought I'd gotten it taken away for good."

"Except now here we are," I said, lacing my fingers with his. "In my bed, no less."

"I want to promise I won't ever make you cry again . . . but I don't know if anyone can make that promise to somebody they're so wrapped up with."

I pictured his face from our last encounter in Cousins, the moment after I'd told him I couldn't see him on the outside. How he'd turned away, looking on the verge of tears himself. I had that power, too.

194

"We can only promise to try, I guess." But in my heart, selfish though it was, I was awed and humbled to even have such powers. Floored to know I made a man feel so much. And one I felt so much for in return.

His jaw was stubbly against my palms. I held his face and kissed him deeply, first with gratitude, then with need. I felt it all returned to me in his hunger, in the heat building between us.

His leg locked around mine and his cock had grown stiff, pressing into the crease at my thigh and hip. My body responded, excitement a rising fire in my belly. He let me explore him with my hands as we kissed. From the soft, loose curls brushing the nape of his neck, to the muscle that hugged his shoulder, to the flat planes of his chest and the whisper of dark hair there. His entire torso tensed as I brushed one small, tight nipple, and the reaction fascinated me. I stroked that hard belly next and set his hips fidgeting. Amazing, how connected his body felt. He must have shut all of this off while he was locked up, sexual pleasure relegated to rushed, furtive acts of joyless necessity. I'd done the same, for just as long . . . though my sexual exile had been a sort of hibernation, not a captivity. How wonderful to know the impulse and synapses were all still here, waiting for us, undamaged by the neglect. Maybe even heightened by it.

I palmed his hip, memorizing the restless flex of muscle and the hard hint of bone beneath it. In turn he only held my head, seeming as lost in my explorations as I was. When I wrapped my fingers around his erection, he moaned against my lips, body tensing in a long wave.

This man wants you, I thought as soft skin glided over stiff flesh, as his excitement wet the heel of my hand. As his kisses turned to nothing more than a distracted brush of lips. *He wants you like no one has before.* He craved me, the way other men craved their addictions. The notion was mesmerizing, as was the undeniable mutuality of it.

"I want you," I whispered against his mouth.

"You ready for me?" He didn't wait for an answer, but instead slipped his hand between our melee of legs. The tips of his curled fingers found me wet, and together we skipped a breath.

I let him go to grope for the bedside table, for the condoms. He took over, sheathed in a blink, his thigh knocking mine wide as he got positioned above me. The world slowed as he gripped himself, his impatience suddenly gone. With his crown he slicked the length of my lips, again and again, his dark eyes drunk. I bucked each time he glanced my clit, the caress knotting me too tight, and I grabbed his arms, prepared to beg.

But I didn't have to. He gave me his head, just that first taste of penetration. My nails bit the swells of his shoulders.

"More?" he asked.

"Yes. Everything."

He granted my wish, pushing deeper, deeper, so deep our hips met, and he held there, palms coming to rest on either side of my ribs. His excitement, hugged in mine. The most perfect design. The sole expression our bodies were made for, it felt just then.

My gaze roamed up his belly and chest to his face, and his mouth twitched in a funny little smile. He freed a hand to brush the hair from my forehead, then linger, thumb tracing my brow, cheek, lips. He tucked his arm close at my side again.

The thick, hard heat inside me retreated, then surged anew. Slow strokes to start, the pace mounting as his breaths became grunts. Eager, I met him thrust for thrust with my hips. The momentum grew frantic as he rushed to give me what I

196

demanded, and I rose to meet him, the rhythm sloppy and all the more perfect for it.

"You like it on top?" he asked.

I sobered by a degree. "I'm not very good at it."

"I want to see you, like that."

I nodded. For this man, anything.

He took everything away, his weight and heat and shadow, lying down. His cock was so perfectly obscene, hovering above his belly and gleaming in the daylight. Shameless. I wanted to feel the same—proud and exposed in the sunshine.

I straddled him and he angled himself, helped me slide into place. I had to shut my eyes a moment, the expression on his face was so intense. His voice opened them again.

"Let me give you whatever you need."

That melted me. That this position wasn't just about the view for him. That he was offering himself for me to use, and take pleasure from. I'd been with guys this way before, but they'd always struck me as . . . lazy. After it for the show and a chance to sit back and do nothing. Not Eric. His body was as restless in repose as it had been above me, tense and ready to deliver. His strong hands held my thighs, his dark eyes waited.

I started to move, just a short slide forward, an easing back. "Tell me if you like it some other way."

"Do whatever feels good to you. That's all I want."

"I'm pretty rusty."

He smiled, so patient in the face of my stalling and insecurity. "Me, too. We'll figure it out together."

I returned his smile, ignoring a fresh sting—grateful tears I wouldn't shed now.

"Here," he said, taking my wrists. "Lean in, so you don't have to just balance up there. It doesn't have to be a show."

I braced my hands at his sides and he stroked my arms.

197

"Just mess around. See if you find a way that feels good. And don't worry about me—I could watch you exploring this stuff with me for days."

I nodded. I fidgeted and experimented, found an angle that was easy on my hips and let me move freely, backward and forward, with total control over the friction. When Eric brought his knees up behind me, the soft bump of his thighs against my butt offered the most unexpected, erotic jolt.

"Oh," I murmured. "That's good."

When I began moving in earnest, he joined me, tensing his body to intensify all my motions.

"Wow." I went faster, finding a sweet little pang on every upstroke when my clit rubbed against the base of his cock. As good as my hand. Better, even, the friction more coarse than smooth fingertips, more exciting. Unmistakably male.

When my back whined, growing sore, I dropped down to my forearms. My entire body caught fire. More friction, only now it was my nipples against his chest. It ran through me, joining up with the pleasure between my legs. I groaned, the sound caught between shock and hunger.

I was going to come. I'd never, *ever* come like this. In fact I couldn't remember ever coming during intercourse without using my fingers, and this was so infinitely more intense. Like I really was using him. Stealing this pleasure from his cock, stroking my desire right against his.

I heard myself say, "Oh my God."

"Take it. Whatever you need."

Fuck, his voice. As good as the physical sensations. "Keep talking. Or moan. Anything."

"Use me," he said. "Use my cock, Annie."

"*Fuck.*"

"Feel how hard you make me?"

"Yeah." The world was tilting, gravity a force concentrated

198

in this man's body, in this sex. Everything was honed, focused, drawn achingly tight against him.

"I've thought about this so many times," he told me.

And that did me in—always that. Knowing that as badly as I'd wanted him all these months, he'd wanted me just as much. That he'd imagined all of this then believed it was lost . . . until I brought it back to him.

I came as I never had by my own hand. The pleasure was a relentless wave, its crest going on longer than I'd ever felt, carrying me out, out, out. Then the crash, the deepest dive before I finally reached the bottom.

The room rematerialized, one object and one wall at a time, and there I was again. Spacey, panting. A mess, but happy for it. Let this man see what he did to me.

As the haze lifted, his own excitement and need stole my focus. The swell of his chest told me how hard he was breathing, and I could feel his pulse inside me as surely as I could see it beating along his flushed throat. His hands were patient, but his eyes wild.

He grabbed my waist and sat up, driving his cock deep inside me, holding me tight as he made it to kneeling. Then it was his hands on my ass, guiding me to ease off, then claim him whole. Inside a dozen breaths he was simply holding me still, the thrusts all his, those hips rising up again, again, again.

Strong. The word echoed in my head with every impact, ringing with awe.

His head dropped, mouth jetting steam against my shoulder. I felt him faltering, muscles losing their finesse. With a surrendering groan he eased me onto my back and came down on his elbows, his big frame dropping over me like nightfall.

His voice was tight, locked up hard like his body. "You ready for it?"

"Yeah."

"Tell me. Tell me to." My God, this man. This violent ex-con, bigger and rougher than just about anyone he might pass on the street, and yet . . . *Tell me to*. Mine to command. So eager to please.

"Let me see it, Eric. Let me see you lose control."

His hips raced, coordination slipping. "Feels so good."

I slipped my hand between us and stroked his cheek. Traced his lower lip with my thumb, and when his mouth opened, I slipped it inside. He sucked a moment, then released me with a groan, gulped a breath. The order implicit in that tiny act of penetration wound him up, same as a spoken command. Another suck, another hot breath, and he was coming apart before my eyes. I swept the wet pad of my thumb back and forth across his lips. Those brown eyes shut as the tendons along his neck stood out, and the hips hammering into me locked up. His moans were silent, their energy diverted to the muscles that clenched and released, clenched again, then finally fell slack.

I touched his face as he caught his breath, tucking his sweat-curled hair behind his ears, loving how heavy his eyelids looked and the pink stain to his cheeks.

He laughed softly and muttered a happy, "Goddamn." Securing the condom, he eased out, leaving me to trot to the bathroom, back seconds later.

With the calisthenics over, the chill of December reasserted itself, and we came back together beneath the covers.

"Let's just hide in here for the rest of the day," I said.

He turned me onto my side and spooned me, his mouth close to my ear. "Deal."

As our bodies came down from the high, I didn't think I'd ever felt so calm, ever in my life. With this awaiting me at home a few nights a week, I could handle anything my job decided to dish out.

After ten minutes or more, a thought slipped through my lips. "Does this feel . . ."

Fingertips skimmed my arm atop the blanket. "Does this feel what?"

"Does it seem crazy to you . . . the way we met, and the way we've connected?" I asked. "Like, what are the *chances*?"

"No, not really."

"No? It seems so unlikely to me. How we got to talking, and the fact that we're here now, still into each other, when the backdrop to everything has shifted so much. Awesome, but unlikely."

He took my hand, kissed each of my knuckles in turn. "Bear in mind, you met me your first day on the job. But for me, I didn't meet anybody who made me feel something like what you have for almost five years. It doesn't feel like a fluke to me. A miracle, maybe, but not a fluke."

"Huh . . . And the fact that what we started while you were inside is actually translating, out in the real— Not the *real* world, sorry. I know that place was plenty real to you. But the big, wide, larger world, or whatever. That doesn't surprise you?"

"Surprise? No. My body knew the second I saw you, you made me feel more than just . . . you know."

"Horny," I supplied.

"Yeah. I mean sure, I was pent up in every way a man can be, but I hadn't forgot how it is, outside, when you meet somebody you're just *really* into. That spark. I felt that the second I saw you. And I felt it in return, when we got close. Felt that energy coming off you, too. So I'm not surprised we've found it out here. Not at all."

I let his words sink in, awed to hear these thoughts. Ones I'd never have expected. "That makes sense. I guess you must trust your body's judgment better than I do mine. I was worried after all those letters, all that buildup, one bad kiss would wreck all the chemistry I'd invented between us."

"Well, I've got a suspicion you think way harder about stuff than I do."

I laughed. "Too hard, sometimes."

"I like that about you . . . Can I ask you something though? About what *does* surprise me some, about us?"

"Sure."

"What is it about me? Not counting how bad we want each other. What about me is . . . I dunno. I don't know if you see me as boyfriend material or anything like that. But what makes me good enough to be with you, this way? To get made pancakes by you, or wake up in your bed?" His voice was tight, shot through with some hopeful breed of skepticism.

"Believe it or not, that's one thing I *haven't* put too much thought into. The why of it. I fell for your aura, first. God, that sounds so stupid. But I fell for this energy you throw off, and it makes me feel so much, now that you're out, the day-to-day details can just be whatever they are." I paused for a breath. "Did that make any sense?"

"I think so . . . I know why I like *you*," he added, and I could hear the smile in his voice.

"Why?"

"Because you care about things. Like helping people."

"Like at Cousins?"

I felt him nod. When he spoke, the words came out slowly, chosen with care. "We live in a really apathetic world. And in a really hurting, extra apathetic corner of it. And you met me in such a shitty place, full of mostly shitty people. And I know you're paid to pretend you care, but I can tell you really *do* care. I could see how excited you were, to read that book to everybody. You really hoped they'd like it, didn't you?"

202

"Yeah," I said, and my throat felt tight all of a sudden.

"And when you helped people, even though they were rude to you, or creeps . . . Well, I'm sure you didn't love that, but you helped them, anyhow. And you helped me. You were *excited* to help me, the first time we talked. I could tell."

My sinuses tingled.

"And it had been so long since anybody looked in my eyes, and I saw that inside them," he added. "Or that I felt, like . . . I dunno. Felt like they saw some potential in me. Something worth polishing up, maybe. Something worth their time, even in a place like that."

I was afraid to reply, positive I'd start crying again. He stroked the back of my hand, then squeezed each of my fingers, one by one.

"You all right?"

"That's just very sweet," I said, a little sob swallowing up the *eet*.

He made a happy sound, a sort of laugh-hum, and rested his head on my shoulder, hugging me closer. "I promised I'd try never to do this again—make you cry. But I can't apologize, since I meant all of that."

"No, don't apologize."

"I think you're special," he said softly, and kissed my neck. "Special to find inside Cousins, special in this crappy city. Special anyplace, though. Somebody who does what they think's important, even if it scares them. Even if nobody appreciates it . . . or is willing to admit they appreciate it."

After a long silence I said, "I was wrong. I do know why I like you so much. Beyond the infatuation."

"Why?"

"You say stuff like that. In your letters . . . You said the most beautiful things."

"You made me see beautiful things again."

203

"See? Stuff like that."

"It's a sign of weakness to feel stuff, in prison. To care. To admit you're lonely, or sad, or that you're aching for somebody. Writing to you was the only time I got to get that stuff out of me. I just wrote down whatever needed to come out."

"I think you may be the most romantic man I've ever met."

"Give yourself some credit. I don't write letters like that to just anybody."

"Write to me, while I'm away. Email me."

"I will. Whatever you want." Eric kissed my temple. "How warm's it gonna be in South Carolina next week?"

"Fifties, maybe."

He rolled onto his back with a lamenting sigh. "Oh, *man*."

"I know. I'm so ready for it."

He shot me a grin. "You gonna tell your father who you've been seeing?"

Guilt cooled me and I met his eyes. "Probably not. But not because of your . . . past. Just because I always take ages to tell my folks about boys. Oh God—it's been so long since I was seeing anybody, it really was a *boy* I'd been dating. Anyway, no, I probably won't. They've been waiting so long to hear about me meeting somebody, I don't want to—" I cut myself off.

"Get their hopes up?"

Shit. How the fuck had I stumbled into that hole? "Sort of. I guess."

"Don't look so freaked," Eric said, and smoothed my hair back. "We're lovers, for now. I know that. And I know a girl doesn't go telling her father about a man unless she thinks he's . . . I dunno. Something serious."

"I don't know *what* we are yet, I guess."

"That's fine. Neither do I."

"But I feel bad. That was really tacky."

204

"Hush. It takes a couple months of seeing a guy for a girl to tell her dad about him. It should take a lot more for a girl to tell her state trooper father about the ex-con she's sleeping with."

I laugh-groaned at that, shutting my eyes. "God, he's going to have a heart attack."

"Let's make it to the spring, okay? By then I might stand a chance at getting permission to leave the state. And by then I can legitimately introduce myself as a landscaper. I'm pretty okay with the lies of omission, as you might recall."

I gave his shoulder a soft whap, admonishing the self-recrimination I heard in his voice. "Fine," I agreed. "We deal with that in the spring."

Spring . . . The season he so longed for. The end to all this snow and ice and biting cold, the promise of green. Of tee shirts and naps on grassy mattresses. Of swimming in still-chilly lakes, I bet, for this man who'd not felt that weightlessness in far too long. Too long to wait until summer. He'd been released from one prison, but the winter was so much the same, gray and dark and hard. But at least for now, I could warm him. I pressed myself deeper into his embrace.

For the thaw he'd brought to my body, and the way he'd coaxed me to bloom again, I'd see him through the harshest months.

I'd bring the energy of spring to him, between these sheets. Rouse the heat of summer between our bodies. Everything a man yearned to feel, and everything a woman yearned to be.

All for a man who truly deserved every last bit of it.

Chapter Fourteen

For the next week, December became June. All the gloom was banished, ice replaced with warmth and vitality; the cold no match for the heat our eyes promised from across a room or a table, the fire our bodies created in my bed.

I wondered, was this how it felt? Falling in love with someone? Or was this still mere infatuation? Was there a difference? It felt so good, it was difficult to care.

That following Thursday Eric let me come to his apartment. It was small, located on the second floor of an anonymous brick four-story on a shadier side of town. Every unit in the building was subsidized, he'd told me, so his neighbors were all struggling in one way or another, and you could feel it as you hiked up the thinly carpeted stairs. It was noisy in the common areas, and there was a certain scent of desperation to the place. I could understand why he was eager to move out, once his fines were paid off and his wages no longer garnished.

But his actual apartment was nice enough. Nothing luxurious, of course, but a medium-sized bedroom, small living area and bathroom, galley kitchen. Not that much smaller than mine, really, just a touch . . . utilitarian. The walls were painted the predictable tired white, and the fixtures and cabinets were all economy. But he kept it fairly tidy, and his windows looked out over a concrete courtyard with a basketball hoop, currently frosted white. A thick old black laptop sat on the kitchen table, looking space-age beside the ancient word processor I'd given him.

"You kept it," I said, laughing. Delighted.

"Course I did. It was a gift. From you." He mumbled the last bit, hiding a smile.

The biggest surprise was his plants. He kept them in his living room, mostly in pots; some in small, covered aquariums on milk crates and cardboard boxes, veiled by the fogged glass, arranged at precise distances from the radiators. He even had an orchid—though it wasn't thriving, to his dismay.

"How did you afford all this?" I asked.

"You can get plants real cheap at the garden store, if they're looking kind of beat. And the fish tanks I got at Goodwill for like a buck apiece. Potting soil was more expensive than the rest of it put together."

"Huh." I imagined him rescuing all these specimens from Home Depot, fretting over them on the unheated drive. Coaxing them back to life.

"My mom gave me the orchid." He eyed it with renewed worry. There were gardening books all over, two dozen of them at least, with Post-its sticking from their pages like rumpled feathers. Hand-me-downs from his boss, he told me. He'd placed several gooseneck lamps around the makeshift garden, and the small inventory of lightbulb boxes told me he'd splashed out for full-spectrum. Watering cans and spray bottles and bags of soil, sticks of plant food, twist ties and slim wooden stakes. The clutter of a man obsessed. It charmed me. So many things a man in Eric's position might choose to

207

throw his precious little spending money at—a nicer phone, car repairs, a TV. Yet he'd chosen this.

This was what had occupied him, his first weeks out of prison. Not women. Not any other thing a man might miss, locked up so long. Just life, and the challenge of fostering it, here in this rough little corner of a rough town. Green against the white walls, under white bulbs, before the flat, white winter sky.

He made me dinner in his narrow kitchen—pasta shells stuffed with ricotta cheese that he insisted he'd overcooked, but that I thought were just fine. We made love on his small bed in his noisy building, and though it wasn't like it was at my place, it was authentic. It was what it was, and the intensity was there between us, same as always.

The next day he drove me to the airport directly after my shift at Cousins. Only two full days in Charleston, plus most of Sunday, but Eric and I said good-bye as if one of us were being shipped off to war, never to return. Kissing one last time for thirty minutes or more, standing just inside the terminal door. We said good-bye so many times, I had to run from security to my gate with my shoes in my hand to make my flight. And it was totally worth it.

It was a late flight, landing just after ten. The sky was crystal clear, the air feeling balmy as I waited along the pickup curb, coat folded over my arm. My phone buzzed in my pocket, having found a signal. I pulled it out, expecting a voicemail from my mom. But no, two text messages.

One from her, reading, Let me know when you're outside.

And one from Eric.

Text me before you go to bed. Give me something to think about while your body's a thousand miles away.

208

Something to think about. I was pretty sure I knew what that meant. It warmed me more than the climate ever could.

I wrote back, Just landed. Give me an hour or two and I'll send some inspiration.

Then I stood there like a dope for two minutes before I remembered to call my mom.

We were back home inside twenty-five minutes, the house I'd grown up in feeling smaller somehow, after six months away. My dad had to get up for work early the next morning and had already passed out in his recliner, but once roused he stayed up to chat for a half hour. My mom taught fifth grade and was already on school break, so she had nowhere to be anytime soon.

After Dad made his way up to bed she asked, "You about ready to crash, baby?"

"Nah, I napped on the plane."

"I've got a bottle of Riesling open in the fridge . . ."

"Well then," I said, perking up, "let's get this vacation under way." I might not get her all to myself again like this during the visit. I had a lot of family to see, and not much time to see them.

She poured us each a healthy glass, and we curled up on either end of the big couch in the den, hugging mismatched afghans. She was wearing a pine-colored velvet button-up, and Christmas settled around me like a spell.

She smiled with that mom-pride, eyes crinkling. "You look absolutely gorgeous, Annie."

I waved the compliment aside, rubbing the heel of my hand across my forehead. "I feel all gross from the flight, but thanks. You, too. I like your highlights, and that cut."

She smoothed her hair, faking outlandish pride. "Highlights? I'm sure I have no idea what you mean."

209

"No, my mistake. Just the natural effect of all that December sun, I'm sure."

"You do look great, though," she repeated earnestly. "I was worried about you, with all the stress of your new job . . . Well, not so new anymore, I guess."

I shook my head. "Nope. Funny how quick I got used to spending my days in psychiatric wards and prisons."

"And everything's okay, at work?"

"Yeah, fine. I mean, it's hard. I won't lie. But nothing scary's happened—nothing dangerous, I mean. It's way easier now, since I've gotten used to the routines, and all the people I work with have gotten to know me, and vice versa."

She sighed, staring at her glass. "I worry about you, every Friday. With all those inmates."

"They're just people."

"Just people who're impulsive enough to make violent mistakes and get themselves locked up in prison."

I shrugged, squirming on the inside. "They're not *all* in for violent stuff. In fact most are in for drug offenses. Anyway, the ones who don't behave have their enrichment privileges suspended. All the guys I work with have good behavior."

"Do they . . . Do they leer at you, at all?"

I nodded. "Oh yeah. Constantly."

She blinked, mouth falling open. "And you're okay with that?"

"Mama, some of these guys haven't been with a woman in *years*. Of course they're going to leer at me. That's like expecting a starving man not to stare at a glazed ham or something."

"Still."

"Seriously, I'm over it. It felt personal for the first few shifts." *Very* personal, with one inmate in particular. "But after a while you chalk it up to a biological distraction and get on with your work. Honestly, there are some days when

210

I'd rather be at Cousins than dealing with the annoying crap people try to get away with when I'm manning the reference desk."

She shook her head, took a deep sip. "Well, I just don't know how you do it. But good for you. It's very important work. And your father and I just think it's so brave."

I blushed at that, not comfortable with the compliment. After all, it was arguably cowardice that had sent me to Michigan in the first place. I'd fled my shame over the abuse I'd put up with, staying with Justin, only to end up surrounded by violent men on a weekly basis. Some of the shrinks at Larkhaven would surely have a grand old time figuring that one out. Perhaps Cousins was my exposure therapy. Perhaps *Eric* was my therapy. Some deep and driving need to prove I could trust a man again—and one who looked so woefully untrustworthy, on paper.

"Enough about work," I said. "What's happening around here?"

My mom filled me in on the usual town gossip and on what my relatives were up to.

"I thought I noticed that on Facebook," I said when she mentioned my cousin's recent weight loss.

She nodded, then sat up straighter. "Speaking of Facebook."

"Yeah?"

"You never post anything."

"That's not true." Close, though.

"Barely at all since you started your new job."

"I'm busy."

"I'm sure everyone would love to see pictures of your apartment and the library. And all that snow you must be getting. And *you*. Don't you have any friends you go out with?" The concern in her voice was as touching as it was infuriating. Mothers.

211

"I have some friends. Mostly coworkers, but a few. It'll take time. The people from Darren are way different than back here . . . they're kind of a slow thaw. But it's not a symptom of some larger issue." I shrugged. "Or maybe I've just outgrown Facebook." Or maybe the most exciting aspect of my life of late had simply involved a clandestine epistolary affair that could've compromised my job and put my parents on anxiety medication.

My mom sipped her wine, then rubbed at some invisible spot on the glass. "I wondered . . ."

"You wondered what?"

She met my eyes squarely. "I wondered if maybe you didn't want him knowing. About your personal life."

I shivered and blushed at once, a queasy feeling. We'd gone so long, never having really discussed this. So many times I'd longed for her to grill me, for an excuse to vent . . . but we'd both always lacked the courage. I wondered why now, after all this time.

I sighed. "It's been five years, Mama. And he was a bad boyfriend, not a stalker."

Her turn to shrug. "You never talked to me about it. I don't know what kind of a boy he was."

"Well, that's not why. I'm sure he barely remembers me by now." Which goddamn burned, in its truth. That Justin had probably moved on, while I'd put my entire sexuality on hold until this summer. "It's not about Justin."

Her brows rose a fraction. "So it's about something, though?"

I sighed again and rolled my eyes. "Oh my God, give it up. Everything's fine. Everything's reasonably great, actually. I'm just sick of Facebook, okay?"

"Is it a boy?"

I froze up. Deflected. "I'm twenty-seven. I don't date *boys*." But my petulant six-year-old's tone gave me away, of course.

212

"You are, aren't you? Did you meet a nice man?" There was a mix of emotions in her voice—a touch of skepticism, probably that such a thing as a nice man existed so far north; and hope, because of course she wanted that for me.

I didn't answer quick enough, and when I did, it only incriminated me further. "I um . . . Nothing official or anything."

Her expression changed, eyebrows drawing tight. "Nothing official? I'll take off the record."

My face burned like we were back on this couch, her giving me the mortifying pre-homecoming-dance talk about making good decisions. God help me, I hadn't listened back then, had I? I'd dated a cruel boy who'd hit me, now a good man who'd nearly killed a human being. And I was torn between the joyous urge to share and the sense that I'd been caught.

"Who is he?" she asked. "Is it new? Are you afraid to jinx it?"

"Maybe. I dunno."

Her head cocked. "Is it not . . . Is it not a man?"

I snorted. "Justin didn't turn me gay, Mama."

"Well I don't know. They say women's sexuality is fluid—"

"No, Mama. It's a man, okay?"

My mother promptly stood and grabbed the open bottle, and I laughed at that, tension bleeding out as she topped us both off.

"Go on, baby. No pressure, but I've been waiting a long time to hear that you've met somebody you're excited about."

I smiled sadly at that. "Me, too."

"So?"

"He's . . . He's great." *Except for the whole attempted-murder thing.* "I like him a lot, but yeah, it's still really soon to know."

"Where did you meet?"

213

"At . . . work." Ah, shit. Time to fudge.

"At the library?"

"Kind of. He works for the city, doing stuff like snow removal in the winter, and landscaping the rest of the year. I ran into him when he was working around the library." How about that? All true. Perhaps Eric was on to something with this whole omission strategy.

I watched my mom process the information, hiding her disappointment well. She wasn't a snob or anything, but I knew she'd prefer her daughter date someone with a more white-collar vocation. Perhaps she was trying to rebrand this job in her head, for when she shared the development with her sisters. What would she do with landscaping? *Horticultural engineer.*

"That must be nice," she managed. "Work that keeps him outside."

I nodded. "Anyway, his name's Eric and he's thirty-two. And he's really handsome and romantic and awesome. But like I said, it *just* started, so don't start getting invitations printed or anything."

She laughed and waved a dismissive hand. "I'm interested, not desperate . . . So."

"Yes?"

"This young man's treating you well?"

"Yeah, he's really . . ." What did my mom want to hear? That he was nothing like the boy who'd sent me away in the first place, of course. "He's gentle." *With me, anyhow. With almost everyone.* "And patient. And the best kisser I've ever met. And he writes me love letters."

Any concerns she had about his profession melted away in the warmth of her smile. She touched my arm. "He sounds wonderful. Tell him he has my approval."

"We'll see. I wouldn't say he's my boyfriend yet or anything."

214

"Do you wish he was?"

I frowned. "I dunno. Maybe." Except then it'd all be so real, and I'd have to break it to my parents what he'd done right around the time I'd been getting smacked around by Justin. I was still only half sure what I felt about all that, myself.

"I hope he's not one of these younger people who believes in dating multiple women at once," my mom fretted. She'd surely seen some talk show or read some article admonishing the modern hookup culture.

"No, I don't think so." If Eric was nothing else, he was loyal. Too loyal, nearly, considering how far he'd taken his defense of his sister. "We just haven't had that talk yet. You know me," I said, dropping my gaze. "I'm taking things slow now. But it's nice, after all this time."

"And what does he look like?" Her eyes narrowed as she prepared to mentally smoosh Eric's and my DNA together and composite her future grandchild.

"He's tall. With dark hair and eyes."

"Oh . . . ?" Lord, what did that noise mean? Though there wasn't any fear in the sound, it was jam-packed with curiosity. She wanted to know if I'd taken up with someone my grandma would refer to as "exotic."

"He's a mix of stuff. French Canadian and German and Puerto Rican. Not that it matters," I reminded her, knowing she was probably making some mortifying connection between landscaping and Hispanic people, one that thankfully she'd have the self-awareness not to voice. But I knew the culture from which I came. My family had some catching up to do with the twenty-first century.

She huffed, rolling her eyes. "I just want to picture him."

"He looks Italian, I guess." *And he's jacked and he's got tattoos and he spent the last half a decade wearing a tee*

215

shirt with his prisoner number stenciled on it. "He's very
. . . sexy."

"What sorts of dates do you go on?"

The kind that go down primarily with our clothes off?
"The usual stuff. Drinks." Though Eric had barely sipped his
beer that time at Lola's. "And he made me dinner last night.
Oh and he drove us out to a lake once. All frozen over, with
the moon on the ice. Simple stuff. Not that there's anything
fancy to do in Darren. Mostly we just . . . talk." *And fuck.*

"And where is he from?"

"Some godforsaken part of rural Michigan. I've never been
there, but he hates it. He's close with his mother and sister
who live back there, though." I tried to picture our two families at a cookout together, to imagine what they'd find to
talk about. Hunting perhaps? Bourbon? "Maybe someday I'll
go, if we stay together."

"Well, he'd be a fool to let a girl like you get away," my
mom said, all wise, probably a little buzzed.

I drained my own glass and craned my neck to check the
clock on the mantel. "I'm crashing, I think."

"Me, too. But it was good to catch up, huh?" She stood
with a dramatic groan, like she didn't swim an hour of laps
every other morning. We hugged and said good night at the
top of the stairs. Our house wasn't nearly as swanky as some
in the Charleston suburbs, but it felt outrageously cushy
compared to my place in Darren. Or compared to any of the
spaces I worked in at the library or Cousins or Larkhaven—
the carpet so soft, the noises so muted.

I shut the door to what used to be my old bedroom, now
the guest room. My lavender walls had been painted taupe
a couple of years ago. My bed was still in its place under the
windows, but my purple checkerboard comforter had been
replaced with a generic toile number. If the rest of the house

felt small, my room felt *tiny*. My single bed especially, since I'd acquired a twin-size frame in grad school. I flopped across the covers and the too-many pillows and pulled out my phone.

You still up? I texted Eric.

Nothing for a minute or more, so I dug my toiletries bag out of my suitcase and headed to the bathroom to scrub my face and brush my teeth.

The little light at the corner of my phone was blinking when I returned to my room, and my heart rose like a balloon bound for the clouds. I ran to the bed, landed with a bounce, and opened his message.

Yup. Been waiting all night to hear from you.

Parents are so selfish, I replied, stealing a woman away from her illicit texting.

Miss you, he wrote. You miss me?

Of course I do. Wish you were here now . . . though this bed is about as big as a yoga mat. No way you'd fit on it.

Bet the floor's nice and roomy.

I smiled. True enough.

I'm gonna think about us, before I go to sleep, he wrote. Tell me what to imagine.

Feeling a twinge of performance anxiety, I wrote, Let me think.

217

What would I want to be doing with him, were we together? I pictured his big body stretched across my bed, back north. Tried to focus on his abs, his chest, his arms . . . but found myself thinking mainly of his eyes. And his mouth.

I wrote, Imagine us, on my bed. Kissing. Then you feel my hands at your waist . . . I pictured it myself, dressing him in what I guessed he'd be wearing on a cold Darren night—his flannel bottoms. I'm undoing the tie of your drawstring, pushing down your waistband. I hit Send and got busy with the next installment.

Just imagine us kissing, and me stroking you between us. That's what I want right now. To feel you, hard and excited. And to make you feel good. If you touch yourself before you fall asleep, imagine it's my hand. That's what I want.

I waited a short eternity for his reply.

Where do I come? In your hand?

A heat wave washed over me, burning off any lingering nerves. My fingers were clumsy now. A little, in my hand. And on your belly. On that warm, taut skin. White on tan. My body clenched at the image. I hit Send.

Would you clean me up? he asked, and the world reeled.

Yeah, I would. I could practically feel his fingers in my hair now, trembling as I lapped at his skin. Whatever you wanted.

Christ almighty, why was he so far away? Why was I anywhere on this planet aside from right up next to that body, that voice, that man? *My* man.

That enough to get you to sleep? I tapped.

218

Plenty. What about you?

I'll be imagining the exact same thing, the second we say good night.

Good. Imagine me saying your name, right when you bring me home, he wrote. Right when you get there, yourself.

I will. Call me tomorrow, maybe? Good night, Eric.

Good night, darling. I miss you.

You too. Merry Christmas Eve. Sleep well. Eventually :-)

And twenty minutes later, I was sleeping like a baby, myself.

By the time I came down the next morning, my dad had already left on his patrol. He was so senior, he was automatically entitled to take the holiday off, but usually deferred. Working Christmas, he could bank a floating holiday and was off by two in the afternoon, all while letting some "young buck" sleep in with his family. He was always up around five, anyway, and my mom operated on the same schedule. I, on the other hand, came trundling down the stairs still in my pajamas at a quarter to eleven.

"Merry Christmas!" my mom chimed as I entered the kitchen. She had the radio on, carols playing, and was wearing her special holiday robe, green with embroidered sleighs and reindeer.

"Merry Christmas. Ooh, thanks," I added, accepting a mug of coffee. "I can't believe how late I slept."

"You must've needed it."

True, though not for the work-recuperation reasons she

was probably implying. I'd been with Eric five nights in the last week, and I doubted we ever got to sleep before 1:00 a.m. If we weren't messing around, we were up talking well past our bedtimes, about everything and nothing at all.

"Want me to make you breakfast?" my mom asked.

"No, thanks. I'll nuke some oatmeal or something after I shower. You relax." We had a couple dozen extended family members coming by for snacks and drinks in the midafternoon, a mix of my aunts and uncles and their kids and their kids' kids, and my grandma, of course. Wine and crudités for the adults, milk and cookies for the little ones, and a whole lot of running around for my mom—though she loved that stuff.

"Put me to work, right after this caffeine hits," I said.

"I will, don't you worry. I need you to wrap some things for the white elephant."

"Aw, crap." She'd emailed me about that over a week ago, and it had fallen right out of my head. I was supposed to have bought a ten-dollar gift for the swap.

"Never fear," she said. "I bought a couple spares."

"Thanks, Mama. I've been distracted."

She smiled knowingly. "So I gathered. Did you get your new friend a present?"

I shook my head. "I didn't, no. We didn't even discuss it."

She looked a touch disappointed at that.

"It's all really new," I said. "But maybe I'll give him something for New Year's."

"What sorts of things does he like? Does he have any hobbies?"

Well, he's really into his civil liberties, at the moment. "He's interested in plants."

"Is he?" She perked right up then. And that there was a major bit of overlap I'd not put together, between my mother

220

and Eric. They might actually hit it off, were they to meet at my family's white elephant swap party some day.

"What kinds of plants?" she asked.

"Everything, I think. He's fairly new to the whole land-scaping thing, but he's got all sorts of pots and terrariums in his living room. He's even got an orchid. Though I'm not sure it's doing especially well. He could probably use some tips from an expert such as yourself."

"Do you think he'd like some back issues of *Horticulture*?"

Before I could tell her I had no idea, she was up and striding for the laundry room. Clearly I'd be going home with my suitcase ten pounds heavier than when I'd arrived. But I had to smile. Two people I cared about deeply were about to connect, even if that crossover was only as thick as a stack of magazines. When she returned with an armload of them hugged to her chest, I asked, "Did you tell Daddy?"

"About your boyfriend? Sorry—your whatever-he-is."

I nodded.

"I may have mentioned you have some exciting news to share."

I rolled my eyes. "Just please don't make a big reveal of it when everybody's over this afternoon, okay? I'm just getting used to dating again, myself. I don't want to get grilled about it in front of half the family. I don't want . . ." I sighed gruffly. "I don't want anybody asking why it is I haven't dated in so long to begin with."

She drew an imaginary zipper across her lips.

"Good. Thank you. I'll tell Daddy tonight, over dinner."

"Your grandma's staying for dinner," she reminded me.

"That's fine. Gram can hear." She'd hear it from my mother, anyhow, if I chose to keep it to myself. They talked about everything . . . Years ago I'd overheard the two of them discussing my breakup, in the kitchen before Thanksgiving.

221

And my gram had called Justin "that little shit." Which for a woman who considered "crap" racy was as incendiary as the C-word. So she must've known he'd hit me. Her never having brought it up with me was a testament to her discretion with the secret, her respect for my privacy, or plain old Southern discomfort.

I chugged my coffee and hit the shower, and spent the early afternoon taking party-prep orders from my mother.

The get-together was as it always was—fun, a touch chaotic, loud, festively spiked. It wound down as the sun began its descent, right as the little kids were crashing from a surfeit of excitement and sugar, and my Uncle Ken was starting to nod off from too much eggnog. My mom and her two sisters tackled the cleanup with the efficiency of a SWAT team while I gossiped with my cousins, and by five everyone was hugging and piling into cars and waving from the end of the driveway, just me and my folks and my gram left on the front porch.

I tried to picture myself with a small child and a husband, like my cousin Kate had. She was only a year older than me. I imagined me and Eric and some toddling, miniature person all dressed up for Christmas, a little family. It was too soon to think about that stuff, of course. Too soon in our courtship and too soon for me in general. Yet here I was fantasizing.

We sat down to dinner at six, and the wine had barely been poured when my mother announced to my gram and dad that, "Annie has some interesting news."

"Oh?" Dad said.

"It's a man," Gram said.

I shot her a look. "What makes you sound so confident about that?"

She shrugged her narrow shoulders, too innocent. "You're

twenty-seven and you've already shocked us by moving up to that godforsaken town. Time's come that you break our hearts further and tell us you've taken up with some grease-stained auto worker."

She was mainly teasing—my gram's sense of humor was nothing if not chiding—and I rolled my eyes at her. "Do you want the announcement or not?"

She waved her fork to say, *Go on, then.*

"Only Mama seems to think this is newsworthy, but fine. I'm seeing a man. He's not my boyfriend yet, but we're dating. And he's lovely, and he treats me great. End of story."

"That's wonderful, honey," my dad said, and raised his glass in a little toast—as much of a deal as he was likely to make on the topic of a man in his daughter's life, I imagined.

"Don't give the milk away for free," my gram warned.

"Shall I grab today's paper," I offered, "and remind you what century we're living in?"

"The two of you," my mom said. "Lord. Let's not talk about this on Christmas, okay?"

"You brought it up," Gram reminded her.

My dad surprised me by being the one to seek further info. "So, Annie. What's this young man do?"

And I gave him the same spiel I had given my mom, emphasis on the landscaping, ix-nay on the incarceration. Thankfully the conversation got dragged off by my gram, who embarked on a monologue on the topic of What's Wrong With Folks from the North, and I was spared further grilling for the rest of dinner. By seven thirty my dad was back from dropping Gram home, and my mom and I had cleaned up the dinner dishes. We switched on the TV, prepared to watch whatever movie was coming on at eight.

My parents took the couch and I curled up in my dad's recliner. George Bailey was just purchasing a large suitcase, when my phone buzzed in my pocket. I slid it out, my heart's eager, hopeful beating rewarded. *Eric.*

"I have to take this," I said, standing. Blushing.

"Is it your beau?" my mother asked.

"Oh my God, Mama. Who says that?"

"That's a yes," my dad said.

I rolled my eyes at them both and headed for the door.

Chapter Fifteen

I hit Talk on the fourth ring, slipping into the hall. "Hey, you."

"Hey, yourself. Merry Christmas."

Fuck me, his voice. It closed around me like a starry night.

"Merry Christmas. What are you up to?" I asked as I climbed the stairs.

"Not a lot. Missing you, mostly. Missing your voice."

I shut my bedroom door, smiling to know the vocal objectification was mutual. "Well, my voice is all yours now. We just finished dinner, and I think I can skip *It's a Wonderful Life*, considering how I could probably recite it from memory." I sat on my bed, suddenly needing to picture him. "Are you at home?"

"Yeah."

"Where? Where in your apartment, I mean."

"Couch."

"What are you wearing?" I giggled and a soft laugh answered me.

"Jeans and a sweater."

"What color?"

"My dark red one."

I pictured him, long legs stretched out, messy hair mashed against a cushion. "Socks?"

"Yup. Two of 'em."

"Okay. Got it."

"What about you? What're you wearing?"

"Damn," I said with another giggle. "This sounds like a prelude to phone sex." Oh man, and *was* it?

"Tell me."

Ooh, and hadn't his voice just dropped half an octave?

"Well, I'm wearing a tan corduroy skirt and a green top, and I'm about to unzip my brown leather boots. And I'm sitting on the bed in what used to be my childhood bedroom, though it's decorated all different now."

"That where you were last night, when we were texting?"

"Mm-hm. What about you?"

"I was in bed. Though after we hung up I wished to hell I had a copy of your keys so I could've driven over to yours and got all tangled up in your sheets, and smelled you in your pillowcases." He paused. "Was that creepy?"

I laughed. "No, I think that's sweet. And a little dirty, depending on what happened next."

He made a low, lazy noise, like he was stretching. "So how was your Christmas? Santa bring you lots of presents?"

"Not too many. I didn't ask for much. I did pretty bad at the white elephant swap and wound up with a harmonica. Plus some good gift cards from my parents and cash from my gram."

"You sound even more Southern than usual," he teased.

"I don't doubt it. Being around my family tends to do that. What about you? Did you see your family?"

"No, just a long phone call. There might be a storm

226

tomorrow, so that was a good excuse to lay low, in case there's some work to pick up."

"Were they bummed, not getting to see you on your first Christmas out of prison?" At that final word, my stomach plummeted as I imagined my parents listening in on this conversation. But I wasn't fifteen, and this wasn't the landline. *Get a grip, girl.*

"Probably," Eric said. "But they'll live. I gotta get them used to me not running home the second they tell me to."

"Sounds wise."

"Plus I didn't feel like seeing my dad, and I heard he's been hanging around. Anyway."

"Anyway," I agreed. "What did you do for dinner? Anything special?"

"Uh, kind of. I guess. I bought a decent steak the other day at the supermarket and made myself that." A soft *heh*. "Steak and beer, in honor of our Lord's birth."

"Whatever floats your boat."

"I got you a present yesterday," he said. "I hope that's okay."

Dreamy. "Fine by me. What is it?"

I heard the smile warming his tone. "You'll have to wait and find out. I wrapped it really badly. So bad it looks like a joke. Don't laugh when you see it."

"I haven't found you anything, yet. But my mom's sending me home with a stack of snobby gardening magazines."

"You told them about me, then?" I could about taste the surprise in his voice. "How much?"

"Not the whole Cousins thing. But everything else."

"I pass muster?"

"Yeah, I'd say so. You mention me to your family, on the phone?"

"My mom already knew about you, from Kristina," he said.

227

"Oh, great. Because she seemed crazy about me when I spoke to her."

"They know you make me happy. That's all that ought to matter."

"Ought to?" I asked, heart twisting a little.

He sighed into the receiver. "Don't worry about it."

"Worry about what?" And how was it that *I*, the mild-mannered librarian, was failing the family-opinion test, when my ex-con lover had basically scored a blessing?

"It's not your fault," Eric said. "They just don't get that my staying away as much as I have is my own decision. Yet."

"They think I'm trying to keep you away from them?"

"They jump to conclusions like that. About like, meddling outsiders. My sister especially. But I told them you're not even in town, that you couldn't care less. It's just their way, blaming the nearest unknown entity. They're threat-oriented folks."

"Jeez." What a bleak prospect, as in-laws went. I mean, not that I was imagining—

"Don't sweat it," he said. "They'll get all worked up about some other thing next week and you'll be off the shit list."

"I'm on your family's *shit list*?"

He laughed softly. "Only my sister's. And it's a long list. Like I said, don't sweat it."

"Fine. As long as my present's really good, I'm over it. What's my present?"

Another laugh, a low one that made me feel all warm and squirmy. "Wait and see."

"I'll make it my mission to find you something tomorrow," I promised. Something for his indoor garden, maybe.

"I like seeing you in lace, if that helps point you in the right direction."

Actually yes, that was exceedingly helpful. "And here I'd

228

been thinking of plant stuff. Well, I'll see what I can do. Any particular color you'd like me to wear?" Though I was only teasing, excitement drew my sex tight and hot. Our game flashed me back to the height of summer, to those meetings in Cousins, stifling for so many reasons.

"That's a good question," he said. "Lemme think."

"It's Christmas. Maybe red?"

Whore. Fine by me. I was quite excited to imagine being Eric's plaything.

"Red it is," he said.

Without meaning to, I let my hand roam low and settle over my mound, cupping through my skirt. After a long pause I murmured, "I miss your body."

"It misses you. Did you read my email?" he asked.

"Oh, no. I haven't even checked my inbox since I landed."

"You made me promise I'd write you. And I always keep my promises."

"Is it . . . dirty?"

"Find out."

I smiled. "Oh, I intend to."

"Last night, after we were texting," he prompted.

"Yes?"

"Did you?"

"I did. Did you?" I asked.

"Exactly how you told me to. Exactly what you said to imagine."

"Good. Me, too."

"Wish I could have your hands on me for real," he murmured.

"So do I."

Nothing for a long moment, so I asked, "Are you . . . *Are* you?"

"Touching myself?" he whispered.

229

My "yeah" was so quiet, he probably sensed it as much as he actually heard it.

"Yeah," he echoed. "A little."

My own hand slid deeper between my legs. "How?"

"Just over my jeans."

I pictured it, his big hand cupping his excitement through his fly. Maybe squeezing gently, stroking faintly. Just as I was.

"That okay?" he asked.

"That's very okay."

"Wish it was you."

"So do I."

"What would you want me to do, if we were together right now?" he asked.

My brain short-circuited, and the nervous energy dissipated like steam. I let the truth flow, speaking my desires exactly as they came to me. "I'd want us both in our underwear. On your couch. Kissing. And maybe I'm on my back, and you're between my legs. Excited."

"That'd be torture," he breathed, voice gone reedy. *Awesome.*

"No, torture for me," I corrected. "You'd be doing it to tease me. Letting me feel how hard you were. But every time I try to touch you or push your shorts down, you stop me." Oh man, this was way easier than I'd expected.

"You want me to tease you?"

"Yeah." Tease me, just as he had with those letters, and with this phone call.

"Wrap your legs around me," he said, and in my mind, I did. His thighs were thick and strong, hips fidgeting as he stroked against me, so slow. I could feel his back muscles under my palms, how they tensed in time with the torture.

"Are you hard?" I whispered.

"So hard."

230

"Still just through your jeans?"

"Yeah."

"Unzip them," I murmured. "But only touch yourself through your shorts."

Distracted breaths came through the line, a soft grunt. "Okay."

My own hand eased up my skirt. I palmed my sex, my hand like ice even through my panties. But not for long. "I'm doing the same," I told him.

"Good. Except you're not, really. Because I'm on top of you."

I shimmied around and flopped onto my back, the fluffy down pillow sighing. I spread my thighs, and just the flex of my hips triggered a rush of arousal. There was an extra pillow beside me, and I shoved it right where Eric ought to be, its weight and softness way off, but thrilling all the same. Jesus, I was humping a pillow in my childhood bedroom. This man really did make me sixteen again.

"I want your hands on my ass," he said. "Begging me for more."

I felt it all—snug cotton over hard muscle, and my nails digging into him. "Please."

"Please what? What do you need, darling?"

What did I need? My mouth knew before my brain registered it. "I want to go down on you."

The softest groan. "Do you?"

"Yeah. More than anything. Get your clothes off."

"Hang on." I heard a tap like he'd set the phone down, then distant rustling, a creak. "Okay," he said, voice tight.

"Make your . . ."

"Make what, Annie?"

"Make your hand wet."

The tiniest, "*Oh*."

231

"Then tell me what I'm doing. And how it feels." I hugged the pillow tight, so aroused I felt a little scared. I liked it. "Eric?"

"Yeah. Okay, I'm ready."

"I'm taking you in my mouth, now."

"Fuck. Okay . . . okay." His excitement was so obvious. And he sounded rattled, just the way I liked.

"Tell me," I whispered.

"You're wet," he said through a moan. "And warm. Feels so good."

I didn't know what to picture—the act we were pretending, or just this man, stroking himself in a spit-slick fist on my orders.

"It's everything I imagined back then," he said. "Before we were ever together. Your hair's so soft, in my hands. And your . . . your mouth. It's hungry. Like you love doing this to me."

In my mind's eye, I released him to speak. "I do. More than I ever knew I could."

"It makes me feel so fucking big, when you do it." His words had sped up, and I imagined his hand doing the same. "I like it with me laying down," he said. "Not above you, like it's something I'm making you do. Like I'm letting you, almost."

Fuck, yes. Exactly. "I'd beg you for it," I whispered. "If you told me I couldn't."

"What d'you like about it?"

"Feeling how much you want me, right there. So close. And tasting it. Smelling it. Feeling how helpless you get, from the way your fingers fidget in my hair, or on my neck."

Heavy breathing, and I was so there with him I swear I felt the heat of it in my ear.

"You," he murmured, voice taut. "You now, or I'm going to lose it."

"God, I wish I was with you. So much."

232

"Me, too. Tell me what you'd have me do to you, if you were."

I shut my eyes, let my free hand wander. "Your mouth, I think. You're amazing with your mouth."

"Whatever—wanted," he said, the connection cutting out in the middle.

I pictured that mouth as it must look right now. Lips parted, pink tongue restless. And the rest of him—that long, strong body stretched along the cushions, big fingers circling his pounding cock maybe, but not moving. Too close to the edge. I kicked the pillow away, hand sliding inside my panties.

"You still touching yourself?" I asked, breathless.

"Just holding it. I'm too close."

And I knew this man too well. "Touch it just a little. Real light."

When his pained groan came through the phone, I knew he'd obeyed. My pleasure drew tight as a knot from that alone. From this weird little kink I'd never known I had, my need to make a man weak. Especially one as strong as Eric. Five years he'd survived in a cage full of angry men, yet I had him writhing from a thousand miles away, from nothing but my voice, my desires. Another soft sound of desperation teased my ear, and my own hand sped, pleasure growing.

"Are you—?" Again, the line cut out a little.

"Am I what?" I asked.

"Are you close? Tell me when you're close."

"Now. I'm close now."

And I could tell from the way his voice went shallow then, he was going to join me. "Good. Keep imagining it."

"You still touching yourself?" I asked.

"Yeah."

"That's what I'm imagining, now." Big dick, big hand, dark eyes closed to slits, lips parted. "Fast?"

233

"Not too fast. Not until you get there."

I slowed his hand in my mind, moving that tight fist up and down in luxurious strokes.

"You're—"

He cut me off. "*Fuck*." And that was *not* the exclamation of a man climaxing. "Sorry. Hang on." The connection went flat for a moment, then he came back on. "I'm so fucking sorry, Annie, but I have to go."

"What? Go where?"

"Nowhere, maybe. But I have to take a call. It's family shit." Ah, that would be the cutouts. Incoming calls he'd been ignoring.

"Oh," I said, deflating utterly. "That's okay. Do what you need to do."

I heard the frustration of ten thousand inmates in his sigh. "I'm really sorry. But go read my email, maybe. We'll talk tomorrow, okay?"

"Sure. I hope everything's all—"

"Merry Christmas, Annie," he said, and then he was gone.

I stared at my phone, at the call duration blinking at me in the dark.

I imagined his sister on the other end, maybe. That brash, mean voice, stealing Eric from me. It was petty to think that after only a week of our being lovers, I ought to take precedence over his family . . . but deep down, that's what I wanted.

I gave the pillow under my head a little punch, annoyed at whoever had ruined our fun. Annoyed at myself for feeling so much about it. Though how long had it been since I'd cared enough for a man to even *get* jealous? I tried to tell myself that was a gift in itself.

The lie didn't take.

*   *   *

The next morning, I rose early and borrowed my mom's car, heading to the mall—though I knew I wouldn't be alone. Sure enough, the parking lot was nuts, everyone on a harried mission to swap unwanted presents and cash in gift cards, make the most of the sales. My mom's little sedan felt like a go-cart compared to my wagon, and I navigated the chaos with ease. It wasn't until I was well inside the mall itself that I suffered a collision.

The crash came out of the past at a hundred miles an hour, in the underwear section of the Gap, of all places. One second I was debating between a scarlet padded demi-bra and a garnet-colored push-up, the next I was staring at my ex-boyfriend.

"Whoa. Anne." Justin's eyes were muddy hazel in the store's lights. He seemed . . . bigger. And smaller. Bigger than I'd remembered him at twenty-two. Smaller since I'd become so acclimated to Eric's body.

"Justin."

There was a girl at his side. Our age. Pretty, blond. Kind of a big head, but sweet-looking. She glanced between us, smiling.

To Justin I said, "Hi," fiddling with the little hangers I held.

"Long time," he said, then turned to his . . . whoever. "Jen, this is Anne. We went out a zillion years ago, in college."

"Hi," I said, and shook her soft hand. To Justin I offered a limp, "Merry Christmas."

"Isn't it just *crazy* in here today?" Jen asked me, trying way too hard to be the poster woman for well-adjusted-girl-meeting-boyfriend's-ex. "But the sales are ridiculous. And I just can't resist a deal."

"Yeah," I said, shaking inside from adrenaline. "Ridiculous."

She had a set of pajamas slung over her arm and held them up. "I'm just gonna try these on. Excuse me," she added with a smile, and headed for the changing room.

"Wow," Justin said as she left. "Home to see your folks?"

"Yup." I turned back to the racks, pretending to seek my size from a lineup of bras. Anxiety was welling in me, hot and frightening, mixing with anger until I was molten. I'd always known I'd feel something, the next time I ran into this boy . . . but this was something else. This was a volcano. A natural disaster churning in my body.

"She's seems real nice," I offered, my face burning crimson to rival the store decorations.

"Yeah, she's great."

"Great. I'm glad . . . Try not to get drunk and beat the shit out of her." I froze but for the tremors quaking through me, and my eyes locked on his. I didn't know which of us was more shocked by what I'd said. I'd slapped myself with my own words. With all the hatred that had suddenly breached a dam in my gut.

Justin stared, looking slapped, himself. "Jesus, Anne."

I shook my head. "Whatever." I wasn't after a fight. Just a release. A way to vent the ugliness I was drowning in.

"I was just a kid back then," he said.

"So was I. Didn't stop you from hitting me, though."

"I was dumb," he said, sounding sad. "You were right to call me on it. I've never done anything like that since. The way you ended things . . . it was a real wake-up call."

"I didn't want to be your *wake-up call*. I wanted to be your girlfriend." I turned back to the piles of holiday-themed panties. Fuck me, this was surreal.

"I'm sorry."

I looked up at that. I'd wanted to hear that for a long time. A *long* time. Had thought it might heal me some. But no, nothing. "I have a boyfriend," I told him, mouth still on autopilot.

"Oh. Well, good."

236

"And if I asked him to, he'd break your jaw."

Justin's eyes widened at that, then panned the vicinity.

"He's not here," I said, suddenly more annoyed than angry. "He's in Michigan. But if I asked him to, he'd drive straight down to this mall and beat the holy hell out of you."

"Jesus, Anne. What the fuck?"

"But he'd never lay a hand on *me*," I told him quietly, leaving the rest of the store to imagine we were chatting about New Year's plans. "Because he's a good man. A man, period. Unlike you were, back then. And I wouldn't ask him to fuck you up, not even if he was standing right next to me now. Because I'm sick to death of hating you. It's so *fucking* tedious, you have no idea."

"I'm just gonna go," he began, but then Jen was walking back toward us. She was empty-handed, and she shrugged dramatically to illustrate her defeat in the dressing room.

"Well," I said to Justin. "Nice running into you." And to Jen, "Good luck with the sales."

"You, too."

"You seem real sweet," I added, my tone strange and grave, matching the crazy swirling in my gut. It wasn't lost on her. She smiled tightly. "Oh. Thanks. You, too."

"You make sure this one here treats you right," I said, and shot Justin a look. Faced with awkward smiles from the pair of them, I abandoned the two red bras I was holding on a pile of panties. "Y'all have a happy New Year." And I marched myself straight out the door.

I was crying by the time I dialed Eric from the driver's seat of my mom's car.

"Pick up," I burbled at the receiver. "Pick up, pick up—"

"Hey, you. Sorry about last night—"

And then I was straight-up sobbing. Throat aching, eyes burning.

"Jesus, Annie. You crying?"

"Yuh," I managed.

"Baby, what's wrong?" I could practically hear him leaning forward, see his brows knitting. "Where are you?"

"I just ran into my ex-boyfriend at the mall," I mewled, sounding ridiculous.

Eric's tone went hard and cold. "He say something to upset you?"

"No."

"Okay. Good. Did you even talk to him?"

"I told—" A hiccup cut me off. "I told him if I wanted, I could get you to break his jaw."

The huff of an incredulous laugh. "Oh. Well, that was . . . assertive."

"I'm so sorry," I sobbed, uncovering the crux of what had me so upset.

"What for?"

"For treating you like . . . like some weapon I've got stashed in my glove box."

"Wait. You're crying because you feel bad about what you said?"

"I think so," I gurgled, dabbing my runny nose with my sleeve.

Another soft laugh. "You know I'd do that, though. If you asked."

"But I'd hate it if you did. Oh *God*, I'm terrible."

"Hey, calm down. You're not terrible. You just got freaked out and said something kinda psycho."

I laugh-sobbed at that. "Yes, I did."

"It's okay. Everybody does it now and then."

"Do they?"

"Everybody I know, anyhow. Listen, Annie."

"Yeah?"

"Don't you ever feel bad about wanting to use me like that. Guys like me haven't got all that much to offer, so it's nice to be needed for what we do have."

"Shut up. You have tons to offer."

"Well, I'm glad you think so."

"I'm in love with you," I blurted out.

Dead silence for two seconds, three, four . . . A sharp exhale.

"Eric?"

"You mean that?"

I nodded, as if he could see. "Yes. I do mean it." All at once, my throat opened like a plucked bow, breaths coming smooth and easy.

More silence, then finally, "Wow. Thank you."

I giggled, feeling drunk. "You're welcome. Thank you for making me feel it." For making me feel so many things again.

A noisy sigh. "Goddamn it. Why the fuck are you so far away? I always imagined if you decided you loved me, we'd be in a position to celebrate it."

"I'll be home tomorrow night."

"Flight six-ten, landing at nine fifty-five," he confirmed. "I'll be waiting."

"Oh—I messed up my quest to buy red underwear. That's where I was when . . . You know."

"Wait. So this asshole wrecked my Christmas present?"

"Or I did."

"I'm definitely breaking his jaw now."

I worked hard not to laugh. "That isn't funny."

"You already home?"

"No, I'm in the mall parking lot . . . I guess I could hike up my big-girl pants and go back inside and try again."

"You could."

I sank back against the seat. "Yeah. And I should."

239

"Not red, though," he said.

"Okay. What color then, personal stylist?"

"Surprise me. Whatever you want me taking off you tomorrow night. Now that you love me."

My smile was huge and shaky. "Okay."

"You read my email yet?"

"No. What happened last night, anyway?"

"We'll talk about that when you're back. For now, buy some sexy underwear, go home, have a glass of wine way too early in the day, then read my letter. Okay? Forget that guy. And forget feeling bad about what you said to him."

"Good plan."

"I have to head out now. Got a gig clearing some of the municipal lots."

"Oh, you got the snow you'd been hoping for? Good for you. It's dry as a bone here. Low fifties."

He laughed. "Rub it in, why don't you?"

"Thanks for letting me sob in your ear," I said. "I um . . . I love you."

A warm *hmm*. "I could get used to hearing you say that."

"Good. Do."

"I love you, too. Talk to you soon."

"Bye."

I did exactly as he'd prescribed. Marched back into the mall, and found the most perfect set of underwear possible in Macy's—sky blue with a garden's worth of little watercolor flowers. I'd been destined for the purchase, really, driven away from those adequate-yet-all-wrong red bras by Justin. I was home by eleven and had a nice lunch with my folks, without mentioning what had happened at the mall. Afterward I went for a drive with my dad, and let him do what he loved most—explain to me all of the incredibly boring construction projects going on around town. The old-man equivalent of gossip. We swung by his favorite truck stop, and it felt just like the old days, cruising around on The Hunt. Except my cup held coffee now, not cocoa.

We headed toward Mount Pleasant, and on Route 526 we passed a crew spread out along the median in orange jumpsuits.

"No rest for the wicked," my dad said.

I bit my lip. *I'm dating one of them*, I imagined telling him. The omission was beginning to weigh on me.

"I look at those sorts of guys all different now," I offered. "Since I've been working with so many inmates. They used to seem two-dimensional to me. I barely noticed them. Or if I did, I thought, 'Good. That's what you get, criminals.' But now they're just like regular people."

"Regular people with a lot to answer for," my dad said mildly.

"Yeah, I know. But they've all got hopes and plans and regrets, just like everybody else." *And I'm in love with one of them. And he loves me back.*

My dad didn't seem especially piqued by the topic, and he pointed to an approaching overpass. "See this here? They're going to be closing that bridge next summer for structural repairs. They say it'll take two months, but mark my words, it'll be closer to six."

I sighed to myself, my chance at confession gone. I settled back in the seat, sipping my coffee, and let my dad discuss the things that moved him most.

Back home, I continued following Eric's instructions.

Have a glass of wine way too early in the day.

At three thirty I poured myself a healthy dose of merlot and carried it and my phone up to my parents' big bathroom and turned on the whirlpool tub. As it filled, I found Eric's email, heart suddenly pounding, just as it had with those paper letters. I set my phone on the tub's wide rim and lit my mom's candles, shut off the lights.

I eased into the hot water, closed my eyes and adjusted. With a deep exhale I pushed out all my angst from the drama at the mall, and let Justin go for good. Let my anger go. Made room for way better emotions, spurred by a man worthy of inspiring them.

And after drying my hands, I picked up my phone and read.

Darling . . . Oh, the things those seven little letters did to me.

> You're in the air right now, headed someplace warm. Can't tell you how jealous I am. But at least you left me with plenty of memories in the meantime. My bedroom's suddenly a lot less depressing since you came to see me here, slept next to me in this bed. I can even smell you in my sheets. Or I tell myself I can.
>
> I was never the kind of guy who wrote love letters before I met you. Hell, I was never the kind of guy who wrote, period. Now it feels like something I can't imagine living without, when you're not here. It's so humbling, good-humbling, all the little ways you've changed me. And thank God for email. This is so goddamn much faster than how I used to write you, on that machine then copied out by hand. I'd get cramps from all that writing. I don't think I ever told you that. I liked it, though. Felt sweet. Does that feel like years ago to you now? When we wrote those secret letters? It does to me. Crazy that it's only been weeks.
>
> I can't imagine what my life would be like if I didn't have you, now that I'm out. Depressing, probably. Empty. Looking forward to seeing you and remembering stuff we did gets me

through my workdays. And being with you for real makes these long, dark nights so much warmer. It's like a little trip to summer in that bed with you.

Everything that we've done, since we got together . . . It's so much better than I ever guessed, back then. And so much better that it's all happened how it did, painful as those first few weeks were. But if that's how it had to go down for you to trust my intentions, then I wouldn't change a thing.

I wonder where you are, as you're reading this. Maybe standing outside the airport, waiting for your ride. Or maybe in bed. I wish I knew how to picture where you're staying. So maybe I could picture myself there with you.

It's late, and I need to get to sleep soon. Lucky I've got you to think about. After I send this I'm going to get into my sheets and fist myself, imagine it's you touching me. Imagine you're on top of me, maybe. Picture your naked body, and the way you look in the light of my reading lamp. Now that I know for real. I'll say your name when I come, then drop off to sleep and dream about you. If I dream at all. Sometimes you send me to sleep so satisfied, it's like my brain goes totally blank. Like a cloudless day. You probably don't know how that feels to a man who spent five years caged in with so much light and noise and anger. To feel that peaceful and cleaned out. But you make me feel it, just from thinking about you.

Hope you sleep well, maybe even dream about me. Miss you already.

Yours,

Eric

I set my phone on the ledge and sank deep into the hot, jittery water, submerging all but my nose and mouth. The world became a garbled, echoing rush, like the physical chaos

243

of an orgasm made audio. I wished Eric were here with me so badly, it hurt. His big body in this tub, talented fingertips turning pruny from spoiling me, below the surface.

I let my own fingertips play his part, and when I came the world was all warm water churning around me, thoughts of Eric's warm body rushing in and out of mine.

When I rose from the tub on wobbly legs, I realized I'd not so much as sipped my wine.

With that man in my blood, no drink in the world stood a chance at getting me even half as high.

Chapter Sixteen

My flight into Detroit arrived early—but Eric was earlier. I spotted him by the baggage claim just as I was pulling out my phone to text him.

Like my childhood home feeling strangely small after all those months away, Eric felt extra big as his arms wrapped around me. Solid and warm and awesome. I was smiling so broadly as we stepped apart, I had to bite my lip.

"Hi," I said, feeling pleasantly shy.

"Welcome home."

Was that where I was? Home? Or was home the place I'd just come from? All I knew was that no matter how ill-fitting Michigan sometimes felt, this man was so damn right.

As we wandered close to the conveyer belt, I said, "Thanks for coming all this way. Saved me loads on parking."

"Best two hours I've spent lately."

I spied my bag coming around on the carousel. I yanked it off, but Eric took it from me before I could even retract the handle. He carried it by the strap like it weighed nothing.

The cold hit me hard as the sliding doors parted and we

hurried to the short-term lot. He let me in first then stowed my bag behind the seat. I rubbed my arms against the chill, remembering it wasn't about to get any warmer in this truck.

"That's what I should've gotten you for Christmas," I said as he buckled up and started the engine.

"What's that?"

"I should have paid to get your heater fixed."

The dash lit up with the headlights, illuminating his smile. "What I need's a new goddamn truck. All the stuff that's screaming to be replaced in this thing . . . Even doing what I can myself, it'd be cheaper to buy a new ride. Well, new to me. Something used, but decent. But not 'til my fines are paid off."

Even if I could afford to front him the money—which I couldn't—he never would have accepted it, so I didn't bother voicing my desire to do so. Instead I asked, "What'd I miss in Darren?"

"Whole lot of the same old nothing. Plus a big drug bust over on Chestnut, the day before Christmas. Oxy racket, the news said, down near the south end of the old plant. Cousins'll be getting some new recruits soon enough."

"Yuck. Glad they're off the streets, anyhow."

He didn't reply, and I realized what I'd said.

"Sorry. I didn't mean that about criminals in general. About what you did. That the more men who get locked up, the better, or—"

"Didn't think you did. Plus I've never once claimed I didn't deserve the time I did."

"Okay. Good, I guess. Drugs are different, anyhow. They hurt vulnerable people. Doesn't sound like the guy you hurt was much of a victim."

"Nope." He said it curtly, but without angst.

"He was on drugs, you said?"

246

"Amphetamines. Not that he was some innocent, the way he got swept up in it."

My stomach curdled a little as I remembered Eric owed me some answers. "So. What was that call on Christmas night about, the one that interrupted our fun? Family stuff?"

"Yeah," he said through a sigh. "Yeah, family shit."

"Who called?"

"My sister."

"And is everything okay, or . . . ?"

A long pause, his eyes locked on the road, unblinking.

"Eric?"

"I dunno, Annie. I don't know if everything's gonna be okay or not."

I felt chilly all at once, and tugged my hat down over my ears. "How come? What's going on?"

"It's nothing you need to get worried about."

"If it's something that's upsetting you, then yeah, it is. Tell me."

He shifted in his seat like a weary old man, and when he spoke, his voice was fifty pounds heavier. "He's getting paroled. The guy who assaulted my sister."

My body went cold. Colder than the air in the cab. Colder than the wind rushing by on the highway. "Oh. When?"

"Second week of January."

"And . . . ?"

He met my eyes for a split second. "And I dunno. Don't know if he's planning on coming back to town—to Kernsville. Don't know if he's got anything to say to me or her. If he's been well-behaved enough to get released, maybe he's okay. But then who knows if his attitude might just change if he gets back on the crank. I got a whole lot of questions, and no answers."

"Is your sister freaked out?"

247

"Oh yeah. But I'll tell it to you like I did to her—there's no guarantee this asshole wants anything to do with any of us anymore. Hardly any of the shitheads he used to hang with back home are still around, and he pissed just about everybody else off, one way or another. It's bad news, but there's not much good in worrying about the worst-case scenarios."

"Are you going to do anything? Like, go home to Kernsville when he's let out, just in case?"

"I imagine so. He's out on a Tuesday. I'll probably see what days I can trade around to try to go over there the next weekend."

"Are you allowed to even be around him, after what you did to get convicted?"

A soft huff of a laugh. "Course not."

My dread warmed over, heating to become anger. "You can't go, then. You can't violate your parole over this guy."

"My sister asks me to, then yeah, I will, Annie." Another glance. "I'm sorry."

"If your sister asks you to, that's pretty fucking selfish of her. Plus that must be a part of *his* parole—not going near your sister."

Eric shook his head. "He got put away for drug offenses. My sister never reported her attack."

"*What?*"

"Her business is her business. That's how she thinks of it."

"Jesus."

A long, long pause. He blinked at the slice of highway illuminated by the headlights. His nostrils flared. "I can't get into this with you. But my family's safety is more important to me than my own skin. So's yours, for that matter. You can argue with me all you want, but you're not going to change my mind."

248

I hissed a sigh, a kettle spewing steam. "If you ever did this for me—risked your neck or your future like this—I'd leave you. I'd *never* ask you to make that choice. And I'd be pissed to hell if you made it against my wishes."

"And I'd rather live without you than let somebody hurt you. There's fundamental differences in the way you and I see things, sweetheart."

Sweetheart. He'd called me that before, but this time there was the slightest patronizing edge to it. The sound of him digging in his heels. Dismissing my point of view. I didn't know what to say, so I just twisted the end of my scarf in my lap, felt the sting of my knuckles going white.

After what felt like an hour, he asked softly, "You gonna leave me if I go home the week after next?"

The world went very quiet and still, my body following suit.

"Annie?"

The question hadn't even gelled in my mind, but it was a good one. A *terrifying* one. "I don't know."

"Don't make me choose between my sister and you. It's not fair. There's no right answer in that."

"I don't want you to choose me—I want you to choose *you*. And what's best for you. Why don't you . . . Why don't you invite your sister to Darren, that week? And get somebody back in your hometown to tell you if the guy shows up or whatever?"

"She won't come."

I got so mad then, I could just about scream through my teeth. I was really beginning to hate his sister. Like, *hate* her. "Then she's being selfish."

"Probably."

"I want to talk to her," I said, though in truth the idea scared me shitless. I wanted to punch her, too, but in reality there was no way I was probably ever doing either.

249

"Not happening," he concurred. "Anyhow, she won't listen to whatever you have to say. My sister doesn't listen to anybody. Not even me."

"She can't really care about you, if she's willing to put your fucking freedom at risk over this."

"Nobody cares about me as much as my sister does," he said, tone stiff.

"I beg to differ." I wanted to think *I* cared more about him, but I couldn't make this into some unwinnable, petty contest. Instead I said, "That's not what family does to each other."

"Keeping each other safe is what my family does. I failed at that six years ago. No way I'm taking that chance again."

"She's not returning the favor, Eric. If you get arrested for a parole violation, or worse . . . What good are you to her then?"

"Annie, we're getting this blown way out of proportion. I'm just going over there to see my family. The fact that I'm not risking my job—ditching shifts to run over there the second he's released—should be proof I've gotten some better boundaries since before I got locked up."

I sighed, fuming.

"Chances are good this guy won't want anything to do with us. He's a coward. He's not after another beat-down from me, and my sister didn't press charges, so he's got nothing to take revenge on her for. Somebody else got him locked away. It's all just a precaution, okay? I'm not an idiot. I'm not going to be doing anything rough unless I absolutely have to."

"Fuck . . ."

"Listen, sweetheart. I love you. But you don't know me as well as you want to think you do."

My mouth dropped open and I stared at him, feeling slapped. He caught it.

"Sorry. I don't mean that you don't know me at all, but this stuff . . . You don't understand me, I can tell. Or what all this means to me."

"No. I don't." *Because it's insane.*

"I wish you'd just trust me. And the decisions I make."

"I wish you understood how ridiculous this is, that you're even *considering* going home."

He didn't reply, a tendon along his jaw tensing in the glow of the dash.

I turned away, attention on the distant lights. Christ, this was going to be a long-ass drive.

When we finally made it to the outskirts of Darren, I had no clue to what to expect from our good-night. Would I just say thank you for the ride, and that would be that? Were we still . . . good?

It was killing me, not knowing. Killing me how quickly we'd gone from warm embrace to cold shoulder. After everything we'd weathered since he'd gotten out, and how close we'd gotten this past week and a half, I'd thought we were rock solid, but now . . . Now I couldn't feel anything from Eric. Like our frequency had gone dead, a wire snipped by my near ultimatum. It hurt as much as a fist around my heart.

"What's going to happen when we get to my place?" I asked, the first words to fall between us in an hour or more.

"What do you mean?"

"Are you just going to drop me off or . . . ?"

"What do you want me to do?"

Christ, always with the *what-did-I-want*. "What do *you* want?" I countered. Much as I'd once needed his deference, right now I was sick to goddamn death of it.

"I want what you want," he said, sounding tired but stubborn, and inside I screamed.

We reached my block and he parked up in front of the bar. He switched off the engine and met my eyes in the streetlight and neon. "I don't want to go without us knowing where we stand with all this. Whether that means we sit in here, freezing our asses off all night, or if you invite me up."

"Come up."

He seemed surprised by my decisiveness. "Okay, then."

We slammed our doors. He carried my bag and I got us into the foyer, no words exchanged until we were inside the apartment.

"Something to drink?" I asked.

"Nah. Thanks." His gaze was moving around the living room—nervous, I thought. Fearful. Like maybe he wondered if this was the last time he'd be invited here.

"I hate this," I admitted. "Are we having a fight?"

"Nobody's shouted yet."

I took off my coat, slung it over the back of the couch then sank onto a cushion with a frustrated sigh. I let my head fall into my hands. Let this man see how I felt. How he made me feel.

He said, "I dunno what to tell you." I sensed his shadow as he sat on the coffee table. "I'd be lying if I said I wasn't planning to go back that weekend. And I won't lie to you, not ever again. Not after I almost lost you, being too chicken-shit to tell you I was getting out."

"It's not about lying or not lying." I raised my head to meet his eyes. "It's about . . . priorities, I guess."

"I love you," he said quietly. "I hope you believe that. But I love my family, too, and I'm going to be there when they need me. When they *ask* me. You can't make me choose. You don't have to like it, but you *can't* make me choose. I'm sorry. I can't tell you what you want to hear from me right now."

I shook my head, frustrated to the bone. "No, I guess not."

252

"You gonna break up with me?"

I rubbed the spot over my heart. "Jesus, Eric."

His voice got real quiet. "I hope you won't. I won't lie to try to keep you with me, and I won't set my family aside for it, either. But I don't want to lose you, believe me." He reached down and took one of my hands in both of his, squeezing my fingers with his big ones. "It'd rip me apart."

"I feel like I don't get a say."

He smiled sadly. "It's not your problem, or your family. So no, you don't."

"But you're my . . . *Are* you my boyfriend?"

"I am if you want me to be. But no, you still don't get a say. The last thing I want is for you to get tangled up in all this bull."

I dropped my head again, groaned, and let him hear exactly how bad I wanted to strangle him at that moment.

"Sorry," he said softly.

"I'm really, *really* annoyed with you."

"I know. I'm pretty annoyed with you."

This wasn't getting sorted out tonight, that much was clear. I was thinking in circles, trudging around and around this stubborn rock of a man, getting no place. "Can we just hit Pause on this for now? Until after New Year's?"

"Sure. Just don't get your hopes up that I'll change my mind by then."

I stared at him, long and hard. "You'd hurt my ex, if I asked you to."

He nodded. "Yeah. I would."

"Why won't you just *not* hurt this other asshole, if I asked you? What's the difference, if both things matter so much to me?"

"Because this asshole didn't hurt you. He hurt Kristina."

"If she told you not to come, would you do what she said?"

He nodded.

"So I'm wasting my energy arguing with the wrong person."

"I guess," he conceded. "But stubbornness runs in my family like brown eyes and bad backs, if you're thinking about talking to her. In any case, enough for tonight. Okay?"

I exhaled, long and weary. "Okay. But I'm still annoyed with you."

"Cousins kinda gave me a high threshold for simmering conflicts," he said with a little smirk. "I can handle that."

I eyed his boots and coat.

"You want me to go?" he asked.

"No. I don't." I wanted him here. If I was stuck feeling all this anger and uncertainty and . . . and helplessness, I at least wanted the comfort of his body with me. And maybe not only comfort. Maybe the release. A chance to take all this aggression I felt toward him and *do* something with it. Something if not productive, then at least entertaining.

"Take your boots off," I said. When he set them aside, his socked feet flexing, I said, "Take off your coat." It hit the cushion beside me. "Take off your sweater . . . Your socks . . . Take off your shirt."

He was standing now, stripping away his undershirt with a slow, smooth pull, staring down at me. I got to my feet. As I stroked his arms, his chest, his throat, he merely watched, hands at his sides. I let my palms roam low, all the way down his belly, and twined my fingers around his thick belt.

"Thought you were pissed at me," he murmured, and his voice gave him away. Light words not matching the weighty pitch of his excitement.

"I am." Fingers still wrapped around his belt, I took a step back. Another. Led him all the way to my bedroom then turned him around. He matched my paces until I had him backed against the bed. I let him go, gave him a soft push.

254

He dropped onto the mattress with a bounce, a smile hiding behind his lips in the ambient light.

I stripped. Not down to the beautiful matching floral bra and panties I'd bought for this, our supposed romantic reunion. I stripped instead down to my crappy travel underwear—a tired old beige bra and navy boy shorts one level nicer than ones I might wear during my period.

Tonight wasn't about seduction, or exploration, or indulgence. Tonight, I wasn't after a man who'd uncover all my desires and shape himself to meet them.

Tonight I was after something I'd never have guessed I'd want: a man's aggression, aimed right at me.

And I wanted it so bad it hurt.

Chapter Seventeen

What do you need?

I saw the question in his dark eyes, in that dim room, but for once he didn't give it voice.

Perhaps he could sense it was the last thing I wanted right now—to be catered to. To be granted whatever I wished of his body, while I was still pissed that my wishes regarding his actions were falling on such willfully deaf ears.

I ditched my bra and panties, and straddled him there at the edge of the mattress. Heat bloomed at the sensation of his clothed thighs against my bare ones, but this fire was more than mere lust.

Those big hands kept me in place, firm at my waist, while our kiss was anything but steady. His hair was between my fingers, our mouths clashing, tongues fighting. Against my naked sex, he was hard, erection pressing into me along with his fly and belt buckle. I felt aggression in him, but no anger. In my own body I felt the anger. The frustration. Resentment. And it felt goddamn good, rubbing right up against his cock.

I wanted him now, now. But more than that, I wanted him

to take control for once. We kissed for ages, well past the point when I felt the wetness between my skin and his fly, well past the point when I might normally have invited him to take things further. We kissed until my lips were tender and my core was aching, until he had to be in pain, taunted by long minutes of stifled friction.

Then finally, just as I was ready to claw him from the wanting, he made a move.

His hands gripped my butt, and he heaved me bodily to the side, onto the covers. Grabbed one of my ankles and hauled my legs wide so he could kneel between them. He worked at his buckle, forearms flexing, and it was the hottest thing I'd ever seen—him sliding that thick length of leather out and tossing it to the floor. A button was freed, a zipper lowered. He shoved his jeans down just enough to frame his straining cock in black cotton, and then that big body was descending on mine.

I'd missed his voice all that time we'd kissed, and he gave it to me now. Not in words—not in the usual requests to hear my desires—but in moans. Rough ones, grunting sounds that steamed against my throat in time with his flexing hips. He taunted me with his cock, every inch as hard as I'd ever felt it, his shorts growing wet from me. I felt his zipper, too, just a hint, and the thick denim of his fly teased my labia.

I wasn't going to give him anything—not a request, not a plea, not an order. Nothing more than my grasping hands on his arms and back, irrefutable proof that I wanted this. But as for what shape *this* would take? He was in charge of that.

He was always taking me where I wanted to go. In this bed. In his truck, to the lake on that moonlit night, or to the airport, wherever I asked. I didn't want a chauffeur tonight. I wanted a *kidnapper*. Needed him to grab me and take me where *he* ached to be, and show me he trusted that I could

257

take it. I needed him selfish. But that meant I couldn't tell him so.

His body was like I'd never felt it. Hard all over, from his thighs through his belly, to his shoulders, all down his locked arms—like I'd seen it from my office window at Cousins, those times I'd secretly watched him. The groans warming my skin were nearing a crescendo, and I could finally hear what I wanted from him. That same frustration I felt.

A rasp of teeth at my jaw, then a growl. "Where are they?"

I nearly came from that alone.

"The drawer," I said, and waved a hand toward my bedside table.

He leaned way over and when the reading lamp came on, I studied the muscles that moved along his side, beneath his ribs. Watched him breathe. The rustle of cardboard and a rip of plastic brought my attention to his hands.

He sat back on his heels, wrapped condom between his lips. He shoved his jeans to the tops of his thighs, thumbs dragging his shorts down with them. His arousal stood between us, a welcome threat. I could see his heartbeat there in tiny tics as he got the wrapper opened. Under my palms, through the denim, his thighs were hot and hard as rocks baking in the sun.

I watched this man sheath himself. He'd never looked stronger, or bigger, or more dangerous, and I'd never wanted him so badly . . . Yet I could never have been with him like this, those first few times. He'd earned it with all that deference and care. And I'd earned it by giving him the chance to make me trust him.

He rolled the condom flush to his base and gripped himself there. "You want me all pissed off, don't you?"

My lips parted, but no reply came.

"Fine," he spat, and moved to the side, freeing my legs "Turn over."

258

I did, settling on my hands and knees, heart thumping hard with excitement, nerves, everything.

He was against me in a breath—cock and hand between my thighs, the other palm on my butt. The penetration couldn't have been rough if he'd wanted it to be; I was too wet.

He drove in deep and smooth, all the way, moaning as his hips met my ass. I felt both hands at my waist, trembling faintly, then all at once, he found his self-control. He planted his knees a bit wider, the fronts of his thighs brushing the backs of mine. One broad palm slid to my shoulder. It curled tight, holding me in a way that brought fire to my cheeks and an ache to my sex.

His thrusts began. Slow and mean, punctuated by a rough little thump each time our bodies met. A thump, and a grunt. I was silent, so focused on how he felt. His jeans slipped lower, bunching against the backs of my legs. I could've killed for a view of that—of impatience personified, of his gorgeous bare ass, denim pooled around his strong thighs.

It didn't feel impersonal this way, not as I might have guessed. As intimate as if we were staring into one another's eyes. I missed his voice, though.

Until it cut through the darkness and straight into my core.

"This what you need tonight?" he asked, words stilted by the impact.

"Why's it always about what I need?"

"Because that's what gets me off, Annie. Being what you need." One hand slid around my hip, dipping low, fingertips tickling my mound then finding my clit.

I sucked a raw breath, head dropping from the shock of it. "I need . . ."

"Yeah?" Those lethal fingers moved in tight, cruel circles. I swore, lost in the pleasure.

"Tell me. Tell me what you need."

"I need to . . ." I wasn't even sure how to put it into words. He slowed behind me then stopped, and his fingers became nothing more than a warm weight against my clit. The other hand was tender, stroking me from my ribs to my thigh, calming the frustration building inside me. As always, just what I needed.

He let me go, sliding out slowly. "Turn over."

I did. And *that* was what I needed, really. An order. A sense that I was his, not the other way around.

I lay back as he got his jeans kicked away, then he brought us together on our sides, his sheathed cock hot against my belly. Only that part of him felt impatient, the rest of him perfectly placid. He stroked my hair and touched the tip of his nose to mine.

"I don't feel right about this," he murmured, "with us angry."

"I do. I want you that way."

"Why?"

"I . . . Because I want to know what you feel like when you're not just . . . catering to me. I want to know how you feel when you're selfish."

He brushed his lips over mine. "You afraid of what you might find?"

I shook my head against the pillow, more certain about that answer than anything else we'd discussed this evening. "No. I'm not."

"You get to see that, sometimes, me being selfish. After I've gotten you off."

"But never before."

"That's just how it works," he whispered. "Ladies first."

"Says who?"

He blinked. "Manners."

I sighed, head sinking deep into the pillow.

260

He traced my ear. "What, baby?"

"Fuck, I don't even know."

"You want to see me angry?"

"Yeah."

"To prove what? That I'll never hurt you, the way he did?"

"No. I already know that."

"To prove I won't hurt you, the way I hurt that piece of shit back home?"

"No, of course not. Just show me something . . . something more than just how . . . How fucking *good* you are."

What the hell was wrong with me, needing proof of an ex-con's flaws? Or maybe that was the disconnect. Maybe this fight had driven home for me exactly how vast the divide was between this man and the one who'd committed that crime. Or maybe . . .

Or maybe, I wanted proof that this man could do something just for himself. He doled out pleasure for me, vengeance for his family. Maybe I wanted another taste of the man who'd come on to me in Cousins, surrounded by guards and cameras and prying eyes. Who'd wanted something badly enough to put us both at risk to get at it.

"Please," I said softly. "Let me see you angry." So much for driving him to selfishness. This was still all about me getting what I asked for.

"I'll give you what you want," Eric said softly. "But I won't pretend I understand it."

"I don't understand it, myself. But yeah. Give me that." *Give me what I feared you maybe wanted from me, way back when we met; feared even as if thrilled me.* "Be greedy. Use me."

"I won't hurt you."

"I'm not asking you to. Just do what *you* want—what you'd do if you just needed to get off."

261

Sounding resigned, he took a deep breath.

I touched his hair, slipping a curl behind his ear. "It's what I want, okay?"

He kissed me in response. First a soft flirtation of lips, then deeper. Far deeper. I felt my body being turned, the cool covers finding my back, but our mouths stayed sealed together. Between us he was touching himself, rousing his cock or checking the condom. His breath flared as he shoved a leg between mine, then the other. He let my mouth go to sit back on his heels. For a long moment he stared down at me, his body looming even curled in on itself, hands resting on his thighs, chin dipped. I quashed an urge to ask if he was upset.

His hands slid to my knees and he raised his head, taking me in. My sex first, then upward, along my belly and breasts to my face. I let him study whatever it was he was after, trying to pinpoint the look in his eyes. Not hunger . . . not that primal. Some sort of fascination, as though he were searching for something.

"I only know one way to make this all about me," he said.

"Okay."

He left the bed, stripping the condom as he strode to my dresser. The vanity mirror pivoted on its stand, and Eric tilted it down. Beyond his shoulder I saw myself, sitting on the bed.

He climbed onto the end of the mattress, kneeling in profile to the watching mirror, and gripped his cock, stroking softly. Those dark eyes caught mine, and he nodded to the covers before him.

With the condom gone, I could guess what he needed. I came to him, sitting on my hip. Brought my face close. He smelled of latex faintly, and far more potently of sex. From so near, I could make out the way his hand trembled, wrapped around his shaft. He gave himself a long, slow stroke.

"This used to be my favorite thing," he murmured, eyes

moving over my face. "When I was younger. Before I cared so much about what a woman wants. Before I got put away and realized how much I'd missed out on, thinking sex was all about getting my own needs met. Back when I didn't know shit."

"I want it to be all about you, tonight." Like that letter he'd written, the one where he'd told me what he'd imagined for his birthday.

"Suck me, then."

The shiver that roused was so deep, it shut my eyes. I opened them, finding him still stroking, still waiting. Ready—a droplet glinting at his crown. I braced myself on my forearm, reaching for him with my other hand. His own hand moved, circling in a lazy frame at the root, presenting his cock. I felt a warm weight on my head, fingers in my hair. Things I'd fantasized about—things I'd felt with him before, even, yet it took my breath away. A new act entirely.

"Taste me."

I did. Brought his head to my lips and lapped him, the flavor pungent from the rubber and lube. It faded with the next pass and the next, until it was Eric, only Eric.

"More."

I gave it. I took him between my lips, welcomed the first couple of inches only to be given a measure more, courtesy of his hips. Not enough to gag me, but plenty to catch me off guard. Yet I'd asked for this. For my catering lover to get pushy. So whatever was in store for me, I welcomed it.

The hand on my head was restless, fingertips rubbing my scalp, palm urging me to take more. Just as I got into the rhythm he was setting, the next correction came.

"Harder."

The word had my throat tightening, but I obeyed, rewarded by a harsh gasp from above. I stole a peek, but didn't find his eyes on me—not directly. On the mirror. At the pornography we were making together . . . or that I was making for him.

"Suck me harder."

I don't know why that excited me, but it did. I'd needed this man's gentleness for so long, in order to trust him. Now that the trust was implicit as a natural law, I wanted the opposite. To explore a man's cruder desires, maybe. To explore the rougher aspects of maleness that I'd been so scared of, for so long. Maybe somewhere along the way, I'd turned terror into taboo. Whatever the reason, feeling a man's bossy hand on my head and sensing his stare refracted off that mirror . . . I could have been getting head myself, for all the fire I felt between my legs.

"Yeah," he muttered, fingers tightening around my hair. "Suck me." His hips began to make demands, thrusting faintly. I could feel the change in him, like clouds drawn over the sun. Felt him shift from excited to crass in a near instant.

I worked to find the best position, to take what he was feeding me, to keep the suction up, keep my teeth covered, keep from gagging. The hand making a ring at his base dipped lower, three fingers seeming to press along his balls.

What did he see in that mirror? His younger self, getting serviced by some anonymous girl? Or was the muscle and the ink too much to edit out?

Maybe he saw us as we were. Maybe he saw through the gruffness of it—saw himself giving me what I'd asked for. Was that what he wanted right now, despite the role he'd adopted? To please me?

"Deeper," he breathed.

Deeper now meant as deep as he could go. Beyond the point where I was giving pleasure, beyond the point where I could act as anything more than a vessel. I hadn't done this in ages—

264

let a man in my throat. I couldn't say I'd ever done it especially willingly. I'd had it sprung on me, and I'd submitted, thinking maybe this was simply what oral was. I'd never made a craft of it. I'd endured it only, feeling ugly—my face sometimes left beet red from the gagging, snot making it difficult to breathe.

For Eric, I'd do more than endure. I'd invite him there, not merely suffer the intrusion. But that required some honesty. I drew back, against the urging of the hand on my head, and he slipped free.

"I'm not good at this," I told him, finding his eyes on my face from miles above. "At going deep. But I want to be, for you. So just go slow at first."

A single nod, though his lips parted and closed and he swallowed. He was holding back words. Reassurances, probably, or an offer to rescind the request. They never came. Instead he said only, "Get on the floor."

I did so on shaky, half-asleep legs, then he tossed me a pillow for my knees and came around the side of the bed.

"I do anything you can't handle," he said, "you just pull away. Okay?"

"Okay."

"We'll just try, real slow." He reached for the mirror, tilting it way down, framing whatever he saw from so high above me. "You see if you can find a good angle. If you do, then maybe I'll speed up. But anytime it gets to be too much, you give me any sign at all and I'll stop."

"I know you will."

"Good." He stroked my hair lovingly, then the hand I'd put on his hip. "Now suck me."

I took him in my mouth once more, so much easier on my knees.

"Nice and hard. Good . . . Goddamn, I think you like that, sometimes."

I told him with my mouth, *I fucking love it*.

"Yeah. Fuck. Do it like you want, baby. Get comfortable, then I'll show you another way."

For a minute or more I took him for myself, using my lips and tongue and hand, showing him my hunger. Slowly, so slowly, he joined in with his thrusts, stealing the reins. As he fed me more, I grew passive. Eventually both his hands were on my head, cradling, then holding me still.

"You're doing so good," he moaned. "You're perfect."

It wasn't easy. It wasn't pleasurable, not physically. But there was something about it, something about the surrender and the submission, the servitude, that turned me on. Something about feeling used by him . . . feeling dirty, little more than a stranger.

His hips sped. I gagged, but only softly. No stinging in my sinuses or tears ducts like I'd felt with other guys, no burn in my cheeks. No suffocation. Only the dark, thrilling size of him, filling me in such a threatening way. His smooth head, stroking the back of my throat. His eyes on me, surely.

"I'm getting real close, sweetheart. Relax for me."

I tried. I didn't quite succeed. As his head bumped my palate, I closed up. He eased out, giving me a few seconds to get loose. He drew my attention off the discomfort, running his slick crown back and forth along my lower lip.

"Again," he warned, and pushed back inside.

Better this time. Gentle fingertips tilted my chin up, and the angle was smoother. I welcomed him all the way in before my throat constricted, and again he eased back. The palms stroking my hair felt nearly patronizing, but I craved it, same as the dirty feeling.

"Again." He eased back in, all the way. In place of the gagging response, I felt only him. The scary size and threat of him, in such a vulnerable place in my body. Also his length, his girth between my lips. The scent of his skin and sweat. The sound of his tight breathing from so high up.

He drew back, then gave me more of the same. Slow. "Good girl."

His kind, stroking hands transformed, fingers tangling in my hair again. Not rough, but not sweet, either. His hips grew restless, a little faster with each thrust, grace ebbing. I gagged. We paused. He gave me more, and I took it.

"Close your lips up tight, if you can." He sounded so excited, and I wanted to please him so bad, it ached. I did as he said, embracing how ugly my breaths sounded, wheezing in and out of my nose. He'd never felt so big, or so crass, or so dangerous. No man ever had, during sex.

And I hoped no other man ever would again, no one except Eric.

"You look good," he told me. I could tell from the angle of his voice, he was watching in the mirror. I tried to picture us that way. Wondered if I didn't need my imagination. I opened my eyes and sought the reflection. It was tilted for his pleasure, so he could watch my mouth on his cock, and what I saw was his face. His neck taut, features strained, his eyes black in the low light. I saw them widen, caught by mine.

"God," he muttered, his thrusts stuttering a moment. My gaze was affecting him, surely as anything my mouth was giving.

I grabbed his hips, digging in with my nails, and he responded, giving me more of his cock. He was losing it now—I saw it in his narrowed eyes and his parted lips.

In his letter, he'd admitted how he'd wanted to come in my mouth. To let me taste it. I waited for that now, anticipating it, craving it. Expecting it.

His entire body shook. "Fuck, Annie. I'm gonna come."

Good. Do it. With an almighty groan he pulled back—pulled

out. Air flooded my mouth and throat, and I watched with surprise as he fisted himself, stroking hard and fast just below his head. Hand jerking, he gasped, cupped my shoulder in his free palm, and let go. His release was long and hot, basting my collarbone and the tops of my breasts.

Dirty, nasty, *perfect*. His arm shook as he came down and I listened to his breathing, the exhalations little more than grunts.

"*Oh*," he sighed, and his hold on my shoulder loosened. Our eyes left the reflection, finding each other's faces for real. His gaze dropped in a heartbeat, to the spoils he'd marked me with.

"Shit. Hang on—"

"No," I said, and got to my feet.

Casual as you please, I snatched my discarded tee off the floor and tidied myself before flopping across the covers. The last thing I wanted was Eric thinking what he'd done was too filthy for my delicate sensibilities.

I smiled up at him. I could barely remember why I'd been so pissed at him, earlier. The things we did to each other always crowded out reason.

"C'mere," I said, curling a finger.

He did, his chest still rising and falling hard, eyes a little dazed. Would he fall asleep, leave me wanting? I half hoped so, I was so strangely infatuated with his selfish side.

"Before you ask," I said, gathering his arms around me, kissing his forehead, "that was fine. Everything we just did. Thank you."

"Okay. Good." He sounded unsure, but not upset.

"I want to see every side of you there is to see. Even the greedy ones and the dirty ones. I want us to be everything for each other that two people can be . . . Everything short of hurtful."

He nodded, expression unreadable.

"You okay?" I asked, cupping his face.

He sighed, eyes closing. "You want to see all these sides of me . . . All except the one that I'm going home for my sister, in a couple weeks' time. The side of me that was capable of what I did to get locked up. And that one might be so bad, I could lose you over it."

My heart pounded hard, all the feelings from before the sex flowing back into me, a cold wind rattling my bones.

Would he lose me, if he went home? Could I do that to him? Could I do it to *me*? I couldn't guess. What was I trying to accomplish, drawing such a hard line in the sand? To prevent him from hurting himself, risking another altercation and more years forfeited behind bars. And for what? His sister's safety, or maybe her honor. I got it; that was a big deal. But so was this man's future. So was what *we* had.

Only it wasn't enough, not to him.

Chapter Eighteen

I stayed pissed at Eric for a while, over a week. No cold shoulder—nothing as childish as that, but I cooled us off. On Friday we spent New Year's Eve apart, exchanging only quiet, strained good wishes over the phone as the proverbial ball dropped.

"Happy New Year," we'd said together.

And from him, "I love you. You know that, right?"

"I do. And I love you." So why on earth hadn't I been with him? Him, in my bed. Him, inside my body. Which of us was doing the hurting here?

I didn't feel I was issuing an ultimatum, or punishing him, or trying to tell him, *Do as I say or no sex for you*. I was just scared and confused, and I needed the space. In time the surprise of it all faded and the situation ceased feeling like a crisis, mellowing instead to a nagging worry.

That Saturday evening I met him down in Lola's for a drink. Upstairs I had dinner fixings ready to go, but hadn't invited him for that officially. I figured I'd see how things went. See if my anger flared over the course of our date.

"Hey you," I said as he strolled over, a gust of cold winter air chasing his heels.

"Hey yourself." He tugged off his knit cap and sat across from me in the booth.

"How was work?" I asked. He'd been off on some special job all day at the airfield.

"Brutal. But extra pay for the holiday, so no complaints. Whatcha drinking?"

"My usual."

He tossed his gloves and scarf on the bench and shed his coat, then went to grab my spiked tea and a beer for himself.

As he sat back down he asked, "How was work yesterday? My old roommates treat you good?"

I nodded. "No major incidents. Some new guy was kind of a dick during book discussion, but a few of my favorites put him in his place." Good old Wallace, my heckler-turned-bodyguard.

"They better."

I smiled at Eric, moving my ice around with my straw. "I remember a certain tall, dark and handsome inmate defending my honor once. In the face of dickery."

He smiled back. "They may stick us in cages, but no need to act like animals."

Man, it was way too easy to get drawn into his warmth, into the memories of our reckless early romance. I mentally waved the fog aside and got down to business.

"What's the plan for next weekend? You definitely going home to be with your sister?"

He nodded and took a long drink, setting his bottle down and rotating it by the neck. "Fucker's out on Tuesday and I couldn't swing any workdays off. Unless something goes down between him getting sprung and the weekend, I'm heading over on Friday night. If anything, it's just so maybe any old buddies of his might see me around. Let him know I'm lurking, that he's on my radar, in case he gets any ideas about intimidating my sister."

"I can't imagine many people stand a chance at intimidating her," I said, remembering that aggressive phone call, me sitting in this very booth, in fact.

"Nope, not many. But he's one of them," Eric said gravely.

"Yeah. Yeah, of course."

He'd been watching his pirouetting bottle, but suddenly his eyes rose to catch mine. "Why don't you come with me?"

I blinked. "What, to see your family?"

He nodded. "I'm going up Friday night, coming back Sunday after dinner. Wouldn't demand any time off for you, either. And what a shame, losing out on a whole weekend with each other . . . I've been missing you this past week."

I shot him a look, admonishing the smooth-guy act.

"C'mon. Why not?"

I considered it seriously, beyond the major issue of how much I resented the entire premise of the trip. "For one, your sister hates me."

"Nah, she doesn't even know you yet. She's just prickly. Plus I thought you wanted a chance to talk to her. Convince her to quit relying on me or whatever."

"You made it pretty clear, that's more than an uphill battle. A sheer vertical drop, in fact."

He cracked a thin smile at that. "Come with me."

"You really want me there? If there's drama?"

"I seriously doubt there will be any. That piece of shit would need to have a death wish to come sniffing around. Not just because of me. My sister's got a couple guns, and more than a couple friends."

"Oh. So why do you need to go back?"

His look said, *We've been over this before.*

"Will you be . . . Will *you* be armed, in case he shows up?"

Eric shook his head. "Those days are over. Says my parole, and says me. Not that I was ever much for packing, not even when I was young and stupid."

"What if he had a gun?"

"Then I'd better be careful."

"Jesus." My hand had gone to my heart, a vision of Eric clutching some bleeding wound knocking me sideways. All these months I'd thought Cousins had desensitized me to such realities, but I went cold as ice at the thought. "Why would you even want me coming with you, then, if it's that dangerous?"

"Because I don't think it's going to come anywhere near to that. Because this guy's a coward. I'm going so I can give my sister peace of mind, and you coming with me might set your own mind at ease."

I did want to meet his mom, and see where he'd grown up. More facets—I was always after those facets, like a magpie scanning for the gleam. And truth be told, the invitation made me feel like his girlfriend, and I wanted that again, after this horrible week apart. And I wanted his family's approval, unpleasant as I knew at least one of them to be. I wanted to charm them. Show them I was good for Eric. Or in Kristina's opinion, show I was worthy of him.

Without even realizing I'd tasted it, I'd finished my drink, straw stirring nothing but ice. Eric's beer was nearly gone as well. "You want another round?" I asked.

"Sure." He drained his bottle.

I waved him back down as he made to stand. "I got it."

Nosy Kyle was working, and my stomach did a flip. He'd grilled me frequently in the past few months about my mysterious, inadvisable romance, but this was the first time he'd been bartending when I'd shown up with Eric. God help me.

He gave his Tigers cap a chivalrous dip as I approached, an odd ritual he'd recently decided paired well with my accent.

"Hey, Kyle. How are you?"

"Just fine, Annie."

"Same as before," I said, setting our empties on the wood.

"So-o-o," he singsonged, cracking open my can of tea. "That's him? Mr. Bad Idea?"

I nodded, eyes on his hands.

"Not so long-distance anymore, huh?"

"Nope. He moved to Darren."

"Jeez. Guess you guys are getting pretty fucking serious, then."

"He moved here for work, actually," I said. "But we're kinda serious, yeah."

Kyle finished my cocktail and rooted in the fridge for Eric's beer. "He treating you good?"

I smiled. I couldn't have stopped it if I'd wanted to. "Yeah. He treats me real good."

"Glad to hear it. And I'll give him this much," Kyle said, twisting the cap free. "Nobody's fucking with you, not with that dude by your side. What is he, like six-three? One ninety-five?" Kyle was a huge pro boxing fan, I'd come to learn. He was always trying to guess people's stats.

"Your estimate's as good as mine."

"Well, good to know you got that on your side in this town."

I raised my glass to toast the ringing truth of it.

Kyle grinned, but it looked a little half-assed. A little hollow. I was pretty sure he had a crush on me, so Eric turning out not only to be real but also gigantic was probably a letdown. I tipped him way too much and said thanks, heading back to the booth.

"He likes you," Eric said, nodding subtly toward the bar.

274

"Probably. But he's a good guy. And an even better bartender—he's been listening to me waffling about you since August."

"He tell you you were nuts, getting mixed up with a convict?"

"No . . . I never told him that much."

Eric looked relieved at that.

"I just said we were long-distance, and that I didn't quite know what to make of you."

He tilted his bottle to his lips, not meeting my eyes as he set it back down. After a long pause he said, "You know, I still haven't given you your Christmas present. I forgot to bring it up, that night I brought you home from the airport, when we were fighting."

"I haven't given you yours yet, either."

That hung between us, the question of where these drinks were taking us. Up to my apartment, where he could unwrap me, discover me clad in flowers and satin? I'd be a liar if I pretended it'd been easy, going without our sex this past week. Five years I'd forfeited it, but now that I knew what it could be like with the right man . . . it felt as vital as food or water or air.

"You need dinner?" I asked.

"I wouldn't mind it."

"I made meatballs earlier. If you feel like spaghetti."

He nodded. "Yeah. I do." His stare was hot, telling me he craved far more than that, after this awful week.

We finished our drinks without speaking much more about anything, and I dropped the empties at the bar and said good night to Kyle.

Up in my apartment, I switched on the living room lights, but as we dropped our layers on the rocker, I was still in the dark on so many fronts. I met his eyes, and held them. Outside

275

a car alarm went off, and the sound of it triggered my frustration all over again. I dropped my gaze to Eric's feet, and he seemed to take it as a hint, crouching to unlace his boots.

When he stood I asked, "Are we still . . . good?"

He features went hard and deadly serious. "I want to ask you the same thing. Because nothing about how I feel has changed, because of . . . because of this stalemate we're stuck in. *Nothing*. I love you exactly the same. You're the one who feels different, so you tell me." He wasn't angry. Not quite. It was a different strain in his voice now. Desperation.

I stared at his wool socks. "I feel the same about you, too."

"No, you don't. Not if you're still considering breaking all this off, if I go to be with my sister on Friday."

I bit my lip. "It's the only way I can think of to maybe . . . To force you to do what's best for yourself. I don't want to lose you, if something bad goes down and you get sent back to prison. *Because* I love you."

"But you *would* lose me. You're prepared to. You'd leave me, if I said I had to go."

I smiled weakly, lips trembling with brewing tears. "I'd say whatever I had to, to keep you free."

His brows drew together, every other feature of that handsome face suddenly softening.

He gets it now, I realized. I'd finally found a way to explain it that broke through that wall of convoluted ethics.

"I'd rather you were out, living a decent life without me, than stand by you and pretend I was okay with you risking everything. And risking everything out of *hate* for someone. Some piece of *shit* who doesn't deserve to have the power to take everything you've worked so hard to get, the last five years." My voice had risen, nascent tears burned away to nothing. "Don't go, and neither of us has to lose."

He didn't need to reply. I knew his answer word for word,

by now. *Don't make me choose between you and my family.* Between his newborn love for me, and thirty-plus years' bond with his sister. Between blind lust and blood loyalty, when it came down to it. I had to admit, I wasn't going to win that fight. But I couldn't help but feel I ought to. I couldn't help but feel I treated him better, cared more. Cared differently, anyhow. I rolled my eyes at that woman in the Gap, threatening Justin with Eric's vengeance. She'd devolved into a persuasion of Kristina, fetishizing or idolizing a primeval code of manhood. Eye for an eye, just like that ink on his shoulder mandated.

"You're still that kid who got that tattoo," I said sadly, gaze on his arm. "You told me you weren't, but all that same revenge crap still applies, doesn't it?"

"This trip isn't about me punishing him. It's about being what my sister needs. And I'm done talking about it, okay?"

I paused at that. I wasn't sure he'd ever shut me down like that before, not even on the drive home from the airport. He'd always been ready to keep giving. Keep proving. We'd reached a crossroads, and while I was left debating which way to go, Eric saw only one path. I could make my threat. I could leave him when he climbed into his truck on Friday against my wishes. But he'd still be getting in that truck. Maybe he'd go, and come back on Sunday night, perfectly fine, perfectly free . . .

He must have read my mind. "You stay with me, everything goes smooth, we still get each other when I'm back."

But for how long? I had to wonder. Until the next time this happened. Until the next call from his sister, the next fight. The next stalemate.

"You make good on your promise," he went on, "we lose each other for sure. I don't get why you can't see the math here, Annie."

He was right. The only way I won was if my ultimatum worked—he stayed safe, legally and physically, and we stayed together. But I wasn't going to win. That was the difference in our two perspectives. He'd already crossed out that possibility.

"I guess I lose," I said quietly, and sat on the coffee table, cupping my elbows.

Eric sighed and dropped to his knees. He leaned close, and I thought he was going rest his forehead on my thighs, maybe, but instead he was unlacing my sneakers. They were double knotted, but he worked the bows free with his big fingers, slow and patient, and slipped each one off. He held my socked feet in his hands, squeezing gently, and sighed again.

"You gotta quit seeing it as you versus me," he said. "Or you versus my sister. I'm gonna go, sure as the sun's gonna rise tomorrow. You stay with me, though, and I'll have somebody I love to come back to."

"And a reason to play it safe next time?" Because we both had to know, there was always going to be a next time, if he refused to change.

He raised his chin and met my gaze. "I dunno."

I sucked in a long, shaking breath, then squeezed my eyes shut, squeezed my lungs empty. "I'll go," I told him.

"You'll leave me?"

My eyes popped back open to find pain written all over his handsome face. "No. I mean I'll go with you. On Friday."

His brow softened. "You're sticking by me, then." He didn't quite sound as though he believed it.

I nodded. "Sure as you're sticking by your sister, I guess. Yeah. I mean, you're right—you go and I leave you, I lose you for sure. You go and I stand by you, and maybe everything will be okay. Much as I'm terrified of that 'maybe.' Much as I worry this is only going to happen again. But you win, Eric."

278

"I'm not trying to *win*," he said quietly.

"I believe that. But I also know how much it feels like I'm losing. And how terrified I am of losing *you*."

His expression fell at that.

"I feel like that's what I'm signing on for," I said, finding my words. "A future where I'll never stop worrying about losing you, over this stuff."

And would I stand by this man through another prison sentence? I had to wonder. Ten or twenty years he might get, for a repeat performance. Then I'd really have a decision to make. Wait for the man I loved and forfeit my sexuality again, any career mobility, my decisions about motherhood . . .

"I'll talk to my sister, when we're there," he said slowly.

I looked up. "About?"

"About how the things she needs from me, the role she needs me to fill . . . What it's doing to you and me."

I snorted softly. "Yeah, because she's such a big fan of mine."

"It won't happen overnight. I have to be there for her, this time. But I promise I'll try to get some of this shit out on the table, in the open."

"Would you?" My heart felt a little lighter, cautiously hopeful. It wasn't the stand I wished he'd take, but it was more than he'd been willing to concede before. It made me feel heard, at least. Made me feel like he was starting to understand.

He nodded. "I promise."

"Okay . . . Good. That makes me feel way better about . . . about staying with you." How those words scared me. Like stopping short and realizing how close you'd come to walking off a cliff.

He dropped his head to my lap and as I stroked his hair he mumbled, "*Oh, Annie.*"

279

"You fuck up and get put away, my letters are going to be short on sweet nothings for a *very* long time," I warned, just the tip of the iceberg of what had me terrified.

His strong arms circled my calves, hugging them tight, and his breath warmed my thighs through my jeans.

I tried to steer us someplace more lighthearted. "At least this way, I can keep an eye on you."

He raised his chin. "Already got a parole officer. Or do you mean with other women?"

I went serious again; deeply earnest, surprising even myself. "I can't imagine you ever doing that. Going with somebody else, behind my back."

He held my stare. "Neither can I."

After a long silence, punctuated by the assorted audio ambience of a Saturday night in Darren, I put my hands on Eric's shoulders, patting. "C'mon. I'll make us dinner."

He got up and I used his proffered hand to pull myself to standing. I felt about two hundred years old, the surrender fitting me like a damp coat. But at least the uncertainty was through. At least I'd scored a tiny taste of compromise.

I made our supper and we ate on the couch, flipping channels then half watching a documentary about fire ants.

Once he'd set our bowls on the coffee table, Eric turned and took my hands in his. "I'm sorry."

"For?"

"For all this. For you having to feel like you've lost this fight."

I shrugged. "I might still get to keep you. That's not the worst consolation prize. And I'm okay, deep down. Just tired. And a little . . . defeated." But if he meant what he'd said, about talking to her, beginning to cut this brutal cord that bound them . . . maybe I could win the war. Just not this nasty battle.

280

"You will get to keep me," he said, and I wondered if he could truly make that promise. "I'll be smart, if anything does go down. And it's real unlikely it will."

"If you were smart, you'd stay the hell away from your sister's drama." I paused, catching myself. Where the fuck did I get off, downgrading a brutal assault, maybe a rape, to *drama*? "No. I'm sorry. That was . . . That was *way* too cavalier."

He cracked a smirk. "Cavalier?"

"That was uncool. Anyway . . ."

"Anyway," he agreed, not seeming offended by my misstep. He looked around the room at nothing in particular.

"Would you do your beat-down girlfriend a favor?"

"What's that?"

"Rub my back?" Maybe those big man-hands could squeeze some of the angst out of me.

"Of course. I'll do the dishes first. You go take a bath or get comfortable on your bed. I'll meet you in there."

"Deal."

I took him up on the bath suggestion, feeling a good deal better as I toweled off. I'd worn the now-thoroughly-belated Christmas underwear today, and it was all I bothered putting back on before I left the bathroom, lotion bottle in hand.

In my absence, Eric had prepped the room.

It looked like something out of his fantasies, the ones he'd written to me about. He'd found three candles and lit them on my dresser, flames reflected in the mirror, their lavender and sage and beeswax scents mingling. All the other lights were out, the curtains and blinds shut. He'd brought my kitchen radio in and it was playing classical music on a low volume. My masseuse was sitting up on the bed, back against the wall, in his jeans and undershirt, hands clasped patently in his lap.

"Wow," he murmured. "Is that it? My present?"

I looked down at the satin garden hiding my breasts and sex. In the candlelight the colors were all muted to mauves and olives and golds. "Yeah. And wow right back at you. This is quite a setup." I crawled across the covers then flopped face down, lotion bottle tossed in Eric's general direction. The soothing voice of an NPR host informed us that Brahms was up next, after a word from the underwriters.

Eric chuckled. "Sorry. Best I could do."

"It's perfect."

I groaned as his palms swept down my nearly bare back, slick with lotion. The world went blurry, reduced to the steady pressure of this man's hands on me. *My* man's hands. Hands capable of tender caresses and shocking violence, of getting lost on my body or in nurturing a delicate plant, capable of threats and of aid, and of composing the most beautiful words I'd ever read.

After perhaps fifteen minutes he moved to my side and said softly, "Turn over."

I did, my body jelly. His touch was different now, more grazing than massaging, fingertips tracing light tracks down my arms, across my collarbone. A whisper of palms over my breasts and down my belly. I shivered in their wake, nipples tensing, breath drawing high in my chest. He palmed my hips, and I saw his reverence morphing to something else above me. Something hungry.

For a long moment his eyes took in their gift, then his body came right down against mine, forearms hugged to my ribs. Leaning close, he made a sound not unlike a growl at my throat.

"Thank you," I murmured, drawing my fingers through his thick hair. "That was amazing."

He sat up some, bracing himself on straight arms, holding my gaze squarely. "I was selfish, last weekend."

282

"Maybe, by request. But you more than made up for it, just now."

"But I haven't gotten you off since before you left for Christmas."

I had to smirk. "Oh yes, you did."

His brows rose. "Must've slept right through it, then. How was I?"

I ignored that. "You custom-made every fantasy I've thought about since then. With your texts and your email, and what you gave me last Saturday."

"Not the same as giving it to you with my hands. Or my tongue. Or . . ." He grabbed my hand, rougher than usual, and cupped it hard against his cock. My blush ran from my hair to my sex, and I swallowed.

"Make it up to me, then."

"How?"

"You show me."

He sat up all the way, looking steeled. Looking ready. I could make out the gorgeous contours of his chest through his shirt and see his hard belly swell with quickening breaths. I felt a warm flush of pride that I'd manifested this—his newfound ability to steer our sex. To worship me without resorting to caution or deference.

He moved back. Moved to his knees between my ankles and pushed my legs apart, ditched his shirt. He slid his arms right up under my thighs, my butt, my lower back, hands cradling my ribs. My relaxation morphed to excitement in an instant, blood rushing to my core. His face was there, right there. A long, hungry inhalation, then his tongue traced me through the satin, nose teasing my clit.

I sucked a gasp and fisted his hair.

The fabric grew wet, his mouth explicit. Until I could feel every nuance, almost as though there were nothing between us at all. I watched his shoulders bunch and release in time with the hands kneading my waist, and felt an entirely different muscle moving against my sex with greedy precision.

He brought me there steadily, with his tongue and his moans and his possessive hold, and when I came it was from nothing more than reality. No highlight reel in my head of fantasies or memories. Just his warm mouth on me, in this set he'd constructed for my pleasure. I came for longer than I could ever remember experiencing—a slow, deep, silent release. His fluttering tongue faded with my spasms, until all that was left was the heat of his panting breaths against my pulsing flesh, through the drenched satin.

He gave my waist a final caress, his palms damp. Bringing his body alongside mine, he wrapped his arm around me. "*Mmmf*," I grunted as his kisses teased my neck, and patted his hair with a clumsy, limp hand.

"Better?" he whispered.

"Yes. Very better. You're forgiven."

"Oh good."

We lay quietly for a time, until the concerto came to a close and the radio host's spiel wrecked the flow. I came to my senses some, wrestling around to face Eric.

"Your turn," I said, then kissed his lips.

"I sent you to bed hungry last time." He stroked my hair. "Won't hold it against you if do the same to me."

"No way. No keeping score when it comes to orgasms, Collier."

"Okay, then. What are you up for?"

I gave it some serious thought. "I've always wanted to watch you," I murmured. "Like we talked about."

"Watch me stroke?"

I nodded, suddenly feeling shy.

"How?"

284

"However you do it."

He sat up, scooting back to lean against the wall. He knees came up and his jeans and shorts went away, then those long legs were stretched across my covers. His cock was already hard, and he wrapped it in a loose fist.

I got comfortable, kneeling by his calves. On impulse, I reached back and undid my bra. I didn't take it off, not yet, just let it hang about my breasts like a promise. The way he stared, I was surprised it didn't go up in flames.

I stared in return. At his hand, at his fingers looking pale against the ruddier skin of his cock. *This is how he looks when he thinks about me.* I did this to him. Drove him to this.

"Show me," I said, grazing the back of his knee and calf with my fingertips.

"Anything you want." His hand began to move. "Anything you want to see, you just tell me."

"All I want is to know how you look, when you think about me. About us."

He licked his lips, eyes shutting for a moment. When they opened them he sought the lotion bottle, pumping a measure into his palm. I watched his cock grow slick in the candlelight, imagined how good that hand must feel. His shaft shone like satin, his head smooth as glass. His abdomen clenched each time his fist crested the crown, muscles standing out.

I muttered, "Jesus," without even meaning to. Then, "What are you thinking about?"

"About you watching me. Do you like it?"

"Yeah," I breathed. "You look perfect."

His hand stilled but his eyes were shut tight. "I haven't come since that last time, with you."

"No?" Jeez, I'd gotten myself off every night since then, I bet. Even pissed off and uncertain, I was helpless against the memories he left me with.

285

"I felt too weird about it," he said. "Or maybe . . . Or maybe I wanted to suffer. As punishment for not getting you off."

I didn't admonish his reasoning, but instead rolled it into our game. I scooted close to stroke his hard shoulder, admiring the round swell of muscle. When his brown eyes opened, I spoke sweetly. "You must need it real bad, then."

He swallowed. Nodded. "Yeah. Real bad." His eyes grew wide as I let my bra fall away, his lips parting.

"Show me how you do it." Rough and fast? Slow and savoring? "Exactly how you'd be, if you were by yourself. So I'll know what to picture, when we're apart."

He breathed, "Sure." And he gave me my show.

Not too rough. Quick, but not too fast. When my eyes drank their fill of his hand and cock, I watched his arm flexing. The muscles of his chest and abdomen clenching. The look on his face. The thickness of his thighs, and his nonstroking hand—restless, rubbing his lower belly faintly. His breathing filled the air, the heavy huffs solidifying, turning to grunts, then moans as his pulls sped. Surely he'd never been able to do this when he was locked up. Not this openly, not this vocally. I imagined the first time he got to touch himself with this much abandon after all those years, knowing beyond the shadow of a doubt that he'd been thinking of me.

"I'm close," he told me, eyes opening a fraction. His face was beautiful and pained.

"Good. I want to see." I ran my palm lightly over his chest, down his belly, the touch telling him, *here, right here.* All over those gorgeous muscles. Let him feel the heat of his own release, the way I'd felt it last week, on my breasts.

His noises changed, long moans becoming clipped and disbelieving. He concentrated his caresses just below his head, the motions twitchy now.

"Show me, Eric."

And he did. His long torso curled, every muscle taut as his hand froze. He basted his golden skin in that perfect, pure white of male surrender.

"Good," I murmured, stroking his hair. Kissing his cheek. "Good."

He sighed raggedly, cleared his throat. Blinked then met my eyes with his glassy ones. "That what you needed?"

"I think we both needed that," I teased.

"Hang on." He left the bed, jogging to the bathroom in that clumsy, postcoital way men do. I heard water run, saw a sliver of light as the door opened, then he switched it off, returning to me, all cleaned up.

We tugged the covers free and climbed underneath, holding each other, watching the candlelight bouncing on the ceiling.

After a time he asked, "So you're definitely coming next weekend?"

I nodded, my hair brushing his neck. "Yeah. I'll come."

He kissed the crown of my head. "Good."

Whether the trip would indeed prove *good* remained to be seen, but having made the decision, I felt lighter. The dread could wait until Friday, until we were in his truck, driving to his hometown. For now, I had my man back. And I wasn't about to trade this feeling for one of anxiety, not for as long as I could manage.

When he yawned warmth into my hair I told him, "Sweet dreams."

"Always, when I'm with you."

And I told myself to bask in that, not knowing when or if the nightmares might catch up with us.

287

Chapter Nineteen

The next Friday, Eric picked me up outside my apartment at six.

"Hey, you." I tossed my bag in the well behind the seat. As I leaned across to kiss him hello, it was a different, welcome caress that shocked my senses.

"Whoa—you got your heater fixed!"

"Yup." He waited for me to buckle up, then pulled us onto the road. "This new guy who's on my crew does auto HVAC on the side. Fellow Cousins graduate. He did the repair in exchange for me helping him move."

"Nice. The CCF Alumni Society has its perks." I took off my gloves and held my palms before the vents. "Oh man, this is luxury."

"Tell me about it."

"So. Work okay?"

"Backbreaking," he said, but didn't sound too down. It had snowed heavily overnight, so he'd surely been busy. It was flurrying now—nothing treacherous, but the visibility wasn't great.

"The guys were all punchy today," I told him. "The exercise yard's all shrunk down from the snow banks. Territorial BS."

"Don't miss those days." He aimed us toward the highway.

"I'm sure." Though strangely, even without the promise of seeing Eric, Fridays were now a highlight of my workweek, probably second only to Thursdays in the bookmobile with Karen. I'd gotten so used to the safety drills at Cousins, outbursts rarely scared me much more than an attack dog tossing itself against a chain link fence. And now that I was a visiting favorite of many of the inmates, and many of them favorites of mine—pet projects even—I looked forward to my shifts. I was never bored at Cousins, that was for sure. And unlike at the library, I didn't have to break up any of the fights myself.

"How long's the drive?" I asked.

"In this weather, over an hour. It's a couple exits past that lake I took you to."

"How does everybody feel about my coming with?"

"Hard to say. I just told my mom, 'I'm bringing my girlfriend.' In case she wanted to clean the place up special or something. She just said, 'Okay. She a fussy eater?' And I said, 'No.' And she said, 'Okay, see you then.'"

"What about Kristina?"

He shrugged. "I told her, too. All she said was something like, 'She's still in the picture, huh?' And that was that."

"Wow. Welcome wagon."

"My mom and sister aren't much for the whole Martha Stewart happy homecoming scene."

"So I gather."

He smiled at me. "But my mom'll like you. She'll think you're way outta my league, and that maybe you'll save me from myself or whatever. She's a big believer in all that love-of-a-good-woman country-music bull. God knows why. Not like she ever managed to reform my dad."

I'd wondered what his family would make of me. I'd be an outsider, for sure. Going home to Charleston after all that time in Darren had driven home how vast the gap was between middle class and poor. I had a master's. I had a very un-Michigan accent, and at least fifty people I'd met via work since my move had commented on how suspiciously polite I was. I was going to stand out on this visit. No fighting it. I'd decided to do my best not to stand out in the way I dressed, at least. Tonight I was wearing jeans and a plaid flannel button-up, sneakers. Hat hair. I'd come prepared to blend in. To recede into the background.

"Where are we staying?" I asked.

"On my mom's couch. It folds out." As if I needed further evidence that this trip was no romantic weekend getaway. "She had my old room done up for guests, but I guess my dad got too entitled about crashing in there when he blew into town, visiting too often. So she tossed the bed and turned it into a sewing room or something."

"Ah."

He shot me a meaningful look across the cab.

"Yeah?"

"I don't know what you're expecting, as far as where I came from," he said, "but lower it by fifty percent."

"I know it's not glamorous."

"I grew up in a trailer park . . . I didn't really realize it back then. Hardly anybody ever called it what it was. It's by this pond and everybody called it Lakeside. Lakeside Estates, that's what the sign at the entrance says. Took me 'til I was about fourteen to realize, shit, I'm trailer trash, aren't I?"

"That must've been a rude awakening."

He nodded. "I guess. And from then on I questioned everything I'd come to think was normal. Compared where I lived to the shit you see on TV, in sitcoms and stuff. Like how just about everybody I knew had a record and a load of guns, and how they drank when it was still sunny out, unlike the people on TV. How when some teenage character on a show got knocked up, it was like, a huge deal. When all around me, that was practically standard issue."

"Not in your family, though."

He was quiet for a long moment. "My mom had us pretty young. Nineteen, with my sister. Twenty-four with me. And Kristina had a baby. Her junior year."

I blinked at the highway. "You have a niece or nephew?"

"I did. Nephew. He passed away when he was still real little. Three."

"Jeez. You never told me."

"And I'd rather you didn't go telling my sister you know. Not this first visit. It's not a secret or anything, just . . . touchy."

"How did he . . ."

Eric huffed out a curt breath. "He drowned. It wasn't anybody's fault. Turn your back for thirty seconds to flip the burgers, and he's gone. Just a tragedy." His tone was sad but flat, as if he were relating a stranger's loss, something off the news. Like maybe he wouldn't let himself really *feel* about the topic, or had burned out all his emotions for it years ago. Or maybe this was like when he'd refused to tell me the details of Kristina's assault. That caginess about sharing other people's traumas. "Could've happened to anyone. Course my sister can't see it that way—what mother could?"

"How awful." And no wonder she was prickly. That changed my entire perception of the woman who'd snapped at me over the phone. Made me wonder if maybe I could come to understand her control issues where her little brother was concerned.

291

A different thought struck me. "It wasn't in that lake—your lake?"

"No, different one. Anyhow. Enough about that," he said, and flipped the radio on low. The topic had made him distant, so I didn't push.

"So where did you live, when you were still in Kernsville? Before . . . you know."

"I moved out of my mom's house when I was seventeen. Rented places. The last one was an apartment above a body shop." He grinned in the glow of the dash, the Eric I'd lost in the last couple of minutes returning to me. "Stank to high heaven, and noisy, but cheap as shit."

"You still have friends back there?"

He shrugged, smile fading. "Nobody too special. Nobody who cared enough to visit me at Cousins, that's for fucking certain."

The rare bitterness in his voice told me loads. "Sounds like there was one or two you'd expected a bit more of."

"Yeah, maybe. Not sure what made me expect loyalty out of those guys. Not when it's in such short supply where we all grew up." And here I'd thought it was a byproduct of where he'd come from, some scrappy tribe mentality.

"Not everyone's as loyal as you," I told him. "In fact, hardly anybody is."

He looked a little uncomfortable at that. Like maybe he didn't love that quality about himself a hundred percent. Like maybe he'd gotten burned by it once or twice. Or maybe all this angst between us had gotten him thinking about it differently. Questioning the instincts that had gotten him locked up, and had nearly had me calling it quits last weekend.

I let silence reign for a time, and Eric broke it perhaps forty minutes later when he said, "Next exit. Then a whole lot of fields."

292

He was right about that. The rural route we took out to his hometown was endless, ice-heaved asphalt—ten miles of juddering bumps that felt like five times that distance with Eric's busted old suspension.

"You've got—to get—a new truck," I said, pitched this way and that.

"Don't I know it."

"We should've—taken my car."

"Nah. You've still got some—shocks left. No sense ruining what actually—*works*. Fuck, that was a deep one." He put his fingers to his mouth like he'd bit his tongue.

After about six years, we reached our destination, the promised sign welcoming us to Lakeside Estates, established 1972. The property was bound by a log fence that gave it a campground feel. We'd passed through Kernsville's main drag, which boasted some okay-looking homes, even a few two-story numbers with cheerful Christmas lights. Lakeside had decorations as well . . . but more of the plastic lawn-Santa persuasion.

I spied a sliver of frosted ice through the pines. "Must've been nice to grow up on the water."

"It's called Green Pond," he said drily. "And not by accident. There's a reason we always drove to that big lake I took you by."

The truck trundled past rows of trailer homes, and the place seemed run-down, but not squalid. Not depressing even, just humble. People had recycling bins and porches and even hedges; the trappings of suburbia, really, just condensed.

"Here we are," Eric said heavily, parking behind a sedan at the foot of a red single-wide. "Home sweet home. Looks like my sister's come for dinner, too. That's her Accord."

There were white lights strung around the large, square window at the end of the house, and I could glimpse what

293

looked like a living room through the open blinds—framed pictures hung on faux-wood walls, a tall bookcase. The single glowing lamp didn't reveal much else.

Eric grabbed our overnight bags from the back and led me across salted flagstones, up onto a narrow side porch. He opened the screened door and knocked on the inner one before pushing it in. A dog barked, and nails chattered against linoleum.

A beagle appeared, pawing at Eric's knees.

"Hey, Scoot." To the rest of the house he called, "Anybody home? Son and heir in need of a hot meal, here."

I heard a female voice but couldn't catch the words. Must've been sarcastic, as Eric cracked a warm smile in profile and shouted, "Good to see you, too."

I followed him inside, into a crowded but orderly kitchen. It smelled great, like chicken and dressing. I stooped to rub the dog's ears, rewarded with much licking. When I stood up straight and stole my hands back, it licked my knees through my jeans. Eric tapped its butt with his boot. "Knock it off, Scooter." Scooter obediently wandered toward his bowls, set in the corner.

Eric dropped our bags by the door and I followed his lead, toeing off my shoes. He was taking my coat when a woman appeared from the next room—his mom, clearly. Salt-and-pepper hair done in flippy layers. She was short, rather round, with strong, feminine, Hispanic features, and Eric's dark eyes. He must've inherited the tall genes from his dad.

"Baby," she muttered as he stooped to hug her. "My baby boy, where you been?"

Eric kissed the top of her head, which melted my heart some. "Working," he answered. "Mom, this is Annie." He drew me over. "This is my mom, Paula."

I was poised for a warm handshake but got a tight hug

instead. When she stepped back she put her hands right on either side of my waist and told Eric, "What a figure on this one!"

I had no idea what to make of that, unsure if that meant I was more or less curvy than expected. "Thanks," I said, gleaning from her smile that whatever the verdict, she approved. "Happy belated holidays."

"And to you!" She looked to Eric. "I tried to keep the tree up 'til you got to see it, but the needles all fell off by New Year's."

"I'll live. Where's Kris? I saw her car."

"She's been with me all week, since . . . you know."

"Since he walked," Eric said.

She nodded grimly. "Just a precaution. She's spooked, of course. Anyhow, she's on the phone with your Aunt Tori." Paula crossed herself in a way that suggested she wasn't a big fan of Aunt Tori. "Better her than me. Who wants to hear about a person's bunion surgery?"

Eric glanced around, hands on his hips. "Smells like turkey."

"Chicken."

"Close enough."

"You eat chicken, Annie?" Paula asked earnestly.

I nodded. "Smells like dressing, too."

"Oh," she said, shooting Eric a look of overdone wonder. "You didn't say she was from down south." She turned back to me. "He hasn't told us much of anything, in fact. He said you're . . . a teacher?"

"Librarian."

"Yes, right, I knew that. Eric told me that much, at least. Anyways, yes—dressing. The box says it's stuffing. I've never understood the difference, though—dressing or stuffing. Is there one?"

I shrugged. "We just call it dressing, where I'm from. My mom makes the cornbread kind."

"Well this stuff looks like croutons but tastes like heaven."

"Works for me."

"Jesus, Eric," his mom said with a grin. "Warn me next time you bring a Southern girl home for comfort food. I didn't study for this test." To me she said, "Now where are you from, precisely, Annie?"

Eric found a screw-cap bottle of red wine from a cabinet and poured four glasses at the kitchen table, and I let his mom grill me. She nodded at everything I said, rapt, like I was an ambassador from some exotic culture. She'd just gotten to the topic of what my parents did, when the missing sister made her entrance, declaring with patented Collier blasphemy, "Fucking Christ, but that woman doesn't understand the meaning of TMI."

Her mom laughed. "Why d'you think I handed her off?"

"Well, you'll all be *riveted* to hear Tori has an ingrown nail on the middle toe of her left foot."

Paula grimaced. "Kris, shush." In a falsely hushed, conspiratorial tone she added to me, "Tori is their father's sister."

"Gotcha."

"They overshare, his family."

"Ha!" Kristina pulled out a chair but didn't sit yet. "This from the woman who gave me a blow-by-blow of the neighbor girl's lip-ring infection over breakfast."

Kristina was tall—easily five-ten—and built like Eric, with long legs and narrow hips. She was a bit top heavy, and though I'd done some math and figured she was thirty-six or -seven, she wore the years roughly. Her black hair was long, loose ponytail brushing her waist. She was dressed not unlike me, in jeans and a plaid flannel, but—unlike me—she looked like she'd earned the latter with some legit wood-chopping

296

cred. With an unsettling shiver, I tried to imagine what kind of a man could've overpowered this woman. Enough to break her arm, even. Then I remembered what Eric had told me on the drive, about her lost son. This woman had had more taken from her than I could begin to comprehend. It made me feel about eight years old.

Eric stood and she slapped his back as they hugged, saying, "Can't get over how big you got, inside."

"It's that luxury health club they got at Cousins." He stepped back to nod in my direction. "Kris, this is Annie. The one you chewed out on the phone."

I cringed on the inside and accepted Kristina's shake. "Nice to meet you. Officially."

"You, too," she said, sounding more resigned than delighted.

Whatever. Close enough. I had a better chance of being hit by a meteorite than of getting an apology out of this woman— that much seemed clear. She scared me, anyhow. I kept my expectations low, hoping for civility.

"Surprised you came for this visit," she said to me, her tone impossible to get a read on.

"I um . . ." May as well be honest. "The whole thing freaks me out a little. Eric figured it might be good for me to come, so I could see there's nothing to worry about."

She shot her brother a *look*. "Nothing to worry about?"

"Probably not, Kris. That shit's a coward—always has been. He doesn't have a death wish. 'Specially not if he's sober—"

Their mom tossed her hands up fretfully, trying to shoo the topic like a cloud of gnats. "I don't want to talk about that horrible man."

"That horrible man's the reason I'm home this weekend," Eric reminded her. "No point sugarcoating it."

"But not tonight, baby. Okay?"

He sighed, dropping his shoulders in a show of surrender.

297

Paula turned to me. "Give me your glass, Annie."

I let her refresh my wine, and the conversation turned to Christmas—what my family's traditions were, what the winter was like in South Carolina. More an interview than a conversation, really, and Eric and Kris kept quiet, preoccupied by a different, unspoken interrogation. I spotted them shooting one another meaningful looks, Eric's probably demanding things like, *Anybody seen him around?* Kris's blasé expression told me nothing, but Eric seemed to read something from it. He frowned at her and sipped his wine. At one point she announced she needed a smoke, and Eric went with her. I could see them through the window when I went to the sink to rinse my hands. I watched him steal her cigarette and take a long drag, though he didn't light one for himself. He hugged his arms against the cold, the two of them trading grave looks and words I couldn't make out over the radio.

I didn't like one bit that a petty part of me was jealous of their obvious bond. It looked nothing like the one I shared with him, like this was a side of him I'd not yet met. A deeply important side—the one capable of his crime. He looked like a stranger out there, a hard, handsome, serious man, breath fogging in the winter air to mimic his sister's smoke. He felt very far away, standing just beyond that pane of glass.

Dinner was served shortly. On paper it was nearly exactly what my own mom had made on Christmas. Roasted and stuffed chicken, dressing, mashed potatoes, green beans. The potatoes were from a box, the gravy from a can, the beans from a freezer bag; all of which might've scandalized my mother, but it tasted fine, just a little different. Frankly I preferred their gravy.

I ate slowly, keeping pace with the others who were talking way more than me. Paula caught Eric up with all the neighborhood gossip, and he pretended to find it all riveting . . .

though I was pretty sure he couldn't give less of a damn about some dispute between the neighbors over property boundaries in relation to unattended dog turds.

After dinner we all tackled the dishes, then retired to the living room to flip channels. Eric and I sat on the couch, Paula in an old wicker rocker and Kristina lounging splay-legged on the carpet with a couple of pillows under her head and Scooter curled beside her hip. We didn't really watch anything, just made fun of stuff and drifted in and out of remembrances triggered by whatever floated by on the screen.

At some point Paula grabbed a photo album from the bookcase, and I flipped through it, fascinated by shots of Eric as a boy, then a teenager. Lots of pictures of him standing on the sand in swim trunks, in front of what I guessed was the lake he'd driven me to. He'd been smaller back then, of course, his narrow frame missing the tattoos and chest hair and punishing build. But the same eyes, same overgrown hair, only curlier. He smiled a lot more in those images than he did these days, eyes often squinted against the sunshine. There were hardly any photos from the winter. And only a few featuring a man I assumed was Eric and Kris's dad. Tall guy, black hair and beard, his frame broader than Eric's and carrying more fat. Not a single shot of Kristina with a baby.

I tuned out of the conversation, preoccupied with questions I planned to save for after the women had gone to bed.

Paula called it a night around eleven, telling Kristina, "You wake me and there'll be hell to pay." They were sharing Paula's bed so Eric and I could have the foldout.

"I'm not the one who snores," Kris called after her mom.

I added, "Good night! Thank you for dinner—it was amazing."

"Yeah," Eric shouted. "Great dinner. See you in the morning."

Kristina swirled the clear plastic tumbler in her hand, her drink drained mainly to ice. I was nursing my third glass of wine in four hours, and neither Eric nor his mom had topped up after dinner. Kristina had switched to screwdrivers, and though she didn't sound especially tipsy, she had to be feeling them by now, at the rate she was going. She left us and returned with a fresh round, taking her mom's spot in the rocker with a lamenting sigh.

"Remote," she said, snapping her fingers, and caught it when Eric tossed it her way. Ice cubes clattered against plastic as she scanned the channels.

"Don't like how quick you're sucking those down," Eric scolded in a lazy tone.

"You my sponsor now?"

"Just saying."

"Oh well *pardon me* for being stressed out. Or have you forgotten who might roll into town at any moment?"

They'd been waiting hours to have this talk, I could tell. Waiting for their mom to turn in so they wouldn't upset her.

"I haven't forgotten," he said coolly. "I'm here, aren't I?"

Kristina smiled, the gesture cruel, and she kept her eyes on the screen. "And color me surprised, what with the company you've been keeping."

Wait. Did she mean me? My balls always took a few moments to gather themselves, and I wasn't fast to snap back. I was always the one who thought up the perfect retort a good two hours after any given spat.

Eric was quicker than me. "Company I keep feels pretty passionate about me not doing anything stupid and fucking up my parole. Which is more than I can say for my family, lately."

Whoa.

Did that mean he was on my side in all this? After we'd bickered ourselves hoarse for the past week?

300

Kristina laughed. An ugly, mean little noise. "She gettin' to you, then?"

"I'm here for you," he said evenly. "She's here for me, much as she hates that I even chose to come."

Mentally, my brows rose at that. He'd never once made it sound like a choice. Had my ultimatum held more water than he'd let me realize?

Kristina demanded, "She the reason you didn't come until he'd been released for four fucking days?"

"No. That's because I have a job now, and a PO to answer to, and debts to pay."

"Debts to pay," she repeated. "Some fines to the fucking feds. What about making that night up to me, Eric? What about that?"

"Jesus." I sat up straight, anger and words tumbling free like a landslide. "Are you blaming your brother for your assault? How the fuck is that his fault?"

She rolled her eyes, not meeting mine. "Stay out of this, princess."

Princess? Oh, it was *on* now. "No, I won't stay out of it. How *dare* you lay that on him?"

"It's okay, Annie," Eric said. "There's no winning with her. Don't bother try—"

"He gave up five years of his life for your . . . for your honor," I told her. I sounded shrill and petulant, but fuck it. "That not compensation enough for however it is you feel like he disappointed you?"

She stared me down. "My *honor*? Jesus, kid. You clearly don't know shit about me, you think I've got any honor. And didn't Eric tell me you threatened to sic him on your nasty ex?"

Oh, great. "I—"

He cut in. "She didn't mean it."

"She said it, didn't she?" Kris's eyes narrowed in my direction.

"I did say it," I admitted. "And I felt so shitty about it I cried after."

"Boo-hoo, pretty princess. Boo-hoo."

And then I said two words I'd never spoken to anyone aloud. I'd written them on a boy's hand in Sharpie, yes, but never actually heard them in my own voice. "Fuck you."

"Christ," Eric muttered and rubbed his thighs, looking to the ceiling as if seeking reinforcements. "Both of you, please."

"Why are you so fucking *mean*?" I demanded of Kris. Too late my brain supplied, *Daddy issues. Dead toddler. Violent assault.*

"Why are you so fucking *surprised*?" she shot back, and she had a point.

"Forget it." I sank against the cushions, standing down. "He's right. There's no point trying to talk to you, is there?"

She stared at me a long moment before speaking, leaning forward to rest her elbows on her knees. "You think you saved my brother or some shit, don't you? Found his sorry ass in prison and shined your happy, rosy light all over him? Rescued him, made him all better? You like a fixer-upper, Annie?"

Scooter whined, sounding anxious.

"I know I love him," I said quietly. "I know he's saved me, in some ways. I know I want what's best for him."

"Turning him against his own family?"

I shook my head, faking a calm I felt no particle of. "Nope."

"Bull."

"I love this man," I said, touching his arm. It was rigid as wood. "And I want him to be safe, and have a future. I don't want him to be treated like some bodyguard or attack dog— no matter what bullshit I might have said to my ex, when I

302

was out-of-my-mind pissed off. I want him to get what he deserves. A future. A good life."

"You think you love my brother more than I do? Bitch, please. Thirty-two years versus five months. Get over yourself."

"I never said that!" So much for my cool act. "And I don't love him more, or better—it's not a contest."

"Coulda fooled me, the way you're so fucking determined to win it."

I glared, anger roiling in my chest. "I think it's selfish, that you ask him to put his life and his future in harm's way, for your own sense of security. If something did go down, he could get sent back to prison for ten years, all because you were too selfish or cowardly to testify or get yourself a restraining order."

"You—"

I plowed straight over her. "And I'm selfish, too. I want him in my life. I want him safe, and free, and not just for his own good. For mine. I'm just as selfish as you, maybe."

Eric stood, cutting off whatever venom Kristina's parted lips were poised to spit at me. "Enough. Kris—get out. Annie, get ready for bed." He flipped the blinds shut. "You two still got shit to say to each other, write it down and we'll deal with it tomorrow."

Kris managed, "She—" before Eric cut her off, a few decibels shy of shouting.

"Shut up. Go to bed."

And wonder of wonders, she did. She stood, tossing the remote on the cushion beside me, and left the room without so much as a muttered word, the dog at her heels. Her silence shocked me more than a hollered curse would have. As I changed into pajamas and Eric unfurled the foldout, I wondered if Kris would wake her mom and tell her what a psycho bitch her son had brought home.

303

"Let it go," Eric ordered, reading the worries on my face.

"Oh sure, no problem."

He clicked off the TV, tossed a layer of sheets over the mattress, then a couple of blankets, and added the pillows his mom had stacked by the wall.

"Get in," he said. The order would've been rude if he hadn't sounded so completely defeated.

I wanted to wash my face and brush my teeth, but my adrenaline was waning, and I didn't relish running into Kris and getting into a fistfight outside the house's only bathroom.

I climbed under the covers and sighed up at a water-stained ceiling panel. Emotions rolled through me, making it feel as though I were lying on an inflatable beach lounger, pitched around by the waves.

It was kind of funny, though. If this evening's main event had somehow gone down before I'd worked at Cousins, I'd be way more of a wreck than I was now. I'd probably be crying. Crying, and desperately trying to figure out what concessions to make to stop Kris from being angry with me.

But not anymore, nope. After swimming for eight hours a week in the Olympic-sized pool of human conflict known as prison, I'd learned to live inside these uncomfortable sensations, as I might force myself to function through a head cold. *Just feelings,* I reminded myself, same as if I'd been spooked by an altercation in the dayroom.

"I'm sorry," I muttered, still staring at the ceiling. "Not for what I said—but for giving you such a headache. I meant everything I said."

"I know you did. And no need to apologize. I always get a headache when I come home. That ain't new."

"Tell me she's kind to you, when it's just you two."

He stripped to his shorts and flipped off the lamp, and the

Christmas lights framing the window. Didn't reply until he'd climbed in beside me.

"She looked out for me, my whole childhood," he said. "She was a bully, but she stood up for me. To other kids, to my dad even. She warned me away from the wrong girls, when I was in high school. Sounds controlling, I know, but looking back, she always knew what was best for me. So it's hard to deny her what she feels she needs from me, now."

"What do you mean, the wrong girls?"

"The kinds who make trouble. The kind who want saving. Or attention. Who get followed around by the drama they make for themselves."

"What kind of drama?"

"One came after me, real aggressive, one summer when I was maybe sixteen," Eric said. "I knew she was a fucking mess, but she was real pretty and I was real horny, and the way she wanted me . . . I felt like I was ten feet tall. My sister told me, 'Don't you fucking dare.' And she just about ran that girl off by force. I was fucking livid."

"Understandably."

"Then that girl had a baby about eight months later. Probably would've believed it was mine, if I'd fallen for it. Would've signed on to be some kid's dad at sixteen, tied myself to some crazy chick for as long as I could've held out." He paused. "That was mean. But you see what I'm saying. My sister saw it all coming. She yanked me back like I was racing headlong toward a cliff."

"Jesus. People actually do that to each other? What that girl tried to do?"

"'Round here they do. And my sister can spot that shit coming a mile away."

"Is that what she thinks I'm trying to do? Trap you?"

"Hell if I know," he said with a sigh. "Maybe she's just

hurt that I've been away for so long, and now that I'm finally out, I'm staying away by choice. She probably thinks that's down to you—she's always looking for some third party to blame. She's always looking for an enemy to butt heads with. But she'll get over it and realize it's my choice."

"I hope so."

"Enough about that shit. You want your Christmas present, finally?"

I blinked in the darkness. "You brought it?"

"Yeah. You want it?"

"Sure. I'd forgotten all about it."

The springs squeaked and groaned as he left the covers. He left the lamp off but plugged in the halo of Christmas lights, bathing the room in their soft aura. I sat up, hugging the blankets. He dug through his bag and came back with a soft package, wrapped ineptly in holly-patterned paper, just as he'd promised.

I squeezed it—definitely fabric. "What is it?"

"Open it. It's not as good as what you got for me," he added, warmth finally returning to his voice.

I peeled at the tape and opened the paper. A scarf—not a warm winter one like I'd made him borrow, but an accessory. It was crocheted out of filmy ombre yarn, the colors shifting between green and blue, with spangly silver thread worked through it.

"It's beautiful," I said, watching the tinselly bits glimmer in the low lights.

"One of my coworkers, his wife makes them. She came by the dispatch office with a bunch, and I saw that one and thought of you."

You look so good in green, my memory read. *Even though you have blue eyes they almost look ocean-colored when you wear green. And I've never been to the ocean.*

306

"I love it," I told him, clutching it in both hands as I leaned in to kiss him. "Thank you."

"Merry Christmas."

"Merry Christmas." I admired my present until Eric crossed the room and tugged the plug free, closing us in shadows.

He rolled me over and spooned me, something weary and needy and sad in the gesture. Something desperate in the stiff arm he wrapped around my waist. I tried to make myself soft, receptive, porous. Like a sponge that could absorb whatever defeat he was feeling, lighten his load.

Like you can save him. I imagined Kristina lashing me with her sneer.

No, I thought. *Not saving.* Just soothing. Just promising him with my body, *I'm not going anyplace.* A promise my brain hadn't been able to make last week, too terrified of this trip and its potential consequences.

Consequences that felt so far away now, with Eric's chest warming my back and his steadily slowing breath in my hair.

Consequences I hoped would never arrive, all just figments of fear and anticipation.

But I wouldn't get my wish.

Chapter Twenty

"I want you and my sister to go out tonight."

I stared at Eric, arms freezing midtousle as I toweled my hair. We were in the living room, Eric folding up the couch, me just showered and dressed. Paula had been puttering around since before we'd woken, and I could smell bacon and coffee, cheerful scents that matched the bright winter sunshine sneaking through the blinds.

"Me and Kristina? Out where?" And *why*? Dear God, why? After last night, the only possible venue had to be the *Jerry Springer* set. *My Brother's Home-wrecking Whore Needs to Butt Out!*

"Get a drink or something," he said calmly. Firmly. He wadded up the sheets and made a pile beside the foldout, avoiding my eyes. "I can drop you two off, pick you up after."

"That's the worst idea I've ever heard."

He snatched yesterday's clothes from the floor, tossing them near our bags.

"I doubt she'd agree to it, anyway," I added, and sat on

the couch to do my makeup. That was one advantage to the way we'd met—no self-consciousness about Eric seeing me with a bare face. *Thanks, Cousins Correctional Facility.*

"You let me worry about convincing Kris," he said. "I just want you two out someplace, together, without me around. So you can hash out your issues, woman to woman."

I dabbed concealer under my eye, keeping my attention on the compact. "Me and her and alcohol . . . You better leave us with a first-aid kit."

He paused in my periphery. "That's not funny."

"Last night wasn't funny, either. One more screwdriver and I swear she'd have decked me."

I didn't see his reaction, but he was moving again, voice still firm. "I'm asking you to do this, as a favor to me, okay? And I'm going to say the same to her. You're both in my life, and you're going to have to get used to each other. I'm not saying you gotta bond and be best friends and get your nails done together or whatever, but I need to know you can survive in the same room without me playing referee."

I couldn't think of a worse favor to be asked. "What if it goes just like last night, only in public?"

"Baby." He sighed and sat beside me, tilting my cushion. His palm was warm as it circled my back, but I kept my attention on the mirror, fussing with my eyeliner.

"Annie, look at me."

I dropped my hands to my lap and faced him.

His smile was goofy and exhausted. "I'm not asking you to do anything scarier than what you face every Friday in Cousins, okay? Have a drink with my sister. Please. Call the closest thing you two can get to a truce."

Through the door came Paula's voice, calling us to breakfast.

"Please?" he repeated.

I surrendered, snapping my compact shut with a sigh and

309

capping my mascara. "I'll go if she'll go." He was right, after all—if I could handle the crew at Cousins, I could handle one mean woman.

Eric smiled his relief, pulling me into a fierce hug just as Paula called us again. We headed down the hall hand in hand, Scooter greeting us along with the mouth-watering breakfast smells.

"Good morning," Paula chimed, setting a plate stacked with toast on the table.

"She's not usually this perky," Eric confided in me loudly as we sat. "Or domestic. Usually it's corn flakes around here."

She waved his snark aside. "It's not just for Annie. I haven't had a chance to cook breakfast for my baby boy in over five years, you know." She came up behind him and smoothed his messy hair, squished his face with both hands. Eric captured her wrists and held her hands to his heart, releasing her after she leaned in to kiss his cheek. I fought to hide my grin, chest all full of cotton candy to watch them.

"How did you sleep?" Paula asked, glancing at me as she collected serving spoons.

"Fine," I lied. I must've played the drama recap over and over in my head for two hours before I dropped off.

"Kris awake?" Eric asked.

"I thought I heard her banging around in there."

And speak of the Devil, Kristina appeared at the kitchen door, finger-combing her long hair. "Morning."

"Morning," Eric said evenly.

I smiled weakly.

Kris headed for the coffeepot. Once she'd set her own mug on the table, she asked, "Anybody else?"

Eric and I both raised our hands, and I avoided Kris's eyes when I thanked her for the cup.

"So, what's on tap for today?" Paula asked the table at large.

310

"Thought I'd give Annie the grand tour of Kernsville," said Eric.

"That's twenty minutes filled," Kris said with a grin.

"I'll stretch it out to a half hour. Take her to lunch at that burger place behind the ice rink."

Kris nodded at that, gesturing with approval as she chewed and swallowed. "That *is* the social center for Kernsvillians under the age of forty. Couldn't guess how many times I got to third base in that parking lot."

Paula shot her a look. "Kris."

"Twenty bucks says one of us was conceived there," Kris returned, fork waving between herself and Eric. I smiled to watch Paula get flustered and change the subject.

Breakfast went okay from there, but I hoped Paula didn't notice how Kris and I refused to look at each other. Once the washer was loaded, Kris announced she needed a smoke, and once again Eric joined her, telling his mom to save him the pans to wash.

They returned shortly, and when Kris disappeared to shower and Paula excused herself on an errand, Eric refreshed our mugs.

"She'll go," he said.

"Yeah? Did she roll her eyes a lot, or did you bribe her, or . . . ?"

"I just asked her nice. Told her exactly what I told you—that it's important to me that you two find your way to acting civil." He smirked. "Just had to ask her like, fifteen times, that's all."

I sank back in my chair, palming my warm mug. "Okay, then. Guess it's a date."

"Good."

"But I still think it's going to be a disaster, so you better show me one heck of a good time before tonight."

*　　*　　*

311

Eric did show me a good time. We drove around his home-town to see the high school he'd dropped out of, the places he used to like hanging out at, a drive-by tour of his old apartments. Nothing thrilling, but it was nice to see all this stuff. He'd been a mystery to me for such a large portion of our acquaintance, even our courtship . . . It was cool to lay my eyes on tangible proof of an ordinary life. And fun to try to picture a younger, more slender version of the man I'd come to love; I imagined his teenage self navigating these streets, or sitting in a booth in the K-Ville Grille, where we got our burgers. After lunch we picked up groceries for Paula, and just strolling down the supermarket aisle with him felt good. It felt like a Christmas present, almost, this little peek at what a life with this man might look like.

Though hopefully our future life might not feature quite so much ice and slush.

Paula made a big, awesome spread of rice and beans and beef and tortillas for dinner, then we sat down in front of the TV for the night. Or Eric and his mom did, as Kris and I had big plans. *Girls' night out!* Cringe.

At quarter to eight I bundled up for the peace summit. It was crazy-cold out, but I forewent my wool scarf, wanting to wear the tinselly one Eric had given me.

When we crunched down the walkway to the truck, Kris let me sit in the middle of the bench seat. Weird. Very weird, me the nervous meat in this angst sandwich. Eric switched on the radio, and none of us said *anything* for the ten-minute drive, not until we pulled into the parking lot of a one-story roadhouse-style bar called The Main Drag.

Then Eric commented, "Busy for a school night," and pulled over to the side, truck idling.

"Here goes nothing," Kris said with a grunt, pushing the door open.

I followed.

Eric rolled down his window and lay his forearm along the frame. "Be good."

"Perfect angels," his sister sang snidely, leading the way, me following.

"No liquor, Kris," Eric called. "You know how you get."

"Whatever you say, Dad."

I could about hear his sigh from twenty paces. "Call me when you're ready to get picked up."

I offered him a wave and a skeptical smile then followed Kris inside the bar.

The place was way nicer than I'd guessed from the facade. Not classy, but cool, with a kind of saloon vibe, bustling but not rowdy. Though it was still early.

"How's this for a cozy little chat?" Kris asked drily, waving to a small booth across from the center of the bar.

"Works for me."

She stayed standing as I slid in behind the table.

"What're you drinking?" she asked.

I didn't feel like explaining my usual cocktail to her. "Light beer. Bud or Coors or whatever. Thanks."

I watched her at the bar as I unbuttoned my coat. The faded redhead behind the taps greeted her warmly, like Kyle did with me. *Bartenders like us,* I thought, scribbling it down on my short mental list of things we had in common. *Bartenders like us. Men have hurt us. We both love Eric Collier.* Please let that be enough to get us through this perverse playdate.

Kris returned with a pitcher and two glasses. I poured and she unsnapped her puffy down coat, shoving it into the corner of the padded bench. She wedged herself in after it, her legs so long I felt our knees brush and angled mine to the side.

"So," she said after a deep drink, folding her arms on the Formica.

"So."

She smiled tightly. "You hate me, don't you?"

"A little, yeah."

"I'm not your biggest fan, either."

I palmed my glass in both hands but didn't drink yet. "I don't know what he expects to happen tonight. But I don't want to fight with you again. It's not going to get us anyplace."

"What should we talk about instead?" she asked, not quite snarky but a touch too sweet. "Clothes? Boys?"

"I don't know who you think I am," I said evenly, "but you've got me wrong."

"I bet you were prom queen and worked summers at the malt shop."

I shook my head. "I tutored. And I went to homecoming, but I wasn't queen by a long shot . . . And it wasn't exactly romantic. My date got so drunk he threw up in my parents' car when I drove him home, then he told me one of the cheerleaders once gave him and his friend head in the school library."

My deadpan delivery brought the shadow of a smile to her face. "Classy."

I nodded. "He was, actually, compared to my college boyfriend." Without meaning to, I gave my formerly bad ear a rub.

"He the one you threatened to sic Eric on?"

I smiled, embarrassed. "Yeah. That's the one."

Kris pursed her lips, gaze dropping to her glass. "I shouldn't have mocked you like I did, last night. About that. Eric called me on it today."

I couldn't help but notice she hadn't actually apologized, but it felt like progress.

I shrugged. "You were pretty drunk."

"Was your ex pretty drunk, when he treated you bad?"

314

"Yeah."

Her brows rose. "Not much of an excuse, is it?"

I shook my head. "No. Popular one, though."

She smirked and held up her glass to that, then took a swallow. I did the same, then laughed as I set my beer down, registering what we'd just drank to.

"That might be the most ironic toast possible. Cheers to the bad decisions people make when they drink."

"It's par for the course, when you're young and stupid," she said thoughtfully. "Bit pathetic when you get to be my age."

Again, a non-apology. Eric must have really worked her over that afternoon. I softened a little in return.

"I was stone-cold sober when I said that psycho stuff to my ex. It was like ten a.m., in the Gap. With Christmas music playing. In the underwear section."

She snorted at that, dropping her head then coming up grinning. "Oh fuck, that is too good."

I laughed, studying the foam lingering around the edges of my beer. "His girlfriend was in the changing room. God knows what he told her about me, after I ran off."

Kris shrugged her broad shoulders. "Fuck them."

Now *that* deserved a toast.

We chatted for a long time about high school—the scandals of forgotten friends, the reputations of notorious classmates. Who the kings and queens of our respective schools had been, and how sad it was that those had probably been the peaks of their lives, everything after a downhill slide.

After perhaps thirty minutes of that and two pints apiece, we fell quiet. I turned memories over in my mind. All the things I'd put up with, when I'd been younger. The things I'd shut out. The things I'd let people get away with. Then I thought of Eric.

"Your brother told me what you did for him, when he was

315

a teenager," I said quietly. "Scaring him away from that girl who ended up being pregnant."

She shook her head. "Poor boys—they stand *no* chance. I saw a tornado tearing toward him at a hundred miles an hour, with that girl. All he saw was a long pair of legs in a short skirt. Way I ran her off, you'd think she was a bear. But I'd just lost my son, not even a year before. I was a bear, myself. A mama bear, and Eric feels like my kid, sometimes. Especially back then."

I was surprised to hear her bring up her child. The way Eric had spoken about it, and finding the boy missing from the family snapshots, I'd assumed it was verboten.

"When I looked through your mom's photo album," I said slowly, then trailed off, nervous.

"What?"

I met her stare and ripped the scab off. "There weren't any photos of you and your son."

She blinked. To my surprise and cautious relief, her eyes didn't glow with anything resembling anger, but rather went a touch glassy and far away. I'd seen her brother's do just the same, whenever I'd pushed him toward ground he didn't feel like retreading.

After a long silence, she said, "I hate that she does that."

Confused, I frowned. "Does what?"

Kristina took a long drink, draining her glass. "She keeps them separate. All the pictures of me, pregnant, and all the pictures of Danny."

"Danny."

She nodded then signaled to the bartender for another pitcher. "Named for his father," she told me. "Shows how dumb I was at seventeen," she added with a wry smile. "thinking that'd get him interested in being the kid's dad. He was twenty-five going on twelve, that asshole."

316

Good God, a man old enough to be in grad school poaching from Kernsville High? But I could imagine Eric's reply if he were watching me process the scandal. *Just how it goes, around here.*

We thanked the bartender when the pitcher was delivered and Kristina sent her off with a twenty. She refilled our glasses, keeping her attention on her drink even after she'd set the pitcher aside. "My mom has all the photos of Danny in this special album—all baby-blue satin with a lacy border and shit. Separate from everything else. Drives me nuts, like he wasn't a part of it all. All our lives, back then."

Her eyes were soft and sad, and I thought maybe she was tipsy. I knew I was. If the options with Kris were angry-drunk or weepy-drunk, I was waving pom-poms for the latter. And I was starting to feel sentimental, myself. My posture was slumped and slack, my emotions loose and wide-open, dandelion fluff. It felt good. I hoped Kris wouldn't turn on me, bat me hard and send all those vulnerable wisps flying.

"Maybe your mom needs to keep them separate," I offered, "so she can visit those memories when she's prepared to."

She swallowed a deep slug of beer, nodding. "I know, I know . . . I get that. But it's been forever. I mean, fuck. Danny'd be turning *nineteen* this March, if he'd lived. Nine*teen*. Older than I was when I had him. He'd be out of high school, but she still can't remember him the way I do. You couldn't keep that kid out of anything—wanted to be the center of it all."

I smiled, her fond grin infectious.

"I wish she'd remember him that way," Kristina said. "Folded in with the rest of our family's memories. We didn't have a lot of money, but we had good times. And that kid . . . He made me feel so goddamn rich, while he was around."

"Yeah?"

317

She nodded, still not looking at me. "Yeah. Most beautiful thing I ever called mine. And sweet—don't even know where he got that. Looked just like Eric, when Eric was little. You put their baby pictures side by side and you'd swear they were twins. Big brown eyes, mess of curly hair." She laughed. "Big fucking heads. Walking around looking like lollipops, with those big heads on those skinny bodies."

"Is that why you're so . . . protective of your brother?" I asked. "Why you're afraid of him taking up with some girl who's not good enough for him . . ."

She finally met my eyes. "I got every reason to feel that way about my brother. 'Cause he reminds me of the son I lost? Maybe. 'Cause he held my baby more than any other man ever did, while Danny was with us—way more than my son's father did, more than my own dad did. 'Cause he's been the one man in my life who ever put me first, and the only one who stuck around."

A shiver moved through me, like someone had cracked a window at my back. God help me, I finally understood her. I sipped my drink, let her go on.

"Maybe 'cause I half raised Eric," she said thoughtfully, "the years when our mom worked two jobs. Maybe because he returned the favor, and stepped up as the father we hardly saw, when I needed him to. Maybe 'cause I was sick of watching everyone around us throwing their lives away on the wrong people. I couldn't pinpoint it for you. But I got a hundred good guesses."

I nodded. "That makes sense. A lot of sense . . . I'd take back some of the things I said to you last night, if I could. Knowing all that."

She shrugged, evading my eye contact once more but looking as relaxed as I'd yet seen her. "I was hard on you." She laughed softly, and for the brief moment, with her cheeks rounded

318

and her eyes crinkling, her mean face was pretty. "I'm hard on everybody. And I know I hold on too tight to him, I do. It's hard not to, when he's the one reliable handhold I got, you know? Or maybe you don't know."

I shook my head. "I don't know. But I can hear what you're saying."

"I'm *glad* you don't know," she said, meeting my eyes for just a second. "I want my brother to be with someone who wants him, but doesn't *need* him. You know? Listen to me, sounding like a goddamn feminist. But yeah . . . someone who's not so dependent on him that they can't step back and see all the good in him, I guess. Fuck if I even know what I'm trying to say. Think I may be drunk."

"Me, too. And I know what you mean. And I do see all that stuff in your brother. In fact, the things I'm the most uneasy about with him are probably the things those other girls might want him for. The protectiveness, I guess. The way he puts his loved ones almost *too* high above himself. And his freedom."

She nodded, brow furrowed. "You mean me."

"Not exclusively. He's shown that side to me, too. It scares me so much, knowing if anything happened to me and he thought it was his job to go after somebody . . ." Knowing how for that bright, burning moment, face to face with Justin, I'd wanted to exploit that side of Eric. "Knowing how guilty I'd feel if he wound up back in prison, over me. He's so black and white about some things. I wish I could make him understand that having him in my day-to-day life is so much more important to me than his payback. But he doesn't want to hear that. He thinks it's all he has to give."

She smiled, looking guilty. "Can't imagine who taught him that."

I softened further. "I think it's just who he is, too." It was

319

in his upbringing, in his genes, in his blood. In the water, around here. Like Kristina's reliance and protectiveness, there was no single culprit to blame, merely a fact demanding acceptance.

"But you see other things," she prompted.

I nodded. "I see lots. He's maybe the gentlest man I've ever met . . . which sounds crazy, considering where we met, and how he got there. He's the most romantic man I've ever known, by far."

Her eyebrows rose at that, telling me that just as I'd envied their bond, feeling like it was out of my reach, there were facets to her brother that only I got to see.

"That's plenty of information, right there," she teased, halting my squishy inventory with a raised palm. But I sensed a pride in her, too, as she realized the man she'd helped raise had turned out that way—kind and romantic.

"He got me this, for Christmas." I toyed with the end of my new scarf, silver strands glinting under the low lights.

She smiled. "It's pretty. He's got way better taste than me."

I let the tail of the scarf fall away and took a deep breath. "I love your brother. A lot."

Her lips pursed, but she nodded. "I believe that."

"I want what's best for him, too. Only the things I want for him look different than the things you want. You want to protect him from getting used by the wrong kind of women. I want to protect him from getting put away again, when he's got so much to offer. Not just what he offers me, but what he can offer with his talents, and his hard work. What he could offer as a father someday, maybe. What he can offer you and your mom, as a free man—just his support and his company and his help. We're both afraid of him wasting his potential. I think we can at least agree on that."

"Yeah," she said heavily. "Yeah, we can. But he's a Collier.

320

What you and I want won't mean shit, if he's got his mind made up."

"Do you think you could let him go, though? Just on this one issue. Give him permission to stay out of this stuff with your . . . your ex, or your attacker, however you think of him."

She stared into the middle distance beyond my shoulder. "That's like asking me to face down a bull with no sword."

"I bet."

We went silent, sipping our beers, watching the people gathered before the bar. It was getting busy. I excused myself to use the ladies' room, and Kris did the same after I returned. When she tried to give me a refill I covered my glass. "I think three's plenty for me."

She eyed her own glass and seemed to concur. She sat up tall and twisted in her seat to address the two men in the next booth. "Hey, Jim."

The one named Jim turned, looking delighted when Kris handed them our half-full pitcher. That left just her glass to drain, and the conversation felt complete. We'd reached more than the truce I'd skeptically agreed to attempt. Not quite a bond, but maybe a seed capable of growing one. Maybe with a little nurturing—or the odd pitcher—every time I saw her, it could slowly blossom into something warm and sturdy.

"Shall I call Eric?" I asked, fishing out my phone. "Get us our ride home?"

She nodded and drained her glass. "Yeah, sounds good. I need a smoke. Feel free to wait inside."

As she bundled up, I dialed Eric.

"Hey." Man, one word and that voice had me as buzzed as those three pints.

"Hey. We're ready to get picked up."

"Cool. Give me twenty minutes? I'm trying to solve this thing with my mom's DVD player for her."

"Sure."

"How'd it go? Any hair get pulled?"

I smiled. "No, we did real good. You should be proud of us both."

"Hey, glad to hear it. I'll see you in twenty. Don't leave me for some dreamboat before then."

I laughed. "Impossible."

"See you soon."

I hung up and got my layers on to join Kris outside. I found her standing a few feet from the front door.

"He's going to be about twenty minutes," I told her.

"Oh good. I'll smoke another, then."

I pulled my gloves from my coat pocket and tugged them on.

"Feel free to wait inside," she said again.

"Nah. It feels good, actually." The night had that rare crispness to it—nothing to do with the cold, just that state of mind where the world felt to be in the finest focus. I looked up into the black sky. "So many stars out he—"

Kris grabbed my upper arm through my coat. Her other hand flicked her cigarette to the pavement and the blue-gray smoke jetted out before us.

"What is it?"

"I dunno yet. Maybe nothing." Her eyes were locked on a red truck with a white cap on its bed, pulling into a spot in the far corner. I studied her expression and the night went liquid-nitrogen cold.

"That's not him, is it?" I didn't even know *his* name. "The guy who . . . ?"

"I dunno," she breathed. She seemed to remember she'd grabbed me, letting my arm go. "Looks too much like his goddamn truck."

"Did he drink here a lot?"

322

She hissed a long, "*Shi-i-i-it.*"

Across the lot, a man had exited the vehicle. Big guy, over six feet, round through the middle under his canvas bomber.

"Let's go inside," I told Kris. "He hasn't seen you. Hide in the bathroom and I'll tell you when—"

"No," she said softly, eyes on the man. He moved slowly and unevenly, a sway in his step. Drunker than us, surely.

"What are you going to do?" I asked her.

"I don't know. Feel free to go inside."

"No . . . He looks wasted. We could call the cops, if he's driving drunk."

"He's not drunk. He's got a limp, from what my brother did to him."

Oh, Jesus. "We can't start something that's going to drag Eric in, when he gets—"

"Wes," Kris called.

The floor dropped out of my stomach. He was close enough that I registered the surprise in his widening eyes. He stopped where he was, maybe ten paces from us.

He said simply, "Hey, Kris."

I could hear her pounding heart in her voice. "What're you doing here?"

He didn't answer that question. "How you been?" His tone was uneasy. He wasn't afraid of her, but he wasn't sneering or cruel or threatening, either. Uncertain. I had to wonder how he might've felt about what he'd done to her, once he'd detoxed in the hospital or prison.

"I was doin' just fine," Kris said, "until I heard they were letting you out."

"I got no beef with you."

"That's funny. I've still got one with you." Her quavering voice undermined the tough words.

323

He changed the subject. "How's your mom?" There was no threat implicit in the question, I didn't think. No veiled, *Be a shame if anything happened to her.* I could guess the reply Kris held back, something to the tune of, *You mention my mother again and I'll gut you.* But she didn't give him the reaction, didn't hand him the ammo. Didn't say a word.

"You gonna sic your brother on me again?" Wes asked, shifting from foot to foot.

I held my breath, worried for what might come next from Kris's lips. *He's on his way now.* But no. Instead she simply said, "You know I could, but only if you give me a good reason. My brother wasted enough of his life on your sorry ass. What're you doing in my town?"

"Meetin' my cousin for a beer." He looked to me. "Who's your friend?"

"None of your business," Kris said, and took a step forward, as though shielding me. She was doing a decent job of acting tough, but I wanted this guy to have every reason to keep being cool.

I kept my voice level, rational, like I was talking to a guy at Cousins. "What do your parole terms say about you going to bars?"

He stared at me a long beat, a hint of aggression in those eyes giving me pause. "Who the fuck wants to know?"

"Kris's friend," I said.

"It's a goddamn good question," Kris said, and she pulled out her cigarette pack and slid one between her lips. She spoke around it. "What *does* your parole have to say about that? 'Cause I got a dozen good friends in that bar who'd be happy to say they saw you drinkin', tonight."

"Well maybe they won't see me drinkin'," he said. "Maybe I'll just order me a ginger ale and have a nice chat with my cousin, call it a night."

324

"That sounds real smart," Kris said smoothly. The fear had left her voice. She sounded oddly cocky, in fact.

"I got no issue with you," Wes told her. "I ain't here to get myself crippled by your goddamn psycho brother again. Just here to see my cousin, so I can borrow his power drill. Okay?"

"Good plan," Kris said. "'Cause if I hear about anybody seein' you around town after this, I'm not gonna be impressed. And if for any reason you get *any* ideas about coming around me, I got a gun, and I know how to use it."

"You sound fucking crazy, you know that?"

"I barely told anybody what went down between you and me," Kris said slowly. "But I could. I could tell every good friend of mine in this county what you did, and you'll be lucky if they don't put my brother's justice to shame."

I held my breath, stunned by that. Stunned because I believed her, that she'd tell. The thing she'd not even been able to confide in the cops, but I heard it in her voice, she'd do it. Take that horrible crime and turn it into a weapon to keep this man from haunting her ever again.

"You heard what I said?" Kris demanded.

He nodded. "Yeah. I hear you. You're fucking crazy, all you Colliers." He spat on the salted asphalt. "I'd have to be crazier than all of you to want any part of your rabid-ass family."

Headlights swung off the main road and into the lot. I froze, and so did Eric's truck. He'd stomped on the brake between two rows of parked cars, and his door popped open.

Wes muttered, "Fuck," then asked Kris, "You got a fucking Bat Signal or something?"

Eric was walking in a way that made him look taller than the bar and out for blood. I waved for him to stop, but it was Kris who actually managed the feat.

"Get back, Eric. It's fine."

"The fuck it is. What the fuck you doing around my sister?"

"Small world, that's all," said Wes. He was playing it cool, but his fear was evident. I didn't blame him. Eric's eyes were darker and colder than the winter sky.

"Just here to meet my cousin. Borrow his drill."

"You get in your truck and you leave," Eric said, "and you buy your own goddamn drill. Get the fuck out of my town and stay the fuck out."

The bar's door opened behind us, the noise inside flaring, light spilling out as two thirtysomething women scooted by to smoke on the other side of the entrance. They were chatting tipsily, but the rest of us had gone silent and somber as gravestones.

"Go," Kris told Wes.

And he did. He skirted Eric's statue-still body, limping toward his truck. We all waited in silence until he'd pulled onto the road and out of sight, then our collective postures slumped.

"Oh my *gosh*," said one of the smoking women brightly. "Eric!"

He looked confused, then spent a moment jogging his memory about whoever she was to him, and they exchanged post-holiday pleasantries. Surreal, but it gave me—and presumably Kris as well—a minute to come down from our adrenaline highs.

The women finished their cigarettes. The one who'd recognized Eric said, "See you around, maybe. You look good," she added, making my eyes roll. "Real good."

He said good night and gestured for Kris and me to get in the still-idling truck.

Once he was behind the wheel and buckled in, he dropped his head and muttered, "Fuck."

"I thought that went real well," Kris said.

"She handled it great," I told Eric.

"Didn't threaten to send you after him or anything," she said. "Just the whole goddamn rest of the town."

"And his parole officer," I added.

"He say anything to you?" Eric demanded. "Either of you. Anything aggressive?"

"Nah," said Kris. "He's a real chickenshit, sober. I'd forgot that about him." She was acting so calm, but I'd heard in her voice, she'd been terrified.

"He say anything to you?" he asked me. "He *look* at you?"

"Not like, *look* at me, no. We did fine. Really."

Eric sighed mightily, like he was exhausted from having hauled us unconscious from a burning house. "Let's get the fuck home."

Chapter Twenty-One

Kris recapped the encounter for her brother as we drove back to Lakeside. About fifty times he demanded details like, "And that's what he said, exactly? How'd he sound when he said it?" before he finally seemed like he was calming. If not satisfied, confident enough to believe maybe he didn't have to stay awake all night, listening for tires rolling up outside his mom's house.

"He's not coming around," Kris said. "I could tell from his face. He's a coward when he's clean. And he's got to be clean, if he's gotten that fat. Goddamn . . . I'd like to know how a man gets that fat on prison food."

The joke seemed to relax Eric officially. I could sense his relief for the confrontation to finally be over and done with as clearly as I might feel the sun on my hair.

"Should I tell Mom?" Kris asked.

Eric looked pensive as he parked the truck. "Not tonight, at least. Let's figure that out tomorrow, maybe."

Kris nodded and pushed the passenger door wide. She intuited from the way he kept the truck running that we needed a minute, and slammed the door without a word.

Once she was swallowed by the light of the kitchen, Eric sank back against his seat.

"Fucking hell."

"It's okay, really. I'm okay. Kris is okay."

"Makes my goddamn skin crawl, to know he even laid eyes on you."

"I'm *okay*. Really. All those Fridays at Cousins prepped me well. And Kris was careful not to tell him who I was."

"Still . . ."

"I'm real proud of you," I said, "holding yourself back the way you did."

Eric didn't seem to hear me. He dropped his forehead to the wheel and made a noise of absolute grief and surrender. "Jesus. If anything had happened to you . . ."

I rubbed his back. "But it didn't. Your sister got in front of me and everything. She didn't need to, but she did."

He sat up and met my eyes. "Did she?"

"She was scared for maybe the first minute, then it was all bulldog." I offered a little smile.

He exhaled, long and loud. I changed the subject.

"Who was that woman who thinks you look *re-e-eal* good, anyhow?"

His nostrils flared with a tiny laugh, telling me I was ridiculous for asking. And that he was grateful for a little ridiculousness just now. "Just an ex of one of my buddies."

"Better be."

We were quiet for a time, me watching Eric, him staring straight ahead.

"It freaked you out," I said, "knowing he was near me."

"Of course it did. Still does."

"Why?"

"'Cause of what could've happened. You know what he did to my sister . . . the gist of it, anyhow."

"You afraid you could've lost me?"

He dropped his head again. "Annie . . ."

"I'm afraid to lose you, too. If you went off on somebody like him, got yourself hurt or killed, or put away." I ran my palm over his back in slow circles. "We're the same, that way."

"I know we are."

"I want you to promise me, if something did happen to me—which it won't—you won't do what you did for her. Because I'd need you with me, helping me heal, way more than I'd need to feel like justice had been done or whatever. Can you promise me that?"

"I don't know."

My turn to sigh, and my hand went still on his back. "I get that you don't value your own neck the way I wish you did, so I'm not asking you to understand, or to do it for your own good. I'm asking you to do it for me. I *need* you, with me. Safe. And free. I don't need to feel avenged. I only need your body next to mine when I fall asleep."

A minuscule nod.

I squeezed the back of his neck. "Promise me."

He held my gaze with those bottomless brown eyes. "I promise." He kissed my mouth, then again. He spoke right there, words warming my lips. "I promise. You get me."

"Good . . ." My heart unwound, chest welcoming a deep draw of air. "Good."

I kissed him hard, more a fierce mashing of lips than anything sensual or sweet, and my arms wrapped around him, tight as a vise. The most powerful body I'd ever known, yet I held him as though he might be lost in a breath. And he could be. Was this why he'd protected his sister the way he had? Because he knew how much this hurt, to come so close to losing someone? That made my demands selfish, but

I didn't care. His safety and his future mattered more to me than anything I'd ever held dear. A taste of what motherhood must do to a woman. A possessiveness so strong, it ached deep down in the marrow and muscle.

He smoothed the hair from my temples and stared into my eyes. "You're the most precious thing in my life. If you want me in yours bad enough to demand the stuff you are, I'll give you that."

"And I promise I won't ever say things to your sister again, like the ones I said last night. We talked a lot, at the bar. And I get what you mean to her, too. And it goes way deeper than I'd ever imagined. I understand how big it is, the promise I'm asking of you. Really."

He nodded once and kissed my temple, then exhaled steam against my skin. "Good."

For a long time we held each other, until the blood pounding in my ears faded to a murmur. Until my vision ceased hopping in time with my pulse. Until Eric's breathing went silent, little more than a warm breeze ruffling my hair.

"You want to go inside?" he asked, so soft it could've been a thought.

"Not yet. Let's just enjoy sitting still, for a while."

He killed the headlights, freed both our seat belts and moved. I waited as he repositioned himself, leaning against the driver's door. He patted his lap and we got comfortable, legs piled along the long seat, two sets of eyes on the rows of modest homes, a few still twinkling with Christmas lights. His mouth was at my ear, his voice filling my entire being.

"I love you," he said, and went on before I could return the words. "More than I'll ever love myself. But I'll try to do what you want. I'll try to value what I have to offer, and my own being here—being free—as much as you seem to."

I swallowed, throat sore. "You better."

331

"And I'll keep writing you letters 'til the day I die."

I gurgled, the sounds of tears drowning a laugh. "Good. I love your words."

"You gave them all to me. Every last one."

"Funny, when they all felt so exactly like gifts." Gifts I'd unwrapped with a thumping heart and shaking fingers; in my own driver's seat, in the bar, on my couch, in my bed. I'd wrapped those secret pages around me like satin sheets and dreamed that the man who'd written them could be so good, could even be real. And here he was, wrapped around me himself. Warmer than my jacket. Warmer than the August sun beating on his bare skin. Hotter than the female eyes that'd watched him then, torn between fear and curiosity.

"When I met you," I murmured, "you were an incarcerated felon. And yet you've only ever lied to me once. And that was so you could hit on me."

I felt his soundless laugh behind my shoulders, then a kiss on my ear. "Guilty."

"The most honest man I bet I've ever known, and I met him in prison."

"The nicest woman *I* ever knew, and she took up with a convict. What on earth would your mother say?"

I smiled at that. "I look forward to finding out."

I'd be telling my parents soon. It was time to stop protecting them—time to stop trying to make amends for the pain I'd never allowed them to share with me.

"My dad might have a stroke," I said, "but they've already seen the changes in me, since I met you. The way I've come alive again, for the first time in years."

"Amen."

After a minute's peace he said, "I think we better head home after breakfast, tomorrow. I'm kinda ready to get the hell out of Kernsville."

332

"Sure." I squeezed the hands clasping my waist. "Maybe we could get up real early and drive out to your lake. Watch the sun come up over it. Grab some donuts on the way back to your mom's." Watch as that watery winter sun rose at its cranky January speed, the sky turning from navy to slate to the periwinkle of my mom's hydrangea. Let the light banish the last of tonight's scarier memories from my mind, fill the gaps with another taste of this man's favorite place in the world.

"That's not my lake, like I said. It won't be my lake again until the spring's here and the water's blue, and my feet are in the sand."

"I'd still like to. And we'll come back, again, when it's warm."

"Maybe even then . . . Maybe it still won't be the same. Everything's so different now, from the last time I swam there. I'm so different."

"We'll come back, anyway," I whispered, "and find out."

I felt him nod, then he kissed the back of my head. "Yeah. We'll come back."

The heat of his words seemed to linger in my hair, but others drifted from my memory, swirling like snowflakes. *I've never been to the ocean.*

I'd take him there, someday, when his parole allowed. To South Carolina, to the coast. To the feet of those restless, lapping waves that stretched out beyond comprehension, under a sky bleached palest blue by the summer sun. To the very end of the land, caged by sand and water and air. No concrete, no steel. A place that seemed to promise that winter would never come again. A pretty lie you didn't mind falling for, not when the lips that delivered it tasted so sweet.

"I hope your sister likes me," I said quietly. "Or at least gets me, some."

333

"Doesn't matter what they think of you, Annie. Doesn't change what I think, anyhow."

"I know. But I want her to think maybe I'm strong, a little. Not as strong as her or you, but enough that maybe she'll think I'm up for this. For being with you. I know I shouldn't care, but they're your family."

"You care about whatever you need to," he said lightly. "Just know that I'm not worried about it."

"Okay."

Eric bade me to sit up. "Let's get inside."

Before we exited, he curved a broad, gentle hand along my jaw, pulled me close. His kiss was soft as snow landing, warm and slow as summer.

We left the heat of the truck, crunching over slate toward the light of the kitchen. His hand closed around mine, strong and possessive. The hand that'd done unspeakable things in the name of brotherly love. A hand capable of the tenderest acts of intimacy and affection. The hand that had penned the most breathtaking letters, for my eyes alone. I'd hold it tight as we went forward together, sure as I clung to it now. Tight as I'd ached to hold it, back when such a thing had been forbidden. I'd never let it go again, no matter where we ended up . . .

Somewhere warm, someday.

Somewhere that belonged to the both of us, far away from the hard cinderblock of Cousins. Out of the cruel cold. Into the light and hope and the excitement of our future, whatever it might look like. Into the bright promises of spring, when the entire world wore green.

Keep reading for a preview of
Cara McKenna's exciting new Desert Dog series

LAY IT DOWN

Available now from Piatkus Entice

The matchstick shifted between Vince's lips as he surveyed the stranger.

Young woman—thirty, tops. Dressed to impress, but not in the way that chicks from Fortuity might. She covered the assets those girls flaunted, held them in reserve. The type who'd make a man buy the cow first, as it were.

The bar had filled up around them, tables dwindling and the volume rising, body heat making up for what sunset had stolen.

Miah frowned at the woman. "Sunnysider. Has to be." Sunnyside Industries was the company that had won the development bid on the casino. Miah wasn't a fan of a project, which had already begun to cause the ranch headaches over road access and construction runoff.

"Well, speak of the devil," Vince muttered, still eyeing the stranger. "Corporate ambassador."

There was a small tech company on the more civilized, western side of the tracks, but the outsiders who worked there didn't look like this girl—they were all doughy, sunburned men in polo shirts and sand-colored slacks. She was too stylish, too pressed and polished. All shined up like a diamond in a place that only recognized coal.

She was here to dazzle.

And sick to death of all the heavy shit running through his head, Vince welcomed the distraction.

"Wonder what the angle is this time," Miah muttered, eyes narrowed in suspicion. The Churches had been deflecting buy-out offers on their land and water reserves ever since the casino had been but a glimmer in Mayor Dooley's beady eye.

The girl was a corporate rep, to judge by the get-up. Crisp short-sleeved shirt tucked under the shiny belt hugging her waist, tailored gray skirt out of a catalog aimed at millionaire secretaries. Wavy near-blond hair—but not the honest kind of wavy, not like Raina's. No, this was the kind of wavy that demanded an early wake-up call and at least two plug-in devices. Raina's hair said, *I just got laid. Eat your heart out.* This chick's hair said, *Hands off. This took me an hour.*

Man, Vince would pay good money to mess that hair up against his pillow. Pretty face, too. The kind of pretty they didn't make in Fortuity. Too clean, too . . . pedigreed.

"Glasses," he noted. Stylish, bold ones, very *hot librarian.* He could roll with that.

The girl gave the entire place a good long study, then Vince—and every other man in attendance—watched as she headed for the bar.

"Chardonnay," Miah guessed.

"Nah, fruity cocktail. Something with a cherry."

"Five bucks says it's white wine."

Vince murmured, "I'll take that," and they shook.

But neither made a dime, as Raina set a double whiskey before the woman.

"Damn."

Vince shrugged. "Just pandering to the local color. Back home, wherever she came from, that would've been a cosmo."

The woman settled herself at one of the small, high tables in the middle of the barroom, and Miah shifted in his seat to face Vince, scrutiny shelved.

But Vince's eyes stayed locked right where they were, questions knocking around his head like pool balls. A different persuasion of curiosity rousing a bit further south.

"Glasses," he muttered again. "How come I never noticed how sexy glasses were before?"

"You're not her type, Vince."

"Like you'd know—you had her ordering white wine a minute ago."

"Leave the girl alone."

The matchstick rolled from one side of Vince's lips to the other. "Wonder what's in that bag." She'd brought a purse, plus another not-quite-purse—a weird shape on a long strap, decked out with zippered pockets like a miniature, misshapen hiking pack.

"That's no briefcase," he noted aloud, and the handbag was too small to be packed with propaganda. Every other Sunnysider who'd come through Benji's had been toting reams of "educational materials" outlining the zillion-and-one benefits of a casino coming to Fortuity. One asshole had even shown a slideshow on his laptop, right there on the bar. He'd been laughed out of the place. That'd been ages back though, before the referendum. Now the project had a name, an estimated opening date, logos. Many former skeptics had since adjusted to the idea, grown curious about the construction and hospitality jobs Sunnyside and the mayor promised to bring to the area, all the money that'd supposedly trickle down into the limping local economy and tempt young people back.

339

"What's your game?" Vince breathed, eyes on the stylish stranger standing in one of the most familiar corners of his dusty little world. The evening temperature had already taken a dive, but Vince shed his old leather bomber and tossed it on the bench, feeling suddenly stifled. "Think I'll introduce myself."

Miah shook his head. "I know that look—leave the poor woman be. Second ago you had her employers tangled up in a murder plot."

"Never said that." Not her employers, necessarily. All he knew from Alex was that bones had been found at one of the construction sites. That didn't mean Sunnyside had anything to do with them. "And putting aside whatever Alex may have seen, I'm anti-Sunnyside as a rule. I like my town the way it is."

"On that we agree, at least."

"And if this innocent woman's gotten herself mixed up with evil corporate monsters," Vince added, "it's my moral imperative to seduce her away from the dark side. By any means necessary."

Miah's eyes rolled. "Oh yeah, fucking Saint Vincent over here. Anyhow, she'd bore you to tears. Look at her."

"Even vanilla tastes exotic when you're only used to rocky road."

"Whatever she's here for, it's not depravity with the locals. I can tell you that for free."

"City girls got needs, too." Vince slid out from behind the table and grabbed his jacket. "Plus I'm an ambassador myself, for this town. This is my civic duty—winning hearts and minds. And any other willing parts that might present themselves."

Miah exhaled in a huff, abandoning the protest. He knew better than anybody, trying to change Vince's mind was a waste of breath. Particularly with the fairer sex involved. "I better head home, check on that fence. Leave you to your lost cause." He stood, abandoning his half-drained bottle.

"Thanks for coming out. This talk ain't over, incidentally."

"It probably is for me, Vince, unless the sheriff gives you some answers worth worrying about. He does, I'm first in line to help. Otherwise, let a good man rest in peace." With that, they traded grumpy good nights and Miah headed for the door.

Vince didn't honestly know what he wanted to get out of the mystery woman—not aside from a sense of her role in the greater development machine. But if a bit of reconnaissance flirting happened to lead someplace interesting . . . ? So much the better. His bottle was empty so he dropped it at the bar and Raina handed him another.

She took in the arms that eight hours a day swinging hammers and hauling rocks had built, and all the black ink that decorated Vince from the wrists to the shoulders. Not her work—she'd done the tattoo on his neck, but been away when he'd gotten the sleeves, not seeming likely to return. Still, the way her eyes always narrowed at them, you'd think he'd cheated on her.

"Funny how you lost your jacket the second everybody else zipped theirs up," she said. "Who's the striptease for?"

"Just hot, that's all."

"Over who?" Like she couldn't guess.

"You served her. What's her story?" he demanded.

Raina broke his ten and spoke quietly, a touch of conspiracy in her voice. "She just got in. Something to do with marketing."

Ah. "Marketing to who?"

He'd leaned in real close and Raina forced him back by the shoulders. "Find out for yourself."

"I love when you get handsy. How come we never started something?"

"Because I know you too well. Go prey on the innocent—you'll stand half a chance."

Vince snagged his bottle and turned, locking crosshairs on his target. She was checking her phone, that pretty face lit blue-white by the screen. Through the speakers, on came Tammy Wynette and 'Run Woman Run'. How was that for mood music? Vince closed the distance in a half dozen lazy paces, but she didn't look up. Not until he set his bottle beside her glass with a *clunk*.

Her eyes found him first, swiveling up above the frames of her glasses. Her chin followed. "Good evening." Sexy voice. Confident, unimpressed.

"You're from Sunnyside, aren't you?"

He'd expected a little taste of intimidation at his tone, but this girl looked cool and dry as the desert after dark. Fine by Vince—he loved a challenge.

"Not exactly." She reached for her tumbler and slid it close, away from Vince's beer. Like her toy poodle had wandered too close to a frothy mongrel.

"Not exactly?" he echoed. "But kind of."

"They've hired me, but I'm a free agent."

Vince hunkered down with his forearms on her table. He caught her scent, something light. The essence of some rare flower he probably couldn't spell. He wanted to curl a fist around her collar and bring his face real close to hers, breathe that perfume in so deep he got drunk off it. Goddamn, when was the last time he'd gotten laid? Weeks? A month or more? Maybe Miah was right, thinking he'd grown irrational—maybe he was going crazy from sex deprivation. Maybe a good tumble would clear his head.

"Free agent?" he asked. "Free to do what?"

She leaned over to lift her weird little bag onto her lap and unzip it along three sides. She opened the flap, revealing a camera with a lens about as long as Vince's foot.

"Don't tell me they're printing travel brochures already?

342

Casino ain't much to look at yet. Bunch of pits and unlaid pipe, far as I've seen."

"No, not yet. They need promotional materials to wow their investors—shots of the progress and the natural beauty of the area and all that. And I need work, so . . ." She tilted the glass to her lips and Vince watched her throat work. Goddamn women had no clue what it did to a man, the way they looked sipping liquor, or sucking a long pull off a bottle. Or maybe they did. Maybe this one could guess exactly how suffocating Vince's jeans were suddenly feeling.

He focused with some effort. "You're a city girl, if I'm not mistaken. You travel far?"

"Portland, Oregon."

He nodded at that, unsurprised. Sunnyside's parent outfit was California-based. God forbid the hypocrites hire a local, eager as they claimed to be to stimulate the town's economy.

"You got somebody showing you around while you're here?"

"No need. Job's simple—take pretty pictures. I wasn't told I'd require a tour guide for that."

"Fortuity's got its rough areas. Though stick to the daylight hours and you'll probably be fine."

"That's generally good advice for landscape photography." Her smile was wry, and it made Vince feel funny. Dirty-funny. Made him want to bite her lip, or maybe get bit in return.

He nodded to the camera. "Hell of a weapon you got there."

She lifted it out of its case with loving care, unscrewed the massive telephoto and replaced it with a stumpier lens from one of the bag's many pockets. The camera whirred to life with a wink of green, and she held it to her face, aimed at Vince.

"Cheese," he offered, beaming her his best panty-melter at the contraption's eye.

343

Nothing seemed to happen, but digital cameras were quiet. Vince dropped the grin, then swore at the sudden flash, then another, and turned away, spots dancing.

She checked her screen, looking pleased. Looking smug, which was Vince's rightful shtick. "They'll probably go with the mountains and hot springs, but it's always nice to showcase the local wildlife. What shall I caption these? What's your name?"

"Vince. Grossier."

She stuck out a small hand. "Kim Paget."

Her skin was just as it should be—all lake-stone smooth in his gravel-roughened mitt. Exactly what he needed to soothe the warm ache she'd stuck him with. "Pleasure," he said.

"Indeed. What's with the match?"

Her gaze had moved to his mouth, and he dropped his own to her lap, smiling. "Got an oral fixation." He hauled his attention up in time to catch her expression of complete and total disinterest. *Fine.* "So, Kim . . ."

She batted her eyelashes, parroting his coy act. "Yes, Vince?"

"How much would it cost a redneck like me to get you to take nothing but photos of the landfill and the sulfur springs and the trailer park, and scare these greedy motherfuckers out of their plans to wreck my town?"

She flinched at the cuss, but barely. "I'm just here to do a job. And I hate to break it to you, but it's an easy one. I'm sure Fortuity's got flaws—every town does. But there's a reason people would pay good money to visit. I got a hell of a preview on the drive in. It's gorgeous country."

"For now, maybe. From down here." Until they cluttered the mountains up with condos and polluted all the water, then caught sight of the east side of the tracks from their hilltop penthouses and decided the trash needed taking out.

"I'm not interested in getting drawn into the politics," she

344

said gently, more calm than meek, and drained her shot in two swallows, scarcely wincing. "I just need the pay day."

"What for?"

Another little smirk, straight out of Vince's own playbook, and she slid from her seat. "I'll see you around, maybe."

"Hey, don't let me run you off, now."

"You're not," she said. "I only came here looking for a quiet drink, and that's just not going to happen." She looked around them, seeming to mean the general volume of a Friday night, not Vince specifically.

In a voice that welcomed no protest, he told her, "Follow me."